EVEN THE FAVORED SUFFER

EVEN THE FAVORED SUFFER

VOLUME III OF THE GIFTBORN CHRONICLES

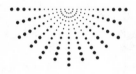

DREW BAILEY

FALSTAFF
BOOKS
WWW.FALSTAFFBOOKS.COM

To the thing within that names me imposter. "Three books in, bitch."

DRAMATIS PERSONAE

HOUSE LANIER

Aiden Ashborough/Prince Desmond Lanier, the eldest son of King Whitman II and Queen Larissa Lanier, the true heir to the Throne of Lancastle, twenty-three cycles old

Princess Marsea Lanier, the eldest daughter, twenty

Broenwjar, Marsea's wolf familiar

Prince Rembrandt Lanier/Yvemathira, the youngest son, eighteen/Queen of the Dracari

Larissa Lanier, Queen of Lancastle (deceased)

Whitman Lanier II, the last and former King of Lancastle, died during the coup of the Midnight Men at the age of fifty

HOUSE HARVER

Raelan Harver, General and High Commander of the Lancastle Royalguard Regiment, Larissa Lanier's husband

Pion Harver, Raelan's son, twenty-two

Julia Harver, the daughter of Raelan and Queen Larissa, half-sister of Pion, Desmond, Marsea, and Remy, nine

COURT OF COUROWNE

Drezhal Dalivant, Emperor of Courowne

Magwyn Lanier, Empress of Courowne, Drezhal's wife, Whitman's sister, Aunt to Desmond, Marsea, and Remy

Rhonyn Waldgrave, Ambassador of Lancastle, Queen Larissa's older brother

Victor Goss, a councilman and the High Magus of Court Courowne

Ender Visbane, Commodore of the warship Belisarius

Wilson Marlowe the Younger, a Captain in the Emperorswatch

SOUTHLANDS

Stella Ashborough, Aiden's step-mother (deceased), a storied magus, and former archivist to Lancastle Library

Vincent Ashborough, Aiden's step-father, a winemaker

Autumn Ashborough, Aiden's younger step-sister, fifteen

Caitlyn Ellsbury, Aiden's former girlfriend

Calem Reid, Aiden's best friend from university

Tabitha Reid, Calem's mother, once Crown of her Order

POTIONS PREFERRED

Edgar Alewine, the troupe's scout

Priscilla "Poppy" Pelvenyn, the troupe's chronicler, Xandria's sister

Xandria Pelvenyn, the troupe's songstress, Poppy's sister

Simon Goodfellow, Xandria's latest lovefool

Niall Latham, the troupe's fiddler

Stringer Paul Finn, the troupe's lutenist

Anson Wordsworth, the troupe's leader and caravan driver

FURTHER PLAYERS

Rhymona Curie/Morgandrel Tully, an ashaeydir battle-magus with a violent past

Xavien Ledgermaine, a barkeep at The Heart House in Port Tavern-mast, a magus and blademaster

Effie Cavendish/Myrenna, a cloth maiden, and friend to Princess Marsea/Yvemathira's closest

Yongrin Tarboril, a magus loyal to Ravenholme

Valestriel Alyfain, an ashaeydir soldier that befriends Aiden (deceased)

Solindiel Alyfain, Valestriel's eldest sister, a soldier in the Ashaeydir Guard

Dysenia Luiryn, an ashaeydir assassin

Elsymir Beldroth, a y'deman huntsman, former apprentice to Malthus Tetherow

Ankaira Severyn, a magus and close friend of Malthus Tetherow and Elsymir Beldroth

Malthus Tetherow, a magus and author tangled in rumors

Yurien Tenbrooks/Hrathgon, a battle-magus of some repute soulbound to a dracari

Lita Drufellyn, a mythical magus shrouded in mystery

WHAT HAS COME BEFORE

REMY: After his duel with Vaustian Harver, Remy Lanier finds himself on the brink of death, but is saved by Rhymona Curie inside an astral plane known as The Spellbind with the aid of a dracari named Yvemathira, who binds her soul to that of Remy's to resuscitate his life force. In return, Thira is released from her imprisonment inside The Spellbind's ward. They return to the physical plane as the blight descend on the kingdom of Lancastle and make it inside the castle by the skin of their teeth.

Inside, Remy searches for his family and finds his mother Larissa and half-sister Julia Harver hunkered down amongst the High House nobility in the King's solar. Queen Larissa reveals that Remy's older brother Desmond is still alive.

The small council meet, but before they can decide a proper strategy of defense the blight breach the citadel and Remy is forced into duty once more. Battling through an endless onslaught of ghouls, Remy eventually meets Effie, who, like him, houses a dracari soul named Myrenna. The two dracari hatch a plan to banish the lichlord controlling the blighted legion and succeed; however, it comes at the loss of Myrenna and her host Effie.

In the aftermath, Remy patrols the castle, searching for Larissa and Julia, but instead finds a demon possessing Aeralie Harver through its connection with the nether infection inside her. It tells Remy his victory here is but a bandage for a death wound, and that the nether will inevitably win this war. It is cyclical and how the story always ends.

Meeting once more with the remains of the small council, they are attacked by a rogue battle-magus named Yurien Tenbrooks, who casts a madness spell amongst the group. Remy gives chase, which leads him through a portal and back to the abandoned shop he and Rhymona arrived in from Palatia. Here he comes upon the corpse of his mother and an ashaeydir assassin named Solindiel Alyfain, who has been waiting for another spellslinger to arrive that knows the name of the ward Dysenia Deadeyes passed through.

Together, Remy and Solindiel go through the portal and arrive in the kingdom of Courowne.

RHYMONA: Rhymona is kept outside the council chamber after she, Remy, and Casilvieri make it inside Lancastle Citadel. She finds herself atop the battlements speaking to Casilvieri about her desertion and all that has transpired since, but the conversation is interrupted by the blight who begin to break through, stacking bodies like mountains to top the castle walls. Rhymona and Casilvieri narrowly escape death with the aid of Effie, who is revealed as Eldnumerian.

Racing back through the castle halls, Rhymona and Casilvieri run into Queen Larissa and Julia Harver. To evade the swarm of chasing blight, they go through a portal in the guest chambers and find themselves back in the abandoned shop Rhymona and Remy arrived in from Palatia. Dysenia Luiryn is waiting for them there. It is revealed that Dysenia is Rhymona's aunt, who left Rhymona to the Alyfain's torments as a child. Dysenia mortally wounds Casilvieri and kills Queen Larissa with a wand strike to the head before leaving through a portal. The blighted claw at the walls all around them, threatening to burst in. Before he dies, Casilvieri convinces Rhymona to take Julia through the portal after Dysenia as he believes she is at the heart of the blight's return and must be put down.

Rhymona and Julia arrive in Courowne and head for an innhouse to regroup. They find some rest and meet some of the locals who report that one of Emperor Drezhal's ships have returned with a man claiming to be Prince Desmond Lanier, also known as Aiden Ashborough, Rhymona's former lover at Perciya University. Not long after, Remy and Solindiel arrive at the inn. They decide to investigate the truth behind Desmond's return.

MARSEA: Moments after Rhymona drops inside The Spellbind to revive Remy, Casilvieri arrives, followed by Yongrin and Davrin Tarboril. The Tarborils have been ordered by Tetherow to meet Vaustian Harver and see Marsea safely through to the Ravenholme enclave. Instead, they find their contact Vaustian butchered and Rhymona and Remy in a deathly trance, Marsea and Casilvieri standing guard.

Marsea decides to go with the Tarborils to the enclave so long as they do not harm any of the others. Yongrin agrees and commands Marsea to bring the grimoire that Remy and Rhymona fought tooth and nail to keep from her.

In the Ravenholme enclave, Marsea meets Tetherow, who reveals he is actually Tetherow's former apprentice. His true name is Elsymir Beldroth and he has been pretending to be Tetherow to keep control of Ravenholme's activities; though the Tarborils have begun to suspect his deception.

Beldroth takes Marsea under his wing as an apprentice, introducing her to his familiar Broenwjar and teaching her how to reach out to her gift. They venture to a nearby hollow named Vinth where Marsea meets Dagmara and Klaus VanLandingham, former Ravenholme loyalists now committed to Beldroth's cause. Beldroth reveals to his old friends he is dying from nether poison with only days, mayhaps hours, to live, and means to leave his legacy in Marsea Lanier's hands.

Marsea eventually agrees to honor him as Beldroth relates his past relationship with Marsea's father, King Whit.

The following day, as she becomes more attuned to her gift, Marsea undergoes a ritual that transfers Broenwjar's bond as Beldroth's familiar to her. Soon after, she begins to notice some of her wounds have healed including the blade cuts on her hand from her duel with Ganedys Harver.

Beldroth takes Marsea out into the woods for one last training session and bestows her with a sentient blade named Blind Widow.

Marsea attempts to communicate with her gift once more. However, during this meditation, Beldroth begins to turn, the nether inside him outlasting his ability to keep it at bay. Beldroth tries to wake Marsea from her giftborn trance as he is being eaten alive by the nether, but is unsuccessful. Broenwjar's fear of his former master's agony pulls Marsea into him through a gift ability known as varging. Ripped from her internal gift ocean, Marsea quickly realizes she is in Broenwjar's body as Beldroth is nearly consumed by nether rot. Unsure how to varg back into her natural body, Marsea races as Broenwjar back through the woods to find Dagmara.

When they arrive back at her body, Beldroth has completely transformed into a creature called a gnaudrylax. Dagmara uses a totem ward and wand strikes to frighten the ghastly horror away and summons Marsea from Broenwjar back into her own body.

Distraught from the loss of Beldroth, they return back to the VanLandingham's cottage only to find Yongrin and Davrin Tarboril waiting for them. Dagmara sacrifices herself in a wand battle to give Marsea a chance to flee with the grimoire. Davrin gives chase. Marsea decides to face him and defeats him with Broenwjar's help. As she strikes him with Blind Widow, a strange creature appears and Davrin's body begins to come apart as though by hemomancy forming a whirling pool of flesh and blood in the air.

Yongrin approaches, following Davrin's death screams, and Marsea rushes away from the bloodbath, deeper into the woods, Broenwjar at her side.

AIDEN: Aiden, Val, and Ledgermaine have boarded Blackhall's Banshee in route to Dorngar, a harbor town off the Vinteyaman coast. They plan to travel to Lancastle, then to The Spellbind in Nocthun, unaware of how dire the war with the blight has become in the north. Aiden learns the truth about his past as Desmond Lanier from Ledgermaine, however, their discussion is cut short by the arrival of the goldcoat fleet.

Blackhall's Banshee is a known pirate vessel and this causes the goldcoat ships to pursue and fire. Desperate to defend the ship, Aiden begins to conjure a spell but is possessed by something within as he taps into his gift. He conjures an impossible amount of magic before falling unconscious.

He awakens in shackles aboard the goldcoat vessel Belisarius. Commodore Visbane interrogates him after claims by the other captives that he is Prince Desmond Lanier, returned from the dead. He admits to it and Visbane decides to keep him alive for now.

Aiden and Val are taken before Emperor Drezhal after they arrive in Courowne. Drezhal's wife, Empress Magwyn, is Desmond's aunt and inspects him. Instantly, she believes he is her nephew, though she doesn't understand how he is still alive. Despite her acknowledgments of Aiden's claim to be her nephew, Drezhal orders them to be taken to the dungeons while he considers what to do with them. Magwyn explains that Demond's uncle, Rhonyn Waldgrave, is also in the dungeons having overstepped his bounds in a violent outburst after the League of Royal Houses voted abdication upon House Lanier.

In the dungeons, they find Uncle Rhonyn beaten and bloody. Rhonyn further explains that there is more at play than they know and that they must remain wary. He divulges some of the prophecy from King Whit's youth, revealing that Whit forged a grimoire that could be used against the dark forces that have returned to their world, and admits to convincing his sister, Aiden's birth mother Larissa, to bring him back from the grave.

Pion Harver arrives and frees Aiden and Val from their cell, but with guards quickly approaching, he is unable to spring Rhonyn as well. Pion leads them back to the city walks and to an innhouse where they can rest and hide for the night, leaving them for another issue he must attend to.

Aiden and Val make love for the first time, giving in to their draw to one another.

The following morning, Aiden awakens to find himself bloody on the floor and Val brutally murdered in their bed. As he tries to make sense of what he is seeing, he is overcome by a voice in his head. Seconds later, Aiden loses the ability to govern his body, fastly realizing he is now the voice in his head and someone else is controlling him.

The creature calls itself Tetherow.

Pion returns with Aiden's grimoire, *Arcanum Volume IV*, in his hand, calling the creature possessing Aiden *master*. Grinning, the master says to his apprentice, "Let's go kill us an empire."

CHAPTER ONE

She died in love.

Such marked the famous last words of *White Wolf, Black Sheep,* some wanky old Chandiian tragedy about a pair of star-crossed school rivals that go from smugging it up proper at a spellslinger's cup to the depths of a penny horror romance in the span of a quintweek.

At best, it passed as sentimental tosh. A classic Caitie heartbreaker. Neither here nor there. The proverbial read at the end of a stack. And yet, for some fel reason, those final words stuck with Aiden Ashborough over the cycles like some cruel manner of crone's curse. Sadly, pathetically, tragically, rubbish as it fell, those four foolish words formed the best explanation he could conjure for why she suddenly stopped fighting him, allowing the fiend to win. Allowing him to unmake her and complete its demented ritual.

She died in love.

And what the fuck would you know of love, fuckwit? All those nights spent flirting and courting and aimlessly humping your way about the university talent. Snogging with the riffraff. Betraying Caitie's trust...betraying Val's benevolence...

She died in love? More like she died hexing your rotten fucking name, you selfish, depraved piece of shit.

1

But this is what we all do in the end, isn't it? When desperation strikes and the luck stones roll against us?

We dissociate.

We deflect.

We bargain.

We compartmentalize.

We pray and give hope to false delusions just so we can feel better about our sins for half a stale breath longer.

We do everything in our power to deny our diseased fancies and return back to a time when the world felt passable and normal and safe.

But the gods know, he had always been a scoundrel, hadn't he? From the very moment he came wailing into this poxy pill of a world. And long before Tetherow sank his nasty fangs in. A King? The mere notion that his name should be placed anywhere near a kingship was absolutely preposterous, and yet here he now found himself...

Val. Her name stretched out in a dreadful lullaby before him, like the crude reflections of an endless carnie mirror. *I should be as the memory. Not you.*

As wounds go, her death dug in deep. Salty as they come. For to the selfish and depraved, as was he, she offered her love freely. Cast forth despite her impossible predicament and in spite of her ugly tangle of emotions. Freely in the face of his ghastly state. Freely as though it were a thing unwanted. Love at its most tender. Surrender in a heart-shaped glass.

I'm sorry. They were words of a sort, he reckoned, though they came out warped and wanting and weak as a used-up murmur.

At least she got in one good blow before submitting, the one that took a tooth from its root. But, of course, Tetherow then spit the prize back in her face, laughing at her pluck as though she'd spun off a witty jape instead.

It was in the moment that followed, her lips yet tasting of his, caught twixt bone and spirit—nay, conception and collapse—that she yielded and in the next thereafter chose submission and sacrifice and lastly, the most disastrous shape of love.

Lies.

He gazed deep into her golden orbs, really gazed, as though for the first time, hunting for some bit of meaning in her final moments, some logical explanation for why she had to be taken in such a vile, senseless manner. But there was no rational answer to be had. No plausible motive. No great, reasonable epiphany. And yet in the place of such foul injustice, of such brazen savagery, he instead found love—of all things—a romantic's reverie, that—chased by hope, and a forgiveness he had no right to claim. Gods' breath, but there wasn't a soul this side of the moon that deserved such a forgiveness as hers.

At once he saw Valestriel's goodness. Like the luminous embodiment of a star maiden. It was a goodness he was wholly incapable of, and in the wake of his actions toward her, it was a goodness he would never ever dream to approach. It was the kind of goodness folk took for granted. The same kind of goodness Stella brandished about with effortless grace. And the same kind of goodness he had always sensed in his baby sister Tam. The kind of goodness that could never be repaid. At least not fully. The kind of goodness only a scant special few were capable of. The kind of goodness that only came naturally and to those that beat pure of heart. The kind of goodness that transcended all other moral conventions.

No, he scolded. *This is not the thing you focus on. This is not the reason you suffer...*

The end of the thought floated away from him and popped like an abscess, leaking away into oblivion's forgotten well of wishes.

It went without saying really, but the nether-madness had long since settled in. Hells, it had uncorked a bottle, propped up its feet, and had a good long drag watching him squirm about like a useless fucking wastrel.

In the corridors of his mind, his thoughts were warring with that of the other swallowed souls for precedence. Or so that was what he presumed they were—the sea of disembodied voices. Thusly, it took a couple loops more to wrest his ruminations from the horror of Valestriel's death so that he could concentrate on what was presently left him.

Ending Malthus Tetherow.

Such was all that mattered now. Such was what remained of his existence. And he *would* find a way to fight back. Any way he could. For Val. For Stella. For those that had been taken by his crooked hand. For those that yet remained. For those that Tetherow would use his likeness to target next. He had to make things right or as near to right as was yet still possible.

Again.

SLIVERS OF VALESTRIEL'S last moments came back in rushes, as they had a dozen times before, beginning with the constricting pain around his calf that would thenceforth slither up the bones of his leg and into the blade scar that marked his belly, forcing Aiden wide awake.

Only it wasn't he that came to call.

Rather Malthus Tetherow, clad inside his gangling form, turning a devilish gaze upon Valestriel and swiftly rolling atop her, inching his knees astride her ribs, casually pinning her beneath his nakedness.

Valestriel stirred upon his presence and dreamily whispered his name. Aiden hated hearing the like uttered so affectionately, especially knowing what lingered ahead. But this was what he had to work with and truth's witness he deserved a punishment that was infinitely worse.

The archivist's hands spoke for his tongue, brushing curls out of her face before delicately tracing the contours of her jawline down to her throat. In response, she grazed fingers gently into the hairs of his thigh, trailing forth toward his manhood, her warm hands finding his hardness.

He began to squeeze, the fingernails of his thumbs stabbing down into her throat like dagger points, drawing forth thin rivulets of blood.

Her eyes came to his—searching—an eternity in an instant—big, lustrous, golden doe eyes housing a cruel panic behind complete and utter confusion. They were as Stella's eyes had been in the downstairs foyer of Ashborough Manor.

Last breath eyes lamenting all the memories that could have been.

And just as abruptly as they appeared, they were gone and replaced by a fist slamming into the side of his chin.

He shifted with the blow, and smiling, spit the blood it bought right back into her face.

She flailed wildly at him, wriggling and writhing as his hands constricted tighter and tighter around her neck, compressing her jugular, robbing her of her screams. But then, suddenly, right before her consciousness embraced the fade, she stared hard into his eyes, one last time, really stared, past the fel creature that straddled atop her and past what came next, deep into the pits of his soul, until she finally found him.

In that instant, her eyes spoke of a love and forgiveness that no one living this side of the moon even partway deserved. Especially not him.

Everything went still.

He watched her for a moment through Tetherow's eyes as the fiend released his hands from around her mangled neck. Tetherow placed a bloodstained finger under her nose and Aiden felt the end of a life whisper across it. The fiend then grabbed the pillow from beside her and pushed it down over her face as he began chanting in a crude devil language.

As it had been each time before, the start of the incantation severed the memory loop, its detachment chased with the sudden sensation of falling from some great height, forcing Aiden's mind back into the expanse of shifting shadows, back amongst the throng of disembodied voices, back into his nothing crippled nightmare.

Frost and flame seized what remained, and a muted wail surged out of him like a monstrous tidal wave.

It went without saying really but knowing the memory did not make the emotions it conjured any less difficult to bear. Though this time the pain brought along something new. Something potentially useful. Something so blatantly obvious he was insulted it took him so many loops through to realize it.

The scar.

Aiden recalled the ache he so often experienced in his side and leg upon stirring.

The scar is your totem.

How many times had he woken to that cold, wrenching agony? How many times had he forgotten it?

That's our bond, isn't it? You skeevy fuck. That's the evidence of your control. That pain is your doorway. It's how you let yourself in and out.

The damp, slithering darkness constricted around his essence in response, and the cramping sensation in his left calf started up again, coiling northward past where his knee might have been, across his thigh, lancing back into his belly...

CHAPTER TWO

...AND THE WORLD tilted once more, looping round and round for another go, sprawling off in a thousand different directions, the colors flickering past with a wholly divergent pattern from before, blurring frantic and bright, hither and yon, bending, sparkling, twisting, burning, until the cry of visions began to repair focus, and the archivist found himself inside the belly of a great ranging tower.

And not just any tower, but one housing the most magnificent ritual chamber he'd ever beheld.

Symbols of the ancient arcana marked the climbing spiral of stone wall, shimmering emerald, ruby, violet, azure, and amber, grasping high into the endless void above, stretching far away from the candlelit cellar.

The fuck is this place?

To be sure, it belonged to no memory of his. Hells, it hardly appeared a real place at all, favoring the fantastic, like some farce ripped straight from the pages of Mervold's *Winterbury Tales*.

He found two others in the tower with him and a most unsettling presence drinking up what little air passed between them. A presence he'd grown lamentably familiar with over the past quintweek.

Tetherow.

By the pair's dated attire, Aiden reckoned if this were indeed a memory, it occurred many cycles past, likely by a few centuries.

"The hour's come," the man rasped, removing his tricorn, disheveled as though he'd just come in from a storm, eyes ranging out of his skull like a resin-fiend on a requiem binge. "We need to cut it out of me before it's too late." Long, pointed ears poked out from the tousled mess of silver-gold hair that ran down like a cloak over his scrawny shoulders, marking him as y'deman. His pallid face wrinkled with fear and mayhaps some manner of sickness—and there was something else there as well. A pall of dread enveloped Aiden as the y'deman's anxieties began to spill over. It was as though the man's apprehensions had suddenly become his own, complete with a comedown fever and the worst case of the cold sweats he'd ever endured.

With a thought, Aiden reappeared across the chamber nearer the pair.

"It's too soon, Malthus," said a gray-haired midaran woman, her face half-hidden behind a floating grimoire. "Besides, we would need a third and likely a fourth."

Malthus?

"Sod it all, Ankaira, it's bloody winning," Malthus grated, twitching about. "We need to bind it to something tonight. Bind it and burn it. You and me."

A page turned on its own before the sorceress as she met the y'deman's eyes. "We've already discussed this. There are too many things that could go wrong without a proper cadre. Namely, we could split the wrong part of your soul. Or worse yet, we could split your mind and leave you a drooling vegetable. What then?"

"I don't suppose you would still dote on a drooling vegetable then, would you?"

"Mal, this is quite serious."

The gods know, but they quibbled like old lovers, didn't they?

"Oh, I'm deadly serious." The y'deman's brow furrowed. "This is what's left us, Annie. I can feel the urges taking over. The hate, the evil, the malice, like a dark thirst. The tonics aren't working. They only dull the senses. And the cutie-penny has nearly eaten through every thought that once made me an actual person. Made a right fine ruin of this wretched soul.

"I nearly killed a man in the bazaar today for merely bumping into me. It was an honest mistake. An innocent little nothing. He even apologized immediately afterward and yet the thing inside urged my hands down toward my wand. Could you imagine it? Striking someone down for such an ordinary trifle? At least as a vegetable I would no longer have the worry of bringing others harm."

"Darling," Ankaira started.

"I mean to do this, Annie," Malthus interjected, defiance stealing through fragments of deranged bloodshot. "I can't trust myself any longer. I understand if you cannot take part. I would be positively unhinged were our roles reversed, but the thought of what this thing is capable of...the thought of hurting you..."

Aiden couldn't believe what he was witnessing. Cutie-penny? Tonics? *This* neurotic junkie was Malthus Tetherow? *The* Malthus Tetherow? One of the most storied sorcerers to ever live?

The floating grimoire snapped shut between them and Ankaira cupped a hand to Tetherow's cheek. "If I lose you," she whispered pointedly, "I will never forgive you."

"If we don't do this tonight, you will most assuredly lose me, and mayhaps much, much worse."

Ankaira frowned. Aiden rather thought she had an attractive scowl for a woman in her silver cycles, her aura fiery and unwavering and full of life despite her age. She turned her back to them and strode to a nearby table cluttered by tomes and parchment and every manner of bottle, vial, urn, and flask imaginable. Each one appeared to contain a liquid of varying shade. A kindleblade lay beside a mortar and pestle, its line of runes gleaming majestically in the crowd of candlelight.

Beyond the table, the chamber was an alchemist's wet dream. A half dozen more such work tables filled the spaces between towering bookshelves and stacks of overflow, each one strewn with a divergent collection of baubles and oddments. Scrolls were nestled neatly inside nooks carved within the stone walls, labeled by school of magic. There was even what appeared to be a golem in the corner. No doubt were Calem to have found this place, he would have been gushing and grinning about like a fawning idiot. He, the man who hated Malthus Tetherow as though it paid his bloody rents to do so.

"I haven't told you everything about me, Annie," Malthus said. "To have it honest, I'd rather hoped to avoid ever telling another soul the tale. In particular, you. Yet, here we are."

"What is it, darling? What haven't you told me?"

"It will upset you and likely change us forever."

Aiden leaned against one of the work-tables, arms folded. The only thing missing from the scene was a grand burning hearth and a fresh goblet of wine.

"Oh, for Veradon's sake, Malthus." Her eyes hardened. "Out with it already. What is so awful you'd never wish another soul to know?"

"It involves the strange circumstances of my birth."

That's never a good sign.

"And the truth about my father."

"Your father? I thought you never knew your father."

"That much was true." Malthus shifted away from Ankaira and gazed directly at Aiden. "In fact, no one ever knew him. There was no account of him at all. No memories, no face, not even a name to claim to."

Aiden pushed up from the work-table and held the y'deman's stare. *Can he see me?*

"Come to find out, my mother was prone to losing time and waking in strange places with no recollection as to how she got there." Malthus glanced away from them both, raking fingers across his heart. "In this, she came to believe herself haunted by a darkly presence not of this plane."

Ankaira held, stiff as a stone column.

"Thereafter, during my youngling cycles, mother would routinely refer to me as devil child and spawn of Sinara, amongst a host of similarly unsavory insults. She was a cruel woman, my mother, taking every misfortune the world ever gave her out on me. And prize well, after my bearing, mostly misfortune was all that found her."

"Spawn of Sinara," Ankaira said, her voice rough as sanded paper. "In y'deman folklore, she is something like a succubus, yes?"

"She is the Queen of all devilkin." Malthus gazed back up into Ankaira's waiting orbs. "Once I reached university, I made it a point to learn everything under the sun and moons about demonology, where I uncovered far more than I should have liked and began connecting dots decades to the rot. I became convinced the creature that tormented my mother was what you midarans name a dream eater and I believe through my conception she passed her curse on to me."

"A dream eater? Are you saying she was haunted by an incubus?"

Fucking hells.

"Oh, I know she was." His eyes shone hard as a whetstone and sharp as the blade it married.

"Which would make you..."

The word echoed behind Aiden's ear a moment before its utterance.

"*Cambion*," Malthus finished, and the revelation burned like a brand of scalding iron down the span of Aiden's essence. "With such information in stow, I thought I could control it. The violent tremors. The sinister compulsions. Mayhaps even overpower them. I thought the greater my ability with magic, the greater my defense. In the cycles to follow, I worked hard as a madman to perfect my gift. A score and ten to the cause. But now it's become too plain to ignore and hope against. The fiend still persists. Nay, thrives. Feeding off of my gift in spite of my efforts. Mocking my attempts to delay the inevitable and laughing in the face of my denial. For the truth remains, that in the end, I am merely a puppet, and the more powerful I become, the closer it gains to completing its possession."

...*session*...

...*ession*...

The word echoed, and without warning the memory began to shift shape once more, blurring like frost on glass...

Wait. No. Aiden drifted forward. *What's happening?*

Focus returned a moment later and Aiden now found Malthus belted to a table at the northern point of the chamber rose.

At the table's end, Ankaira was reciting from the largest grimoire the archivist had ever beheld.

On a plinth beside her lay an opened timber box, laced in iron and warded on each side with glimmering ruby sigils.

By the old tongue's beck, a soft mist the shade of stone malachite arose from Malthus's writhing torso like steam from a boiling cookpot, darkening as it expanded. The leather belts strapped around his wrists, waist, and ankles were barely keeping him in place. Fever poured down the y'deman's face as he ground his teeth against the wooden bit and clutched frantically at the edges of the table. It wasn't long into the ritual that the vapor began to form the outline of another.

No, Aiden quickly realized, almost sensing the shadow-thing slithering about his own ethereal flesh. It wasn't forming. It *was* the vapor. The gods be damned. The faceless apparition reached out from Malthus as though it were crawling up from the bloody grave.

Despite Malthus's unnatural clicking and strangled cries of agony, Ankaira never looked up from the grimoire. The words, recited in what Aiden could only presume was Dracthonir or Chandiian, had the fiend rapt under its spell, drawing it forth from Malthus's convulsing body like a siren's song.

The chamber withered inside the creature's wraith-like presence, the tables started to crack, splinter, and warp, glass bottles shook from their perches, smashing in chorus against the flagstone depths, the little plant-life that lingered about wilted to dust in their pots. Though, within seconds the chamber altered from that of a wintry abyss to a sweltering oven well on its way to combustion, defying the proper nature of the elements. The fiend was fighting back, its presence like a hammer to anvil upon the sorceress's musical chant, but even still she couldn't halt the ritual now, there was too much bottled magic at play, were she to break by even the smallest of margins the effects could prove catastrophic.

Ankaira held to the grimoire's passages, not a word wasted, leaving the archivist in complete awe. Never before had he beheld such extraordinary wizardry. It was at that point Aiden realized the sorceress was employing an old lecture hall trick. One Calem taught him during his first semester at uni. The grimoire itself was nothing more than a red herring, an object to focus on to keep her mind on the task at hand rather than the horror show it bought. While the words may have indeed found presentation, the archivist had no doubts Ankaira knew the lines well before their count. Truth's witness, she seemed precisely the sort to memorize pages forwards to back and last to first if only to cover all fronts.

But this particular creature was an ancient and formidable being, and it was not to be outdone. Not now. And certainly not by some old nan's half-cooked storybook incantation. It stretched out across the table, silhouette darkening, grasping for its present master, desperate to silence the calling.

Malthus spit the bit out, raw. "Annie, stop!" he yelped through clenched teeth and gobs of mouth foam.

The whole of the fiend's murky form set about swallowing the void behind its appendage, picking up pace in Ankaira's direction. It was coming for her, sucking her in. Aiden could feel it too, as he could feel Malthus, and quite suddenly he understood where all the y'deman's fear rose from. The presence was pure malevolence and escape was precisely what it desired.

The sorceress paced back a step, drawing forth her kindleblade, but the effort came much too late.

Malthus unleashed an ungodly howl as the presence tore itself free, invading Ankaira's orifices, halting her chanting like glass in the throat, piss pooling at her feet, before a deafening crack flung the entire chamber into complete disarray, sending tables, cabinets, and bookcases toppling over, tomes flying, and the sorceress careening violently backward.

Moon-eyed, Aiden watched, utterly powerless.

Loose parchment floated down around them like falling leaves.

Malthus croaked out to Ankaira, but his voice proved as uncooperative as his restraints.

The sound of metal scraping across stone silenced his struggle as Ankaira staggered back up to her feet.

:*Sodding hells,*: the sorceress groaned as she turned back toward them, multiple voices coming out of her simultaneously. Blood bubbled up and streamed down her face from a nasty gash across her temple. Though as gruesome as the wound was to bear, it paled by comparison to the misshapen expression she presently wore.

"Annie?" Malthus whimpered.

:*How does one know where the devilkin goes when the devilkin knows you're awake?*: she answered, her many eldritch voices merging into one guttural tone midsentence.

"No."

:*Mother always did have an odd sense of humor, didn't she?*: Ankaira said before pressing a finger into her head wound and licking its contents. :*Oh, but what to do when the thing from within has its own thing within?*: The sorceress halted at the table's midway point and gazed down at Malthus. :*Every one of them obeyed us. Everyone, but her.*: She trailed her fingers delicately through his hair. :*Do you recall what mother named us?*:

"Rot in hells," Malthus spat through the slobber, jerking away from her.

:*A mistake.*: Ankaira studied the kindleblade's serrated edge, running a thumb across its jagged teeth. :*And do you recall what we did?*:

"What you did!"

:Well now, I can't take all of the credit. You had the thought after all, didn't you?: Ankaira shifted the blade so the bottom of her fist wore the deadly end. *:But you never had the bollocks, did you? Even when you still physically owned a pair.:* She lowered the blade point against his heaving stomach. *:Was it like this, I wonder?:* By her command, the kindleblade eased into Malthus's belly all the way down to the quillon.

"Ungh…" Malthus wheezed, blood discoloring the froth caked to the edges of his mouth. "I was only a boy…"

:Thought you'd given your last fuck about me, didn't you, Malthus? Thought you'd had me bested.: A grin full of menace and mischief played upon her lips. *:The cutie-penny was a clever ruse for a time, I will grant you, but not near clever enough.:*

"I was…a good man…"

:You were some Lord's fool motley, Malthus. You were a slave, a cockless nursemaid at best, and a fucking kneeler. All the talent in the world and you've squandered it, bending to the whims of hags and heathens, no better than the leeches they set to feasting on the dying and unwell.

:I am what got you this far, the only reason we've lasted as long as we have, and yet you strive to rid yourself of me? You dare to bury me away as the monster? To keep me dormant? You, who are nothing without me? Now you can suffer as such. Just as our whore mother did.:

At the words, an eerie ghoulish noise pulled at Aiden, gnawing at him from the memory's edge.

Ankaira twisted the blade out cross and messy. *:And here's one more fuck you to linger on.:* She made a second wound within the wellspring of blood and left it there to fester. *:Be seeing you, Mal.:* She drifted away, orbs glistening bright as untouched snow, swaggering off toward the great sparkling crimson doorway. *:Or maybe I won't.:*

Aiden watched in terror as the sorceress disappeared from the tower, and when he turned back to Malthus, he found the y'deman once again staring directly at him, laboring for breath. It only lasted a moment, but the archivist asked anyway.

Can you see me?

Malthus made no response. Instead, he screamed for all the hells' nine furies and shimmied his body toward a hand, stretching the opposite restraint to its limit, just far enough to free the dagger from his belly. A fresh gout of blood gushed out of him as he shifted the blade so it dug into the leather belt fastened to his wrist, and he began to saw away at it.

Suddenly Aiden felt as though he'd taken a blade to the gut himself, and a scream the color of shimmering starfire spilled out of him. A jagged pain bloomed inside his belly, clawing down his abdomen, shredding through scar tissue, splitting meat from bone across the length of his hip, separating the flesh of his thigh all the way down into his calf.

The tower started spinning again as he staggered forward, through blinding agony, away from the strange, muffled voices behind his ears, catching himself against an overturned bookshelf, and finally crumbling to the floor. The shadows descended, feasting after his fear afresh, fast as a preying spider, tendrils swathing him in razor-sharp gossamer, swallowing up all to sight.

And once more, like maggots on a corpse, the creeping darkness crawled inside...

CHAPTER THREE

THE CRONE'S promise danced along the fringes of Magwyn's recollection, almost toying with her for all its cycles spent in blatant disregard. Still, it was all she had thought on since Desmond's arrival. Something about Selwyn Shawley's prophetic telling had always troubled her, and never more so than after her nephew's untimely death. Though news of Whit's beheading only days later vastly overshadowed the former. At the time, it was all she could do just to cope with the loss of her brother. She hadn't enough strength in her to accept both. So, she closed herself off to Desmond. And then she closed herself off to Marsea and Rembrandt and Larissa and House Lanier entirely.

Admittedly, she'd been weak back then, and until his death, still bitter toward her brother for selling her off to the Dalivant's like so much livestock, knowing good and well her heart belonged to another.

As the cycles fell away, the court of Courowne hardened her considerably, altering her personality in ways she couldn't have possibly imagined whilst living so sheltered in the high halls of Lancastle. Made a right proper Lady of her, they did.

The Empress sat up straight, brushed the ruffles from her green velvet dress, leveled her lace collar, and eased her shoulders back against the smooth stonework of her throne. A deep breath followed, and she closed her eyes to block out the bickering council in the pews below. She tried to mouth the crone's words to life as her mind wandered deep into the folds of her past, deeper than she would have preferred, deeper than she'd allowed herself in nigh on a score.

But the gods know, she was just as unfair to Whit as he had been toward her. Oh, how she wished she hadn't been such a wretched little shit back when, so wrapped up in her own little problems to ever bother with that of her brother's, to ever attempt at relating to the pressure and scrutiny he lived under every single breath of every single day. Then again, she'd counted just north of fourteen at the time and was yet still fresh in the throes of her first bout with lovesickness.

Maggie clung, rapt, to those feelings and tethered them to those associated with the crone's encounter, sending her gift hungering after it, determined to unlock the hag's prophecy.

It wasn't long into her focus that her husband's quarreling began to fade away, replaced by her dead brother's voice and the whine of a cold winter wind.

"I TOLD you that you would need your heavy cloak," Whit scolded as they passed from Marion's Courtyard and into the arcade just outside the Lancastle Cathedral.

"You live and you learn, I suppose," Maggie answered smartly, at least as smartly as one could through chittering teeth, bundling up her shivers, and rubbing her hands against the outsides of her arms. Truthfully, she had just been so excited to finally spend some quality time with her brother that she'd completely forgotten about the drop in weather.

In one fluid movement, Whitman shouldered off his Royalguard coat and draped it across her shoulders. "There you are."

"You don't have to do that."

"I'm fine, honestly," he replied in his best older brother tone. A tone, as she recalled, that bore little use quibbling against.

"You're sure?" She had to admit, Whitman had filled out considerably in the months he had spent away at officer training. At a score, he was already taller than their father and almost as broad. He even sported a full beard now. She rather thought it suited him handsomely.

"Positive," he answered with a noble grin.

And by the gods' good graces, the guard hadn't yet taken anything away from her brother's warm smile. She was greatly thankful for that bit too.

Maggie clutched at the buttoning point of the oversized coat and swayed her shoulders about playfully so the sleeves flapped around her from front to back. "You know I rather think I'd make for a dashing soldier." She stopped to make a heroic pose. "Wouldn't you agree?"

Whit snorted. "I agree that you are absolutely ridiculous."

Mid-pose, Magwyn crinkled up her nose and stuck out her tongue. It went without saying really, but she had long since settled into her role as the family clown.

"Careful sticking your tongue out too far, sis, else you may catch a fly for it." He ran a hand through his dark wind-tousled curls, brushing the length from his eyes.

"Are you joking? Not with these gnashers in defense." She smiled big, emphasizing her most defining facial feature.

Whit simply rolled his eyes. "You should've seen some of the women at Maidstone. They'd eat a soldier like you for breakfast. Hells, they'd eat a soldier like me for breakfast. One in particular, Hilda Veranski, she'd take the cup off any tourney bracket."

"A woman soldier is top of your class?"

"By a few dozen marks."

"I should like to one day meet this Hilda Veranski."

"You may be in luck then. She will be attending the upcoming springtide oathing ceremony. I will have to introduce you."

"Please do." Maggie delighted at the prospect. "Mother says you are home until the New Cycle," she offered a breath later, her mind horribly astray. "Mayhaps one of these days coming, if the weather warms, you could train me to the bow. That is if it won't be too much of a bother."

"It would be my pleasure." He stroked his bushy beard. "Honestly, I could stand a bit of practice over holiday and what better reason would I have than teaching my little sister the huntsman's game?"

"We may have to go out ranging farther than you and Elsymir typically did to avoid the guard," she added. "Mother has been less than enthusiastic about my inquiries into the like."

"Is that so?"

"They are not ladylike, she says. She rather made it her intention to embarrass me in the tourney yard last week, scolding me in front of Sir Phillip and the Ellorys, in typical mother fashion. I don't think she much cared for my jokes about it later at dinner either."

"Maggie…"

"I know, I know, I'm a shit."

"You bring it on yourself is what it is."

It was Maggie's turn to roll her eyes.

"And what does Father say about it then?" Whit indulged.

"Haven't the faintest. I don't think we've spoken a word to one another since you left."

"Truly?"

"He keeps himself locked away in the solar most days, unless the small council is taking the round."

"I suppose he did seem rather distant at the banquet last night."

"That's how he is now. He's become a bit of a hermit these days."

"A King returns," a voice croaked from the churchyard as they neared the cathedral entrance.

Both brother and sister halted in unison and stared at the short, frail figure hobbling up between the gravestones, prodding forth with the assistance of a strange shimmering sword, her cloak flapping in the frosty air.

"Who goes there?" Whit asked.

A misshapen hand pulled back the hood from over the figure's head revealing a crudely-cut, scraggly silver mane of hair and a porcelain face with milky-white eyes that were wreathed by a series of dark scabs.

"Begone from us, hag," Whitman warned, reaching for his hilt. "How did you even get inside the upper yards?"

Maggie could not believe what had become of the woman before her. In truth, it had been some many days since the last time she'd seen Selwyn Shawley, and though the woman had always cast a rather sickly guise, she now appeared as ghastly as death warmed over.

"That's not a hag. That's Selwyn Shawley. She's one of the scullery maids." Maggie swallowed. "At least she was."

Whit placed himself between Selwyn and Maggie. "Well, she looks a proper hag to me. Just look at the state of her, Mags. She's positively ghoulish. And she's wielding a naked blade within the upper yards—"

"Whitman Lanier, Second of his name," Selwyn rasped through a deathbed wheeze. "By the powers three, you are bound. Three Houses linked. Three tombs to share. Three lines of fate. Gods' fruit to bear. Nine cycles hence the first of three heirs will arrive. Three faces they will be. Three forms they will wear. The crow. The wolf. And the serpent."

Here it is. The Empress felt Selwyn's foretelling rise up inside her like the lyrics to an old song.

"One will die before their time. One must go alone. One will cede love's greatest gift in turn to spite the throne. A ruin by starlight. A blade from the stone. A door from within, rent straight from the bone. Frayed are the threads that cast shadows. Lush is the drear in their unforgiving—"

"Emperor!" a voice cried from outside the throne hall and Maggie's eyes screamed open.

A moment later a panicked goldcoat crashed through the great iron doors, clattering to his knees, before pushing back up into a mad scramble. Behind him, in the corridor beyond, a second soldier burst apart above his waist spraying black and crimson gore across the ivory walls as the rest of him plunged with grisly violence to the marble flagstones. A hush took them all as they watched a portion of the soldier's blood-spatter hang in midair, devoid of gravity, briefly floating about like a feather on the wind, before it shifted directions and solidified, shrieking into the throne hall after the first goldcoat, impaling the crier midway down the walkway as though it were a bolt fired from a crossbow.

The goldcoat caught himself hard against the outside of a pew and looked down at the crystallized blood that was now eating through him like acid from the space between his ribcage. He looked up at them, bulging eyes spilling tears of black ichor down his cheeks, and let out a harrowing scream that was cut short by a sudden explosion of blood, bones, brains, and nether dust.

The council members scurried for the hidden passage like a mischief of rats, leaving just the Emperor and a handful of goldcoats to fend against what was coming.

Silently, Drezhal motioned for his men to flank the doorway. There were two to a side and one that remained in the walkway with her husband, all had their officer's blades drawn and were noticeably shaking. The Emperor retrieved Val's mae'chii from the pew beside him as a series of dark appendages slithered through the doorway and into the throne hall as though some great sea beast had been summoned forth somewhere inside the palace. The long shifting tendrils of flesh marauded through the flanked goldcoats in seconds as though they were merely flies on the wall.

Maggie rose to her feet as the corridor beyond disappeared inside a pall of ink and shadow and a tall, lanky figure appeared from within the unfurling bed of tentacles.

Desmond.

Her nephew looked anything but the same beggar wretch that had been brought to his knees in chains only a day ago. Though the gods only knew, he barely looked a living thing at all anymore. He wore his robe open, unveiling a painfully thin, malnourished torso complete with a pronounced ribcage and a scar that screamed sallow white obscenities against the pale empty plain of his grotesquely emaciated abdomen. Wet ashen hair lay slicked back out of his gaunt face accentuating bright icy eyes that glinted with a hatred centuries in the making. Even across the throne hall, Magwyn could feel the malevolence emanating off of him as though from a dark alien mist.

He raised a red right hand and blood from the nearest guard's corpse clotted, then coiled up like a charmed snake and sprang out at the remaining goldcoat's face, swallowing the poor bastard from head to toe in a matter of seconds.

Backing away, Drezhal made to unsheathe the mae'chii, but before he could fully draw it, Desmond was on him, traversing the space between them in a blink and snapping the Emperor's arm at the elbow as though it were little more than a rotted branch. The scabbard clattered back to the floor as Drezhal collapsed to his knees in screaming agony, clutching at the ruined arm that now hung limply from its tendons.

Desmond cackled. *:You bend the knee awfully fast for a man that names himself as emperor.:* He turned his attentions up at the Empress and paced leisurely forward. The proud look on his face bordered on the obscene.

"What have you done to my nephew?" Magwyn asked, repulsion contorting her lips.

:Oh, he's still in here, shoved off somewhere amidst the lot. We are bonded, after all, your Desmond and I.:

His voice had changed nearly as much as his appearance, projecting throaty, yet sharp, and swathed inside a most unsettling manner of sophistication. Every word a carefully placed incision.

"Did you kill her?"

:The ashaeydir? But of course. It was her sacrifice, in fact, that allowed me to complete the possession ritual. And the hallows know, they don't come easy these days, do they?:

"Ashaeydir?" Maggie's mind couldn't seem to accept it.

:Oh, yes. Turns out the betrothed was not quite all she appeared in the end.:

"Did Desmond know?"

:He did, believe it or not. This one rather proved herself an oddly honest sort.:

A scratching sound drew both of their attentions as Drezhal unsheathed Val's mae'chii. The ka'rym chii certainly made far more sense now.

The fiend glanced over his shoulder. *:And just what the fuck are you going to do with that?:*

The Emperor stood, the one arm bloated and bleeding, a sliver of broken bone poking out near the elbow.

"What I should have done already," Drezhal answered through snot and tears and a warrior's grit.

"Drezhal, don't," Maggie implored.

The Emperor staggered forward, his working arm wobbling as he made to raise the blade at Desmond.

Desmond gazed up at Maggie. *:He keeps on, I'm going to shove that blade up his ass.:*

"Let's get it done then," Drezhal grunted.

Desmond dropped his vision to the floor and let out a condescending chuckle.

"You think this is a joke, do you?"

Desmond flexed his red right hand. *:I think you're a fucking joke, all things honest.:*

"Then face me, you bastard. We'll see who has the last laugh."

Desmond shifted ever so slightly to his left and spoke in a tongue Maggie hadn't heard in many, many cycles. *:Thas'kon ech vira dhu xarma.:*

"No!" the Empress howled, recognizing pieces of the incantation.

Instantly, Drezhal's ruined arm bubbled up as though it was boiling from

21

underneath the skin. The mae'chii clattered to the floor, and the Emperor let out a bloodcurdling cry as his body began to betray him, lesions bursting black and yellow pus amidst warping flesh, dark blood twisting out of the opening where the bone had punctured through the skin, and blooming into something like a second half-formed appendage. Red moving eyes blinked out at them from the freshly summoned oily black growth.

:And now look what you've brought me to. Spitting old sweepings from a misspent youth.:

"W-what...have you...d-done...to me?" the Emperor managed through a series of clicking sounds and tics that bent the shape of his neck to a horrific unnatural angle.

:I'm bringing us round to the matter then, aren't I? Is that not what His Lordship bade me?:

Drezhal vomited and glanced up at Maggie, his eyes leaking the same black substance that trailed down his jaw. "Maggie..."

:Besides, every man should know the sum of his true self before the end. Pity there isn't a rodent-filled ditch within range to have yours.:

An inhuman screech shredded its way through the clicking noises as Drezhal's arm expanded into a giant mass of netherflesh causing the rest of his torso to convulse and atrophy until the thing tore itself away fully, ending his mad shrieking and leaving in its wake a pile of skin and bones and torn silk rags.

Maggie had never beheld hemomancy to such a scale before. Bile started for her throat in response, prompting Emyria to take the reins. A moment later, Eldn flame sparked to life in the Empress's hand as though from muscle memory and the giant maggot-like abomination that was Drezhal Dalivant became engulfed by crackling hot azure.

Desmond cut back to her with a dark smirk as the thing that was her husband burned to ashes under the bright angry flames. *:And what have we here then?:* he inquired.

"Not another step, devil," Maggie warned, and with a wave of her hand a sphere of fire cast forward, trailing along the lowest step of the throne staircase, expanding to create a barrier of azure flame between them, tall as a wngar shield wall and bright as a flash of lightning.

:There it is again. That fucking accusation. Devil. Monster. Fiend. Abom-ination.: The smile—if one could name it such—vanished from

Desmond's face. *:I unfuck your little warlord shitshow and yet I am named as the devil? If nothing else, you Lanier's certainly hold fast to your high morals, don't you? Fucking class, truly.:* Blackened blood flowed like melting wax from the minced corpses of the council guard into a hole cut through his red right palm. *:I've vilified the ashaeydir for much in my time,:* he began as he approached, *:but they never would have let such an unworthy mongrel as Dalivant sit the top House.:* He halted just before the flame barrier. *:Was it not that sort of passive, backward-ass thinking which led to the dracari's demise in the first place?:* The flow of blood stopped, the last of it spitting steam as Desmond flicked it into her magical buffer. *:These creatures feared you once and now you hide amongst them, cowering from them, and allowing them free rein.:*

"It's been my experience where one tyrant falls another will soon have his place."

:Ah, the whole wretch you know approach, is that it?: The wall of Eldn flame was pulsating in the space before Desmond's dark presence, almost as though it were trembling away from him. *:I must say, I expected better. But then again, I suppose they did always name you the desolate one, didn't they?:*

He knows, Magwyn thought.

NO MATTER, Emyria returned.

A war horn's call echoed throughout the palace walks and carried into the throne hall as though across a large, open plain.

:Mmm, a bit late on that one, I'd say,: Desmond said, presenting a ghastly gap-toothed grin.

Tentacles, thick as redwoods, poured into the throne hall, clogging the entryway, sowing its putrid disease. The great shapeless mass wormed along the pews and up the walls and pillars and ceiling like devil's vine soaking in nigh every drop of daylight from outside, until all that was left was the flicker from Magwyn's wall of Eldn flame. In the fire glow, she could faintly make out small, viscous goblinoid shapes creeping along the beast's formless legion, hatching like larvae from within the nether's many red eyes.

DO NOT LOOK DIRECTLY INTO IT.

:You shoulder Fyr's passing well considering your role in her folly. Or was it actually Farador?:

23

"...Dredging up the past will serve you little advantage..." The Empress held her position, wary.

:Look around you. I assure you any advantage to be had here is already mine.:

Outside, beyond the blot of nether, across the courtyards, from the belfry above the barracks, a bell began to toll against the war horn's rumble.

:And I know you won't kill me. Not while there's hope yet for your host's nephew.:

"...You presume much about me..." Emyria spoke.

:Do I? And have the cycles spent as a parasite finally made you a cynic then?:

Emyria, what's the plan?

WE RETREAT. AS SOON AS WE CAN.

Retreat? How is that even an option? Maggie had shared all manner of emotions with Emyria in their cycles together, but never once had she felt the one that presently found her.

HE IS TOO POWERFUL NOW. WE MUST LET HIM WASTE A BIT LONGER. WE MUST LET THE POSSESSION WEAKEN HIM.

You mean to let him roam free?

FOR NOW.

You can't be serious, Em. We can't just let him just run amok. Think of all the lives that will be lost.

THE OLD BLOOD MUST SURVIVE, MAGGIE. WE WILL NOT OUTLAST HIM. NOT AS WE ARE NOW. NOT WITHOUT CANDLES AND TRAPPING WARDS AND...

Em...

WE MUST MAKE TIME TO DEVISE A STRATEGY FIRST. I WILL NOT RISK LOSING YOU BOTH.

:Fuck's sake. I can almost hear the two of you from down here. Some bollocks about how the old blood must survive, I would imagine. The hallows know, how predictable you've all become.: As Desmond spoke, one of the goldcoat corpses near the doorway rose into the air like a marionette, and took flight, soaring through the flame wall directly at her.

Maggie leapt to the side, spinning a swift pirouette, as the burning body slammed into the throne with a wet thud. Gore ran down the seat from the smoking mass of flesh and pooled at the base.

You say he will weaken. Can a possession of this nature be reversed?

I CANNOT SAY FOR SURE. I SUPPOSE IT MAY BE POSSIBLE IF THE HOST WANTS IT BAD ENOUGH AND HAS THE WILLPOWER.

"...I have seen this sickness before..." Maggie served Emyria's words to the fiend. "...You have mutilated your soul and let the darkness consume you..."

:And so I have.:

"...You are but a fragment of your former self..."

:I cut away the fat, as they say.:

"...How many times?..."

He's split his soul?

YES. A MOST DANGEROUS ENDEAVOR.

:You act as though the darkness is a plague. Such juvenile ignorance from one that should know better. The darkness is not a plague or a curse or even an affliction. Not to those that take the proper time to listen and pay attention. In fact, the darkness can be a boon when minded fairly. For the darkness hews away all of the needless distractions and allows us to see what we really are.:

"...It manipulates..." Maggie returned. "...It feeds off of our fear. It turns the mind toward lunacy..."

:It shows us our truth and the value of suffering.:

"And it just ate my husband alive, where is the value in that?"

:Spare me the platitudes, bitch. Dalivant was as unsavory as they come, playing at a lordship and titles well above his merit. He succumbed to his ego ages ago, abusing the favor of his forebearers' stolen nobility, and the nether showed him just how unseemly his pride had become. All of that vanity. All of those cycles of forced idolatry. That was the true evil.:

"You're mad."

:Madness, fear, control. Fancy words, those. Used far too liberally, by my estimation. Romantic tosh, more like. Fairytale folly, Old Nan fables, and card stock for poets and bards to frighten unsuspecting damsels between their bedsheets. For creating fear only goes so far and control is but a notion. A false comfort. And fighting certainly won't protect anyone. Fighting swallows more than it saves. Every time. And hope. That fucking slag. Hope doesn't give a fuck about you. It doesn't give a fuck about me. It doesn't give a fuck about any of us. This world, it's all about what you know and what you are willing to endure and sacrifice to stay alive. Before my master cut me

out, I suffered through an invasion. And then I suffered through the pestilence to follow. I watched helplessly as the ashaeydir enslaved everyone I ever knew. And if enslavement wasn't reprehensible enough, they also brought their diseases to our moon. Trust, nothing will dehumanize you faster than a good ol' fashioned plague. It reaps without mercy or remorse. And what the ashaeydir didn't take from us through violence, their diseases did instead. I watched as thousands of my kin suffered and perished, most living out their final days in empty fear, clinging to the delusion that what awaited them beyond had to be better than what found them in this existence. Praying to gods without ears.:

"Enough! No matter what your past may have found you, this is not the way."

:Not the way? And who are you to preach at me the way of things? You, who play at games with shameful sycophants. You, who dawdle at daft politics and trivial successions. You, who've taken a host yourself. A queen host no less. And you've had a dozen more before her, I'd wager. Oh, but I do so wonder, now that we're at it, does the bonny Empress know what befalls a human's soul bound to that of a dragon's?:

Just then a fold of nether came coiling down from the ceiling near her. Though it had suckers formed amongst its underside, the thing appeared more tongue-like than tentacle. Maggie followed it to the source, a gaping mouth with rows upon rows of razor-sharp fangs. The tongue lashed out at her quick as a whip, and she scarred it with an angry lick of Eldn fire, carving a scalding blue line down the length of its slimy form.

The mass of netherflesh bellowed.

:Embrace the fate, Emyria. The dracari are the past. We are the future, as nature intended, and our time is inescapable. Inevitable. Mind the heavens. Ashira will attest.:

The fiend was savoring this.

:Nothing sane can stay.:

Another tentacle thrust out at her from the vast dark beyond, a pair of sucking maws near its other end, and Maggie reached out toward the far wall with every ounce her gift had left to offer, an animal cry erupting out of her as she psychokinetically ripped the giant shield away from its massive iron anchors. It arrived in the nick of time, denting inward at the nether's impact, and she was off to the races, without a second glance, striding down the stairs two at a time, ducking razorblade tendrils and dodging little half-formed spriteling abominations, fast as she had moved in decades, away from Desmond and the suffocating mass of nether, toward a seldom used back passage that she knew would eventually open up to the upper courtyards.

:That's right, run and hide, Emyria,: Desmond's demon-drenched voice chased after her. *:Just as you've always done.:*

Maggie didn't dare look back, bare feet slapping down hard and harder still against each passing flagstone.

She could kick herself senseless for leaving her leathers in the bath chambers after wash, the fool she was. But she'd become so damned distracted with Desmond's arrival, and the crone's prophecy, and then Lady Esme had been so bloody adamant about her haste and attendance at the afternoon's council summit...it was truly a miracle more hadn't been missed...

:One of you will not be enough to stop what's coming.:

But Maggie was no longer listening. She just kept repeating Selwyn's promise over and over again in her head, clinging to its heresy like some mongrel meld of fresh gospel.

One will die before their time. One must go alone. One will cede love's greatest gift in turn to spite the throne.

CHAPTER FOUR

FUCKING PROPHECY, Maggie huffed as she approached the other end of the hidden passage, the soles of her bare feet burning all manner of unholy hellfire. *Nothing about the dead one coming back a demon's puppet, then Selwyn? No, nothing about that bit at all.*

The gods know. She cursed her younger self for letting Whit usher her off to the cathedral away from the crone. But how could she have possibly known Selwyn's words would come back to haunt and with such ferocity?

Maggie tiptoed the last few steps as she approached the corridor's end. She lifted the wooden beam from the iron latches and the oak door creaked inward. A horrible, quivering scream blustered past her from the courtyard just outside, echoing long into the passageway recesses whence she'd come.

"Leave him." She heard a voice say. "He's gone."

"Tommy, I'm sorry," a girl's voice called over the coinciding chaos.

"Laurie, please," a terrible little noise cried out in response followed by a wet, grisly sound and that of bones crunching.

Heart in her mouth, Maggie reached for the door handle, gripping it with a shaking hand, and pulled it open.

She found the voice's owner between a pair of ghouls, one tugging at the boy's arm, the other buried nose deep in his neck, spouts of blood spraying skyward, bright as a ripe orchard apple. The arm snapped free from the shoulder in the feeding frenzy, causing both ghouls to fall roughly to the ground with their uneven shares, and the Empress watched helplessly as two more blighters descended upon what remained of the poor squirming child.

Several such clusters of the fiends were scattered in the courtyards beyond, feeding on their friends and families alike. In the distance, she found a few others fleeing from a chasing pack of blighters.

WE MUST KEEP MOVING.

I know.

THE TOWER. IT WILL TAKE US TO THE MIDDLE BAILEY AND THE LOWER HALLS.

The Empress hurried forth as Emyria guided, racing the open walkways between clots of ghouls, cutting through gaps in the garden hedges, slipping and sliding in the slush of blood and viscera, blisters screaming across the expanse of her feet, as though she were stepping on broken glass, dirt and blades of grass sticking to the fresh cuts in the softer spots near the middle.

Nothing a few candles can't cure, she told herself. *Nothing to worry on. Just keep moving.*

As she neared the tower entrance, a pair of goldcoats tumbled out of it, grappling at each other. Tearing, punching, snarling, before the larger one spun the lanky one around, tossing him into the shrubbery like a ragdoll.

"Fucker!" the standing soldier growled, ripping the bloodstained golden helm from his head.

But the fiend was back on his feet in a blink rushing back at its foe. The larger soldier cracked the blighter across the side of its head with the helm then followed its descent into the patch of garden and bashed the helm down into its gnashing face again and again and again until there was nothing left but a dark red puddle of brain mush and skull fragments.

Afterward, the soldier rolled off his dead comrade, into the pink and white roses, and lay there, panting.

Maggie cut the space between them with a series of light, swaying steps, slinking into the flowerbed, and dropped to her knees at his side. She recognized him as Wilson Marlowe. "Are you all right, Captain?"

Marlowe glanced up at his company, his long, disheveled hair plastered against his sweaty face. "Empress," he grunted in pain, followed by a tick that bent his neck crooked and turned his head away from her.

HE IS INFECTED.

Yes, I can see that.

LEAVE HIM.

"I mean to make the undercroft," she said. "Do you know how it is that way?"

Marlowe motioned out into the courtyard around them. "It's like this..." tick, "bugger. It's like this everywhere, Majesty. Worse even." He lifted up to an elbow with a groan and shimmied a dagger from the sheath at the dead goldcoat's waist. "Where is the Emperor?"

"Dead," Magwyn said. "Killed defending his throne." *And his foolish pride.*

Captain Marlowe nodded grimly. "I don't mean to..." tick, "become one of them." He offered the dagger's hilt out to her. "Majesty, will you..." tick, "will you see it through?"

The Empress blinked at him, momentarily caught off guard by the ghastly request.

"Majesty, please."

Her eyes sank to the shining silver in his trembling glove. She had never taken a life before, at least not with her own hands, and never so directly as what presently lay before her. All the dirty work and dark decisions had always been left to Drezhal's decree, far away from her perfumed chambers and honeyed concerns.

A thunderous crash quaked across the courtyard near the throne hall and her head jerked away from Marlowe to take it in. Palace chunks rained down from the explosion as the mass of netherflesh poured through the gaping fissure in the stone wall, baying for blood.

"Gods." She heard Marlowe utter as the first of the beast's many maws appeared with jagged teeth like giant shards of glass, its countless black tentacles slamming down upon the flagstones below, twisting out amidst the throng of ghouls, and spewing little goblinoid spritelings from the many crimson sacs lining its fel form.

The goblins began to attack both the living and blighted causing strange black appendages to sprout forth from the infested portions of their bodies.

The next thing Magwyn knew, she was descending the tower steps, tears in her eyes, icy cold sweat trailing down her backside. She hadn't the faintest inkling what happened with Marlowe. Hells, she couldn't even recall standing, much less how she arrived inside the tower. And before she had a chance to partway consider a plan further, she found herself out amidst the madness of the middle bailey.

At first, the path was clear, as she dashed forward in the direction of the next tower down. Though as she passed inside the settling mists, she was unable to make out much beyond a few feet in front of her. Still, she pressed on, fast as her feet would carry her, sure as the gods did suffer.

A goldcoat darted past her, back toward the way she'd come, his face gushing blood through dark red fingers. A second soldier, crossed her path, yelling unintelligibly at the top of his lungs, chased by a knife-wielding cloth maiden riddled with streaking blade marks carved up and down her countenance. The third soldier slammed into her, sending her stumbling wide of her original route, though, somehow, she managed to keep her feet under her. Only just.

A heartbeat later, she found herself within a swarm of bodies. They were crashing into one another, crashing into her, ghouls, the living, men, women, children, jostling her, crushing her, pushing her, suffocating her, sending her spinning in violent circles.

Silver flashed out, missing her by a whisker, sinking into another shape inches to her left, both blighted and barmy. The sword-wielding ghoul ripped the blade from its brethren and came at her again as she collided with another distorted figure, the impact wrenching her neck back. And another form shouldered into her immediately after, driving her down into the muck.

White and yellow stars danced across her vision as she began to crawl, her eyes fixed to the mud and the gods only knew what else, clawing in some direction, desperate to just keep moving.

A blighted woman, missing most of her body below the waist, locked eyes with her from the depths of the fray. Despite the fresh alterations, the Empress recognized her as Kenzi Stanchion, a distant relative to Drezhal that had come to court some many quints ago seeking a noble husband with deep pockets. Oh, but those horrible milky-white eyes. A moment more and Lady Kenzi let out an even worse sound between broken teeth as she began dragging her legless torso toward Maggie.

Before the Empress could think to react, someone stepped on her shoulder blade, forcing her back down into the mud, and something else kicked into her side. She cried out, gasping for air, her stomach contracting sharply, as her sight blurred into a jumble of formless colors...

Emyria...I'm sorry...

I...I can't...

...rage flared forth to spite The Hood's invitation, flooding through her veins like a tide of wildfire as the dracari roared to the surface, pushing her host back up to her feet and conjuring forth a ring of blood from the strewn about corpses, from any corpse that would heed her call. And with a well-placed whisper, the floating stream of gore ignited, cross with dragon's fire, and she sent it whipping out into the ravenous host.

The Eldn flame separated the blight from the living in an instant, causing the nether to boil and bubble up where it had infected. Nearly half the surrounding populace began to writhe and screech as their insides began to stew and burst apart, their blood spill sending a wave of poison rippling out into the farther crowds.

Emyria chased after the dragon's kiss, weaving through the rupturing blight like a practiced stage dancer, conjuring forth a second egg to light the way.

Magwyn Lanier couldn't believe the movements that sprang forth from her body. In truth, she was out of shape, rarely finding time for the training of her youth. Though, even then, she was never much one for sport and always came off a bit hopeless when it involved any activity that required her to show a modicum of grace or nimbleness. But now. Oh, now. If only her dance instructors could see her turning about this fel madness.

Em, how are you doing all of this? Nigh on a decade bonded, and she hadn't the faintest inkling anything like this was even remotely possible.

I AM TAPPING INTO YOUR GIFT. THOUGH I CAN ONLY SUSTAIN IT FOR SO LONG. WE WILL NEED TO FIND A PLACE TO REST SOON.

If you can get us to the tower. I know the perfect place from there.

To her astonishment, Magwyn found the lower halls eerily empty, near quiet as the crypt, as though every creature within had somehow become winked out of existence. It quite reminded her of a spooky old manor she and Wils explored some cycles ago in a township named Gravesend Hollow, back when hunting murder houses still found a fashion, back before Whit discovered their affections, back before he made Wils choose between a friendship and a romance and her world became tossed on its head.

Bramlett Manor, the old tales named it.

The supposed birthplace of The Stranger. It was said the Bramlett's bought a former fool to play as the heir's servant, and over the cycles, the son, growing into a dreadfully cruel master thence drove the fool further and further toward madness, until finally, the fool awoke one nightfall, upon the hour of the witch, stalking the halls in a catatonic stupor and butchered the entire family in their beds, mother, father, sister, brother, each a sight worse than the last, before escaping thereafter into wilds of the Kingswood to forever haunt the forest shadows.

Despite the tale's creepiness, Maggie crept through the dark corridors cautiously, cupping the egg of Eldn flame close as she hugged the walls, only stopping at the corners to check what lay ahead.

Of course, there were signs of a recent struggle and all the hallmarks of the blight. Blood and hand-prints were smeared across the walls, portraits knocked from their places, and the runner rugs, which normally trailed the center of the walkways, mostly lay ruffled about and out of line. But nothing remained yet to define the foul unrest.

Fretful, the Empress let out a heavy breath as they reached the quarters of one of her handmaidens.

ILFAEYDA'S CHAMBERS.

The door hung slightly ajar. Maggie peered in through the crack, hovering the firelight left and right to observe as much of the chamber as possible. But it was too dark inside to see anything properly. She rapped a knuckle against the wall, in consequence, to see if anything moved.

Nothing. Almost less than nothing.

A shiver crawled the length of her spine at the hush and she entered the room, fastly closing the door behind her. Emyria spoke in Dracthonir, and the door complained, the wood compressing ever so slightly under the protection ward's pressure.

The Eldn egg shrank and reappeared at the tip of a finger growing tall like an untrimmed fingernail. Maggie waved it about to light the space and found a candle half-melted on the vanity table. She married the azure flame to wick, and it sputtered to life.

It was a simple space, Ilfaeyda's chambers, housing a bed, a trunk, and a vanity. Enough for a pair of lovers to get on, she supposed, knowing the truth of Rhonyn's lustfulness, but it also served as a safe haven for Maggie and Rho to convey messages and supplies to one another behind the privy council's watchful eyes.

As you might recall, I had Rhonyn stash some bags and candles here last summer, she relayed to Emyria as she snuffed the azure flame between thumb and fingertip.

The room shifted from flickering blue to gold.

She caught her reflection in the vanity mirror and held, gazing deep into her dracari eyes. Quite a many cycles had passed since the last time she'd seen her eyes in such a manner. She stepped back and surveyed herself, finding her favorite dress a ruin. Soiled on one side from her stumble within the bailey and torn on the other by something she would likely never have the truth of. She put pressure on the side with the mud stain and found it woefully tender. No doubt she would find it covered in lumps once the time for a proper inspection presented itself.

Further down, her legs and feet fared little better. She began to count the cuts and bruises within the dirt stains but stopped once she reached a dozen. There were far more than she would have liked for, she decided, and left it at that. She was still alive, after all. At least for the moment. And that would have to be enough.

She lifted a foot off the ground and curled her toes, in and out, one foot then the other, working the ache from her arches as much as could be had.

"I may never go without leathers again," she muttered to herself, wishing for a pair of boots, as she opened the trunk at the foot of the bed.

Inside, she found fresh linens, and mercifully, a pair of leathers she prayed would fit close enough. Tucked underneath one of the piles of handmaiden garb was a coin sack. She lifted it and found what she needed. No wax bags, but eight candles and a pair of ring razors.

I could kiss you right now, Rho.

Magwyn slid the ring razors onto each middle finger. They fit tightly on her, but there were far worse matters to contend with just now than the comfort of jewelry.

Next, she slipped her arms from the sleeves of her dress and gingerly lifted it over her head. Once again, she caught her reflection in the mirror. Bumps and lumps ran down through the folds of skin from shoulder to hip. She turned back to the trunk, shaking the sight from her mind.

Nothing to be done about it now.

She grabbed a shirt from the trunk and began scrubbing the mud from her face, then her legs and feet. *Em, how are you holding up?* She asked, noticing her dracari companion had become uncharacteristically quiet.

AS WELL AS CAN BE EXPECTED, CONSIDERING, Emyria answered. I PULLED A BIT MORE FROM YOUR GIFT THAN I WOULD HAVE PREFERRED.

You did what you had to. She withdrew a fresh black undershirt and golden surcoat from the stack of handmaid clothes. *I'm sorry about—*

NO. NONE OF THAT NOW. THERE IS NO NEED FOR APOLOGIES.

Maggie pulled the undershirt over her head, punching hands through sleeves, letting it settle down near her ankles, and chased it with the surcoat. Together, they fit about as snugly as the rings did to her fingers but certainly smelled better than the filthy rag her favorite dress had devolved into. She blew loose curls out of her face as she reached back into the trunk for a belt, stockings, and leathers.

We need to get to Rhonyn. Maggie plopped down at the edge of the bed and pulled the stockings up to her knees.

IT IS LIKELY RHONYN WAS KILLED BY YOUR NEPHEW ALONGSIDE THE BETROTHED.

You don't know that. She laced up the leathers that mercifully fit just right.

NO, BUT RHONYN IS EXPENDABLE AND YOU ARE NOT. I WILL NOT ALLOW YOU TO RISK YOUR LIFE FOR A FOOL'S ERRAND.

You mean your life, the Empress thought.

"This is not up for debate." She stood, wrapping the belt around her waist. "It's ghastly enough we let them take him to stocks in the first place." She knotted the pouch of blood candles to the belt and gazed back up at herself in the mirror.

Her eyes no longer burned with dracari nightmare, and an uneasy silence followed.

I know the godsblood must survive, Em. Maggie loosened the ribbon in her hair, letting her dark curls fall loose over her shoulders. *But what's the point of surviving all of this if everything we hold dear is gone afterward?*

I ONCE THOUGHT AS YOU DO. BACK WHEN I HAD A CLUTCH. BACK WHEN I HAD SISTERS AND BROTHERS. HOW MANY MEMORIES HAVE I SHARED WITH YOU OVER THE CYCLES? YOU CANNOT SAVE EVERYONE, MAGWYN. NO MATTER HOW MUCH YOU WANT TO. AND THERE ARE TIMES WHEN LEAVING A THING TO ITS FATE MAY ACTUALLY BE FOR THE BETTER.

AS YOU WELL KNOW, I TRIED TO PLAY PEACEKEEPER FOR EVERYONE IN MY FAMILY, AND IN THE END, I LOST THEM ALL.

EVERY DAY I WONDER, IF I HAD SIMPLY KEPT TO MYSELF, COULD THINGS HAVE TURNED OUT DIFFERENT? MIGHT I STILL HAVE A FAMILY? MIGHT I STILL HAVE MY OWN BODY? MIGHT I STILL BE ME?

Emyria.

I KNOW HOW MUCH RHONYN MEANS TO YOU, BUT YOU HAVE SEEN WHAT WE ARE UP AGAINST HERE. AND YOU KNOW HE IS IN NO SHAPE FOR A WAR. EVEN IF HE IS STILL ALIVE, IT WOULD TAKE SOME DOING TO BRING HIM BACK AROUND TO FORM. AND WE SIMPLY DO NOT HAVE THE RESOURCES TO TAKE SUCH A RISK.

Maggie fumed as she placed the ribbon against her neck, raised it up around her curls, and collected them into a ponytail.

I UNDERSTAND WHY YOU ARE CROSS WITH ME, BUT—

"What happens to my soul now that it's bound with yours?" Magwyn blurted. "What's going to happen to me? To us?"

MAGWYN.

"No, Emyria. I won't let it go. I'll no longer ignore a thing just because it frightens me."

VERY WELL. DO YOU RECALL WHEN I TOLD YOU THAT WE SHOULD ONLY USE MAGIC SPARINGLY? THAT YOU SHOULD ALWAYS TRY TO CONSERVE YOUR GIFT?

"Yes, of course. You made quite the deal of it, all told."

THIS IS BECAUSE THE USE OF MAGIC DRAINS MY SOUL. TO

COMPENSATE FOR THIS, WHEN I PULL TOO MUCH, MY SOUL INTRINSICALLY BEGINS TO LEECH FROM YOURS. AND WHAT IT TAKES CAN NEVER BE RETURNED.

Maggie lowered herself down on the bed. "You're saying when you conjure magic, it's slowly killing me?"

WHEN I CONJURE TOO MUCH MAGIC AT ONCE, IT TAKES FROM YOU, YES. THAT IS WHY WE CHOSE THE CHANDII AS OUR FAMILIARS ALL THOSE CENTURIES AGO, BEFORE THE DRAG-ONSFALL AND THE GIFTWELL. IF A DRACARI ATTEMPTED TO MELD WITH AN UNGIFTED HUMAN OUR SOUL WOULD BOIL THEIR BLOOD AND BURN THEM ALIVE FROM THE INSIDE OUT.

YOUR BLOOD, THE GODSBLOOD, IS DESCENDED FROM A SIMILAR LINE TO THE CHANDII.

"That is why you chose me, isn't it?

BECAUSE OF YOUR LINEAGE, YOU STAND THE GREATEST CHANCE TO LIVE OUT YOUR NORMAL LIFESPAN WHILST STILL HOUSING MY SOUL.

"And what happens to you if I die?"

THAT I DO NOT KNOW. I HAVE ALWAYS BEEN ABLE TO PASS ON TO THE NEXT FAMILIAR WITHOUT TROUBLE.

"What about other dracari? Surely, it's happened before."

I CANNOT SAY. I HAVE BEEN ISOLATED FROM MY KIND SINCE THE DRAGONSFALL. SINCE I FORSOOK MY ORIGINAL FORM. AND I HAVE ALSO BEEN GREATLY FORTUNATE TO MELD WITH A MOST CONSUMMATE CIRCLE OF HOSTS.

"How many hosts have come before me?"

YOU ARE MY NINTH.

Ninth, goodness me. "And do you know what happens to a familiar if somehow the dracari dies first?"

ONCE SOULMELDED TO A DRACARI, A HUMAN CANNOT SURVIVE BEYOND IT. NOT EVEN THE MOST GIFTED OF THE CHANDII COULD ENDURE THROUGH. MY SOUL WILL DEVOUR EVERYTHING IT CAN FROM YOURS TO SURVIVE BEFORE SUCCUMBING TO THE BLACK.

Magwyn rose to her feet, sucked in a breath, and exhaled.

I REGRET YOU HAD TO FIND OUT THIS WAY.

"Don't be absurd, Em. I'd be a corpse already if it weren't for you. Yes,

I'm cross, but prize well, I am thankful to have you in my life, no matter what the sacrifice."

AND I YOU. ALLOW ME AN HOUR OF REPAIR, AND THEN WE WILL CHECK ON YOUR FRIEND. BEYOND THAT I CAN OFFER NO PROMISES.

Thank you, Emyria. Maggie adjusted one of the ring razors at the base of her middle finger. *Beyond that, I will ask for no more.*

CHAPTER FIVE

ONCE MORE AIDEN found himself inside the tower.

By the chamber's repair, he assumed the memory took place sometime after Ankaira's possession. It emerged from the surrounding depths a woeful shadow of its former self, not unlike the figure hunched against the edge of its entryway, clutching his stomach, staring out into the deep emerald moonlight of vast Y'dema.

Aiden charted the winding trail of blood spots to their owner and filled in the remainder of the doorway's opening.

Beyond the thin veil of rolling cloudworks, Y'dema near swallowed the horizon whole. A titan amongst titans. Ashira occupied the scant sliver of space over her broad shoulders. And the gods only knew, Aiden had never beheld the hunter's moon under such magnificent spirits. So close, one could almost reach out their hand to grab her up.

Beguiled by such an ethereal splendor, he'd drifted halfway down the tower steps before realizing it, gazing out into the mass of heather that glistened like a painter's canvas under the soft trickle of rainfall, and further still to the dark, smoky-topped shapes of the township out yonder.

He could almost smell the springtide and raised his nose to the heavens fusing his own memory to that of Malthus's. A smile came round for the haunt. *What a foolish indulgence,* he chided. Though after all the horrors of the past few days, after all the darkness, drear, and disease, such a scene seemed wholly impossible.

The sound of coughing returned his attention to the tower entrance as the hobbled figure disappeared inside.

Aiden offered the sister moons one last glimpse, nodded his appreciation, and with a thought, returned to the tower's sea of candlelight, watching Malthus as he began to unwind the bloodstained linens wrapped crudely around his abdomen. The y'deman winced as he reached the final layer, peeling it gingerly away from sticking skin. Aiden couldn't hold back a grimace of his own having felt a similar pain before.

"Gods, you old fool," Malthus grumbled once the bandaging was off.

Aiden felt the ache in his own belly, crawling the length of his death scar. *Fucking bastard*, he spat at Tetherow's ghost.

Malthus took up a half-empty bottle of black, limped over to the nearest armchair, and eased himself down in it with a heavy sigh, sweat pouring down his forehead, dribbling off the end of his nose, in considerably worse condition than the last memory they'd shared.

"One more," Malthus slurred as he turned the bottle up, chugging it down to a quarter. After weathering another coughing fit, he gripped the jarred candle next to him and blew out its flame, then fitted a bundle of cloth in his mouth.

The stab wounds Ankaira left him had formed a grotesque black hole the size of his gut that appeared to be alive and spreading across the length of his entire torso. Weeping scab marks and melted candle resin surrounded the patch of mutilated flesh from where Malthus had attempted to burn it shut and mend it with his gift before, but the curse gave as good as it got, it would seem, and refused to be defeated so easily.

A wand thrummed to life at Malthus's side, as he dumped the jar of candle resin over the wound, grunting and gasping at the agony rippling through him. His scorched skin bubbled up and hissed in consequence. He brought the tip of the wand to the center of the opened flesh and howled bloody murder as it tasted the char once more.

A lesion swelled to a large blinking red eye atop his breastbone, shrieking like a kettle at the wand's touch, expanding beneath the skin until it burst, spraying dark pus about the chamber.

Trembling, Malthus withered in the armchair, the wand's magic dying as it clattered to the floor.

The chamber blurred around them, as it did in the previous memory, fading with Malthus's consciousness, and returning thus moments later inside the expanse of a dissipating fog.

Daylight sat ill upon the strewn-about chamber, only bested by the broken y'deman slouched like a corpse in the gore-soaked armchair.

The state of him. It wouldn't be long now. In the lapse of time, the disease had ranged to his neck and around his sides.

A shadow approached, growing as it ascended the steps toward the entryway.

Malthus groaned, head lolling as he eased himself upright in the chair.

A figure in dark huntsman's attire halted at the top step, a crook-shaped dagger shimmering at his side. "And here he is," the man muttered, removing the hood of his cloak, unveiling a canvas of scars between long silver-gold hair.

Another y'deman?

And one Aiden had never seen before, to be sure. The man cut a rather unforgettable shape, all told. Tall and broad-shouldered as though he'd lived it rough working hard labor ever since he was a youngling. And yet, something about his presence rang oddly familiar.

"Brother," croaked the whiskey frog in the back of Malthus's throat.

Aiden shifted toward the sorcerer and found the shaky wretch working himself up from the armchair, every measure as frail as his company was fit.

"Do not dare name me as your brother, Malthus. You forfeited that privilege when you severed part of your soul." The man's grasp tightened on the dagger's hilt, his leather glove emitting a daunting scrunch sound. "And what you did to Ankaira…"

"Annie?" Malthus wheezed. "You must stay away from her, Elsymir. She's not herself. She's—"

"Dead," the man named Elsymir finished. "Do not play the fool with me, Mal. We found her in pieces. Parts of her anyway. A ritual dagger left in the space that formerly housed her heart." He flung the blade down at the stones between them.

"Where?" Malthus swallowed. "Where did you find her?"

"The Marrovard crypts. One of the groundsmen found her."

"And you believe I am responsible?"

"I know you are."

41

"I would never harm Annie," Malthus rattled. "You know this. I loved her."

"You are incapable of love, Malthus. You were meant to guide us to a better world. A more enlightened world. But all you've wrought is death and violence."

"All *he* wrought. All *it* wrought." Malthus stumbled forward, clutching an arm across his belly. "It did this to me after it possessed Ankaira. The demon. And try as I might, the wounds will not close. It meant to have us both in the grave."

"And who is the man on the table behind you? Another corpse for your demented cause?"

Aiden turned to the table across the chamber. *How did you not notice?*

"I found this man expired in an alley on the edge of town," Malthus said.

The archivist sensed the truth in his words.

"Found him, did you? And you were going to what? Bind your soul to it because you went and ruined your own with all this dark-dabbling."

"Only if it came to such."

"And did it?"

"We must stop it. This demon. Whatever it takes. It cannot be allowed—"

"*We* won't be doing anything. You've grown reckless, Mal. Gods' breath, I don't even recognize this man before me. Hardly a man at all, by the state you're in. This experimenting, these rituals, look what they've made of you. And Ankaira tried to warn me."

"My experimenting has forced the demon's hand and rid me of it. For that, I will not apologize. I regret Annie's ill fortune in this ungodly affair, but you haven't the faintest inkling of what it takes to beat back such a fiend for every breath of every day. Not knowing which one might prove your last."

"Stow the fool's charade. It was you, Malthus. You're the demon. It's always been you." Elsymir stepped inside the tower. "You were family to me. To Annie. To Ravenholme. Our bond was thicker than blood. Greater than mere master and apprenticeship. But you've betrayed that now. You've betrayed everyone."

"You're not listening, Elsymir."

"I've heard more than enough through your actions."

"You're still caught up in morals and societal expectations, constructs our enemy cares nothing about. You have no idea what we're up against here."

"Do you hear yourself, Malthus? *You* have become the enemy." Menace layered his tone, thick as pond scum.

A swell of anger passed through the archivist, bought of Malthus's emotions, and he didn't necessarily disagree with their placement.

We aren't so different after all, are we?

The sorcerer held next to Aiden in the middle of the chamber. "Have I." Spoken more as a statement than a question. "Are we now enemies, brother?"

"You've made it so," Elsymir eyed the barely standing, shambles of a man.

"And I suppose in your mind you're the bigger man in all of this?"

"I am what I have to be."

"How does it feel, brother? To always have to be the bigger man?" A step closer. "To always have to make the hard decision?" Another step. "To always be the one to sacrifice?"

"Do not condescend to me."

"Then find your proper place, apprentice."

"And thusly you're reduced to juvenile insults. I must say, Mal, if this is your best attempt to get inside my head—"

"Oh, I have no doubts I will live inside your head for many cycles to come. You never quite got a handle on the letting go of things, did you?"

"There's a farce, coming from you."

"I will not cross steel with you, brother." Malthus squared himself. "I've had enough violence. Enough loss."

"Then death will have you before the dusk settles."

"Will you not hear me? Will you not allow me to make this right?"

"It's too late for amendments, I'm afraid. And I've indulged your deceptions long enough. I reject your mentorship, your pleas, our friendship, our brotherhood. And for Ankaira's butchering, I cannot allow you to endure."

"This goes far beyond me. Far beyond the pair of us and Annie's murder. That creature was inside of her, pulled from my flesh, meaning if she is dead, it's likely jumped bodies again."

"You're deranged, Mal," Elsymir argued. "Digging up old hearthfire haunters from the beggar's stack. An exorcism requires a ritual, not to mention willing participants."

"You don't think the demon has loyalists within our ranks?"

"You're the only demon here."

"You're wrong," Malthus roared and Aiden sensed something pass through his specter and into the y'deman's hand, called by a whispered name. A burst of golden light screamed from the wand's end met by a second bright white stream conjured by Elsymir.

Aiden rematerialized between the pair, called to the colliding forces of magic like a moth to the flame, as gold and white surges smashed up against each other like waves on a sea wall, sputtering hot molten sparks to the flagstones.

Malthus gripped his wrist to hold the wand steady as pus and gift-blood cracked through the burned plain of his chest.

Aiden could feel the sorcerer's pain radiating through him, through the entire chamber, like rapid heartbeats squeezed shut at the end, too weak to remain upright, too feeble to overcome the stamina of his apprentice.

With a flick of the wrist, Elsymir sent the jet of magic shrieking down to the floor, killing both streams, then raised with an incantation and fired once more.

The strike burst through Malthus's out-stretched wand arm before he could return a proper defense, severing the limb at the elbow and sending him spiraling violently sideways, through Aiden's apparition, smashing the back of his head against the armchair's edge, where he sank limply across the front of it, the shortened appendage leaking from a few spots where the cauterization didn't quite catch.

Elsymir's wand was spitting and whistling an instant later as the apprentice advanced on his fallen master.

"Not how I saw all of this playing out," Malthus rattled, his chest heaving.

Somehow the detached arm still clung to the wand, pushing what remained of the gift within to the instrument's tip, though it was swiftly dying out with the lack of blood supply. Elsymir stamped down on the spark to kill it, smoke rising from beneath his boot.

"If you kill me, my soul and gift go to the entity," Malthus uttered. "I will become part of its legion."

"And you deserve a damned sight worse by my estimation," Elsymir returned.

"It grows weaker by the cold. The demon. So, it will stay to the south." Malthus said, his words drying up.

The apprentice stared down in grim silence at his master, a mixture of grief and disappointment in his violet orbs.

"It can be banished…under a holy ward," the master continued as the memory began to blur and dim around them. "Like those from the old y'deman temples." Numbness replaced the pain. "Those used against…the snatchers and the dream…"

Elsymir released the spark at the end of his wand, the stream of magic snapping like a bolt of lightning into the oozing black scar covering Malthus's heart.

And thusly, the darkness returned afresh to reclaim its boldly scheming stray…

CHAPTER SIX

AN OCEAN COULD HAVE PASSED between the misfit trio for all the conversation they'd managed since noontide.

Julia sat in the middle of the bed, running a brush through her hair, her countenance shifting between vacant and troubled. Rhymona occupied a chair in the corner, marrying a stone to Fucker's bit. And Remy leaned against the wall by the lone window, puffing at his pipe, waiting for the night to come.

Where is Thousand Names? Remy thought for the thousandth time as he watched an elderly man locking up the shop across the street below. *She should have returned by now.*

After setting the plan for dusk, Solindiel decided to have a little scouting excursion, grumbling something about being cooped up in a shithole tavern all day and drinking the place dry. No one this side of the moon had the heart to argue, so they let her go. Though with the brand of devil she harbored within, it was highly unlikely she could have been stopped had one of them actually taken exception.

A few hours within the surly ashaeydir's company and Remy couldn't quite decide who was more vulgar and unruly, Soli-shan or Rhymona.

He turned from the shop owner to Julia, who now sat still, staring down pensively into the rumpled blanket at the end of the bed.

"Julia." His voice came out rough from the endless smoking.

Slowly, she shifted her blank expression toward him.

"I know this must be a lot for you," he said. "It is for me too."

"Yeah," she returned glumly, plucking clumps of hair from the brush's bristles.

"How are you holding up?" Remy asked after a long drag. "And it's completely all right if you don't want to talk about it. If it's still too soon."

It certainly would have been too soon for him were their roles reversed. The sight of their mother's corpse was one of the most dreadful images he had ever beheld. It took him to his knees in an instant; he couldn't imagine what he would have done had he actually been present when it happened.

"I don't really know what to say. Mum...she..."

"She did what she could," Rhymona finished, grazing a fingertip down Fucker's freshly whetted fang.

"She didn't do anything wrong," Julia said, anger swallowing sadness.

Remy couldn't help but notice how hard she was gripping the hairbrush's handle. For some reason, the memory of Marsea in Alistair's Courtyard came back to haunt, clad in his tweed hunting jacket, clutching a skinner's knife, her other hand a wretch of its former self.

"She was on her knees, pleading. I've never seen Mother so low." Julia sat the brush down trading it for the boot knife Rhymona bestowed upon her. "And then Dysenia made Rhymona choose. But it didn't matter what she said. The witch killed her anyway."

Remy looked from Julia to Rhymona. The magus held his stare, and her frown deepened.

The image of their mother's death played through a sequence of horrors in his head. He knew Dysenia. Wade's harlot, he'd gotten on naming her after Brymshire. He recalled her violence in the Krueger Street Innhouse, carving up his old swordbrother like a holiday roast. And then again in Palatia where she revealed her truth, toying with him further, making a mockery of his station, before burying a blade in another poor, hapless simp unlucky enough to cross her path at the wrong time.

Was there a chance I could have prevented this? The question couldn't be helped. He'd certainly had the opportunities. Had he only been even the smallest bit brave. He could have at least made an attempt. But on both occasions, he was weaponless, and both occasions came before...well, before Yvemathira.

"She will get what's coming to her," Rhymona promised, her scowl darkening.

"I hate her," Julia added. "Dysenia Deadeyes. I hate her guts." The words were pure venom. Nothing at all like what should be filling the thoughts and leaving the mouths of younglings.

Selfishly, Remy wondered if that was how the little one in Brymshire felt about him, some loose dog brandishing a sword about her father's face, threatening violence.

"She could have just gone," Julia kept on. "She could have just left us, and we wouldn't have stopped her."

"What she did was senseless," Rhymona agreed. "And unforgivable. And she will be dealt with accordingly."

"I know I shouldn't want to hurt someone," Julia said. "But whenever I imagine the witch's face, I just want to cut it, and punch it, and kick it in. I can't stop—"

"I know," Remy said, in awe of her mounting hostility. It was her Harver side making its presence known. "As horrible as it may sound, if there is any one thing I've learned in my nineteen cycles, it's that you should never hide from who you are and how you feel." He held her gaze. "I love you, Jules. And I'm here for you, whatever it is you feel like you need to let out. However awful it may be. We're in this thing together, yeah?"

One big, happy, fucked-up family.

"Thanks, Remy," the girl offered. Though, by her tone, Remy couldn't help but wonder just how much of that girl was still left.

An earsplitting cry from beyond drew Remy's attention back outside the window. The shop owner was tussling with another larger man before being thrown down to the stones. At once, two others descended atop the fallen shop owner and began to tear him apart.

"Blighters!" a voice howled from downstairs. It sounded like Goldcoat Pip. And a raucous followed. The sounds of a vicious scrap. Tables scratching against hardwood, bottles smashing, voices yelling and cursing, and finally the unforgettable clicking sound of the blight.

The watchman spanned the room in a heartbeat and was halfway down the upstairs hall when the barkeep appeared at the landing's edge, slamming hard against the opposite wall. Remy stopped cold at the sight of him.

"They're dead," Ozzie said, loon-eyed. "They're all dead." He approached. "Lucian. Lizzy. Pip. He...he killed them all."

Remy had seen that look before. Those eyes. Hells, he'd worn them himself only a few days past.

"Compose yourself, lad." A haggard man appeared after the barkeep, hobbling behind a blood-spattered golden shield, sword at the ready, all manner of gore dripping down from its deadly end. "This ain't even close to done."

Mayhaps the only thing more astonishing than the man's unsightly appearance was the fact that Remy actually recognized him. He'd grown a patch of salt and pepper across his jawline and put on a few dozen pounds since their last meet, but there was no mistaking it.

"Ledge?" uttered the watchman. The gods wept. How he looked anything but a Lord Magus now.

"Highness," Ledge returned. "Pardon the coarse tongue, but what in the nine fucks are you doing here?"

"I could ask the same of you."

A fresh commotion poured into the tavern downstairs, joined by the distant bellow of a war horn. "No time for that now," the Lord Magus said. "We must keep moving. The blight has taken the courtyards and the Noble district."

"How could they possibly be in the courtyards without having passed through from the outer city first?"

"How do you think?" Ledge returned as he shambled past the group to the window at the end of the hall.

"You believe it started there?" Remy inquired.

"Aye, and since we're playing at old mates, I believe your brother to be involved just the like."

"Desmond?"

"He has a strange connection to the nether. And...wait a tick, why is it you don't appear to be the least bit surprised by this?"

"Long story."

"Aren't they all?" Ledgermaine said as he entered the last room over-looking the back side of the innhouse. "We need a way out of this place."

Remy followed to the doorway. "So, what is he then? Is he a lich?"

"I didn't believe so. Truth be told, I don't know what he is. But we're well past lichlords and ghouls now, I'd say. At least those fuckers I can halfway understand, but this shit here...these nether demons, or whatever the fuck they are, they're an entirely different animal altogether.

"I was in the barracks when this all began. Rumors from the guard were that the false prince was the one responsible for the blight. But there were also other creatures, eldritch abominations like nothing I have ever seen before. I fought with a small group of pisscoats against the first wave, but the bastards just kept coming. We had no choice but to retreat into the city. But there were too many at once there. And one by one the others dropped off..."

"...*We have to go to the palace...*" Thira spoke through Remy, turning back to Rhymona. "*...Now more than ever. We have to stick to the plan as best we can. Remember the godsblood may be the only thing that can stop this...*"

"Your eyes," Ledge uttered. "Fucking hells, you've a snake in your head, haven't you?"

"*...That is one way of putting it...*"

"Yeah, well dracari or no, there's no way back to the palace from here. You won't even make it through the Nobles, the way things are."

"I've seen this play out before, Ledge," Remy said. "In Palatia and Lancastle both. If we run now, Courowne is as good as lost and the blight will be on to the next kingdom. We must make our stand here."

"You've no idea what's out there, boy."

"Oye. You can stow the bloody condescension, yeah. And I'm not your fucking boy. I'm your King. Or something damned close to it. And you're a high magus sworn to my liege, by my father's sword. Now you were one of father's most trusted once, not to mention one of the best swordsmen to ever grace the halls of Lancastle proper, so pull your head out of your ass, sack the fuck up, and—"

"Oye," Ozzie dared and the group turned to the barkeep in unison. "Yeah, hi. Hate to ruin this merry little circle jerk you lot have going here, but I may know a way to get us to the palace without going through the Nobles if that's your fancy."

"Well, *do* keep us waiting then," Rhymona said.

"The Emperor and I...well, we..." He eased knuckles into a palm. "Well...you've got it now, haven't you?"

"You and the Emperor were together?" Remy asked.

"Prize well, Drezhal is not all the horror the moon paints him as," Ozzie answered. "Though I wouldn't imagine that should come as any surprise to *you* of all folk."

"Have a care then, yeah," Remy said before he turned back to the former Lord Magus. "What say you to another round of madness, Ledgermaine?"

"What say I? I say you've all gone fucked in the head then, haven't you? But I reckon what's an old fart left to do these days anyway save find a proper deathbed?"

"There's a legend, there," the watchman said.

"Besides, knowing what I know, I can't in good conscience leave you all to it, now can I?"

Remy turned back to the barkeep. "Right then, Ozzie, the plays on you."

Only the fate of civilization at hand here. No big thing. Go figure, it might come down to the passage quality of a secret lover's rendezvous.

"Time to go play in the chaos."

CHAPTER SEVEN

FUCKER GORGED through the widow's peak of another scalp and came out easy, blood, hair, and brains splashing out at the crack in the scud. Oh, but for the whetstone's kiss, what a ghastly awful mess it made. Though it was just enough time before the next blighter came for her throat. Rhymona spun around the attack, giving the gangling, one-armed goldcoat an awkward elbow forward, before jamming a knife into the temple of the next ghoul thereafter. She ripped the shard of steel free, chasing what motherly instincts she'd cobbled together over the cycles, whirling about quickly to find Julia as the girl kicked the second blighter's knee out and followed the creature's descent with the nasty end of Old Trusty.

Well taken, the magus thought, sheathing her knife. Julia's movements were nearly flawless. Just as Rhymona had taught her.

Though her pride in the girl's grit was fleeting as she yanked a sword up from the gnarled dead hand of a nearby dwarfkin then stood back and took the poor bastard in. Something had burrowed a grisly path into the back of his head and eaten the brain clean from his skull as though it were a bowl of roast stew.

All of this horror, this loss, this death, and for what? Because some swaggering cunt-rag fucked with the wrong god an age ago?

Grimacing, she turned away from the scene. "Here." Rhymona offered the dwarf's sword to Julia as the girl wriggled Old Trusty from the side of the blighter's head.

"Thanks." Julia took the hilt and gave the sword a measured swing. It looked as natural to her as would a folding fan or sewing needles to most royal girls. Three cheers for the Harver bloodline, born to weather even the worst of civilized states it would seem, no matter what the age. At that moment, little Julia Harver, flecked in blood and nether residue, looked every measure a pit dog as did her father and uncles. Three red smear lines ran unevenly down from the side of her nose across her cheek where at some point she must have scratched at her face. *The warpaint would not be denied, not even from the younglings,* Rhymona thought. Though she couldn't imagine she appeared much cleaner herself.

"Go at them from the front when you can, yeah," Rhymona added. "I've seen some come back from side and stern blows."

"All right," Julia mumbled as she slipped Old Trusty inside a slit she'd made in the belt Lizet had given her.

A pair of looters burst out from a shop entrance across the street, bulging sacks slung over their shoulders, and stopped to take in their company. One wore a skull face and the other a long-nosed plague mask.

Rhymona stared them down, head tilting slightly to the side. *These fuckwits.* Slowly, she raised Fucker out at them, and they scurried down the cobble in the opposite direction.

"Courowne's finest," she grumbled to Julia. *Good to know the end of the fucking world wasn't even enough to dissuade the greed of man.*

"We're clear for a moment," Ledgermaine called out from up ahead, strands of gray hair plastered across his weathered countenance.

For a fat, old geezer, Rhymona had to admit, he knew his way around a sword and board, leading the charge like a seasoned soldier. But he certainly wasn't blowing smoke when he said getting to the palace would be a whore mother. The first couple streets outside the innhouse showed promise. They were manageable, easy pickings even, only a few patches of ghouls here and there. And she thought mayhaps the old man had oversold it. But such hopefulness found itself a lamentably short lifespan. For with each block nearer to the courtyards they drew, the more of the blight they had to cut through, and the more vicious the bastards became. These were not the same as the blighted in Lancastle or even Palatia. They showed signs of further mutations from the Lancastle wall-crawlers and some of the lot reacted as cleverly as the living, dodging and strate-gizing their own attacks. One, a few blocks back, had sprouted a third appendage from one of its shoulder blades, ranging long and black with red blinking eyes and three dagger-length talons at its end.

Remy referred to the abomination as a phase of drylax named a phaedrylax, a sort of half-formed gnaudrylax, and proceeded to Eldn flame the clicking bitch back to whatever foul abyss it crawled up from.

"How much further?" Remy pressed their guide.

"We're close," Ozzie answered, awkwardly clutching his sword. It was obvious he had never trained with a blade before. At least not properly. "Another couple of blocks and we'll reach the woods. It won't be but a stone's throw from there to the hedge maze."

"Hedge maze?" the watchman scoffed. "Your lover's meet is in a fucking hedge maze?"

"Name me a romantic," Ozzie answered, wiping a dirty sleeve across his damp forehead.

There was a crashing raucous behind them and an eerie shriek to follow. Rhymona's skin goosefleshed in its wake. It instantly reminded her of the cry she and Remy unbound in The Spellbind. Then the thing was upon them, tearing across the rooftops, ripping up wood and shingles with every movement. It leapt past, overhead, a shadow against the dying sunlight, a vaguely humanoid silhouette, like the thing in The Spellbind only scaled down. Soiled rags like a tattered cloak trailed the glint of a massive broadsword as its tentacles retracted and stretched out from its black and red form, propelling it forward with ungodly speed.

"Bloody hells!" Ozzie's voice cracked. "What the fuck was that thing?"

"Did you see its blade?" Rhymona asked. "Have you ever seen a sword like that?"

"It looked almost like wngar's iron," Ledge said.

"Fuck me, if that thing's a fucking wngar," Ozzie said.

"For now, thankfully, it appears to be going in another direction," Remy said, frustration riding the azure brand of his dracari orbs.

They crept down a skinny back alley, halting about a third of the way down as a thunderous rumble shook the buildings around them. Rhymona had to steady herself against the wall.

"What was that?" Julia asked.

"Nothing good, to be sure," Rhymona found herself saying.

"And it's only going to get worse," Ledge put in, readjusting his shield. "Keep your guard up."

The group kept moving, cautiously weaving through the carnage of corpses, stabbing blades down from one skull to the next. And the gods know there were so many one could barely make out the cobblestones any longer. One wrong step and it could fastly become a shitshow. But what other choice was there?

"There." Ozzie pointed forward as they neared the end of the alley. "See the trees? That's where we're headed."

Lovely, fog-covered woods, Rhymona groused. *And here I was just beginning to think the fates were starting to go easy on us.*

"It'll be dark soon," Remy said. "We need to be off the cobble by then."

"What are you suggesting?" Ledge countered. "We make a run for it?"

Cautiously, Rhymona poked her head out from the edge of the alley and found a blood bath in both directions. She could hardly see the horror of it any longer, such imagery had become so commonplace. It all felt more like a dream or a nightmare or a hearthfire haunter. Like some old nan's tale. Or rather, like she had been dragged out of her own story and placed into that of another's.

Upon pulling back, she froze, her heart clogging her throat at the phantasm in the alley's continuation across the thoroughfare. *Fia.* She blinked, but the specter of her sister remained fixed at the corner of her eye. Rhymona swallowed the lump of her heart back down. "If we're going to do this, we need to go now," she said. "Straight ahead."

"What are you talking about?" Remy asked. "What did you see?"

"You just have to trust me. You and Thira both. Straight ahead, full sprint, no stopping, no stabbing corpses, not until we reach the woods."

Remy held her gaze. She could almost always tell when he and Thira were in conversation and something was certainly being discussed presently.

"Rally up, you lot," the watchman said a moment later. "You heard her. Stay close and do not stop until you're past the tree line."

JULIA SKIDDED to a stop just short of a wandering ghoul, sword extended, silver sorrow locking them six paces apart.

Rhymona caught her up and held her side as they took the ghoul in. It was quite near Julia in age, barefoot and clothed in rough spun attire, which led the magus to believe that she may have been a crofter's daughter, though it would appear her turn to the scourge was freshly born, for aside from her opaque orbs the remainder of her visage shown wholly unaffected. She may not have been much to behold in her days amongst the living, but by comparison to her atrophied and limbless legion, she was an absolute vision.

Mystified, Rhymona and Julia watched as the pristinely unscathed ghoul shambled passed them without conflict like she was drunk off lotus milk.

"She...she..." Julia started.

"I know," Rhymona said.

"That could be me."

"That could be any one of us," the magus corrected.

Rhymona stalked after the pristinely unscathed ghoul, using the trees as a buffer, cutting a quick path around the front of it, and drove her knife into the girl's temple before easing her tiny, limp body down to the forest floor.

Seconds later, a burst of blinding light rippled through the pitch from up ahead, from the direction of Remy and the others. The light shone with such an intense glow that Rhymona had to shield her eyes until it softened. An otherworldly screech raged through the trees.

Rhymona and Julia rushed toward Remy and they found another phaedrylax writhing and melting in azure conflagration at the edge of the woods. This one had multiple black appendages, a few only half-formed, stemming from its flanks and backside like some sort of fucked-up human-spider hybrid. Despite its doomed predicament, it kept digging toward Remy, its shrill language defiant, until the watchman lowered iron mercy atop its smoldering crown.

He glanced back at Rhymona and Julia, and his mouth thinned with distaste.

In the distance beyond, the palace loomed like an ice-capped mountain. Somewhere inside its belly, something dark and dreary grew, soiling its once shimmering, translucent magnificence. It was netherborn without question, black as a crypt, consuming nearly half of the great diamond-shaped citadel. *Welcome to Courowne*, the magus thought. *Home of the moon's largest gravestone.* A thin, shit-colored mist was unfurling from the soaring tower, spreading like a beggar's cloak over the hedge maze between them.

As they scrambled across the open field, sidestepping corpses, scraps, screamers, and feeding frenzies, the last of the sunlight snuffed out like a glass-covered candle, giving way to the dark tower's ever-expanding shadow, where a strange static cling awaited them.

The wind in her throat, Rhymona's blood was pounding ear to ear, the air popping loudly back and forth with every swallow taken.

Twenty yards away.

Ten.

Five.

And they were inside the hedge wall, breathless and bleary-eyed, only slowing once the entrance disappeared fully from sight.

Beneath the nether-smog, she found the maze itself was surprisingly lush. The hedges stood a head taller than anyone in the group. Yews of an impossibly vibrant green were spotted in an alien navy-blue shade, as though some cheeky artist had skipped along, running her paintbrush here and there without taking proper measure. The serpentine rows were dense and seemingly impassable. And somewhere amidst the hedge paths, a weeping willow could be seen like a giant lording over its vast twisting kingdom.

Keeping a swift pace, it wasn't long in that they reached a fork. Cries of agony filled the clicking gaps of the blighted hive. They crawled out from both directions, echoing up and down the sylvan walkways like a devil's omen.

Turd for your sandwich or turd for your soup? Rhymona thought. *Choose wisely.*

"This way," Ozzie guided, and the group followed left, like a flock of braindead sheep.

Turd for your soup then.

At first, the path was clear, but they weren't in long before stumbling upon a pack of blighters. Three of the fuckers in the middle of the path gorged over a fourth. They would have to be dealt with to pass.

Rhymona raised Fucker for the task, but Ledgermaine was the quicker, chopping into the nearest two with their backs turned, taking

their scalps with a deft one-two strike before finishing the third with a
blade between the eyes as it made to stand.

Reflexively, Rhymona swung around to the space behind them. A light
breeze, like a whisper, danced past her and a shiver ran her length from
nape to arse. "You hear that?" she breathed to Julia.

"What?" the girl asked, owl-eyed herself.

Swallow. Pop. Exhale.

"Nothing," the magus answered, eyes darting hither and yon. Though
she couldn't shake the feeling that something far worse than the blight
was lurking not so very far away, nipping at their heels. It was as though
the hedges had eyes of their own. Thousands of the beady little bastards
behind every branch, full of mischief and murder. But there was no time
to mind them, no time to rest, no time to bandy threats, and even less
time to investigate.

"Rhymona," a tiny voice said.

"Coming," she answered, snapping back from paranoia's parade. *Keep
it together, fuckwit.* "Stay as close to the center of the walkway as possible,
you hear?"

"I hear," Julia returned.

*Preach, preach, preach. What the fuck are you doing, Morgan? This isn't you.
Pretending like you're the girl's mum. Pretending like you give half a toss about
these posh fuckers. What is your number one rule? What has always been your
number one rule? You. Don't. Fucking. Participate. And you never let them in. At
best you fuck off and tell yourself you've done them the favor. Have you learned
nothing since Val? Since Skagaten? Since Aiden and uni?*

The further inward they traversed, the thicker the mist became and
the deeper the shadows. The heavens had all but abandoned them now for
the hedgerow abyss. They scurried along to spite it, headfirst, driven by
some pact between the fates and the unknown, coming to another fork,
and another left turn, trailed by a third and fourth iteration before they
were back ranging near the outskirts of the maze again.

"I would imagine we will need to take a right at some point," Rhymona
called up ahead, mopping sweat from her face with the cloth she used to
polish Fucker's blade.

Ozzie held at the path's end, made a face at her, and placed a finger
against his lips.

The hideous sounds of bones crunching and flesh ripping could be heard around the bend, promising another rousing spell of Fuckwit Garden tomfuckery.

Rhymona dared a glance around the corner and found the path crammed with the blight. It had to be a dozen, possibly more. Some were merely standing idly in place or staggering aimlessly like the pristinely unscathed girl in the woods, but the most of them were feasting upon the fallen.

"We approach in waves," Ledge whispered. "Two ghouls at a time then back off for the next one of us."

The group marauded forward, holding to the plan like scripture, Ledge to start, then Remy, then Rhymona. Fucker to the first one, Bellend to the next. Bellend wasn't Old Trusty, but she was still a massive cunt when it counted and she'd cut through bone just as quickly as a carrot. In for two, out for a breath, in for two more, smooth as butter, like pinching pennies from the lowly town tosspot.

All the while, Julia and Ozzie kept watch behind them.

The group moved as a proper unit, without a word between them, just reading each other's body language, and it wasn't long until they were through and moving with pace again.

Rhymona listened intently as they finally trailed right, and then right again, past the weeping willow, and past another handful of wandering ghouls that each found a silver fang waiting.

All the while, the whispers had progressed from a passing dancer to a fully arranged masquerade, whirling her about this way and that.

Rhymona bit back a curse.

Swallow. Pop. Exhale.

It was around this juncture that the magus began to question the flow of time. How long had they been in here? It felt like both hours and minutes, and every path looked damn near the same. As usual, the sister moons proved little boon, as their hazy glimmer only served the mist's increasingly unsettling iridescence. She felt eyes burning on her skin, like the scald of a shufa stick cherry, as she swiveled about behind the group to make sure they hadn't taken on any unwanted company. She thought she saw the hedgerows shift and reshape, turning about all wobbly and weird, closing where it once was open.

It's only the mist, she told herself.

They finally came to a dead end, but Ozzie motioned to a soft spot in the brush. Remy disappeared inside.

"Something's not right about this place," Julia said.

"You just keep following your brother, yeah," Rhymona murmured. The words were rough as sandstone across her tongue.

The girl nodded, following the others through the makeshift fissure.

Rhymona gazed into the spiraling maze behind her and found Fia there, where she always was, just at the edge of her vision. "Dammit," Rhymona muttered as she backed into the branches and wormed her way twixt the brambles after Julia's shadow.

On the other side, she found a dark-skinned man on the ground dressed in fine silk robes. He was whimpering over a woman in his arms, caressing her pallid cheek. It was obvious they were nobility, and by the pendant he wore, he was likely some high-ranking councilman.

"They...I...I did my best..." he said to her, looking her dead in the eyes. Purple wax caked an exposed arm, which revealed a series of oozing cuts carved east to west. "There were too many...they...I've never seen anything like it..."

Rhymona approached cautiously, clutching Fucker warily between them, unsure if the man was actually real or if she was beginning to hallucinate. The others seemed to take no notice at all, which put her closer to the latter.

"We need to keep moving," Ledge barked from the mist ahead.

"Do not push further inside the palace," the man warned. "It's a death pit. You won't last an hour."

A shriek blasted through the hedges. Far too near for comfort. It sounded like the thing they beheld back in the township.

Shit. Rhymona cocked her head from the robed man to the others, drew in a deep breath, and tried to steady herself as the world began to spin sideways again, bending almost upside down. At once, her chest felt tight as a corset fitting and her lungs fumed like an ashy old hearth. Suddenly the hedges were closing in around her, vines of ivy unfurling, reaching out, trying to catch her up and suck her in. *You're fine. Just breathe.* She took a staggered step forward, the urge to faint causing her to list. *It's only the mist playing tricks.*

Swallow. Pop. Exhale.

"Rhymona?" Julia said.

"I'm fine," she wanted to say, but her throat closed around the words like a noose, choking them back. *You're not fucking fine, fuckwit. None of this is fucking fine.* She swayed from hedge wall to hedge wall.

Remy conjured an egg of Eldn flame to better light their way, and her eyes flicked over to his.

"You've made it this far," he said to her before starting forward.

Ledge and Ozzie returned from their scout further ahead.

"There's a legion of the bastards up around the bend," said the old man. "Too many to take on in such close quarters. Especially with this infernal fog."

"Then we'll burn our way through," Remy said as he ignited the wall in Eldn fire, carving a pair of bright azure lines a meter apart before kicking a doorway into the hedgerow to the next path over.

Forcing her fears to fuck off and willing the numbness to devour what weakness might betide her, Rhymona kept in uneven stride behind Julia and the others, into the slog of tallgrass. The world was an unending spiral, spinning, spinning. Spinning. It was all she could do to ignore the glower of hedgerow eyes as she pushed through their unblinking sea...

Here, amidst the tallgrass, there was no wind, the blades curling high as her waist in places, their weeds tearing raw across her weary ankles. The air hung heavy and humid, weighing her down, though not nearly as much as the flurry of disembodied murmurs.

A blood-smeared arm burst through the yews up ahead, grabbing Ozzie's sleeve and jerking him hard against the wall of foliage.

Rhymona's eyes cut to the attack, focusing. "Pull forward." She strode into action, swinging upward through an arm that came reaching for her, and hacking back down through the one that seized Ozzie.

The barkeep stumbled to his knees as more hands and arms, like broken branches, breached through the shrubbery from the other side. It wasn't long before faces and bodies began to follow.

"They're pushing through the walls!" Ledgermaine shouted.

Remy blistered another door into the next path over and the others scurried through, ever closer to the palace steps. Rhymona remained behind, mindlessly chopping and slashing, severing limb after limb and braining a few of the bastards in between. It was all she could manage just to give the others some measure of distance.

The unexpected clang of steel ringing out against its kin ripped her away from the wall of growing flesh and just as she made to step through the opening opposite, Julia shoved back in at her, dropping them both down into the tallgrass.

She heard a deathly cry and a dense, black mass hummed past the opening, dragging what remained of Ozzie with it, sending a wave of gore lashing out over them. *Fuck me!* The poor bastard continued to wail to his lung's capacity before the blood-curdling sounds of bones snapping in the distance silenced his terror.

"You all right?" Rhymona asked for lack of anything better to say.

"I think so," Julia said.

A blast of Eldn flame followed after The Shriek and Rhymona scrambled to her feet.

She cracked a skull with Fucker, the bit sticking, then a second with Bellend, the blade breaking away from the handle in its noggin. "Shit fucking day," she spiked the useless cut of wood into the ground.

Ledge appeared ugly in the doorway, his shield covered in blackened blood, his blade aflame with Eldn fire. "Get her the fuck out of here," he ordered before hobbling off in The Shriek's direction.

"Rhymona, watch out!" Julia shouted, her raven-hair whipping about wildly.

A third ghoul wielding a knife came at her, crazed yet calculated, and she caught the blade through the palm of her hand, seizing its other wrist as it gnashed its broken teeth at her face. *Fuck.* Its breath was rank as a chamber pot. *Not like this.* They crashed into the wall of leaves and limbs, twigs and fingernails from the other side raking up and down her backside, carving poison curses across her jerkin. *Not here.* The bastard thrashed at her, threatening to push her back through to the next passage over. *Not by this arsehole.* She dug in, a roar heaving out of her, as she shoved back against the fiend's assault from the soft flesh beneath its jawline, keeping its hungry maw at bay.

You promised the drink your death, remember?

Swallow.

Pop.

Scream.

Suddenly the bastard went limp, slumping loose down her body, and there was Julia Harver, tugging her dwarven sword free from the back of its head.

Rhymona lurched forward, out of the ghoul's nest, and ripped the blighter's knife out of her hand. "G-get...get her loose. Fucker. Get her loose now! That one over there."

Julia moved quickly, almost methodically, stabbing her sword down into the tallgrass before stepping on the blighter's head and wrenching Fucker free.

Rhymona shifted to the wall of blight and drove the ghoul's knife into the first face she saw, once, twice, a third time, smashing its temple into sauce, then left it jammed in the second dumbarse cunt to rear its ugly fucking mug at her.

"Still alive, you fucks!" she shouted through the sting of sweat in her eyes.

Julia had Fucker waiting for her as she reversed momentum, twisting awkwardly into the next path over. *I can't feel my hand,* she thought as they passed between Ozzie's lower half and Remy as he spun up another crackling sphere of celestial horror.

You've healed worse, she reminded as she cupped the blood spill in her fist, pressing her hand into her stomach as little rivers poured through the gaps between fingers. *You just need a binder. Half a candle and you're right as rain.*

The mist was thinning up ahead.

"This way," Jules bade as they raced toward the yawning expanse at the path's end.

Remy called out something from the space over her shoulder, but she couldn't half hear him. It sounded like, "I'll be right behind you."

Rhymona tossed a quick glance back the other way and found the old man cutting at a tendril with his flaming sword before taking a blow against his shield that sent him reeling into the hedge wall. The fiend raised its sword high, poised for another strike. And the gods know, the blade was longer than she was tall and nearly as wide, its form more akin to a slab of raw metal than any manner of smithy-forged weapon.

"He won't survive that thing," she thought she said.

"I don't reckon he plans to," she thought she heard in response.

CHAPTER EIGHT

Vesper.
Danica.
Seren.
Yvaine.
Asteria.
Tana.
Celeste.
Hester.
Stella.

AN AGE HAD PASSED since the last time she'd counted maidens by burning, but, verily, it was just about all her mind would allow her in its wearied state, their midaran names passing over her like gentle waves on exhausted shores, her footsteps treading in their wake, slogging, plodding, until one caught…

Shit.

Marsea stumbled over another stray root, her ankle twisting through a fresh pain, as she crashed against a redwood, shoulder first.

A flood of curses followed as she pushed away and dug another step forward, followed by a third and a fourth.

Hours had passed since her mad dash into the Kingswood, away from

Vinth and the Tarborils. A dash that unbound all manner of forest terror as she scrambled, hurdled, and stumbled her way from starlit patch to starlit patch until she'd put enough distance between herself and the township to risk catching her breath.

In the after, she found her body riddled with an untold number of knocks, cuts, and bruises, as though it had been torn to slivers amidst the trees and put back together in a slightly crooked fashion. Likewise, her head was thrumming to a vicious ritual song and her nose wheezed like the whine of a boiling kettle pot. Still, she trudged forward, her legs like wet clay, pushing through breath cloud after shrinking breath cloud, her gran glasses fogging up in consequence, the damp ground below threatening to make her a fresh grave with every stride taken.

As though all of those worries weren't problem enough, the shivers had found her after a time and her body had begun to gradually hunch and stiffen as the snowfall continued to collect. It went without saying really, but she needed to find shelter and soon or she would snag a sickness for her efforts, mayhaps worse, and that was if she hadn't done so already.

A whisper caught at the edge of her consciousness, and she halted for the thousandth time, her hairs standing on end and knees locking, as she swayed forward and then peered over a shoulder, her eyes blinking past delirium into the suffocating pitch.

"Sod off, you," she gritted to the black, having long since grown weary of whatever it was that had taken to their tail.

Nothing responded.

The princess wiped her running nose against her dirty sleeve and took an unbalanced step forward as Broenwjar turned back to take her in.

"I know, I know. I'm coming," said Marsea through clenched teeth and aching gums.

Old Boy had been leading the way for a while now. For how long exactly she hadn't the faintest. Mayhaps an hour. Mayhaps longer. Impossible to say really. The forest all looked about the same to her at this point besides. A tree was a tree was a tree against the woodland shadows. And this part of the wilds appeared as dense and untraveled as they come, with layers of unbroken white stretching far into oblivion's embrace. It was mayhaps the only thing that convinced her they hadn't been milling about in circles all this time.

Once upon a dream, she loved the sound of snow crunching underfoot. The quiet sinking sensation, the instant return to safety, the funny little misshapen hollows that ensued. But no longer. Not after this fool's charade. The effort had grown more akin to stepping through a sea of glass shards. And how the maidens knew, she could pass along a dozen lifetimes more without hearing the detestable crunching sound again and it might yet be too soon for tolerance.

Time.

Oh, Time.

Such a useless construct that cruel mistress Time. Especially when one had become exhausted and adrift and utterly without charge. And having traipsed this long through the wilderness in such a state, she was beginning to feel like she had crossed over into some completely different plane of existence entirely.

All the while, her mind had become fixated on the following whispers and the lingering woodland presence.

Were they actually one and the same somehow? Why was it following her? What could it possibly want stalking her all the way out here?

Or was it actually Yongrin that had put her to the chase?

Had the sorceress managed to slay the wood witch?

Marsea tried placing herself in Yongrin's boots. If their roles had been reversed and Yongrin had murdered Remy or Jules, would she have come out here hunting after the woman?

The image of the haxanblade sinking through Davrin's leg flashed through her mind. And the stars know how he howled at the strike, baying even louder when Yongrin sent up a flare of magic in their direction. Then louder still as Marsea found herself scampering off through the brush and thicket like a madwoman off her elixirs.

Broenwjar made a low growling sound and came to an abrupt halt. Marsea paused at his side and nudged her glasses back up her nose as she stared into the starlit clearing up ahead.

"I really hope this isn't the fever taking hold." Marsea toed out of the darkness into the wan expanse and approached a wall of layered stone. She placed her palm against its cold surface and exhaled. "I think you've done it, B. Maidens' mercy." She trailed the wall to an opening and squeezed past the rusted gate, which hung at a crooked angle, its top hinge having been broken by some manner of brute force and discovered within a massive cemetery.

Through a thin purple fog, she scanned the field of graves to verify that they were alone. Her vision eventually halted on a crow that was cawing atop one of the nearer stone crosses, its black feathers dusted in snow. Her eyes trailed down to the patch of broken dirt below. It appeared as though the grave had been dug up freshly. As she approached, another far more terrifying thought filtered through. Had it been dug up or had something dug itself out? The way the world was spinning these days, one was just as likely as the other.

"You see anything?" she asked Old Boy in their special language.

Broenwjar let out a troubled snarl and began to scout further ahead, disappearing inside the fog.

Marsea followed in her companion's wake, unsheathing Blind Widow, though nothing else moved about the cemetery save the murder of scattered crows. The princess cautiously navigated the tombstones, the ground heaving up and down beneath each footstep, until she reached a mausoleum that appeared horribly misplaced amongst the sea of smaller plots. It stood as the largest structure within sight and the comparison wasn't particularly close. Twixt withered strands of ivy, the name engraved above the opened entry read 'SHAWLEY' in large, bold letters. Just inside there was a sconce on the wall with a torch in its holder.

"Finally, some bit of luck," the princess breathed as she fished inside her satchel for the flint and tinder Elsymir had forced her to bring and collect during their trek to Vinth from the Ravenholme enclave.

She removed the torch and set it down atop the altar in the mausoleum's depths. It took her a few strikes, but she managed to bring a flame about and grew a smile inside its paltry warmth. She ran a hand through her hair and pulled away a pair of tiny twigs. For a moment she forgot its new length and forced herself to swallow the ensuing panic. "Well, you've certainly gone full savage now, haven't you?" *Only a little more blood and war paint and the transformation would be complete.*

She glanced around the mausoleum's innards studying the nearest tombs. *'Chandler Aloysius Shawley.' 'Selwyn Peth-Shawley.'*

"I hope you don't mind my company," Marsea said as she closed the doorway to a half and made herself a spot in the mausoleum's corner. *The stars save me.* The stone floor was somehow, impossibly, colder than the snowfall just outside. *Suck it up, buttercup.* She bundled up as tight as she could and brought the flame close, the last of her energy ebbing away. She then closed her eyes, knitted her hands as best she could in prayer, and began to recite The Omedran Canticle, if only to settle her mind by the smallest measure.

During the third verse, Broenwjar returned and his casual demeanor provided her with some small measure of comfort as he came to a rest next to her.

They remained quiet for a time, tucked away inside the stink of stone and decay, so quiet she could almost hear the moon turning, as her eyelids grew heavier and heavier still...then her stomach decided to let out an ungodly loud lurch. Broenwjar lifted his head and blinked at her.

Good gravy, Marsea. Were they not in such a horrid predicament and had she not been so sleepy, she might have had a laugh at the face he made. "Don't suppose you've got some spare rations stashed away inside that big furry coat of yours," she japed. Broenwjar eased back down, resting his snout over his outstretched legs, clearly unimpressed. "No?" she asked. "Too soon for a shot at gallows humor then?"

A bear-like yawn forced its way out at the end of the sentence. Sadly, it was about the last of her strength. Her gloved hand drifted onto Broenwjar's flank, and her exposed fingers combed through his fur, leaving a pair of trails. Underneath, his body was so warm. Meanwhile, hers was beginning to overtake her mind against every effort she could muster to stay awake.

The guttering torchlight cast queer shadows along the walls of the crypt, tall and skinny and full of fancy...

THE NEXT THING Marsea knew she was back atop her endless ocean standing next to Other. They stared out together into the ocean of trees.

"**Frayed are the threads that cast shadows,**" Other finally said. She turned to Marsea and clapped her hands together then spread them apart as though she were opening a book. "**Faceless man. Master. Stranger. He who dawns the endless night. She.**"

"She?"

"**Tetherow.**"

"Tetherow?"

"Tetherow is both. He and she."

"Both? How do you mean?"

Other shrugged.

"Do you believe Father knew of this?"

"You believe—"

"Me? I believe?"

"Us."

Just then another passage struck her.

And so, the pages were scribed in its blood and sealed with a sacrifice and a pact, their words thieved, and bound to a new master.

"No." Marsea spun into a pace, tiny eddies forming at each footstep. "But it can't be."

"It can."

"You're saying Tetherow literally wrote himself into the grimoire's pages. That he...she...it's somehow bound itself to them." Immediately she wanted to set fire to the dreadful thing.

"Blood magic, soul magic," said Other. **"Phylactery."**

"How many times?" Marsea uttered. "How many times can one fragment their soul?"

"Open your eyes."

"What?"

"You will know the page," Other spoke in Dagmara's voice. **"Just open your eyes."**

"I can't—"

"You will."

At the telling, the ocean gave out beneath Marsea's feet like a trapdoor and she plunged below the ice-cold surface.

Water filled her lungs, freezing her last breath inside the base of her throat, as something grabbed hold of her ankle and began to tug, something hot as a boiling cauldron. She made to investigate the scalding touch and splashed down inside The Cupboard, sodden to the bone. A torch burned against the hardwood and yet somehow it didn't catch fire. There was a book opened on the ground before her, its barbed chains reaching out from its underside like spider legs. *Dusk.* There could be no mistaking it. The pages fluttered this way and that as though stirred by a phantom wind finally stopping about midway through.

Marsea dared closer.

Etched unevenly in the faded parchment were strange incandescent markings that burned with the inimitable ire of a thousand magi, stinging her eyes and warming her face.

Despite their temper, she found she could not look away. Some invisible force compelled her to stare at the page and into the glowing runes. Tears rolled away from overgrown eyelashes. A moment later, she sank to her knees, seemingly at *Dusk's* behest, and her fingers stabbed down against the page starting with the first symbol in the uppermost right corner. She began tracing its arches and edges until it met the next letter just below. They were y'deman script all. She recognized that much from her father's glossaries. Though how she was now able to interpret them, fell some rest well beyond her wit. Last she'd checked, of the fifty some odd characters comprising the y'deman alphabet she understood maybe a quarter. That, and it was widely believed impossible for one to see proper languages inside dreams.

Still, she traced, on and on, until...

"You know the answer to that. You've read the words. How many times now?"

Marsea shifted toward the voice in the doorway. "Father?"

There, in the dying torchlight, holding the *Kingstome*, stood the thing that had been made of Whitman Lanier. The blood spots in the bandaging around his head almost gave him a sack doll face, but, at least, he still had his head on his shoulders.

"This...these words..." she stammered her way through his unsettling appearance, "they're a soul-binding curse, aren't they?"

Her father said nothing.

"Does this mean you've split your soul as well?"

"You know the answer to that. You've read the words. How many times now?" A voice echoed and her father opened the *Kingstome* to a page about a third of the way in.

"What does that mean?" Marsea implored as she came to her feet, holding *Dusk* close. "Are you still alive then?"

"You know the answer to that. You've read the words. How many times now?"

"I don't know anything. I'm barely staying alive myself." A silence stretched between them. "If part of you still lives…can that part be brought back?"

"You know the answer to that. You've read the words. How many times now?"

"You keep saying that," she shouted at him, becoming cross. "Is that all you can say then? After everything we've been through? Why even show yourself if you're not going to help? What am I supposed to do here? Where am I supposed to go?"

"You know the answer to that. You've read the words. How many times now?"

"No, I don't know the answer. And I've read thousands of words. You'll forgive me that I haven't memorized all of them or unraveled each specific purpose."

Whit extended the *Kingstome* toward her and she read the words aloud.

"One will die before their time.
One must go alone.
One will cede love's greatest gift in turn to spite the throne.
A ruin by starlight.
A blade from the stone.
A door from within, rent straight from the bone.

"What am I supposed to do with this?" she said with a groan. "What does it mean?"

"He can't actually speak, you know," another voice spoke from behind her and Marsea spun toward it. "He had his tongue ripped out as you might recall."

The voice belonged to her younger self, little Marsea Munch, clad in a collared dress and pigtails, before the gran glasses and all the pretty, pretty scars.

"You're…" Marsea turned back to her father to find only empty air. "But…"

"You truly don't remember those words?" Marsea Munch asked.

"No. Why would I?"

"Because they were the last words father ever said to us."

"No, they weren't."

"They were. You just didn't understand this at the time."

"Seems to be a rather common theme with me."

"Father split his soul. You know this to be true." Marsea Munch offered her hand. "We noticed the difference immediately, remember? Those words were the last words he spoke to us as his true self."

Marsea took the younger version's hand and stepped out into the Lancastle Library. Only the archive was now shrouded by a lazy mist that was far more befitting of a swamp than the inside of a castle. The walls were indeed bookshelves, but the further into the boggy labyrinth they traversed the more fen-like it became. Hanging moss ranged down from the darkness above and the aisles were littered with cattails and mushrooms of every color. Not to mention the colony of fireflies. At one point, Marsea thought she saw a swamp rabbit, hopping along just ahead of them, leading them onward.

They passed aisle after aisle, sloshing through the muck, occasionally taking a right turn here or a left turn there, until they came to a wall of books that couldn't be passed. Here she found a face she hadn't seen in ages. "Desmond?" He was standing on a bright red toadstool the size of a footrest, pressed against the shelves, spying through an opening between books just like they had done so often way back when.

Marsea Munch stopped beside him and removed a tome so she could see through to the other side. Marsea followed suit, slipping a lichen-covered book from its cranny before glancing into the candlelight beyond. Amidst the dreary haunt of the other side, she found her father from a time before his torture standing next to Stella Critchlow. He appeared to be cradling a youthful version of the *Kingstome*. Marsea's eyes widened as their faraway words, hushed and ethereal, carried into the bookshelf alcove.

"I will only help you this once and then we are even," Stella said. "The soul is not a thing to be toyed with."

"It's the only way for me to understand him," Whit replied. "To understand what he has done. And it might be the only way for me to stop him."

"If you pull too much, it could make of you an even more dreadful creature than he is."

"It is a necessary risk."

"Think of what you're saying, Highness. Think about Desmond and Marsea. About Rembrandt. You do this, the man you are will be no more. Do you think this is fair to them? That they should have to grow up with a father missing a piece of himself?"

"It must be done. And I won't ask another to take on such a damning charge. The godsblood will keep me together. In this I trust."

"Well, I won't let you do it alone."

"You will and that's an order. Ledge has already volunteered his services, and I turned him down. And I would far sooner risk his neck than yours."

"Whit—"

"Besides, things go sideways, it will have to be you or Ledge that puts me down, won't it?"

"And what of Elsymir?"

"He is not to know of this. Is that clear?" Marsea had never heard her father take such a sinister tone before.

"Perfectly," Stella said.

"He cannot be trusted any longer. He has made his decision, taking league with Ravenholme. It should only be you, Ledge, and—"

Whit and Stella both turned to something in the opposite distance, glaring in unison.

"**You should open your eyes now**," a voice said from the shadows behind her.

Marsea turned to find Other, all the whites of her eyeballs swallowed up, black as fish eyes.

Both Desmond and Marsea Munch had vanished, leaving just the two of them.

"Is this real?" asked the Lanier princess. "Did this really happen?"

"**You know the answer to that**," Other returned. "**You've read the words. How many times now?**"

In the muck between them, *Dusk* began to call out, her symbols smoldering anew, bright as dragon's flame.

"**Open your eyes**," Other said. "**You will know the page.**"

Marsea knelt before *Dusk* and picked up where she left off tracing the symbols.

"**I said open your eyes**," Other repeated in a warped snarl.

Marsea glanced back up just in time to see Other's jaw unhinge impossibly wide and lower down to take her head off.

CHAPTER NINE

"WOULD you mind seeing to the vineyard duties today?" Stella asked as she shuffled into the kitchen.

"Not even a day home and you're already putting me on the vines?" Aiden teased from his old spot in the quaint little nook overlooking the side yard. "For shame, Mother. For shame."

"I know this isn't exactly how you saw your visit going, but Matthew says your father will be on bedrest for at least the next few days, and it would be a huge help." She produced one of her many famous motherly expressions. This one landing somewhere between kind and commanding. "I have to head into town for most of the day or I'd see to the picking myself."

"And what pray tell has you in town all day for?" Aiden asked.

"What do you think?"

"You know the Apothecarium will survive a single day without you, right? It might even survive two if you let it."

"If only," Stella grabbed an apple from the countertop, then the oilskin satchel at the table's end. "So, you'll do it, yes?"

"Yes, of course, I will do it, *Mother*," he offered with an eye roll. Stella had won this little exchange long before its conception and she bloody well knew it.

"Thank you, *son*." She smirked. "I'm sure Tam won't mind lending a hand."

"Don't hold your breath," Aiden said.

"Maybe try asking nicely."

"Yeah, yeah." He waved her on.

"I'll grab some sweetmeats and pie from the confectionery on the way home. What'll you have?"

"Caramel tarts."

"Of course, it's caramel tarts. I don't even know why I asked." She stopped at the doorway that led into the foyer. "It's good to have you home, Aiden. Truly."

"It's good to be home," he returned.

"I'll be back sometime before supper," she called as the front door opened and then closed.

Aiden scooped up the last bite of blueberry porridge and tossed the bowl and spoon into the wash bucket. Milling the downstairs, he grabbed a matchbook from the hall table, nicked one of his father's aprons from the coat rack, pulled a shufa stick from a tin case in his trouser pocket, and sauntered off to the front porch with a shimmy and a shake.

Outside, he gazed across the yard and found his mother on her mare Dargol in the distance, nearing the road for town. He drew in a fresh breath of country air and let it out. Only the faintest whisper of yestereve's rainfall. "There it is," he said before tucking the shufa stick between his lips, lighting it with a match, and sucking in the first pull.

"Seriously?" Autumn said from a chair at the other end of the porch.

"And there's the betrayer," he said dramatically to the fat ball of fur curled up in her lap. "You missed out on a quality breakfast, you lazy little shit."

"I fed him some chicken shreds from supper, so I'm sure he'll survive," Tam said.

"Sister," Aiden greeted.

"I think he's found himself a new favorite." She scratched under Grandpa's chin.

"Awfully early to be after my good mood, wouldn't you say?" Aiden took another drag.

"I'm not after anything."

"Mmhmm. And we're fast at the page today then, aren't we?"

75

"I rather find that a good book is the best way to start the day. Isn't it, Grandpa?" She rubbed his little noggin and made kissy lips.

"A good book, hunh?" Aiden said as he approached her. "And that better not be fucking Mervold I see in your hands there."

"I don't care what you say. I like them."

"*Our Knives Hide Scars,*" he managed enough of the title between her fingers. "At least you've chosen one of the better stories."

"You're such a book snob."

"I can't help Mervold is a bloody hack. And you can blame Mother for my book snobbery. It's a wonder her highbrow affinities haven't rubbed off on you a little more, to have it true."

"It's not for lack of trying, I'll tell you that now. But what can I say? Sometimes I like a bit of lighter reading. Not everything should be all doom and gloom, you know."

"You say doom and gloom. I say realistic."

"And Mother says useful. But usefulness has many meanings and what may be useful to one person may not be to another."

"Rot, rot, bloody rot, spare me the lesson," he said before circling away from her, back down toward the stairs and the backyard, puffing at his shufa stick, big clouds of smoke trailing after him.

"Where are you off to?" Tam asked.

"Mother's asked me to go grape picking for the old man," he grabbed a pair of shears, dropped them into a bucket, and lifted the handle. "Care to join?"

Autumn thought on it a second before closing the book. "Sure, why not?" She inched to the edge of the chair, but Grandpa wasn't budging. "Come on Grumpy-bum, move it along." Grandpa yawned and stretched, taking his sweet time about it, impeccably defiant in his laziness. "I know, I know, I'm awful, aren't I?" She picked him up from her lap and set him back in the chair behind her. "I swear, he's nearly the cat version of you."

"He should be so lucky."

They strolled toward the vineyard, brother and sister, side by side, down a broad dirt path in the tall grass that stretched out from the egg-colored manor, Aiden swaggering through smoke clouds, Tam lost in one of her lilting songs.

Autumn's voice carried across the open fields with effortless grace and a gentle breeze did follow, as though spellbound by her heavenly sounds.

Hers was a voice that belonged on a stage in the highest of courts, not lost amongst the wilds of some backwoods hollow. And the gods know, but Aiden missed her singing dearly whilst away at university. Kanton, he'd come to find, proved rather light on musical flair. Every once in a maker's moon, during Harvestide or Midwinter, a halfway decent troupe would stroll through town for a night or two, but that was typically about as good as it got.

"I don't think I recognize that one," he said as they neared the vineyard's edge, a sliver of sunlight working its way through the gray above.

"I don't know how you would," Tam said, bending auburn locks behind an ear and presenting a clever smile. "I just made it up."

"You're taking the piss."

"Nope."

"Either way, it was quite good. You might even consider a name for it."

"A name for it." She shook her head. "What's with the world and naming everything these days? Maybe once in a while, we can just let a thing be what it is and not force a title upon it."

"Ease her on back then. I was only trying to give a compliment."

"A compliment? From the moon's biggest grouch? I daresay, graduating university has turned you into a right proper tenderheart then, hasn't it?"

"I don't know about all that. But I can certainly appreciate talent when it finds me." Aiden puffed the last bit of green from the roach of his shufa stick and made a little grave for it in the dirt. "The gods know, you sound just like Calem."

"Oh, how is Calem?" Autumn asked.

"Well enough, I suppose."

Autumn clipped a cluster of grapes into her bucket. "And Caitie?" she cooed.

Aiden shrugged. "Caitie is Caitie."

"You mean she's not Rhymona?"

"Rhymona, she is most certainly not."

"Is that a good thing or a bad thing?"

"You know, I've been asking myself the very same question since Caitie and I started on."

"It's just so strange her leaving like she did," Tam said. "So unlike her."

"Honestly, I think that's the part that vexes me the most. That we never broke it off. At least not properly." He found a ripe bunch and snipped. "One day we were bingeing about the typical haunts, drunk as lords, and the next she's gone. No note. No goodbye. No fuck off, fuckwit, nice while it lasted. Not even an argument to give it purpose. Just gone. Like in the end I wasn't even worth that to her."

"I'm sure that's not how it was."

"Well, however it was, it's been almost two cycles. If she were ever going to show herself again, she would have done so by now. Not that I'd have the faintest inkling what I'd actually say to her after all this time."

"It's brave to let a thing into your heart," Autumn said. "It's the bravest thing one can do. Especially when you already know how it feels to lose such a thing."

"Awfully wise words from one with so few cycles and suitors to her count. What pretty page did you readily pluck that bit of dross from, I wonder?"

"Rhymona, actually. It's what she once told me when I asked her if she loved you."

A brief pause settled between them. "Yeah?" he mustered, shaking his head. "Perfectly Rhymona, that. Always expect the unexpected."

"If you say so."

"In any case, you shouldn't have to hear me go on like that."

"It's all right. Truly. I'm your sister, aren't I? I won't pretend I'm much help with such matters as the heart, but, at the very least, I can listen."

They were making quick work down the row, given to conversation. Though, to have it true, Aiden had always gotten on with Tam pretty effortlessly, despite their eight-cycle age gap, especially when it was just the pair of them. Autumn Rose had a certain air about her, a certain empathy and comfort, only rivaled by their mother, which made it far too easy to open up to. As for the picking, once he got started it was all muscle memory from there, the rhythm of moving up and down and side to side along the vines like he'd done it every day of his life since birth.

"What about you?" he asked. "Still planning for uni in harvest?"

"More than like it'll be pushed back to next cycle."

"What?" He turned around to face her. "Why?"

"Well, with father's health issues, I can't just leave them to it, now can I?" She brushed her hair out of her face and met his gaze.

"Mother said it's just the turn of season. Just like last cycle."

"Last cycle? Oh, Aiden, do wake up. She's coddling you, like always. Father has been sick for months now. *Since* last cycle. Since before that. He's lucky to see two days of work a week most weeks. And mother is reluctant to pay for a spare hand because we aren't pulling the coin like we used to. Why do you think she's been working so much at the Apothecarium?"

"You could have told me this, you know. *Someone* could have told me, at least. You could have written a letter. If you knew mother was coddling—"

"That's just it. No, I couldn't have. And you know that. You know how she is. Mother made me promise not to. At least not until you graduated." Tam's eyes became watery. "And now, you're on for assistant professor, aren't you? And then tenure...and then who knows?"

"Tam."

"I'm sorry." She shifted away, striding down between the rows of vines toward the other end.

"Shit," he mumbled. "Tam, wait." He dropped the clippers down beside the bucket and followed after her. "Don't be sorry, all right. You needn't ever feel sorry toward me. I'm glad you told..." He halted next to her before the great oak tree at the vineyard's far boundary, his head slowly listing. Magic dust glittered inside a series of cuts made in the bark. "I'm a little high right now, but are you seeing what I'm seeing?

"Glowy yellow stab marks."

"Brilliant, not hallucinating." Aiden approached the oak tree and traced a finger against the shimmering residue. The carving began to flare brighter at his touch, showing a similar shape to an X etched through an S. "Fuck me." He backstepped as the strain of magic tingled down his arm and across his body. "It's definitely active."

"Active?"

"Living, working, serving." He glanced at Tam over his shoulder. "Do you know what this is?"

"It's some sort of enchantment, obviously."

"Well right, obviously. Have you seen it here before?"

"No, I haven't," she answered.

"I wonder if mother made it."

"Do you know what type of ward it is?"

"I don't recognize the sigil itself. Could be part of an obscurity circle. Though I've also seen similar symbols with translocation wards."

"Translocation wards? Like a portal?"

"Precisely. Step back a bit. Let me see if I can call it forth." Aiden approached it again, dragging a ring razor across his palm, and placed the bleeding cut flat against the carving. If only he'd thought to bring the last of his blood candles home with him. He closed his eyes. "Let me know if you see anything." He concentrated on the symbol, forcing it to appear in his mind, and attempted to compel his energy toward it. After a series of breaths, a faint hum began to resonate within. "Anything yet?"

"Nothing."

He pushed harder against the tree, plundering deeper into his gift, blood pumping through him like waves to the shore.

A thundering sound approached from somewhere off in the distance and his heart set to the races. "Come on, sing to me, sweetheart," he called, ignoring the sudden itch across the scar on his stomach.

"Aiden." His name pierced through the sigil's vibrations.

"Quiet," he returned.

"Aiden, what in vaelnation are you doing?" his mother's voice shouted and Aiden's eyes burst open as she slowed Dargol's trot to a halt. "Take your hand away from there this instant."

Aiden pulled away, defiantly holding Stella's harsh glare, the fresh cut across his hand stealing the itch from his abdomen.

"What is this, mother?" he asked.

"By the looks of it, I'd say you know damned well what it is."

"And did you make it?"

"It was conjured by someone I trust and that's all you need to know about who made it." Stella dismounted. "How could you be so foolish?"

Aiden cupped his bleeding hand against his belly.

"You know what horrors can happen chasing after another caster's ward without knowing its key. Gods' wounds, Aiden, it's the first precept of ward magic. And with your sister here, no less? How do you suppose she might have reacted had it been hexed? Watching her brother become boiled alive or torn to ribbons?"

In all of his cycles, he'd never beheld his mother so furious.

"Tam, take Dargol back to the stable." Stella handed the reins over to her daughter. "You, sir, with me, right now."

Stella stormed passed the great oak toward the tree line on the other side; and Aiden followed, wrapping his hand in his father's apron.

They walked for a while in silence, traipsing through mud and leaves, the terror stewing, until they came to a clearing, and it dawned on him where they were.

Twixt patches of ivory and lavender bellflowers, amidst the grove's opposite edge, rose a series of identical stones that climbed up well north of the waist.

Mother had brought him to the Critchlow Plot.

It had been many cycles, nigh on a decade, since Aiden last bothered a visit, though it looked exactly the same as he remembered. Evidently, daughter and grand had kept it up proper.

He stalked through honeysuckle and foxglove, following after his mother's trail until she came to a halt before Nan's grave.

Marion V. Critchlow. 1756–1818.

Aiden stopped next to her, before his grandfather's headstone.

Aiden X. Critchlow. 1757-1812.

"You're a man grown now," Stella said, staring down at her mother's headstone. "I cannot pamper you any longer, and I cannot protect you like I used to."

"I'm not asking you to."

"I know that, but..." She let out a heavy breath. "One day you'll likely have children of your own and maybe then you will understand."

"I was a fool back there, mum. I understand that. I honestly don't know what came over me."

"Mayhaps the shufa," Stella said pointedly.

Aiden winced. "That obvious?"

"I could smell it on you from the edge of the yard. I was young once, too, you know. It's a harsh habit, smoking, but you're a man grown, as I said, so it's your habit to contend with."

"So, it is."

"Gone are the days of me trying to govern your every move. I accept that. But Autumn. She is still a child. Try as she might to act older than her few cycles."

"Tam was the one that found the ward."

"And you were the one begging after it, were you not? You should have taken her away from it immediately."

"It wasn't a translocation ward, was it?"

"No, it was not. It was a protection ward. And there are dozens more around the property."

"A protection ward from what?" Aiden asked. "Is someone after us?"

"No, nothing like that."

"Then why have them? What aren't you telling me?" He finally took her in, just as the wind found them.

"I swore an oath to a friend," she answered. Her long ruby hair ran the course of the breeze as it lessened. "An oath of secrecy. An oath I cannot and will not betray. Not even to my own son. Prize well, they are there for a damned good reason. And promise me you will leave them be from here on out."

"I'll leave them be, hand to heart. But you should probably have the chat with Tam about them."

"I suppose I will have to." She met his stare.

There was a sadness in her eyes. A sadness and something else.

A distance, maybe...

No.

A fear. Try as she might to mask it.

Do you fear me, mother? He wanted to ask, daft as the question felt to consider. *Is the ward intended for me?*

"Why did you come back home?" he inquired instead.

Stella Ashborough was amongst the most renowned of Midara's living magi, after all. What fear could a novice barely off his scholar's robes possibly invoke from such a marvel?

The daughter turned back to her mother's headstone. "I forgot a delivery for Dom Bailes."

"Rotten Dom? Gods know, that one takes me back a turn. He's still milling about these parts, is he?"

"He is. You wouldn't even recognize him now. Cleaned himself up proper, got himself a bride, and took over Rendyll's smithy a couple cycles back."

"Dom's married?"

"Aye. To the Trevathyn girl."

"Madeline?" Aiden turned back to his grandfather's headstone in full bewilderment and stared at the name they shared. "Punching out of his league with that one, you ask me."

"Your father said the same."

They shared a smile as a murder of black birds began to caw in the halo of branches around them.

"I should have told you about the wards," Stella said.

"Yes, you should have," Aiden replied. "But I should have thought better than to hunt after it." He unwrapped the apron from around his hand. "Tam told me about father. That he's been sick for a while. And that's why you've been working the apothecary all hours of the day and night."

"He has his good days and his bad."

"Mum, you can be true with me on this."

"I am being true."

"Is he dying then?"

Her composure slipped, if only slightly. "What sort of question is that?" she asked. "We're all dying, aren't we?"

"Is he going to get better?"

She shifted away from him. "What he has, tonics won't cure, and neither will the gift."

"What is it?" Aiden took a step closer, halving the space between them. "What does he have?"

Stella turned to take him in. "There are these growths inside of him. Between Matthew and I, we've done everything we can to remove them, and for a time, in the after, your father does improve. But the growths eventually return, and in recent months we've found they are spreading. Matthew believes with continued and constant treatment he may still live for a while relatively pain-free, but…"

"Dare I ask how we're affording all of these treatments?"

"We're not? I work the Apothecarium in return for supplies and access to their laboratory. And I've been teaching Autumn the treatments. She's come along quite fast with them."

"Gods' wounds. Why haven't you told me about any of this?"

"For a multitude of reasons. Namely, you're graduating university. You've worked so hard, Aiden. And your father didn't want to be a distraction from your studies and trials."

"Fuck the studies and trials. I could have been here helping you."

"Oh, don't be so dramatic. The last thing your father wants is another fusspot roaming about his bedchamber feeling sorry for him. I promise you that. He feels bad enough as it is with all the work Tam and I provide. And he would have felt worse with you having missed out on graduating having worked so hard all these cycles."

"Well, now I'm graduated. So, there's no reason—"

"No."

"No? What do you mean, no?"

"I mean no. Your father and I have already discussed it. At length, mind you. And you can have it out with him just as well if you must. He is aware of your professorship and we won't have you throwing your future away for something that cannot be helped."

"I don't mind doing more, mother. Especially after all you've done for me. I'd like to help in some way."

"Then work hard at your professorship. Gain tenure. Stand a legacy. Honor us with success at university."

"And what about Tam? What about her success? What about her dreams?"

"What about them?"

"Next cycle," he said. "Next cycle then it's Tam's turn. She deserves a chance at uni too, every bit that I had. A cycle at the professorship and I will make the most of it. I will honor you and father both. Auror's oath. After that, I'll come home to help out and Tam can have her go."

"Two cycles," Stella said evenly. "Two and she's fifteen. That's how old you were when we allowed you enrollment."

Aiden simply nodded. It was a small victory, but a victory nonetheless. He couldn't wait to talk with Tam again and give her the good news.

"All these cycles away and still you are as your sister's keeper," Stella said.

"I wonder where I got that from."

"She is lucky to have such a caring older brother." Stella lowered herself down upon her knees before Marion Critchlow's grave, clutching the amethyst pendant that hung down from her neck.

Aiden glanced up into the high branches at the legion of blackbirds, cawing as though in symposium over their latest guests, their count doubling in mere minutes.

He knelt next to his mother as she began to recite an old maiden's canticle, one Nan used to recite every nightfall before supper. The moon went black behind his eyelids and he envisioned the words like burning sigils against the endless dark.

Maidens, make me thine instrument
Where doubt may dwell, may I find faith
Where despair may haunt, may I find your hope and grace
Where hate may tread, may I find your gentle love
Where the nether grows, in blackest dark—

A sharp pain stole the last of his words and he pitched forward, plunging through a whirlwind of black and white feathers that cut about him like a swarm of hungry knives.

Strange, savage images followed, splitting the slender spaces between, distorted like a watercolor painting left to the run...images not of his own leaving...images of unspeakable acts and twisted faces...faces deformed by Tetherow's insatiable hate and malice...

CHAPTER TEN

...UNTIL HE SLAMMED BACK into his own body, white-hot pain bursting from behind his eyes as his vision restored to Vaelsyntheria's plane.

He spun around and his red right hand clasped at the throat of a young woman, driving her back hard into the wall, the impact of her skull cracking against stone pulsating through him.

Blood spurted up around the knife blade she'd lodged in the soft tissue between his neck and shoulder, but his possessor paid it little mind.

Against his pleas, Aiden's nails dug into the woman's sweaty, slippery skin, gripping a chunk from inside, and ripping it back out the front of her throat.

"Alice!" a man howled.

Alice gurgled the last of her bloody breaths in response as she slid down limp to the floor.

At his beck, gore began to spiral out midair from the gaping tear in the woman's neck. *:Thas'kon ech vira dhu krell.:* Aiden vaguely felt the words spring from his tongue as the blood spill solidified and shrieked at the approaching soldier cross as a crack of lightning.

It found the poor bastard dead center, devouring a third of his torso in an instant, and sending the remains flying violently backward. A wet thump accompanied the sound of clattering steel.

Tentacles unfurled from the ceiling of netherflesh, cradling the goldcoat's freshly undone corpse, as a series of lesions on one of its appendages burst open, birthing a clutch of little misshapen goblinoid creatures that fastly infested the soldier's orifices, crawling inside his mouth and slithering into the gaping wound upon his chest.

Tetherow started away and an eerie clicking sound arose from the hallway behind them.

Have you not yet had your fill?

:There he is. And here I was beginning to think you might have actually accepted your fate.:

I know what you are, Aiden dared. *And who you are not.*

:How exciting. By all means, regale away, young master.:

I know you are not Malthus Tetherow.

:Malthus, you stubborn little worm. Spilling our secrets about like the courtyard scandalmonger then, are we?:

He named you cambion.

A terrible grin bowed his lips.

So, it's true?

:The grave will sooner have an answer to that one, boy.:

Ankaira, who was she?

:Ah, yes, the Lady Severyn. That does take me back a turn. She wore a dirty little soul, that one. All that promise and power. But she knew better than to meddle with old-tongue rituals. And she should have known better than to trust a magus as brainsick as our dear friend Malthus.:

Tetherow paused before a window, catching Aiden's reflection in the emerald radiance of Y'dema's moonglow, shaking its head at the sight of the knife hilt jutting out from their shoulder.

:Well, that one's a problem,: Tetherow said. *:Though, I reckon, death by mangy whore seems about what you've earned from this life.:*

Aiden remained silent, unable to overcome his nightmare appearance long enough to muster a proper riposte. Lesions spotted taut skin that shrunk his face to the protrusion of bone, his hair blanched from black to ash, and within a pair of sunken hollows, his irises burned a ghostly white in place of their prior icy blue. Scarlet-stained fingers rose to inspect his gaunt, husk-like cheeks, and he found in the middle of his hand a hole the size of a Commonwealth copper.

:I will award credit where credit is due, however. Your gift has made for a most handsome destruction.:

And her song found him at that. The cry of his gift. Her anguish, her fury, her lament, echoed throughout the halls, and into the palace ruins beyond. The fiend had made of her a woeful wretch, every measure as dreadful as her unsightly master.

My gift is my own.

:Don't talk like one of them, boy. Not to me. You're nothing like them, try as you might to match their expectations. And you know damned well the gift doesn't belong to you. It doesn't belong to anyone. We belong to it. And one way or another it belongs to the nether.:

Fuck the nether. I'll not play slag to its sinister games a breath longer.

:The golden age of the gift is over. Gone...: Suddenly Tetherow turned a snarl into the far reaches of the corridor, toward a second song. *:Emyria,:* it hissed as they strode after the fresh force of magic.

I said, no!

Aiden's legs came to a halt, briefly obeying his instruction.

:Don't make me bury you again, boy.: Tetherow growled, as it broke through the archivist's command.

I may be bleeding out, but you're losing your strength, just as well. I can feel it.

Tetherow said nothing as they stalked forward.

You couldn't bury me back if it meant your bloody life.

Shrieks and battle cries chased the sounds of explosions up ahead as a dark-haired woman in a black robe spun out into the hallway. She spat a curse, raised her wand, and fired it back inside the chamber.

Breath held, Tetherow sprang into action, unsheathing Val's mae'chii with a crisp ring, and sliced it at the spellslinger, nicking her upper arm before she could think to mount a sufficient defense.

The blackcoat managed to avoid a deathblow and called another spell to her wand behind them, forcing Tetherow to guess the proper course for evasion. It pushed off to their right, colliding into the near wall, and the blast screeched past with a keen wind.

:Thas'kon ech vira dhu leckt,: Tetherow bellowed as they whirled about to face her, commanding the nick in her arm to consume. It was in that moment Aiden realized the fiend had coated Val's mae'chii end to end in nether residue.

The woman's arm began to bubble up from the inside out as black ichor poured from the expanding wound.

Oh, how the spellslinger wailed at the horror, crashing into the wall opposite as netherflesh grew in the place of her mutilated arm. She chanted a series of anti-magic spells against it, but there was no such invocation or ward to stave off such a greedy hunger. Not for long anyway. Once the nether crept far enough inside, it was only a matter of time.

Tetherow flicked a sluice of dark blood from the mae'chii and left the screaming woman to misery's minding, passing through a pair of large iron doors into the palace library, determined to uncover the dracari presence within.

Bookshelves, thick as ramparts and twice as tall, rose from the marble, chessboard flooring, stretching out deep into the cavernous shadows, putting Withers' paltry stacks to utter shame. A bright azure glow emanated from some place deep within, twixt gaps in the rows of tomes.

At the sound of approaching footsteps, Tetherow darted down an aisle, fleet as a hillside haunter, stepping past a smoldering corpse, skirting by a rolling ladder, and deftly navigating the spaces between fallen books.

"Curse the devil's whore!" Someone said from the library entrance.

"Shit, what the hells happened to her?" a second voice replied just before a fresh set of screams and death cries became them.

Tetherow rounded the end of another aisle and paced down the far wall of the archive. They were nearing the light's source and found fist-sized orbs of magic floating lazily within the fog of drifting dust particles.

More voices rose from up ahead as the fetid odor of burnt flesh found them, and Aiden reckoned they managed to slay some creature of the nether's design.

Tetherow came to a halt against the end of a bookshelf and peered down the aisle, finding a phaedrylax in the clearing ahead burning under a towering azure flame.

"I can sense you there, sorcerer," a gravelly voice said. "You may as well reveal yourself. The archive is warded to all who stand against us. So, what comes in, stays in, unless I dictate otherwise."

Aiden's lips thinned to a hard line at Tetherow's irritation. It daubed a hand in the blood running from the knife wound in their shoulder, and placed it against the wall, revealing the spell. It rippled like the surface of a pond, iridescent glyphs trailing the chamber, far as the eye could see.

:Motherfucker,: Tetherow muttered, starting down the aisle toward the burning drylax.

"He's here," a blackcoat announced from the other end, training his wand on them, a golden spark sputtering to life at its tip.

:Lenore, thae rendae,: Tetherow hissed, and Aiden felt an itchy, burning sensation on the inside of an arm.

Within a blink, a flying abomination came swooping down at the blackcoat's face.

Aiden couldn't believe the creature before him. It was Dalivant's pet crow, without a doubt, but the nether's disease had transformed it into a pale, deathly thing, its feathers whiter than unblemished ivory, its beady orbs opaque as ocean-washed pearls.

In the slender space between bookshelves, Tetherow bolted forward, mae'chii poised, halving the distance, as they dodged a coil of earsplitting magic, Lenore affording them just enough distraction to play the heedless halfwit. Before the blackcoat could recover, Tetherow was on him, driving the blade into the spellslinger's heart and guiding him back out into the clearing.

There were three others waiting, blackcoats all. A man hiding behind a queer silver mask, a bald woman, and a dark-skinned man in burgundy robes, eyes emanating the unmistakable azure flame of the dragonborn. The two non-dracari aimed their wands at them, as Tetherow ripped the sword free from their dying spellbrother, drawing blood from the wound with its offhand, and sending it lashing out into the trio, as the nether expanded the screaming blackcoat's poisoned body into a shield wall of flesh, absorbing their wrathful wand strikes.

The bald woman dropped to the floor shrieking, blood pouring out of her, as Tetherow spun around a bookshelf for cover and tore down the next aisle over. Behind them, azure flame sent the diseased spellslinger into a fearsome rage and caught fire to the row's end.

"I wondered if we would meet again," the dracari called out from somewhere within the web of tomes.

Tetherow held at the end of an aisle, looking around for any measure of advantage. *:I rather thought you opposed taking midaran hosts.:*

"Desperate times, as they say."

:They are, indeed.:

Lenore croaked from the edge of a bookshelf a few aisles down and Aiden realized the bird was divulging the dracari's location to them.

:The fuck are you doing here, Hrathgon?:

"Oh, you know, ending a bloodline. Yourself?"

:Ending an age.:

"That a fact?" An air of dry amusement coated his voice.

Bastard! Aiden concentrated on the ghost of pain in his red right hand, usurping a breath of control, bringing the hand up before him, and forcing Tetherow to stare into the hole it had carved within.

:Fuck off.: Tetherow clenched the trembling hand into a fist and drove knuckles into the wall, the new pain sending Aiden's paltry effort whimpering back down.

"And lumps to luck stones, by the House Eternal, you have brought one of them right to me," Hrathgon continued.

:Have I?:

"A peculiar strategy wearing the skin of a godsblood. Dangerous and reckless. Though, I suppose, I should expect nothing less from one of your ilk."

:This one's about spent as it is,: Tetherow rasped. *:Though, I'm afraid, I'll require his services a trifle longer.:*

"Then you will share in his oblivion." Hrathgon was gaining nearer.

:And more's the pity.:

Tetherow edged the corner away from Hrathgon and found the silver-masked blackcoat approaching. It spun back out of the aisle as a shrill wand blast came thirsting after them, charring the stone wall across from them. Knowing it would only have a few seconds before the next spell was primed, Tetherow pivoted back into the aisle, pulled a tome from a shelf, and hurled it at the blackcoat, disrupting the conjuring enough to get close and take a swipe.

It missed, as Silver Mask proved himself halfway competent in the melee. Instantly, a kindleblade found the blackcoat's hand and they were at contest, Silver Mask driving Tetherow back down the opposite end of the aisle. The space was narrow, limiting their exchanges to swings and parries until they were out of the aisle and back into the clearing, passing through the sea of study tables and nearing the archivist's counter.

As they came upon a long slab altar, a creature tackled Silver Mask and pinned him down to the floor with a pair of crimson appendages, the ghoul-half stabbing a blade into him again and again.

Silver Mask convulsed in his own shit and entrails, screeching bloody murder as dark fluids pooled on the floor beneath them.

Tetherow sheathed the mae'chii and Aiden attempted to grasp control again, reaching for the knife handle protruding from his shoulder, ready to pull it free and have it done with.

In response, Tetherow swung their body in the opposite direction and drove busted knuckles into the stone altar, forcing Aiden back down again, and then began chanting and guiding their fingers through a series of movements the archivist recognized as a blood-whispering spell.

Such was a form of spellcasting he and Rhymona dabbled in for a time. RC could manage it well enough, but he never caught on to it, and truthfully never much cared to. When done properly, the movements allowed the conjurer to use their own lifeblood as a source while the incantation linked it to the lifeblood of another allowing the spellcaster to claim control. Whatever they did with their own blood offering, the linked blood would imitate.

Bright arterial plasma rose from inside his wrist filling the gap of missing flesh in his hand and it became horribly clear why Tetherow cut the chunk from him. The fiend pinched a thread of blood from the hole like jelly from a jar and began drawing a shape atop the altar slab.

As rivers of blood flowed forth from Silver Mask's slaughter, the shape began to form around the clearing. Within seconds, a massive gory warding sigil the breadth of an innhouse bedchamber formed around him, the altar, and a strange opening in the floor behind the altar.

A breath later, both Silver Mask and the nether creature erupted into screeching azure flame as Hrathgon approached, a black wand in his offhand leaking steaming green bile across the checkered marble.

:*You're running short on fuckwits,*: Tetherow mocked.

Hrathgon's host halted before the sigil. "A dracari hedge ring. Impressive. Honestly, I thought such a spell given to the grave a millennia ago."

:*I bet you did.*:

"It may keep me at bay for a time," he raised his wand, training it on the archivist. "But not this."

A blast of foxfire hungered after them and Tetherow ducked behind the altar as it screamed overhead, narrowly missing them.

:Is that madness I smell on you, Hrathgon?:

"You are wise to fear me, heathen," said Hrathgon's host as he rounded the blood ward's edge. "Best to make peace with your devil queen. You will be reunited forthwith."

Tetherow glanced down into the spiraling stairwell as it wrapped around the altar away from the advancing dracari. *:Curious to know what lies down this fancy hole in the floor here.:* it called out. Another strong aura radiated from some rest below.

"You are more than welcome to have a look-see if you like. Save me the trouble of waiting you out."

Sensing a sudden fragility in Tetherow from the warding incantation, Aiden concentrated on the song of his gift, hunting after her call, as she guided him from the beat of his heart, into the blood vessels of his arm, and back toward the hole in his hand. He felt the void of missing flesh as the melody pushed him through the tainted blood conjuring to wiggling fingers.

"Fuck you!" Aiden erupted, the poisoned plasma plunging from the gaping hole at the stolen movement and he fastly directed the fingers up to his shoulder, gripping the hilt tight, and wrenching the blade free.

:Fool!: Tetherow thundered, blood spurting up from the open wound.

"Val sends her regards, asshole."

:You've only killed yourself in this, boy.:

Reclaiming control, Tetherow melted against the altar's flank, retrieved a wineskin attached to their belt, and removed the cork.

Concurrently, an image of Autumn standing before the great oak tree at the vineyard's end flickered against Aiden's mindscape. A portal rippled from inside the tree behind the ward's glowing sigil.

Aiden felt the name of the familiar brand prickle on the inside of his forearm again as a plan materialized between them. Tetherow's movements flashed quickly in spite of his pain as Lenore let out a croak and a streak of foxfire lit the chamber behind them. From tip to pommel, Tetherow doused the knife in the black oozing liquid from the wineskin, tottered back up to its feet against the altar, took aim at Hrathgon's host, and let loose.

:Thas'kon ech vira dhu nethros.: Came the hex as the blade spun sideways, end over end, curving in its flight until it struck its target true.

Hrathgon's host stumbled a step, frantically reaching for the hilt bulging out from under his shoulder blade. A distended silence sucked the air from the chamber just before his screaming began and the blade disappeared inside the wound as it opened up into a fanged mouth, the growing maw separating his robe at the seams as it spread the length of his spine.

Tetherow sank low behind the altar as bolts of foxfire shot out in all directions.

Tam?

:All these centuries. You didn't think you were it, did you?:

What do you want with her?

:Spirits like ours, we were born to defy ages.:

What does that mean?

:This is not going to end how you think. You haven't lost nearly enough yet.:

What do you want with her?

An impish smirk sprouted as Tetherow clutched a hand over the gushing wound in their shoulder, lifeblood welling between their fingers, and it smeared it down the archivist's chest.

:Be seeing you, Desmond.:

You stay away from her, you sick fuck.

Lenore landed next to him as he slumped against the altar, watching petrified as a dark malachite vapor rose off of him like a thin morning mist.

:Or maybe I won't.:

Within a beggar's breath, the fiend's miasma dissipated and a vast emptiness followed as blistering pain boiled across his shoulder. The presence was gone, as though nothing more than a night terror, leaving Aiden a dying mess, in worse repair than it left Malthus.

Feeling returning to his extremities, Aiden eased down to his better side (if one could truly name it such), and lay still, save for the shakes that wouldn't be denied.

Lenore watched him with a queer tilt of her head.

It was at that moment he realized that the screaming and wand spells had ceased and he dared to look back the other way.

Nothing moved save Lenore.

"Piss off, you," he spat. "I've no taste for—"

The remaining words caught in his throat sending him into a violent fit of coughing. His mind went blank as he curled into a ball, gasping through chattering teeth, fighting against the agony of each tried pull of air that followed.

Lenore croaked at him and Aiden blinked through the shivers realizing he'd just understood the hideous abomination.

The realization expanded as he glanced at the ugly black scar tissue carved into his forearm.

You've got to be shitting me.

But there was no mistaking the mark...

Tetherow had burned a fucking familiar brand into him. As though the warlock's well cut through his palm weren't damning enough.

Of course, he'd read plenty about familiars, being some manner of scholar for a time, but for the most, he knew shit all about the process of actually gaining one. Such knowledge was placed under black magic use and subsequently found banishment from the universities under Ministry Law. The usual hijinks of one bad egg, chased by another, followed by a few dark tales of human enslavement, rot, rot, bloody rot, the day become rue. Though, as much as he despised the Ministry for their typical flavor of hidebound hysterics, Aiden couldn't say he entirely disagreed with this particular decision.

Notwithstanding, two facts concerning familiars were commonly known amongst the university halls. One: Familiars shared a special language with their masters. A language between proper languages so to speak, that only they could understand. And two: When the master dies, so too does the familiar.

Lenore rasped at him again, imploring her master to cauterize the wound.

Get up, you useless twat.

He worked himself up into a sitting position, a miserable grunt tearing out of him. First step, he glanced into the distance, he had to temper Val's mae'chii in the Eldn flame before it died out.

And then the hard part.

It was a bastard of a plan at best, but what other choice remained? Another few minutes and he wouldn't just look like a corpse. He'd actually be one.

He thought of Autumn and Tetherow's cryptic response to his vision of her. He couldn't let Tam down as he had his mother and Val. He wouldn't. He had to rally on. He had to fight and he had to survive. For Tam. For Marsea. For Rembrandt. For the mother he'd forgotten. The one yet left him.

Tucking in the arm from his mangled shoulder, Aiden shifted his better side toward the altar stone, propping himself against it, and slid upright, groaning until he found support atop it.

"Gods' bones," he wheezed, blood dribbling from his lips.

At least, the wound had slowed in its weeping.

From his post against the altar, he scanned the chamber. Not hide nor hair of Hrathgon's host, though the drylax and Silver Mask lay in a heap of shared ashes, a portion of the drylax corpse still aflame.

There's no way he survived. Aiden told himself in regard to Hrathgon's host as he edged around the altar, judging his steps. It would take at least five or six to reach the carcass. He unsheathed Val's mae'chii and stabbed it down into the floor, measuring his weight against it, meaning to use it as a cane for support. Once he got started, he knew he'd have to move quick, as his legs were already beginning to wobble at a mere stand.

Lenore joined him, alighting atop the altar stone, and they shared a look before he turned back to the task at hand.

Here we fucking go.

He sucked in a shriveled breath and released, preparing himself for the coming agony, long ashen curls hanging down like loose threads before his withered countenance.

One. He lifted up, straight as he could manage, ignoring the vicious tingling sensation racing up his side from hip to neck.

Two. Val's mae'chii chiseled into marble.

Three. He pushed off unsteady, bumbling drunkenly forward, somehow spanning the distance before collapsing onto his hands and knees beside the burning drylax.

"Fuck," he grated before spitting a mass of dark blood from the back of his throat.

Blinking through shots of pain, he retrieved the mae'chii and raised it into the guttering flame, watching through a watery haze as it ate through the nether residue and tempered the steel, bestowing the blade with a majestic azure glow.

Mother, please forgive me.

Tears, salty and severe, rolled from the corners of his sunken orbs as he removed the mae'chii from the dying blaze.

Val, please see me through.

Gingerly, he peeled the robe down from gore-stained skin, thick, red ichor from the wound bubbling up anew.

And you gods. You keep me going. Come what may.

This time he swallowed the rising lump of bloody mucous back down.

You keep me up long enough to make sure Tam's safe.

He gripped the hilt in both hands, his teeth clenched, heart pounding into the crown of his skull like a battering ram, blood pacing the dull ache between his ears.

You do that and I'm yours.

The blade drew nigh, and the world began to spin and dim.

Yours to stay.

Glimmering steel pressed onto the throbbing pit of opened flesh and a sharp, inhuman whine forced itself out of him as his skin bubbled and hissed. He couldn't say how long he'd managed to hold the blade in place before his body dropped from the shock, but he hoped long enough.

He lay perfectly still in the after, numb to the hurt coursing the entirety of his body, staring up at the high ceiling, studying the archive's esoteric artistry. *Fitting you'd find The Hood's Door inside a fucking library.* Screaming crosses and stars with eyes centered the gilt crown molding panels, the shapes turning like the wheel of a watermill, shifting to form runes he'd read somewhere before, but did not fully comprehend.

It had to be an effect of the dracari's ward...

Or you're dying and losing your shit.

A low, tortured sound resonated from some haunt deep within the hole in the floor as though in response and Aiden's head rolled over to the opening.

Something's down there, his mind shouted as his focus began to fail. *Something large and long suffering...*

CHAPTER ELEVEN

A SCREECH ECHOED from the shadows up ahead and Maggie halted, her eyes growing wide as dinnerplates.

DRYLAX, Emyria warned.

An image of the mutating creatures back in the upper courtyards flashed through Maggie's mindscape.

I knew this quiet was too good to be true.

"Come on, you ugly bastard!" an approaching voice growled.

At the company, Emyria conjured a blazing egg of Eldn flame into Magwyn's palm.

A second alien cry echoed throughout the crawl of lower corridors and past her. Another heartbeat and a man turned the corner in her direction, brandishing about a sword that burned bright as a fallen star, its cast and scent unmistakable.

"Go left!" Magwyn bellowed as the shrieking horror filled the space behind him, her hand splaying out wide, enlarging the crackling egg to the size of a cannonball before she slung it into the pitch ahead.

The swordsman lunged to the left, slamming against the wall and hefting his shield up for cover as the entire right side of the hallway behind him burst into a brilliant azure inferno, partially engulfing the riled creature.

In response, the gnaudrylax hurled a mass of steel at her as it came tumbling violently into the corridor, curling harshly past the man and into the space between them.

Maggie reeled a shoulder back, spinning away from the flying metal monstrosity, narrowly avoiding it as it whistled past and split into the stones behind her, setting firm.

The gnaudrylax flailed and flopped toward her, shrieking madly, desperate to put out the flames, and that much more to turn Magwyn a fast, ugly tomb.

But the Empress held all the advantage, calling forth another egg of Eldn fire as she backed away, flinging it at the thrashing creature.

The swordsman regained his footing and cut his fiery sword at the beast, severing one of its appendages as he leapt passed to Magwyn's side. The netherflesh writhed and hissed on the floor as it wilted beneath the devouring conflagration.

"Behind me," Maggie said as a third egg of Eldn fire appeared in her hand, and once again her fingers expanded, augmenting the conjuring before she hurled it at the squirming wretch.

Black goo and nether dust erupted out of the formless mass, spattering across the walls and flagstones as the shrieking eyesore made one last desperate attempt to get at her, lurching forward, sending tendrils of charred netherflesh striking out from multiple angles like a giant cat o' nine tails.

Within a blink, the swordsman stole past the space between them, flowing like a fish in water around her, unnaturally fleet of foot, his shield absorbing most of the lashes, before he lunged toward the viscous heap, his blade sinking in all the way down to the hilt, burning what remained of the foul abomination from the inside out. He ripped the extinguished blade out through the beast's belly as it cratered in a pool of its own ashes, popping and crackling like logs in a hearth, its screeching dwindling to that of a pathetic whine.

And then there was silence.

The pair sagged at the same time.

"Fuck, I'm old," the swordsman wheezed, brushing long, dangling strands of gray out of his eyes. "Bastard nearly had me." He cut the blade out to his side, sending slick gobbets of nether fluid splashing across the wall.

"Lord Xavien?" Magwyn uttered, taking in the rough, bearded face for the first time. "Is that really you?" The gods know, he'd filled out considerably since the last time she'd beheld him, though by his swordplay, he hadn't lost much from the tourney champion of old.

"By some fel miracle," he answered.

"The gods be merciful, it's good to see a familiar face," she returned. Though, in truth, it had been cycles since last Magwyn had heard anything of Xavien Ledgermaine. Back then, rumor was the Lancastle lord magus had been put to the chase by Ravenholme for some ambiguous offense and thusly disappeared into the eastern wilds.

"Empress Magwyn." Something like a chuckle ambled through labored breaths. "And here I was thinking surprise could no longer find me."

"Maggie will do."

Ledgermaine bowed his head. "As you wish."

"What's back the way you came?" she asked.

"Nothing good, rest assured." He leaned his leaking sword against the wall and unbuckled the shield from his arm. "I daresay, have all the Lanier's been hiding snakes in their heads for all these cycles?" He massaged his wrist and forearm, clenching and unclenching his fist.

INTERESTING FRIENDS YOU KEEP.

Ledge was one of Whit's old swordbrothers. He served as lord magus and blademaster in Lancastle for a time some cycles back.

CAN HE BE TRUSTED?

He was warring against one of those nether beasts, so my coin is on yes. And if he's preserved any of his prior talents at all, he could prove us quite the useful ally.

"It's only been a few cycles, if you must know," Magwyn said as she retrieved a blood candle from the pouch at her waist. "Can I assume you've retained some of your healing studies, or shall I see to your wounds?"

"I can manage."

She tossed him the blood candle. "And your sword. 'Twas kindled by Eldn flame, yes?"

"Your nephew's work there." Ledge winced, squeezing the candle against a fresh cut in his palm and letting it sink into his bloodstream. "Remy. He's one of you lot swimming around the upstairs just as well."

"Remy's here? In Courowne?" Magwyn asked, pacing back to the wall where the mass of metal stuck.

"Oh, yes. Bent wrong by what's all gone on the past quintnight. With a temperament every measure as rash as Whit and twice as cross. The little one's here too. Larissa and Harver's girl. And a rogue named Curie. They make a strangely formidable trio, all told. We were en route to the western gatehouse when fuckhead over there found us. I got separated in the hedge maze leading it away from the others."

She turned back to face the former lord magus. "You mean to say they're in the palace?"

"More than like. They mean to banish the nether and kill a man they believe to be housing Hrathgon."

BROTHER. Given her sudden swell of emotion, Magwyn withdrew for Emyria's stead. "Hrathgon is here?"

"Thira believes so."

SISTER. The name sent a chill through Magwyn's entirety as Emyria took Ledgermaine's meaning. "Yvemathira has bound herself to Remy?"

"Evidently," Ledge retrieved his shield and began the process of buckling it back to his arm. "Honestly, we were only together a few hours and most of that was on the run. But the lad's slit-eyed and wielding Eldn flame, same as you. Roasting ghouls and nether beasts like its bloody sport on summer holiday, so take from that what you will."

"...And Hrathgon has bound his soul to a human as well?..." IT CANNOT BE. SUCH WOULD GO AGAINST EVERYTHING HE HAS EVER STOOD FOR.

"A magus named Tenbrooks to have it from your nephew," he said, reclaiming his sword. "Which begs the question, yeah. Which one are you?"

"...Emyria..."

"Gods save the old ones," Ledgermaine said. "And I am in your debt, Emyria. Truly. Though one has to wonder what it is you and the Empress are doing down in the undercroft all by your lonesome."

"We were on path for the cellar," Magwyn answered before running a ring razor across her palm and clutching the candle tight until it disappeared inside her.

"The cellar? Whatever for?"

"Lord Rhonyn. He was imprisoned for treason and threatening the Emperor. I meant to see to his injuries and restore his services."

"Chuffing hells, but of course he was," Ledge muttered, glancing past the gnaudrylax carcass into the torchlit darkness beyond. "Shall we on then?"

Magwyn started forward, minding her hand until the cut sealed.

"Treason on what grounds?" Ledge asked, taking to her wing.

Maggie couldn't hold back a sigh. "Drezhal put to council an order to remove House Lanier from The League of Royal Houses."

"Remove House Lanier? To what end?"

"To quell any chatter of Vaustian Harver taking a seat at the High Council summit come summertide. Or so that was how it began. As you might have already suspected, Rhonyn was not best pleased to have the news, and my husband—"

"Pardon the ill-tongue, Highness, but your husband is a fucking twat."

"He's also dead." Their pace quickened. "Murdered by the demon possessing my other nephew. So, I will advise you to find some restraint in your disdain. I'd be a corpse all the same had it not been for Emyria."

Ledgermaine stopped cold. "It's true then. Desmond's at the heart of all this?"

Magwyn could almost smell the guilt rolling off of him. "And you know something about it, don't you? Something about how it all began."

"Mayhaps it'd be best had from Rhonyn."

Something about those words sat ill with her. "No, Xavien, piss on that." The old, crude version of Maggie leapt from her lips as though plucked from the halls of Lancastle yore. "What in the nine hells did you two do?"

"You know what we did."

Magwyn shoved Ledge into the wall, his sword clattering to the stones, and she pressed in hard against him. "You had no right." Her mouth arched in disgust.

She knew she should slow down and let rationality take its turn, but nothing about any of this was rational anymore, and she would not be kept in the dark about her family's affairs, not after all this.

"I know." His gaze lowered.

"That poor child. How could you think such a thing would possibly end well?"

"It wasn't my decision."

"Then whose was it?"

Ledge opened his mouth as though he might respond, but nothing came forth.

"Was it Larissa?" Maggie asked, unable to quell her distaste for the woman. "Always the frivolous busybody, that one."

"Larissa took some convincing if you must know," Ledge returned.

"And which one of you foolhards brought him back?"

"Stella."

Magwyn pulled away. "Stella?" Her memory repaired a ruby-haired vision in Royalguard livery. "The archivist? Your Stella?"

"Stella was never mine. At least not in the way I fancied it. But, yes, that Stella."

"I don't believe it. She was far too clever to entertain such drivel."

"I think you underestimate Rho's charm and spirit, not to mention his cycles of diplomacy."

"You mean to say you lot forced her hand to it?"

"That was your brother's doing, Magwyn. Long before the deed came to fruition. We merely reminded her of our pact." An undertone of irritation endured within his voice.

"What pact?"

"Whit named it the Shawley Accord."

"Gods' wounds, I knew it had something to do with that damned prophecy. How could you all be so heedless?"

"You know how Whit was about it." Ledge retrieved his sword.

"Whit was mad." Magwyn's fists began to shake at her side, nails digging into her palms. "You all knew this. He had what sickness ailed Father. And he was wrong. Lest you forget I was there for the telling just as well."

"And, thusly, we found ourselves indebted to a madman, didn't we?" Ledge answered. "Your brother made us all, Maggie. Surely, you must understand. Larissa, Rhonyn, Stella, myself. He made all of us. He gave us everything we had. Every chance. Every coin. Every comfort. And how many others could claim the like? Not one of us noble. At least not in the eyes of the Commonwealth. But Whit's view of nobility proved far from traditional. For Whit sought out nobility of character, not blood. That was always his game. Every soul he let in. That was how he found his most loyal. And because of this charity, he was owed."

"Owed my eye. 'Twas a damned fool's charade. It's one of the first laws of the gift, Xavien." She recalled how Wils Gilcrest would go on about the magic precepts during their trysts. "You never fuck about with dead things. Ever."

"I argued the same when the time came. Trust, I argued against bringing the boy back."

"Do not lie to me, Xavien. You should have died to keep Desmond buried. Instead, you all thought to play gods."

"Now who sounds a nutter?"

Magwyn's upper lip quivered. "Do not dare attempt to turn this around on me. You all fucked with my family while I was pushed away and left here to rot, and this is how I find out? This is now what's given me? I've two brothers, two loved ones, I haven't seen in cycles to decades, on course to butcher one another, and I'm just supposed to let it happen, and then see to the one that remains? Assuming they do not kill each other before I find them."

"Maggie, you must understand, this was not—"

"Was not what? Was not what was intended when you desecrated my nephew's passing? As though Harver's savagery weren't ugly enough."

"Highness..."

"You were a fucking magus. You may have been shit at it, but you were a magus nonetheless. You took the warder's oath. You and Stella both. And you both knew better than to gravedance."

"You can sink your fangs in all you like, milady, but it shan't change where we presently find ourselves. Desmond is still in there fighting," Ledgermaine said. "I've spent the past few days with him."

"You what?"

"I was aboard Blackhall's Banshee and the Belisarius with him. During that time, we spoke on matters. And before that, I watched over him from afar, while he attended university and lived with the Ashborough's in Gallea's Grace. Trust, his life is worth every ounce of wrath you believe I'm due. He's ill-tempered and angry and he's horribly, horribly mistook in nearly every aspect of the word. But he is strong-willed and steadfast. And his heart screams Lanier with every lasting beat. I was wrong to argue against bringing him back all those cycles ago, and you are wrong to doubt him now. He's earned the name of his blood without even knowing its truth. And for that, I will lay down my life for him as I would you, Highness. I will give everything I have to try to save him and make this right. Everything I can to exorcise that fel bastard bewitching him—"

"Fine words, indeed. But you do not know the power of that creature. I have seen it firsthand. The gnaudrylax that nearly ended your life back there is merely a speck on the floor by comparison to the devil in that boy. He's killed Drezhal and the gods only know how many others. And he sacrificed his betrothed—"

"Val?"

"Knew her too, did you?"

"Val's dead?"

"The fiend claimed as much."

"Fuck all."

"It named her ashaeydir."

"Aye, and she was. But prize well, she was like no ashaeydir I've ever heard of. I daresay, by the by, she was rather beginning to grow on me."

"It knew Emyria. It knew dracari lore. And it controls the nether as we control the elements. As though it was bloody born to it." Magwyn said as they started forward again. "Despite your foolish optimism, I can't help but wonder what will be left in the event we do actually manage to save him."

"We must try."

"And what of Marsea?"

"Marsea? What of her?"

"I don't know, just a thought. With Desmond and Remy and Julia being here, I only assumed." A horrible notion wormed its way to the fore. "Do you suppose she's still alive?"

"I have to believe it so. Not a one of them said anything about her."

Selwyn's foretelling returned once more. *One will die before their time. One must go alone. One will cede love's greatest gift in turn to spite the throne.*

Not so daft now, is it? she thought in spite of her aversion to prophecy.

One must go alone. Is that you, Marsea? Magwyn pondered, her heart shrinking in her chest. *Or did you find love's greatest gift?*

Or…

A third possibility occurred to her. What if she had been misinterpreting the prophecy all this time? What if Desmond wasn't the death before his time? In a manner of speaking, he was actually still alive, after all. What if instead that death belonged to Marsea?

The question made her ill to consider.

Marsea Anne Lanier. Truth was, Magwyn never gave her only niece much of a chance to make any sort of impression on her. Marsea got unfairly lumped in with her mother because she came out the spitting image, such was Magwyn's loathing for Whitman's slag beloved. Thereafter, Desmond received all of the preferential treatment from Aunt Maggie. As for Rembrandt, she and Whit were no longer on speaking terms by the time he came along.

"This way," she said.

Magwyn Lanier had never been more disappointed in herself than she was at that moment.

You're every bit the monster you war against, Maggie. Marsea was only a child. And now you may never see her again. An image of young Larissa, belly fat with Desmond, played through her mind in Marsea's place. *I don't even know what you look like now to pick you from the crowd. Mayhaps you look nothing at all like your mother.*

She slowed, noticing the patches of gore strewn about the walkway ahead, leading out of the dungeon. Rhonyn's dungeon. Her palms became sticky with sweat burning the skin made raw by her Eldn fire conjuries.

"Rhonyn," she called, rushing to the opened iron door.

Inside, the smell was stifling, reeking of piss and curdled sorrow, and she found all the telltale signs of a struggle. More blood and a faint hum of magic dust. Though no traces of the blight.

"Someone took him," Ledge deduced. He set his blade against the wall and lifted one of the torches that had been left burning in its holder beside the entrance.

"And there's no telling how long it's been," Maggie said. "He could be anywhere by now. Assuming he's still amongst the living." She bit down hard and began chewing on her lower lip. Old habits returning along with old faces.

"Which cell was his?" Ledge asked.

"This one."

Ledge stepped inside, kneeling beside a large puddle of blood on the floor. He ran a finger through it. "It's not completely dry. Though it's been some time, mayhaps a few hours, were I to venture a guess. And this is an awful lot of blood." He stood and kicked through the patch of hay in the cell's corner. "Nothing."

Maggie scanned the rest of the cells, but they were all empty save for trodden hay beds, old cloth blankets, and a few loose stones.

THE WALL BETWEEN ROWS.

Magwyn trailed back outside the last cell and stopped at the end of the walkway as Emyria raised a palm, bringing a glistening gold symbol to life from within the stone. She pressed her hand against the wall and a pond rippled out from the ward.

"A translocation portal," Ledge uttered as he occupied the space at her side.

"Someone took him," said Magwyn.

"Could it be your husband's work?"

"Doubtful."

"Who else knew he was here?"

"By now, I'm sure the entire kingdom had gained wind of his arrest."

"It's your choice, Maggie. You want to chance it and start jumping puddles, you have my blade. And I'll follow just as well if you plan to find Remy. But one way or another, we can't stay down here. We have to keep moving."

THE MAGE IS RIGHT.

"I know."

Her head was screaming for her to go back for Remy, all the old Lanier House watchwords running through her head afresh. *Family first. Blood before bravery. Kin before courtesy.* She shook them from her thoughts. For her gut told her she was brought here for a reason and that she needed to go through the portal after Rhonyn or something far worse would follow the horrors that had already found them.

The gods be with you, nephew.

Maggie's hand pushed through the wall, like sinking through cold pudding, and she followed the momentum into a dark, soundless pitch that smelled of rotten eggs and death rot.

CHAPTER TWELVE

THE NOONDAY BELL tolled rousing Rhymona from a deep slumber, and seconds later, a stab of fear found her a fast friend for company.

"Shit," she rasped through the stench of yestereve's binge. "Shit. Fuck." She jolted up and stumbled from the bed, buck naked, sweeping up her trousers. "Shit fucking shit-fuck." She managed the first leg through, and nearly fell over with the second, steadying herself against the wardrobe.

Baka.

Aiden groaned something unintelligible into his pillow.

"Aiden, we overslept."

Baka. Baka. Baka.

His head lifted toward her, one eye still closed, bed hair in fine form. "Mmm."

"Your mother and sister, we're to meet them at noon outside Withers."

"Brilliant. Yeah."

"Yeah, brilliant, fuckwit. Listen to it out there." The final toll from the Velmont Tower belfry resonated. "That would be now." Rhymona flung his shirt at him before finding her own and bringing it round for the button. Of course, it was rumpled with creases and plagued with every ugly fucking tavern stain imaginable.

"Shit," Aiden grumbled with a composure she would have slapped right the fuck out of him had she not been so bloody rushed and hungover.

"I need to borrow one of your robes," Rhymona said as she flung the wardrobe open and began cycling through a dozen some-odd coats, robes, and academic regalia pieces before plucking forth the smallest of the bunch, a tawny-colored robe with white interior lining.

"Hm, that's fine," Aiden said, clearly still half-asleep, nary a fuck given.

"I thought you set a timepiece."

"I did." He sniffed the shirt, shrugged, and pulled it on. "Though debatable where said timepiece currently resides."

Rhymona halted before the desk mirror to adjust the robe's fit (mercifully, it somewhat held her form), and began brushing down her long, dark hair as best she could. A black streak of kohl trailed down from one eye where the other was a clouded smudge that made her appear half raccoon.

Just one pint and we're off stool, Rhymona mocked her past self. *Knowing good and well there isn't a cup in existence deep enough to keep the boozehound bitch at bay. Well done, baka.*

She scrubbed at her face with her crumpled shirt until the makeup appeared partway even and turned to Aiden with a hopeful grin. "How bad is it?"

"Shall I find my trousers first to answer? Or are you just ready to have it from an idiot with his cock out?"

A smile took its mantle. "Fuck you, that's hilarious, but I'm not in a laughing mood just now."

"You've nothing to worry about," Aiden returned, locating said trousers. "She's going to love you."

"Because I'm so fucking loveable," Rhymona said, sarcasm at the bowstring.

"Precisely, and because I love you. Tam will too. Hand to heart."

Rhymona's lips pursed. "I appreciate the rally on, but maybe save any further compliments for when you've covered your dangly bits, yeah?"

"Right."

"And hurry the fuck up already." Rhymona licked the end of her fingers, turned back to the mirror, and eased the dampness over the fade of kohl a mite more.

A song later and they were out amongst the madness of the midday crowds, crossing through the sprawling bazaar toward the university's old archive, only stopping for a dash into the Brass Lantern Pubhouse to beggar breath mints and a fresh kiss of perfume from Trixie's hangover remedy kit.

For reasons Rhymona could not reconcile, her mind had set Stella Ashborough apart from the rest of the world. And there was no denying it, despite her loathing of pedestals and placing folk atop them.

Mayhaps there existed a similarity between them that found some meaning beyond mere surface-level understanding. Or mayhaps it was simply good, old-fashioned elder reverence.

They passed Scarlett, Herb, and Sage, The Magnificent Mask, and Lulu's Confectionary, the scent of sweets, chocolates, and sugar cookies lifting her from the cobble as they crossed the threshold of districts from the market to the university outskirts. The gods know, but she would have absolutely destroyed one of Lulu's custard cream pies if there were even the smallest occasion for it.

Somewhere on a distant street corner, 'Last Lovers Left Alive' crooned out beautifully with the soft pluck of mandolin strings reminding her of the coming holiday but a few hours away. The Loverstide Moon. Yet another silly midaran tradition.

"There she is. What a sweet Autumn Rose. Though she'd be a lot sweeter with the finger out her nose," Aiden called playfully as they passed into Adevir Square.

A fiery-haired girl, sitting primly at the fountain's edge, glanced up from a book. She wore a sleeved, olive-colored dress that would have found fame at the Harvest Light Festival back home for sure.

"Oh, hush up with that," the girl said pointedly as she stood and approached with a dimpled smile. "You know how I dislike your sorry excuses for japery."

"And why do you think it is I call upon them so?" Aiden teased as he wrapped his younger sister in a hug. "Gods, I missed you."

"Missed you too." Tam pulled away and gave him an odd look. "Is that perfume you're wearing?"

"Bottled sunshine," Aiden answered with a goofy grin.

"I don't even want to know."

"Probably for the best," he nodded. "Anyway, where's mum?"

"She's talking with Dean Brumfield inside the archive. You know how she is, once she's on one. I got bored." Autumn eyed Rhymona up and down. "Is this her?"

"Good day," Rhymona said with an awkward hand wave, realizing the last time she spoke with someone so young was likely half a score ago. "I certainly hope I'm her."

Autumn smiled. "Your clothes are...interesting."

"Are they?" Rhymona answered. "I hadn't noticed."

"I mean I like them. They're very...unique." She smiled away her mortification.

Absolutely darling, this one.

Rhymona quite approved of little sister already. She was odd and bashful and mayhaps a little feisty, yet bonny in a garden party proper sort of manner.

"And your dress is quite smart," Rhymona found herself saying.

"Mother made me wear it. Singing something about first impressions."

"Truth is, your brother made me wear this," Rhymona joked as she pinched the edges of the robe and offered a poorly formed curtsy.

Tam giggled.

"What were you reading there?" Rhymona asked.

Autumn offered the book to her. "Mother just gave it to me yestereve. She names it *Noon*. She said it's mine, just as *Dawn* was Aiden's."

Rhymona turned to Aiden with an arched eyebrow, *"Dawn?"*

"It's a really old grimoire passed down from her father and her father's father," he answered. "I've shown you before. I know I have."

"No, I think I would've remembered." Rhymona studied *Noon's* exterior. It appeared the color of a cornfield husk, as though it had been left out drying in the sun for every angry second of the past century of summers. She leafed through a few pages, noting spells, formulae, and logs.

"Aiden," a voice called from behind.

Rhymona turned and instantly her heart set to the races as a flawless vision in midnight-blue magian robes strolled up to them from the archive's entryway. She'd beheld the woman before by way of a framed family portrait Aiden strangely kept on the floor beside his bureau, but the artist's rendering did her class of beauty woefully little justice. For Stella Ashborough in the flesh was an absolute stunner, especially by midaran standards, standing out like a cloth maiden at a harbor end whorehouse. Long, ruby curls trapping breath-catching eyes with plush lips that instantly set Rhymona's lady parts to the tingle.

"Mother," Aiden greeted warmly as they embraced.

"You've gotten taller," Stella said. "And may be in need of a fresh wash and visit to the barber."

"Definitely the former-former."

"And this must be Rhymona." Stella said as she pulled away, offering her hand. "Aiden has spoken quite highly of you."

"And of you, milady." Rhymona took the sorceress's hand, bearing a slight squeeze, and shook. Handshaking between women was not commonly performed in midaran society and almost never in ashaeydir culture. Thusly, the experience sat queerly with her.

Is she toying with me?

"I see Autumn has shared with you one of our family heirlooms," said Stella.

Rhymona handed the grimoire back to Autumn. "She mentioned it was named *Noon*, and Aiden has one named *Dawn*."

"Yes, there were four in the set, each one formed from a different hide of beast, then bound, stitched, and blessed by my third great grandfather. *Dawn*, *Noon*, *Dusk*, and *Haunt*, they were named."

"I've always found a curiosity for bookbinding, though I've never tried." *There you go, love. Keep it nonchalant.*

"Mayhaps I can teach you the basics sometime," Stella said, casually dancing through her carousel of courtly charms. "It's been some ages since I've had a go at it."

"I'd quite like that." *Stella Ashborough, you are a shrewd lass, aren't you?* Rhymona glanced at Aiden, and he offered a sheepish smile and nod.

"I've heard tale you are quite the healer as well," Stella continued.

"I'm passable, I suppose."

"Passable? Aiden says they name you the master of Myers Infirmary," Autumn added. "Rhymona Curie, the queen of curing."

Fucking hells, Aiden. Ease up the flattery, yeah. "I wouldn't go that far." She put on a pair of rosy cheeks.

"He said you even mended a bone that broke through the skin using a single candle," Autumn said.

"Well, that part is true."

"And no easy feat," Stella said. "Tam fancies herself a healer once she comes of age for university. You'll have to pass on some of your secrets."

Rhymona's mind ran down the sea of scars strewn about her flesh. *Be careful what you wish for, milady.* "I'd be delighted."

"That being said," Stella resumed, "I was rather hoping I might borrow you for a stretch, Rhymona. Just the pair of us. If that isn't too forward or uncomfortable for you."

And so, the games begin.

"Not forward at all," Rhymona said forcing a desolate smile. "It would be my pleasure."

Stella ran a motherly gaze over her children. "Can I trust the pair of you to behave yourselves for an hour?"

"Oh, but an hour is definitely going to be pushing it," Aiden answered.

"Must you always act so beastly, brother?" the sister teased.

"I must." Aiden let out a ridiculous growl to the accompaniment of clawed hands.

"I'll do my best with him, but no promises," Autumn said with a sigh before the Ashborough siblings turned away and Aiden began rubbing his stomach and describing Lulu's caramel tarts and how the girl absolutely had to try one post haste.

"I take it you two had a festive evening?" Stella inquired, wasting no time at all, as she strode back toward Withers.

"It was a friend's birthfall," Rhymona offered, following like a leashed pet.

"And is that Aiden's second-semester robe you're wearing?"

Straight for the throat then? Though how could she fault any woman that spoke her mind with such candor? "There was a bit of a mishap."

"I see." Stella glanced over a shoulder at her, picking up her pace. "I'll be plain with you, Rhymona. I like you. At least what I know thus far. You seem to have made a positive impact on my son for the most, which this day and age is a most undervalued prospect. But I do not yet trust you."

Dagger meet heart. "As I recollect, I haven't had an opportunity yet to earn your trust."

"A clever answer. Trust should be earned, never given," Stella said, as they passed under the arcade and back into the archive. "Which makes what I'm about to show you all the more mad-capped and wholly against my nature, but we may never get another chance."

They filed past the reception desk without so much as a glance from the scrivening archivist.

"Is everything all right?" Rhymona offered.

"Presently, yes. But the coming conversation has naught to do with the present." Stella led them down a row in the historical section, one that Rhymona found painfully little familiarity with, all the way to the dimly lit back wall of the archive. A little further down to the left, she stopped before a bookshelf, trailed her fingers against the bottom of one of the shelves, stopping near its end, and retrieved a skeleton key.

Rhymona only saw it for an instant, but she noticed the key's bow was shaped like a clover and engraved with writing she couldn't quite distinguish.

"Onward then," Stella said, as she marched down the back aisle toward the wall of study chambers.

Rhymona shoved her hands inside her trouser pockets and tried to push down the waves of anxiety that seemed to spike with every other footstep taken. In mere minutes, Stella had leapt from the most striking woman she had ever beheld, to the most forthright, to the most secretive. A terrifying concept indeed considering the trials of her own past life as Morgandrel where she found the company of more soldiers, assassins, and torturers than not.

Stella halted before the last study chamber door on the far wall and inserted the key into the lock. Once the door was opened, Stella entered, and light followed the clicking sound of an oil lamp.

"Hold this." Stella offered the oil lamp and Rhymona took it.

Quickly, Stella locked the door from the inside behind them and produced a deadly serious countenance.

"Now be true with me, Rhymona. Have you ever gone through a portal before?"

"Yes," she uttered as though compelled by some wicked cast of old magic, and couldn't help but wonder if she could actually lie to this woman if the occasion rose for it.

"You have?" One eye narrowed and the other eyebrow arched.

"Yes."

"Grand." Stella fished a ring from her pocket and fitted it to a finger. "You are just full of surprises then, aren't you?"

That's one way of putting it. "I reckon."

"Nevertheless, things should be a mite less messy for you on the other end then. But this will be a discussion for another time." She scratched the ring razor across her palm, calm as the breeze in springtide, daubed bright red wax from a pouch across the cut, and stamped it into the stone wall across from the doorway as she whispered something under her breath.

Instantly, a gilded sigil crackled to life, chased by a rippling watery doorway. Rhymona studied the ward but did not recognize its shape.

"I'm unfamiliar with the ward's language," she said.

"Are you possessed of the nether?" Stella asked.

"I hope not."

"Trust it true, love, you would know."

"And where exactly are we passing through to?"

A fox-faced smile played across Stella's lips. "The archive of archives, of course. Lancastle Library. I presume you've never been?"

"Withers is tethered to Lancastle?"

"It is. Amongst other places of import. Marrovard, Palatia, Courowne to name a few."

"Why would you show me this? I don't—"

"Because you may need it one day. Especially if you carry on with my son like you have. And I may call on you to use it."

"Does House Lanier know of this secret ward in their library?"

"It is known by those who need know of it. By oath, those folks shall remain nameless. And for the time being you are not to mention any of this to Aiden, is that clear?"

"Aiden doesn't know?"

"He does not, and it shall endure as such."

"Understood."

"Fantastic. Now douse the lamp and through the puddle you go then."

The portal proved unnaturally kind. The kindest she'd ever jumped through, in fact, dropping her like a feather from the warded ceiling into a small store-room. Stella was but a blink behind her, their silhouettes stretched inside the sigil's glittery golden glow.

The space was stacked wall to wall with tomes of all shapes and sizes and scarce wide enough for more than two.

"What is this place?" Rhymona questioned, measuring her hand against the fore-edge of the thickest tome she'd ever beheld.

Stella drew a finger to her lips and hugged a wall listening intently.

"It's a hidden cupboard," she murmured after a time, moving something between tome piles, and a section of the wall eked out like a doorway. "Quickly."

Gods' breath, Stella Ashborough, hidden portals and secret passageways? I can't tell if you are some bridge beyond brilliant or absolutely batshit barking mental?

They both passed through the low opening out into the massive library.

"This way," Stella commanded with a whisper.

"Where are we going?" Rhymona matched her voice.

"Try not to make this odd, but I've dreamt about this. About you. About us. Here. Dozens of times. Likely before you were even born. By the manner Aiden described you, I had my suspicions, but I knew it for certain the moment I took your hand."

"My hand?" She recalled the odd handshake. "How?"

"Your vibrations, they were the same. Unforgettable really."

"You mean to say you read my blood through my skin?"

"A nothing spell used far too seldomly, but I had to be sure."

"Of what exactly?"

"You have a curse on you. How this came to be, I cannot yet say, but it's there and it's undeniable."

"What curse?"

"A blood curse. You've caught glimpses no doubt. Of the banshee's labyrinth. Inside the dream with all the cobwebbed innards and crimson mirrors."

Rhymona halted, a lump rising in her throat.

"That dream is only said to appear to those championed by the Hand of Vengeance."

Rhymona swallowed hard. *How could you possibly know?*

"You are a soul out of time. As am I. And I've only found one other to match our vibrations in all my cycles."

Does she know who I am? What I am?

Does she know I know Aiden's true identity?

How fucked am I?

"What does that mean?" Rhymona's voice rose.

"Lower. We cannot risk being seen here by the wrong sort of folk."

116

They held for a moment before she started again. "It means that you are destined for something of great import. And I was destined to tell you as much. Though your purpose has not yet arrived, it will soon find its teeth. Stay close." In silence, they strode forward to the end of a row and hurried down an empty aisle. "I haven't unraveled all of it yet," she continued as they resumed by the cover of bookshelves, "but I've pulled at a few strands here and there, and in the process, I managed to come across one of yours."

"Are you some sort of dream eater?"

"Heavens, no. More of a dream walker. A night drinker, as the magi name it. Prize well, there is literally a world's difference between a dream eater and a night drinker. For one, I am not a demon. And I've only just dabbled in the mold of my mother. Though she was far more adept at the craft."

They halted at the end of a row.

"Around the corner," Stella continued, "you'll find a girl. Take a good hard look at her, for you and that girl are linked by this curse. She is the other. Forged by blood threads and gallows glass. Again, I have no specifics as to why, only the bones of it. Observe the tome in her hand. That, too, is one of my family's grimoires. *Haunt.* Unlike the other three, it was left incomplete and unblessed and in such a state of disrepair, I forced it upon the girl's father for safe-keeping. My instinct was that the girl felt a calling to it because of this blood bind."

Rhymona gazed at the girl. She was mayhaps fifteen cycles, cute as a button, with shimmering blonde hair, and sporting a dress that was worth more coin than she could count in her wildest fantasies. To the contrary, the tome appeared a dark purple bruise of a thing, handsome as a rotted plum. Rhymona's face scrunched up at the image.

"That girl..." she began a breath later.

"Is Marsea Lanier," said Stella. "And that grimoire is the answer to its siblings' glut of questions."

"Do you mean to have it back from her?"

"It's no longer mine to have. Though, in truth, it was never mine to begin with. Whether she knows it or not, that tome now belongs to the Princess. It chose her, assuming I've read the leaves correctly. Just as *Dawn* chose Aiden, and *Noon* chose Autumn."

"And what of the third?"

"*Dusk? Dusk* chose me. At least for a stretch. But after a time, I refused it and sent it far away."

"You refused it?"

"A tale for another jump, mayhaps. Just know they cannot be destroyed by natural means."

"Should they be destroyed?"

"That is unclear. But such musings are not why I've brought you here. For now, we're on your curse, Rhymona. There simply isn't time for anything else."

"Pardon the tongue, but how the fuck did I...did we get cursed in the first place? I've never seen that girl before. Obviously. She's the bloody princess of Lancastle. By caste, I wouldn't be allowed within a stone's throw of such a name. Hells, I wouldn't be allowed within a stone's throw of her ruddy handmaidens."

"Would that I could name it."

"Then how do you know we are?"

"Through my connection with Marsea. I was once an archivist here. During that time, her father had me put my talents with oneiromancy to her slumber."

"To what end?"

"He was afeared of a prophecy regarding his heirs and had me hunt their dreams for answers. Children have the most vivid dreams, after all. It was through her dreamscape that I found you. And how I found the curse that links the three of us like a hillside haunter."

Rhymona thought of Fiandrel and she could feel her eyes peeking out from some rest within the stacks. As though her life were not already fucked up enough. Half an hour ago she was worried she'd drank too much to provide Stella Ashborough a proper dance amongst the catch and courtlies. Now she questioned if there existed enough drink in all the Vael to tolerate this fresh cup of lunacy.

"Much of this I am still trying to puzzle out myself. To flay back the fabric of the fates is a most daunting proposition, after all. One cannot be too careful."

"And what exactly am I do to with all of this?" Rhymona asked. "Am I meant to protect the girl?"

"I do not yet know. It's just as well she may be meant to protect you."

Rhymona watched Marsea as the girl flipped a page.

A dainty shrimp like that. Doubtful.

"I was meant to bring this to light, to guide you here. What you do with this knowledge is entirely up to you. Your bond will reveal itself in due course. You will hear it like thunder through the stone. Feel it deep inside your core, pulling at every fiber of your being. Taste it like an abscess in your mouth. And when it comes, you must let it move through you. For only then will you move through it. With it. As it."

"Do you know what I am, Stella?" Rhymona asked, taking in the battle-magus once more.

"I know what I need to know of you. What is important for my path. I know you are not who you claim to be, but you keep that bit to yourself. What you are and who you pretend to be has no consequence in what's to come. The only thing that matters is who you are truly."

Rhymona gave Marsea Lanier a second glance, pulling back behind the bookshelf when the girl turned toward them.

"Hello?" Marsea called out. "Is someone there?"

Without a moment's delay, they hurried back toward The Cupboard.

"The name of the ward is *sylvoth'yka*," Stella said as they reached the hidden doorway and squeezed back inside. "In case you ever have need of it."

CHAPTER THIRTEEN

THEIR VOICES FOLLOWED the fever as she chased the spinning palace halls after Fiandrel's shadow.

"Sister, you must slow down," Rhymona begged, as she staggered forward, prodding Fucker's head down like a walking cane, a trail of blood painting the marble floor behind her with each passing footfall.

The words echoed in her head noxious as a nightmare devil and she couldn't dismiss their familiarity. The familiarity of everything that had come to pass since they entered the hedge maze. A feeling like she'd been here and done all of this before.

"I've got you," Remy said, taking her up under a shoulder. "We've cleared the pack that tailed us."

"Aye. Collecting quite the trail of corpses, you and the youngest."

"Not by desire, mind you."

Ah, funny thing that desire. But we're all dancing at the knife's edge now, aren't we? She imagined a ballerina figure in a music box spinning on the tips of her toes to some grotesquely sad lullaby. "Toff, have I ever told you I'm mad?"

They hobbled forward as one, one step then another, Julia watching the corridor just behind them.

"No offense, yeah, but I puzzled that one out nigh on an age ago."

"Right, but I mean proper mad. As in around the old barmy bend mad.

As in I see and hear shit that I know isn't there and I humor it all the same."

"Can I assume there's a point coming to your rather poignant confession or—"

"Point is we've been chasing after a ghost all this time. Since the Nobles. The ghost of my dead sister." Rhymona shifted her head slightly and found the familiar shiver of movement in the corner of her eye. "She's just ahead there. I think she means to lead us to some manner of sanctuary."

"Fucking hells, Rhymona."

"What's that then? No witty slag for that one?"

"All things honest, I don't suppose your ghost can do us much worse."

"You better find some wood to knock with that shite—"

They froze in place as a figure emerged within the moon-drenched mist up ahead. Ghoulish clicking noises filled the space between them as the figure shuffled its feet in their direction.

Julia strode cautiously past them, the dwarf's blade locked tight inside a pair of tiny fists.

"Jules, be careful," Remy called after her.

"Always," she whispered.

Though despite Julia's approach, the figure made no intent to attack.

"I think it's a turncoat," Rhymona said. "Like the girl in the forest." As they drew close, she recognized the figure as the dying noblewoman from the hedge maze. "You?" *How is this possible?*

"You recognize her?" Remy asked.

"I saw her back in the hedge maze. She was dying."

"What?"

"At least I thought I did, but..." Fia materialized before the opened doorway next to the woman drawing her attention. "That room. Fia wants us to go in there."

"Should I kill her?" Julia asked.

"Yes," Remy said, "when it comes to the blight, always, yes."

Julia advanced on the defiant ghoul, and as though in agreement with its pitiful fate, it bent down to its knees before the girl.

"It's yielding?" Remy uttered.

Rhymona turned away from the scene and into the torchlit chamber as the woman lowered all the way to the ground.

121

"They...I...I did my best..." a voice called from the room's corner. "There were too many...they...I've never seen anything like it..."

"I saw you in the hedge maze," Rhymona said to the man. Indeed, he sported the same pendent and silk robe embroidered in the heraldry of some unfamiliar noble house, but there was no mistaking the desperate incisions and purple wax residue ranging the span of his exposed arm.

Next to him lay emptied phials and an untied pouch with blood candles spilling out of it. Rhymona limped away from Remy and found the floor next to the man, resting Fucker upright against the wall beside her.

"Do not push further inside the palace," the man wheezed. "It's a death pit. You won't last an hour."

"So, it's been said," Rhymona returned. "Mind if I nick a few of these?"

"Take what you need. It won't matter much longer."

Remy closed the door behind Julia, and immediately Thira set to sealing the chamber with a warding spell.

"What's your name?" Rhymona pressed the man as she crushed a pair of blood candles inside her ruined palm and called after her gift.

"Victor," he began.

"Victor Goss," Remy said as he circled back upon the group, his eyes burning azure.

"And you are Prince Rembrandt," Goss rasped. "Gone Eld then, have you?"

"The union was unavoidable, old friend," Thira offered.

"Majesty?" Goss lowered his eyes in reverence before rising once more upon the Crown Prince. "Can that truly be you, Yvemathira? Returned to us at last."

"As the fates decreed."

Rhymona inhaled sharply, the air tasting decidedly different than any other breath she'd ever pulled before, and she pushed back hard against the wall as the blood candles sent a series of diverse sensations undulating through her, both cutting and kind. She could almost feel her pupils dilating as the blood melted fully into her own and goosepimples chased the foreign substance racing throughout her bloodstream.

"Fuck's sake." She clenched her teeth and felt her cheeks flush. "Buggers are potent, aren't they?"

"Chandii stock," Goss said in a far more matter-of-fact tone than she cared for. "Best to just ride out whatever it needs from you to get you right."

Whatever it needs from me? There's a comfort.

The heat in her face turned raw in an instant.

Typically, a blood candle was hot inside the veins, its warmth but fleeting, like the passing touch of a hand over the tip of a candle's flame. The Chandii blood, by contrast, burned so fiercely it was cold, as though she'd fallen through a lake of ice and the frozen water below had come flooding in.

She closed her eyes, clutching a fist to her bosom, fighting through the freezing fever, concentrating on the rush of frigid waves, until they settled about her chest, and began crashing against the wall of her heart.

***

VAL, her thoughts rang, and the lapping waves began to ebb.

There's so much I want to tell you.

Her muscles relaxed from screaming to singing as a field of lilac and cintas flowers opened up around her.

So much I've locked away for so long…

Valestriel swayed amidst the meadow in her best springtide dress, humming some old ashaeydiri lullaby, tossing a dashing smirk over her shoulder, and offering her hand out gaily…

Why couldn't I accept that I was enough for you?

"With me, you'll never walk alone," Val whispered.

Alone.

Lone.

One.

The word echoed all around her as though spoken from within a maze of glass corridors.

The only one to make me fall in love twice.

At Valestriel's touch, a keen breeze twirled around them, and Rhymona had the sudden sense of falling backward, gently, like a floating feather, until a bed caught her, and she found Val cradled underneath an arm, a head of curls resting over her shoulder, warm, absinthium breaths wandering across her naked breasts and down her span of self-made scars, to a hand that rested comfortably atop her mound.

Faint music could be heard outside the window of their bedchamber from some haunt down the avenue. A sound so familiar, unmistakable really, and particular to a certain kingdom.

Rhesh?

"I thought you'd never wake up," Val said with one of her best-placed smiles as she propped herself up on an elbow, fingertips roaming up Rhymona's belly to a breast where she pinched a puffy nipple, still burning so sweetly from the prior eve's frolic.

Cintas flowers and lavender soap invaded Rhymona's nostrils and the taste of Val and mint remained upon her lips like a fresh coating of winter balm.

"Val..."

"Shhhhh."

Val crushed her mouth against Rhymona's, their tongues entwined, as fingers trailed back down into her soft hairs parting her lower lips, slipping inside her wetness, caressing her folds, in and out, delicately, faster, then faster still, forcing a series of moans and sighs between kisses that kept on until they were both out of breath and forced to break for air.

She found Valestriel's eyes thereafter, ever on the verge of tears. Happy tears. Sad tears. Maddeningly unreadable tears. But always tears. Betraying the curvature of her silky lips.

Possessed of their passion, Valestriel shimmied down Rhymona's side, nestling her nose against the space just beneath her navel, her mouth following an inch lower, pillowy softness pressing deep into her waist, tickling her in the best way, leaving a faint wet mark before repeating another inch lower, and then she felt the softness between her legs chased by the thrill of an eager tongue.

Want gasped, buzzing about her swimming mind...

As need found the gods' names for playthings...

And thusly she surrendered...

Valestriel was all the world to her. All she could ever desire.

We can be enough for each other.

Chest heaving, heart hammering, toes curling, her lover's tongue and lips ran the length of an inner thigh, agonizingly slow, toying with her, teasing her, reveling in her, nuzzling the places where her scars ran the deepest, lapping up their names and crosses, drinking in their everlasting pain, culminating with an intense sucking kiss against tender, untarnished skin.

Rhymona's spine arched at the warmth of Val's tending, eyes rolling back in her head, whispered curses filling the spaces between panting breaths.

Hundreds of times Rhymona had fallen on blood candles to heal a wound or heighten a shufa high, but never before had she experienced something so intoxicating as this. She wanted to stay in this place forever. With Valestriel. In that tiny little bedchamber on the outskirts of Rhesh, amongst the undesirables, where nobody knew their names and less cared to have them. She remembered the old innkeeper and her slow-witted apprentice. Country folk with no business running an establishment anywhere near a city as grand as Rhesh, and yet to Rhymona it was as near to perfection as she could imagine.

But that's not...

how it...

happened...

The kissing and licking began to hurt at the realization and Rhymona gazed down at her heart's delight.

Valestriel?

Baleful eyes glared up at her, one ashaeydir gold, the other lilac and loathing.

Valestriel...

Slowly, Val pulled away from her, gobs of gore smeared across her lower face, and running down the length of her chin. A fel grin bubbled up from within.

What the fuck?

Rhymona jerked back from the abomination, blackened blood trailing her squirm up the lily-white bedsheets.

Voices began to break through the blood candle's fade.

No. Rhymona shoved up hard against the headboard, imprisoned by the creature's stare, unable to stand, her legs swollen and impossibly heavy, weighed down by her lover's fervent attentions.

The thing that was Val pursued. Deliberately unhurried. A taloned hand stabbing down into the mattress, cutting the linens as she crawled forward, followed by a second.

No!

Rhymona's eyes slammed shut and her head wrenched to the side as Valestriel dove at her…

HOLD THE DARK, *my dear.* Her mother bade. *But only half as near as the light.*

SWALLOW.

Pop.

Exhale.

"Tell us, Victor," Remy began as the real world materialized around her. "What have you seen further inside the palace?"

Shit-fucking cunt whore.

A fresh breath of old air filled her lungs and her scars burned like the hells' endless furies across the span of their count, worse than when she first made them.

"All manner of terror. Netherspawn, ghouls, goblins, drylax, your host's brother ripping folks apart from the inside out."

"Desmond?" Rhymona's words came out scratchy as though they hadn't quite caught her up yet from the bloodmare. "You saw Desmond?"

"I did. Briefly. But I was not fool enough to contend with such a deranged creature. My wife and I fled, but it only bought us a short reprieve." Goss glanced away.

"What was her name?" Julia asked as she advanced from her brother's side.

"Esme." He swept, woeful chestnut orbs across the room stopping on the girl.

Julia knelt on the floor between them. "I made it clean if it's any comfort."

Rhymona watched Julia closely, both terrified and impressed by the youngest Harver. As fucked-up as her own childhood had fallen, she'd never once come close to uttering such a thing. Though the magus couldn't help but wonder, if the girl actually did manage to survive all of this, especially given her lineage, what sort of monster might come stabbing out the other side.

"Aye, and for that, young one, you have my gratitude."

Rhymona's jaw set and she gazed at Remy.

"My Esmeralda," Goss sighed. "Beautiful, even in death. I couldn't stop the infection once it got in her, and I'd planned to let her take me with her, but you can see how that went."

"She didn't attack you."

"No," said Goss. "And not only that, but she refused my requests, walked away from me, and let herself out. I've seen others like this. Few and far between. As though in some way they've managed to reject their godless masters' cruel commands."

"And we plan to find those godless masters," Remy said, "be they Desmond Lanier, be they Hrathgon the betrayer, be they The Hood her fucking self, and we plan to send their sorry asses back to whatever fel cesspit they skeeved out of."

"Only death awaits you, if you push into the palace. Even for a gods-blood stowing a dracari soul."

Rhymona grabbed a blood candle from the pouch and offered it to him. "Death awaits us all, but there is time yet for one last fuck you."

Goss offered her a stern expression before trailing down to the blood candle.

"What my friend is trying to say is we could use your help, Victor," Remy expounded. "And you know this palace better than any one of us. We've already been through the northern kingdoms fighting and running from this horror and still it persists. I fear it won't stop until it has the whole of the moon. Unless we stop it. *We* must make a stand here. In Courowne."

"Maybe this was why Lady Esme let you be," Julia added. "Mayhaps, somehow, she knew there was more left for you to do here. Mayhaps this way you can still honor her."

Rhymona met the girl's eyes and nodded her approval. *Try saying no to that shit, Victor.*

Goss slipped the blood candle from between her fingers.

Aye, that's what I thought. Rhymona opened her palm and found the knife wound restored to a bright white line of warped scar tissue. It was ugly as fuck to be sure, like the bastard who bought her, but she could see to that bit of clean up later, if indeed a later actually found her. With a grunt, she pushed up to her feet, jerking Fucker up by his jagged timber scruff.

"Better?" Remy asked as she rose to equal height.

"Still high off Chandii ichor," she arched a cramp from her freshly mended hand, "and better seems a most ill-fitting term, but the bleeding's stopped, so there's a thing."

"And your sister?"

"Back in her coffin for now." Rhymona squeezed around Fucker tight as she could, testing her gift's quality. The hand still felt a little stiff, but otherwise retained most of its normal flexibility.

"Last I saw of him," Goss said, "Desmond was carving a path to the eastern wing."

"And what is there?" Remy asked.

"Most notably the library."

Remy returned his attentions to Rhymona. "It's a start."

"It's no coincidence you found me here," Goss began, easing his disfigured arm back inside the sleeve of his robe. "This chamber is a repository for the Emperor's guard. Plunder the cupboards and stacks and you'll find all manner of enchanted items, potions, and tonics."

"And some shit about prospering luck stones?" Rhymona opened the nearest cupboard to find row upon row of bottles and flasks containing various colored liquids. She turned back to the group, smirking. "Now this is my kind of party." She shoved Fucker down inside her belt, picked up one of the bottles labeled as *frost powder* and held it up. The substance inside appeared like any ordinary handful of crushed snow.

"Be careful with that one," Goss said as he rose to his feet. "It's an explosive. You drop that in here, it'll turn the entire chamber into a block of ice."

"If we're going out, we may as well go out with a bang, yeah?"

"In the chest, you will find belts, gloves, satchels, and pouches." Goss drifted over to it, mumbled something under his breath, and a collection of runes burned to life across the iron banding. A clicking sound followed and the chest yawned open. He retrieved a belt and strapped it around his thin frame then buttoned a hardened leather pouch to either side of his waist. "And here I thought my Oathsworn days behind me." Next, he joined Rhymona before the cupboard and collected a mixture of phials and flasks, placing them neatly inside the pouches, then he passed over to an alcove at the end of the wall, from which he retrieved a gnarled cherrywood wand. "Yes, you'll do nicely." He muttered another enchantment under his breath and a bright golden language chased the stalk of the object. "Well, what are you lot waiting for? If you mean to war, we best be getting to it."

Rhymona followed course, throwing a satchel over her shoulders, before sliding into a pair of leather gloves and looting the potions cupboard.

"I believe your brother is the nether's champion," Goss said. "The one prophesied in Tetherow's works. The bastard born of summer's blood and winter's kiss."

"This shit again," Rhymona muttered. *Fucking Tarborils.*

"You're familiar?"

"I've read a number of Tetherow's fictions and accounts, including *The N'therN'rycka*, but nothing about this bastard champion." Rhymona let the satchel's flap down. "Though we know that Desmond fits the part, don't we? We know he was murdered and brought back. And we know he is likely possessed as a result, possibly by Tetherow himself."

Owl-eyed, Goss turned from Rhymona to Remy. "Majesty? Is this true?"

"Just as you and other giftborn have communed with me in The Spellbind over the centuries, so too did Malthus Tetherow. I cannot recall specifically when, but at some point, I began to notice a difference in him. Marginal changes over time. A slight edge of menace. Almost as though he were becoming another man entirely. It was by no means obvious back then. In fact, the thought never once occurred to me, having never felt sinister urges from him before. But I believe at some point Tetherow split his soul and part of that severed soul became entwined with the nether. As you are aware, one must sacrifice a part of their gift to gravedance another. And that sacrifice draws the nether in like a beacon during a tempest."

More like a wolf to a shepherd's flock, Rhymona thought.

"I believe this is how Tetherow found the young prince," Remy served the dracari's words. "Now, how he was able to splice himself from the nether and attach to Desmond is another story altogether, and certainly not one I can rightly explain."

"He is a master of hemomancy," Goss said. "And I am sure many other forms of black magic less familiar to our annals. His attack outside the throne hall was unlike anything I have ever beheld. Calling blood from corpses and the living all at once, using their spill to paint the walls with wards and impale their swordbrothers. Though how he managed to sustain the host from such a massive pull is wholly beyond…"

"Carnomancy," Rhymona said, recalling the games she and Aiden would play on each other whilst shit-housed after lessons. Using the gift to briefly control the other's body parts and movements. A fist to the bollocks here, a misplaced footstep there. Mostly harmless, innocent fun by a couple of flirty, drunk fuckwits with too much time on their hands. But, history told, carnomancy had proven a rather nasty penchant for turning shitshow and more often than not. Which, honestly, back then, was half the thrill of it. And, also, why its study and practice were banned under Black Magic Law by the Ministry. "Aiden knows carnomancy."

"Flesh manipulation?" Goss asked. "How do you know this?"

"We were mates once," Rhymona said as she took to a lean against the opposite wall from the cupboards.

Remy and Julia began to kit up, the older brother helping his sister with the appropriate potions and tonics.

"Do not use these unless you absolutely must, Jules," Remy ordered. "Is that clear?"

"Yes, brother," Julia responded, the words like an eye roll.

"You mentioned seeing Aiden…Desmond," said Rhymona. "Any chance you happened upon a dark-skinned girl with strange markings?"

"Not that I recall. It's possible back in the higher halls, but there were so many faces, both blighted and living, and everything passed by like a blur until we found ourselves here. The gods only know, we didn't even notice Esme's wound until—"

Everyone stopped moving for a small instant and Rhymona could see the pain welling up inside the man as he stared off into his own personal void. She could almost feel the hurt herself, it was radiating off him with such a ferocity.

Her chest tightened as her own emotions regarding Val began to surface. Still nothing about her friend and love, and the further this progressed without news, the more she began to fear the worst, especially with all she'd already been given about Aiden and knowing they'd come to Courowne together.

Rhymona stepped forward from the wall, placing a hand on the man's shoulder. "Thank you, Victor. I know this is shit asking for your help given your loss, and I know there are no words I can offer you presently, but I promise, if we make it out of this alive, I'll help you give Esme a proper burial."

Goss's eyes hardened as they met hers. "I appreciate your cares, but where we're going, what we're going up against, we won't be coming back from it. Not as we are. Even if we do actually manage to survive."

The bitch in her wanted to make a biting comment, but she glanced down thin-lipped at her leathers instead.

"Help me bring her in?" Goss asked.

"Of course," said Rhymona, following the battle-magus to the crackling azure ward.

"*Ghathrovira*," Remy called from behind them with a shift of the wrist and the ward faded.

Rhymona lifted Fucker for the task if needed and eased the door open. She stared long into the dark corridor, waiting, listening, before quietly slinking out. The silence sent a chill wandering through her.

Goss joined her, kneeling next to his wife, who lay flat on her stomach, a pool of blood and nether dust having formed a gory halo around her head.

Like a fusspot master, Rhymona studied Julia's bladework. The iron entered from the temple, driven straight through, leaving but a thin red opening that had run down her jawline to the seepage below. It was quite well made, all told, and doubly unsettling, when considering the girl hadn't yet found a decade in age.

Goss cupped a hand against the stab wound and gently rolled Esme into his lap, stroking her cheek. The image mirrored that which Rhymona saw in the hedge maze and from the corner of her eye Fiandrel watched.

Heat claimed the space behind her eyes, and a heaviness settled in her heart, sending her broken parts spiraling once again. *You sappy ass bitch.* Though despite the dreadfully tragic circumstances, she saw a twinkle of beauty within that desolate moment.

Halion flashed before her eyes. Her beloved. Her first heartache. Hells, her first thousand heartaches, to have it true. Long inky-black hair, piercing hazel orbs, disgustingly handsome smile. He was not unlike Aiden in appearance, her Halion, especially whilst donning his midaran mask, and he was always quite keen for a good haunt anytime something romantic and even partway emotional found her.

Fuck off, Halion. Twist the knife another night.

She knelt next to the ill-starred couple and glanced over at Julia, who appeared all manner of nervous and ashamed. They locked eyes and Rhymona mouthed, *you did good.*

A scream from down the corridor drew all of their attentions.

"It's time we start moving," said Remy in response.

Rhymona set Fucker down and helped Goss lift Esme up from under an arm, guiding her back into the store-room and laying her down against the wall where they first met.

"Rest easy, my love," Goss said to his wife, tucking a loose strand of hair behind her ear.

Julia had Fucker waiting for Rhymona as she turned back toward the door.

"Cheers," the magus said.

"Please tell me the library is away from the gods-awful shrieking," Remy said to Goss as he joined them in the corridor.

Goss returned a grim expression.

Wrong story, Toff, Rhymona thought, admiring that he still held out some measure of hope despite the ungodly heap of horrors that continued to find them. *And this one only ends one way.*

CHAPTER FOURTEEN

SHARDS of pale emerald starlight poured through a pair of cracked windows illuminating the least damning sections of the dank, dusty space.

Magwyn shielded her nose with the back of her hand to cut the stench as her eyes adjusted, but still her stomach wouldn't stop turning. Something in the room's shadows produced the worst stink she could ever recall crossing.

Fastly, she spanned the room to the door on the opposite end, letting herself out into the lazy mist of a desolate clearing.

She halted once the smell was off her, inhaling the forest air like a kiss of incense. Though, truthfully, it proved scarce better.

Past the clearing's gloom, she scanned the dark ring of surrounding trees in an effort to gain some understanding of their whereabouts, but nothing stood out. The weather was still reasonably warm though, which likely meant they were still south of the highlands or possibly east of the Morrigar Mountains.

And there was something else. She squinted, azure returning to her eyes.

A SPELL HAS HIDDEN THIS PLACE FROM WATCHFUL EYES, Emyria said and Magwyn's vision flickered between the open field and forest.

"Maggie?" Ledge called after her.

"I'm fine," she answered, as he appeared in the doorway. "What is that unspeakable odor?"

"Place looks like a butcher's shop."

"I daresay, do butcher's shops smell worse than dungeons these days?" In the light of the sister moons, she noted numerous plots between them where holes had been dug up and refilled.

"I should rephrase, milady. It is a chamber for interrogating folk." He followed her gaze. "And this clearing is likely its potter's field."

"I thought I saw a body in there."

"Aye. There is."

Ledge turned back into the cabin and the Empress forced herself to follow, conjuring an egg of azure flame inside her palm. "Is it Rhonyn?"

"No, it's female. But she's been flayed something horrid."

Maggie brought the Eldn light close and forced herself to inspect the body. She was stripped above the waist and shackled to the wall beside a scarred wooden table cluttered with every manner of ungodly blade and torture instrument imaginable.

Ledge retrieved a torn golden surcoat from the floor beside the wood-stove identical in make to the one Maggie now wore.

"No," the Empress uttered upon the sight of it.

"Milady?"

She sighed, a terrible sadness settling in her chest as the contours of the skinless face became all too familiar.

"Did you know her?"

"Her name was Ilfaeyda. She was one of my handmaidens and a damned good one. One I trusted."

"Sympathies."

"She didn't deserve this." Magwyn paced back to the doorway, extinguishing the ball of magic flickering in her hand. "What in vaelnation could possess someone to commit such a ghastly act?"

"I'd say someone had an agenda here and needed answers."

Magwyn glanced at Ledge over her shoulder. "From a chambermaid?"

"These are hard words, milady, but it's been my experience that chambermaids of a certain quality typically harbor the most valuable bits of information."

"What are you insinuating?"

"I believe the girl was tortured because of her closeness to the crown, though what for I couldn't much say. Mayhaps you know something about that?"

"She and Rhonyn were together. Intimately. Nothing serious that I was privy to, but—"

"Do you reckon she might betray Rhonyn?"

"Betray him? To what end?"

"Now there's a question. But the ends are endless down this rabbit hole, aren't they?"

"Whatever his cares for the girl, I doubt Rhonyn was foolish enough to confide secrets with her."

"Only a thought, milady."

A queer notion struck her. "Do you believe Rhonyn may have been responsible for this?"

"Do I believe him responsible? No. Not for a second. But do I believe him capable?" Ledge pursed his lips and offered a slight head tilt. "Honestly, I believe nothing can be ruled out. No one is above suspicion. Not anymore. The world as it is is not how we once knew it. Not even close. The only things I can trust are what I see plainly before me, and even then, most of that is in question."

Magwyn wandered back deeper into the cabin, chewing on those words as she brought forth a fresh egg of Eldn flame, and silence stretched out between them as she combed the walls end to end for any other evidence of Rhonyn's passing, halting at a cobwebbed bookshelf in the corner and sifted through the tomes and scrolls and spider leavings. A collection of useless old junk from what she could tell. Most of the tomes were works of fiction and the scrolls were of cooking recipes.

YOUR FRIEND IS RIGHT, MAGWYN. YOU MUST BE CAREFUL WHO YOU TRUST. THERE IS A POSSIBILITY RHONYN IS LOYAL TO TETHEROW. YOU HAVE HAD THE THOUGHT BEFORE.

I had the thought that he was out for himself, but never that he could—

Her eyes wandered back to the front of the room where Ilfaeyda remained.

"Maggie," Ledge called from outside the cabin.

"Gods be good," Magwyn uttered, startled by the shout. "What is it?"

"I think I know where we are."

135

She followed his voice and found him behind the cabin staring into the distance.

He pointed out to the west. "You see those spires just over the trees there?"

She nodded. They were by no means obvious, especially in the darkness, but once they were revealed, there was no missing them.

"Those are the spires of Marrovard University's admissions hall."

"You're certain?"

"It's been a few decades to have it true, but I'd never forget the architecture. Stella used to name them The Onion Towers."

The Empress had heard countless tales of Marrovard's unique building structures but had never found the good fortune to behold them.

"Further north there." Magwyn turned with Ledge toward a tall black shape that disappeared into the patch of clouds. "That's Wyrmswold Tower."

From this distance, the dark pillar appeared like a stake driven down from the heavens deep into Vaelsyntheria's hide.

"And these tracks here are fresh," he continued.

Magwyn glanced down at the drag marks and boot prints leading off into the forest in the direction of the university.

"I'd say we're roughly an hour away if we keep a good pace."

SEEMS AS GOOD START AS ANY, Emyria offered. WE CERTAINLY SHOULD NOT STAY OUT HERE MUCH LONGER.

Agreed.

Magwyn's attentions returned to Ledgermaine as they set off toward Marrovard. "Since we'll have the time now, mayhaps you can learn me up on Whit's dealings with black magic."

"Milady—"

"No more milady bollocks, Ledge. I will not be put off a moment longer." They passed into the woods. "The time for secrecy has long since passed." She swiped up a branch from the forest floor and clasped the azure flame to it until it caught like a torch. "And as far as I see it, if I'm to be of proper use in any of this, I may as well have the whole of it."

"Elsymir Beldroth," Ledge began. "I'm sure you recall the name?"

"Of course. He and Whit were practically inseparable back when. I may have been a youngling, but a blademaster of y'deman descent in the old kingdom rather makes for a lasting impression, wouldn't you agree?"

"Aye. And in the cycles following your betrothal to Dalivant, the relationship between Whit and Beldroth began to unravel."

"A happening of which I'm still unclear about. They were thick as thieves for cycles, bound as brothers—"

"Pardon my brashness, Maggie, but you know the sting of betrayal better than most. And Whit got in his head that Elsymir would betray him —in fact, was betraying him."

"How? Why?"

"Elsymir started hobnobbing with Ravenholme again, playing at mediator between Whit and Tetherow. Or so the story went. I wasn't around much in those cycles. But this was about the time things took a turn for the worse and Whit became convinced that Elsymir and Tetherow were somehow the same person."

"The same person? How could that possibly be?"

"Hells if I know. As you've said, your brother had a sickness, and he was fully off his nut in those days, but you've seen what the bastard's done with your nephew."

"You believe Elsymir was possessed?"

"I don't know what I believed back then, but mad or no, Whit wasn't entirely wrong. There was something foul afoot. Something horribly off. And Elsymir wasn't doing himself any favors by consorting with the enemy. Though I doubt Old Whit saw all of this shit-fuckery with the nether being at the other end of it all, it wasn't possession your brother was concerned on, rather that Elsymir and Tetherow somehow housed one side of the same soul. Naturally, he became obsessed with soul-splitting in the after, and through that gateway other forms of dark magic began to sink their teeth in.

"When he questioned Elsymir about the split soul, Elsymir denied the accusation. He explained that Tetherow was merely a guise, an act, a means of crowd control. But Whit wouldn't hear it. Thusly, Elsymir was banished from Lancastle on pain of death, ending their long-held friendship.

"This would come to haunt your brother more than any of us could have possibly foreseen. Casting out Elsymir was only the beginning of Whit's descent. He became mistrustful of nearly everyone until there was only a handful of us left that he would permit into the council. All the while, he became consumed by his study into soul magic, believing it was the only way to understand the truth behind Elsymir and Tetherow. It wasn't long afterward that the rest of us were pushed out of his circle, until only Stella remained."

"Why Stella?"

"Because of her Chandiian lineage. And because of the grimoires. Both of which made her indispensable to Whit."

"What grimoires?"

"Some fel miscreations the Critchlows stole from the Morrigar Mountains generations ago. They were created during the Dragon Age, an apparent response to the elemental magics of the dracari and the spread of the gift. It's said each one houses a different manner of spell, spells of the soul and body."

"Each one? How many are there?"

"Four that I know of, and Stella gifted one of them to Whit during her tenure as head archivist. Whatever possessed her to do so, I couldn't say. Around this time, I was in Palatia for a summit and the winter that cycle was fierce, this would have been roughly 1812. I stayed in the north for months, and when I returned the change in Whit couldn't have been more obvious. I pressed Stella about this after Whit's death, and that was when she confessed to helping him split his soul."

Magwyn stopped, Ledge halting just ahead of her and glancing back.

"He actually did it then?" she asked.

"Yes."

"Does this mean part of him yet lives?"

"Part of him remains, but living he is not. His soul is bound to the grimoire Stella gave him."

"Meaning he is limited to its magic and placement."

"Precisely. It would take some barmy level of magic to move it from the grimoire to another object, much less into another sentient creature."

"But it can be accomplished?"

"By the right quality of sorcerer, yes. Though none that I know of. None still living anyway."

NO, Emyria argued. IT IS UNNATURAL. NOTHING GOOD CAN BE HAD FROM SUCH A DEED.

We at least need to consider finding the grimoire.

I CAN AGREE THE GRIMOIRES NEED TO BE FOUND, IF ONLY TO BE BURNED OR BURIED.

"As you're already aware, Whit was obsessed with the prophecy and Tetherow and he became obsessed with the grimoire just the like. He believed the three connected in some way. And he was convinced one could be used to correct the other. He became erratic, talking to himself, some noting screams and strange laughter from the king's solar in the middle of the night, stealing down the lengths of the high halls. It was around this time that I lost touch with him completely. He kept me out on this little summit or that little training retreat, oftentimes with Desmond. I knew it was his way of limiting my knowledge into his studies, but what could I do but allow it?

"Not a one of us stood up to him. Not a one of us argued, even after the supernatural began to creep the castle walls. We allowed him to drown. Anyone else would have been sedated or kept in confinement under watch, but not the king of Lancastle. Not a one of us held him accountable, and eventually, that bought him a terrible death."

They started forward again.

"First we find Rhonyn," Magwyn said. "Then the grimoires."

"I believe Desmond had a second one on him," Ledge added. "The sister Autumn, the third. No clue on the fourth."

"A bridge we can cross if we get there," the Empress returned as they pushed deeper into the wooded darkness, praying that the dawn would soon find them some measure of good fortune.

CHAPTER FIFTEEN

MARSEA SNAPPED awake just as Other's teeth began to sink through flesh, falling backward, away from the attack, catching herself just before her head slammed against the mausoleum floor.

The stars keep me.

She blinked through honey-thick eye crust as she eased herself down flat and lay still on the cold stones staring up at the vaulted ceiling, her heart stabbing out of her chest, as the rest of the conscious world came flooding back into existence. Slowly her head swiveled toward the door, which had been left ajar, letting in a finger of fuzzy, golden dawn light that crooked up once the knuckle met with wall. She was alone, but through the Mark of Shyraithka she could still sense Broenwjar ranging somewhere close by.

You will know the page. She heard Dagmara's husky voice from some misfit place within and her vision trailed back over to the opened grimoire. She could feel the arches and edges of the symbols against her tender fingertips. The maidens only knew how long she'd been there scritching and scratching them raw against *Dusk's* innards, collecting Tetherow's sacrifice beneath her nails like so much dust. Never before had she so desperately yearned for a warm bath and a sturdy scrub brush.

Wincing, she hauled herself back up into a sitting position and removed her glasses, digging sleep muck from her eyelids with her remaining pinky.

You will know the page, Other echoed.

The princess returned her glasses to their rest and slid soiled fingers back under *Dusk*, placing her thumb against the page to split the beast back open. She read the page title aloud. "Chapter Thirteen: The Hour of Dark Things."

She continued to the next page where it began like a memoir:

"If you have read this far, you have no doubt caught mention of the between hours in various parts of prior pages and chapters. Where *Noon* and *Haunt* represent the peak hours of midday and midnight, *Dawn* and *Dusk* embody the between hours. Dusk, for which this very tome is named, belongs to the realm of shadow. It is known in some cultures as *The Hour of Dark Meetings* and in others as *The Hour of One Thousand Devils*. Dawn by contrast is known as *The Time of Banishing and Blood Cleansing*. Together, they act as the balance between our plane and the planes beyond."

Pretty words and utter nonsense, this.

"During dusk," she kept on, "the shadows swallow up all to sight and the eyes become our opposition, prone to our excitement and our fears and doubly more so to the deceptions of the darkland creatures. For dusk is when the boundary between the planes is at its thinnest and can be breached by evil creatures and nether beasts at will, allowing them to materialize on this side of The Pale where they can both commune with and terrorize the living.

"This can't possibly be it. There's no mention of a door." She flipped ahead, through what almost appeared like a bestiary, skipping past pages describing spritelings, goblins, oni, djinn, nymphs, golems, something called a drylax, of which there were numerous variations, until one of the monsters caught her attention. She sat up straight and stared hard at the illustration. It was of a naked figure with dark, stringy hair whose body was unnaturally long and thin as though stretched on a torture rack. The creature was named a wraith. It was described as a vengeful presence bound to the mortal realm by an object, typically to a tool of war and savagery. Marsea's eyes flitted over to the haxanblade before returning to the page. "Their like typically come into creation by some manner of dodgy spellcasting," the princess read, "yes, yes, yes, blah, blah, blah." She skipped ahead. "A wraith is known to harness horrific magical abilities during the twilight hour for it is one of the few dark creatures powerful enough to manipulate affairs across planes. Most notably, they can create gateways and pocket dimensions that do not obey the laws of nature."

"Pocket dimensions…"

Marsea glowered into the band of sunlight, chewing on the inside of her lip, and something of her dreamscape returned to her, like a poem of some sort, each line spilling into the next as though she'd heard it a hundred times before.

One will die before their time.
One must go alone.
One will cede love's greatest gift in turn to spite the throne.
A ruin by starlight.
A blade from the stone.
A door from within, rent straight from the bone.

She paused.

Why is this so familiar?

A glint from the haxanblade restored her attention, and that was when she heard it. A voice in soprano, straight from the choir's heart, achingly sweet.

Ears perked, Marsea tensed as it continued into the next verse. *What a lovely voice*, she mused. It hardly mattered that she didn't recognize the melody. Its pitch quite reminded her of her mother's. It was said Larissa Waldgrave possessed the lilt of an angel back when, though she seldom found time for song these days and rarely gave her gift life whilst in Marsea's presence. The voice that stole a king's breath, hers was named. Rissa the Rin who fastly became one of the Lancastle choir's most renowned, catching her father's ear, and soon after, his heart. Or so the story went.

Another voice trickled in as the song progressed, answered by a third. The fresh sound of living, breathing, singing creatures both thrilled and terrified her. They would be the first outside of Lancastle, save Elsymir and the VanLandingham's, she had come upon. But more significantly, they would be the first that she would have a choice whether or not to interact with. Instantly, she began wondering what they looked like, how old they were, if they were kind and friendly, where they hailed from.

She shoved *Dusk* back into her satchel, plucked the haxanblade from its rest, and hurried out into the sunlight, toward the endless stream of cheerful banter. Darting between the gravestones, she trailed the paths of glistening snow, careful to avoid the clusters of dug-up hollows. Broenwjar joined her as they neared the other end of the cemetery. The gate on this side was missing entirely, and the pair passed through toward the tree line ahead. The princess could see movement the second she reached the woods and heard another new voice join the conversation. As nimbly as her aching ankles would allow, she dashed from tree to tree until she had a clear view. The voices belonged to a troupe. But, of course, they did. She swiveled around toward Old Boy and pressed a finger to her lips. Broenwjar responded by lowering into a serious prowling stance.

Marsea nudged her glasses back up as she turned back to the travelers, squinting through swaying pillars of gilded sunshine.

She counted a pair of horses pulling a caravan. An elderly man sat on a platform at the front of the wagon, clutching the reins. Two others, a man and a woman, walked ahead of the horses. They appeared young, mayhaps near Marsea's age. The woman sang a new tune now. It was slower, but considerably more euphonious than the last one, reminding Marsea of the maidens that would tend to the castle gardens just below her bedchamber window.

On the side of the caravan, in faded crimson paint, read 'Potions Preferred.' An absurd name to say the least, and one Marsea had certainly never heard before. Though to have it from the hens of court, there were so many troupes roving about these days, swapping names and players, it was impossible to keep up with all of them.

Just as Marsea worked up the nerve to dare closer, another man dropped down from the back of the caravan, lighting a pipe. This one carried iron at his hip and looked a mite more dangerous than the others. It was only a skinner's knife, but a blade was a blade was a blade in Marsea's opinion, and they were meant for one thing and one thing alone in the end. If nothing else, Cas had never let her forget that much.

Marsea shrank back behind the tree and let out a nervous breath.

"What are you thinking?" she whispered to Broenwjar.

The wolf angled his massive snout toward the travelers and let out a low growl.

"I agree. Who better knows the roads than a troupe? I mean the girl is serenading about like it's the bloody Springtide Ball out here, how bad can they be?" *Famous last words, those.*

Broenwjar offered a guttural rumble in response.

"I'm well aware it could be a trap, but if we just follow, mayhaps they will lead us to the next township without bother."

The princess peeked out from the side of the tree. The troupe was well ahead now, and the smoker was up by the horses.

Marsea charted her path forward before shifting back to Old Boy. "You keep to the black for now, B. Just in case. I'm hopeful, but campfolk are campfolk and I won't show them a lick of trust until we better know their character."

BY THE AFTERNOON, Marsea had a name for each of the troupe members, seven in total. The songstress was named Xandria, and the poor lovesick fool that never left her side, Simon. The old man at the reins replied to Wordsworth the one time and appeared to be something like the group's leader. The two who looked the most like trouble were named Niall and Stringer. Then there was another girl named Poppy, who hadn't yet left the caravan's confines despite Xandria's incessant pleading. "Still writing," Poppy would yell back. Even without having seen the girl, Poppy was the early frontrunner for Marsea's favorite of the bunch. The seventh, Marsea thought Niall named Unsung. But then Wordsworth later referred to him as Eddie. So, she landed on Unsung Eddie. He was the troupe's vanguard, she presumed, having apparently scouted ahead before she found them. Though, half the day gone, she hadn't seen hide nor hair of him yet.

She counted the names again like characters in a book, as she held for a breath behind an ivy-covered oak. Xan, the walking lullaby. Simon, the tomfool. Niall, the knife. Stringer Paul. Old man Wordsworth. Writer Poppy. And Unsung Eddie.

Another breath brought in the scent of burning wood and she turned her nose up to it, drawing it in like a spray of perfume. A spirited smile graced her lips. *Could it be?* She paced forward, a spring in her step. *Civilization, at last.* She closed her eyes, inhaled another lungful, and for some reason a vision of the VanLandingham's stove flashed through her mind, followed by the sound of a cookpot boiling, and the twinkling of the Yuletide tree. A warmth fell over her at the memory. Then the other side of the coin beckoned. *So what now?* Her eyes shot open. She'd become so fixated on merely finding civilization again that she hadn't a clue what to do with herself once it was actually upon her.

She raked her good hand through her freshly chopped curls, butterflies taking flight from the expanding pit in her stomach.

As it stood, she had no money, she couldn't reveal her true identity, or rather she knew she shouldn't, and she still hadn't the faintest inkling where the devil she was. Debynshire remained her best guess, but for no other reason than it was the only hollow she'd even halfway heard of within a few days of Vinth.

She flexed her bad hand, her skin peeling away from the glove's interior. It ponged of something awful inside, causing her nose to crinkle up. Given the assortment of odd smells within, she couldn't be sure if it came from her hand or the glove. More than like it belonged to both, but such was a worry for another time.

Just stick to the plan, Marsea. Easy peasy. Follow the troupe. They won't be staying long. Mayhaps only a night. Or so she suspected. *And try to find an in if you can.*

Much of the morning conversation between the troubadours centered around the Midwinter festivities in Courowne and finally making a name for themselves. The princess knew Courowne was roughly a week's travel south from Lancastle, which meant at least four or five days onward if, indeed, they were now just outside of Debynshire. And even that count was generous, providing they found no trouble along the way. Uncle Rho always called the southern highlands the most dangerous patch of road south of The Scar. Densely forested, it was the perfect hunting ground for the wolld tribes, many of which settled in the area after the ashaeydir invasion during the mid-1700s.

Marsea started forward.

Uncle Rho. The thought of seeing him again gave her renewed hope. And her Aunt Magwyn would be in Courowne as well. Not that they were ever very close. But blood is blood. And she would be something of a familiar face. An increasingly rare commodity in this day and age.

"Not another step," a steely voice called from the woods.

Marsea froze, eyes darting to and fro, her prior excitement catching at the base of her neck. *Shit.* Her mind began to race. *Are you running? Are you drawing?* Blind Widow's ghastly wail soared to the forefront of her thoughts.

He's only a man, Other snarled.

No.

"Who are you and why have you been following us?" a figure in brown leather armor stepped inside the edge of her vision. He had an arrow trained on her.

Calm and collected, Marsea dear.

"You must be Eddie," the princess said as she tilted her head toward him and took him in.

Cool as a cucumber.

He had a youthful face, dark skin, and a wild mass of salt and pepper locks that must have once favored the Royalguard cadet fashion (short on the sides and thicker up top), though presently his iron-hard eyes betrayed any measure of innocence that youthfulness might have claimed.

"I mean you no injury," she added, barely staving off utter panic from her voice—or so she hoped.

"Could have fooled me," his stare dropped to the haxanblade. "I say again, name yourself."

Despite his menace, there was something oddly familiar about him. Something about his voice, his body language, his energy.

"I'm no one," Marsea said. "Just a wanderer. An adventurer, one might say."

"Bullshit," he stepped closer, the bowstring creaking back ever so slightly. "I've been watching you for an hour now, creeping around, no doubt plotting."

"Plotting?"

"Sizing up the take, yeah?"

"No, it's nothing like that. And I'm no bandit if that's your insinuation." Logic forced its way through Other's survival instincts. "I mean, how would I even pull off such a take anyway? The numbers aren't exactly in my favor, now are they?"

"Spare me. The numbers don't mean shit out here. You could be a ruddy gravewitch for all I know. Or a warlock."

"A warlock?"

"Aye, have us all in bags before the sun goes to rot."

Marsea could sense Broenwjar coming back for her now. "I could be, but I'm not. And you bloody well know it. Now listen to me, I'm not out here alone. I tell you this now for your benefit. You need to rest that bow before my friend comes back. He won't be happy to see you threatening me."

"You must think me a complete bloody simp. You're the only one I've seen out here for a league. Now toss your blade over there."

"You don't understand," Marsea said. "You don't see my friend. He sees you, and then it's a problem."

Eddie swallowed, clearly growing more anxious by her warnings.

He's playing hard, she thought. She'd seen it a thousand, thousand times over in the tourney yard, scabs too big for their trousers, talking a big game because they finally made it to the king's cobble, not taking into account that everyone else had just the same.

"Now I can tell you don't wish me harm, Eddie." She could practically taste his fear now. "Nor I you. Please trust me on this."

The bowman glared her down as he came within a few feet. "Toss your sword and I'll think about lowering the nock." Slowly, Marsea unclipped the scabbard from her belt, and let it fall to her ankles. "All right, now palms out where I can see them," he ordered. Marsea obeyed and Eddie fixated on the bad hand. "What happened there?"

"Where?"

"Your hand."

"Wildkin attack," she found herself saying.

"Mmm, I bet. Or it could be you're hiding a warlock's well." *A what?* "Or you fucked up a mugging."

"Fucked up a mugging?" *Not far off, actually*, she thought. "More like self-defense."

"Oh, and there she is. Thought I saw a bit of the crazy in there."

"How dare you," she hissed. "Don't act like you know me, sir. You don't know the half of it."

"Maybe not, but I know a killer when I see one."

"Yeah? And it takes one to know one, rot, rot, bloody rot, and onward, right?"

"Something like that."

Stop trying to hold on to normalcy, Marsea. Embrace the madness as it embraces you. "Prize well, he had it coming."

"Did he now?"

"I won't apologize for it, and I certainly won't be made to feel less by the likes of..."

"The likes of what? You complain about my judgments, yet suddenly you know me?"

They locked eyes, holding, and Marsea found herself collecting the surrounding features of his face. The bags under his eyes. The scar that split an eyebrow. The tuft of black hair jutting out from his chin like a spearhead. The last thing she wanted was another argument or another enemy.

"Go on," he goaded.

All those cycles kept to a cage, all those cycles spent dreaming of the world beyond Lancastle, and this is your first interaction? This was where you landed?

"No," she said.

"No?"

"I'm sorry." She produced a duckling frown. "I'm sorry you don't feel like you can trust me. I'm sorry I've put you in this awful situation where you feel like your life and the lives of your friends are in danger. I promise you they are not. At least not from me. Take my sword, if it pleases. Take my satchel too. But know their ownership requires a great deal of responsibility and an even greater degree of sacrifice."

Eddie's jaw clenched, and it was obvious he was debating something internally. A moment later, he looked up to the heavens, whispering something she couldn't quite hear, then lowered the bow away from her. "The gods know, I'm going to regret this," he muttered. "All right," he turned back to her, "let's have it then. Where are you from?"

"I told you I'm a wanderer. I have no home."

"A fetching girl like you has no home? I very much doubt that."

Not exactly the response she expected, especially considering some of her more recent beauty alterations. "It used to be up north if you must know. Before all this business with the blight began."

Another Casilvieri lesson. *Always give a little truth, but never, ever the whole of it.*

He nodded. "Well, you already have my name it seems, though I much prefer Edgar to Eddie or Unsung, or whatever you've heard from the others." He separated the arrow from its nock. "Edgar Alewine, properly. And you?"

"My name?"

148

"Yeah, you have one of those at least, don't you?"

"I don't know." *Nothing. No one. Nameless girl.* "Dolly Damsel Ray-of-Sunshine. It doesn't matter. Call me whatever you like."

"Come now, a posh girl like yourself. I'd rather have the truth of it."

"Fetching? Posh? You are forward, indeed, sir, aren't you?"

"Are you saying I'm wrong?"

"Egregiously so, yes."

"And there you go with egregiously. Could you be more obviously bookish? As though the glasses weren't already a dead giveaway."

"I said I didn't have a name, not that I was an idiot."

"Damsel it is then."

"No." *Sweet mother of irony. I mean truly, could you imagine?* "I think not."

"Dolly then?" He turned up a fish-eating grin, all puppy dog charm. "Or Ray. Oh, or Sunshine? I do like that one. It has a certain—"

"Damsel will do for now," Marsea interjected. *Maidens' mercy.* What did she care anyway? As long as it wasn't her birth name, and no one suspected her true identity, why should it matter?

"All right, Damsel, if I may so inquire, what exactly were you and your imaginary friend doing out so far in the woodland depths then? Why were you stalking after us?"

"I wasn't so much stalking as I was casually following at a safe distance. I'm sorry, do you mind if I lower my hands now? I wasn't sure if that was implied by you with the bow or..."

"Yeah, it was sort of implied."

Good gravy, Marsea. "Cheers." *Fitting in brilliantly.* She snorted. "Was beginning to feel a bit ridiculous there."

"The blade stays where it is though, yeah?"

"Of course." She scratched at the scar on her upper lip before repositioning her glasses.

"You were saying about you and your imaginary friend?"

"Right. Well, this is rather embarrassing to admit, but we ran into some trouble outside of Vinth last night during the snowstorm, and in the process, I seem to have gotten myself a bit turned around."

"I'll say."

"Then when I heard you all nearby this morning, I thought who better to lead me to the nearest township than a troupe."

"I suppose that tracks."

"Like I said, I meant no injury, and I certainly had no intentions of thievery. If anything, I was hoping I might join along. I was just trying to work up the nerve before, well...before," she pointed back and forth between them, "all this."

"Join along?"

"I may have overheard Niall and Wordsworth discussing a hired man at the next township."

"First off, it's a little disturbing you know all of our names already. Secondly, that hired man is nothing more than wishful thinking."

"Is it though?" An eyebrow arched.

"You?"

"Me."

"Fancy yourself a sellsword then, do you?"

"I don't necessarily fancy it, but if it's useful." Her lip quirked up. "I'm better with a blade than you might think."

"You'll certainly have to be where we're going."

"You're going to Courowne, are you not?"

"We are." His eyes narrowed. "Though rumor is the blight has become a problem on the main roads south of here, so we're planning to push through wolld territory. The lesser of two shitshows according to the Old Man. Just thought you should be aware of what you're signing up for before you go on making it all official."

"You think the troupe will have me then?"

"Oh, I know they'll have you. Niall and Paul, they might boast a tough game, but they're a couple of dandy sweethearts once the fire's going and the drink leads to song. Wordsworth was once a soldier, and a damned decent one to have the tale, but that was an age ago. An age and counting. And you'll sooner catch a blade from one of the Pelvenyn sisters than the wantwit bard. So yeah, I'd say the job's yours if you truly want it. Besides, I've passed through this town a handful of times over the past few cycles. Mostly cravens and drunkards and the like. Useless folk where the road's concerned. And certainly not the sort you want watching your back when the cards are stacked. The pay will be shit, too, especially given what we may be in for, but I reckon you help us get there and things work out, you may fetch yourself a fine purse for it in the end."

"I don't need coin," Marsea said. "Though if you've any food to spare,

I'll take that for services rendered. It doesn't have to be much and it doesn't have to be quality. I eat like a bird most days anyway."

Edgar inspected her head to toe, shoulder to shoulder. "You're an odd one, Damsel. A sellsword that doesn't take coin and talks both brigand and highborn?" He smirked and shook his head.

"I can't tell if that's meant to be a compliment or..."

"Take it as you like. Stay weird, as far as I'm concerned. But you may want to rein in the highborn once we get into town. Too much of a good thing is likely to find you a blade around these parts."

"Edgar."

"Yeah?"

"Don't move." She took a step toward him.

"What?"

"Broenwjar, tae haeru." *Hold.* "He is a friend." Marsea stopped in the space next to Edgar. "Now slowly, turn around. And don't look him in the eye. At least not to start."

"Are you fucking with me, right now?"

"Not fucking with you."

"What is it?" Edgar asked.

"You remember my imaginary friend?"

"Mmhmm."

"Well, he's a good boy most of the time, but he doesn't take shit from anyone."

"That a fact?"

"So, don't give him shit and he won't have a reason."

"A reason for what?"

"Just turn around slowly. Let him get a sense of you."

"Gods, I really hope you're fucking with me," Edgar murmured as he shifted around toward Marsea and found the beast waiting, "Balls of Agault, you're not," the words pushed through his teeth. "What the actual fuck am I looking at here?"

"His name is Broenwjar. He may not be the prettiest prince at the party, but he's a pup once he gets to know you."

"A pup. Right." The bowman's eyes stretched wide.

Marsea placed her hand under Edgar's, her knuckles spooning against his calloused palms.

"What are you doing?" he asked.

"Just trust me." Gently, she guided his trembling hand forward. Broenwjar brought his massive snout up to them both and wrangled in a heavy sniff, breathing out warm and wet.

"See," the princess purred. "He's a big softie."

"Yeah, big softie," Edgar echoed. "Emphasis on the big."

Broenwjar padded a circle around them before settling at Marsea's other side. Force of habit pulled her gloved hand through his thick, gray coat of fur. "He's no sellsword, but you get me, you get him. We're kind of a package deal."

"Yeah, and lost damsel my sorry left ass cheek." Edgar backed away, his gaze lifting from Broenwjar to Marsea then back down to the wolf again. "You know, I was wondering why you smelled so much like wet dog."

Her expression soured. "No, I don't."

"Now your turn to trust me." His expression brightened. "It's bad."

Marsea pinched the collar of her shirt and brought it to her nose then sniffed under her arms. It smelled like forest and sunlight to her. Mostly.

"Fortunately for you, there's a hot spring nearby. I can take you to it. That is unless you prefer to put everyone off their supper once we get into town."

Marsea thought on it a moment. "Shall I pick up the sword then...or?"

"No disrespect, but I'm far more concerned about your imaginary friend than anything you can do to me with that blade."

"As well you should be," Marsea said, nestling the toes of her leathers beneath the scabbard and guiding it up into her hand.

"Fucking hells," Edgar snorted. "The girls are going to love you."

CHAPTER SIXTEEN

"If it's revenge you're after," a man spoke from outside The Cupboard, "you better dig up two graves."

The boy put out his candle and kept perfectly still inside his little nook, each breath slow and easy, unwilling to be heard.

"If that's what it takes to protect my family and end this then so be it," a second voice returned.

"Majesty, this is not the way." The voice lowered. "Splitting your soul will only lead to ruin. You know this."

"I do not require your consent, Ledge. The decision is final." The men came to a halt just outside the dark place. "I am too far gone to it now besides. My conscience will not allow me back even if I chose it."

"This is a mistake."

"I appreciate your cares, prize well, but the future of my family, of House Lanier, lies in the balance, and there are enough schemers and bladehands already among us."

"Give me leave, and I will have Beldroth in chains within a quint. Ravenholme can yet be brought to heel. Or disbanded. Or whatever it is you deem necessary. We have the forces to combat them."

"It's only the worms for Beldroth or Tetherow or whatever the hells he is. He can no longer be trusted. And I won't have my council giving chase to a lost cause. Ravenholme has too many heads as it is, and I'd sooner let them devour each other in their lust for fame and clout than risk a single bluecoat life."

The boy backed away from the doorway until he felt the opposite wall press against his spine.

"The same can be said of all others outside the accord," his father continued, "and for the time being Larissa. My spell-work stays between you, me, and Stella. Is that understood?"

"Understood, Majesty."

"Besides, there's fresh work to be done here in Lancastle. I've been meaning to discuss Desmond's tutelage with you."

"Desmond's tutelage?"

"He lacks discipline, as I'm sure you've beheld, parading about the halls between tirades playing childish games on the staff, and making undue trouble. It's simply unbecoming of a prince and heir. As such, the time has come to expel these juvenile manners before they set, wouldn't you agree?"

"True, he's a bit boisterous, but he's only a lad, yeah?"

"He's practically a man grown by Lanier standards. My father put me to the silver lesson the second I could stand." Hard words, indeed, as were most that fled the tongue of Whit Lanier. "At least, he's found half a normal childhood. But such comforts are not long for future kings. I've seen the way he bullies Marsea, and the ugly stares he aims at Remy when Larissa has taken to his favor. Desmond needs to be taught expectations before he becomes too unruly. He needs to be taught duty and honor and the way of the knight. Especially with the turn of things here lately. He will need the ability to defend himself from this world and likely sooner rather than later. Properly, I mean. And I can think of no man better suited to the task than Xavien Ledgermaine, the finest swordsman this side of The Scar."

The latch clicked, and the boy felt his heart jump into his throat. A sliver of light expanded across the wall of books from the doorway, chasing after him, and blinding him as it caught him up.

"Desmond?" the misshapen figure said from behind the glow of lantern light.

AIDEN OPENED his eyes and found the world horribly skewed and cloudy, as though he were gazing through a frost-covered window on a cold wintry morn and the same old daily questions followed, right on schedule.

Where am I? How long was I out for? Are my trousers still on?

His head twitched to the side, and he found himself on the floor in the distance next to the half-dusted phaedrylax, trousers still on, but...

Bugger all.

He was back outside his body again. Though this time it passed differently than the dead man's rift aboard Blackhall's Banshee. For this time, he still felt corporeal.

What fresh hell?

And the realization left him in the form of a high-pitched croak, as a third something or other regarding familiars crashed over him. A particular something he'd dismissed as total bollocks back when. And yet here it was twisting the knife anew, another tally on the list of things he'd gotten completely and utterly wrong about the gift's capacities.

But the gods only knew, Aiden, there's halfwits, quarterwits, fuckwits, and then there's you.

Offhand, he couldn't quite evoke the actual name for the spell, but he recalled hearing on several occasions from a number of reputable sources that masters of a certain aptitude had the ability to transport their consciousness into the body of their familiar. Now how his primitive ass had managed to see it through was anybody's guess...

Just a wee bit more tomfuckery for the young master then. I mean, how much more shit am I going to have to eat today?

His little bird chest puffed out as he awkwardly walked across the altar to its end and glanced down at the stones below.

Bloody hells, this seems quite high, doesn't it?

He cocked his head to the side and told a wing to move. To his surprise, it did. Ever so slightly.

Simple as walking, right?

Next, he urged both wings to span out wide and they answered his command.

How about that?

Slowly, he motioned each wing up and down like he thought it might be to flap them and they obeyed. Then he thought about what he must look like, cawing and flapping his wings about like a nutter that took a hard one to the back of the crown.

Fucking ridiculous, mate.

He managed a clumsy sort of hop-walk toward the center of the altar stone and aimed himself over toward his human body.

Easy does it.

Tam flashed through his little bird brain. All smiles and songs.

Then Stella. Smart and confident, with the breeze at her beck and whim.

And Val. Great, big golden orbs behind dark, shining curls.

You've got this, Aiden.

His claws dug in as he pushed toward the altar's edge, one hop-step at a time, fluttering his wings furiously. *You're definitely doing this.* And he found flight.

Sweet, glorious, short-lived flight, as he came to an ungainly landing midway between the altar and his withered human body. He'd made it down in one piece, though, and rasped out an ugly victory cry at the effort.

He halted before his side-turned face, catching a deathly wind through dried, crusty lips.

Haven't pissed off yet, so there's a thing.

On the other hand, I look like a fucking corpse and I'm trapped inside a creature that eats dead things, so there's obviously room for improvement.

A low rumbling sound echoed out from the hole in the floor, deep as the wail of a mountain, sending a keen shiver through his feathers.

And then there's whatever the fuck that is. Shifting back to his unconscious body, he began pecking himself on the forehead. *Hey, asshole, wake up.*

Nothing.

No. That would have been too easy, wouldn't it? He snapped Lenore's beak down against one of his fingers until he tasted fresh blood, but no reaction followed. *Lenore, if you're in here, you might want to learn me up on how to trade back bodies before I fuck up royal and kill us both.*

He spread out his wings again and began to beat at the air.

At least show me how to fly this damned thing.

Just then he felt a prickling sensation on one of Lenore's wings and noticed the familiar brand. It burned twice as bright on the inside of his pale white human arm.

But, of course. A thought occurred to him. *The gift. It's just like calling your gift into play. Like a song. Just chase after it like you always have.*

He followed the cacophony of sirens and crows in his head as he hop-walked forward and worked his wings, and before he could even think it into existence, he was sailing amongst the bookshelf tops as though they were the shops and homes of some great sprawling kingdom.

Cheers, Lenore.

The sensation of flying was beyond exhilarating, almost godly, lording over all.

Controlled falling.

Soaring above the sea of motionless carnage.

The illusion of safety.

Mayhaps he could find help in the halls. Possibly a surviving battle-magus that could call him back into his body and see to his myriad assortment of wounds.

Gods' bones, Aiden. Flying about for two seconds and it's made of you a rotten hopeful simp, hasn't it? You've seen it out there. Who do you reckon could survive against such a beast and legion?

And the tale was a grisly riot once he'd abandoned the library's walks. Even with vision in black and white, the bloodbath below could not be denied.

The nether had spread everywhere, like a spill of tar, coating the entire corridor, from floor to wall to ceiling hanging down in oozing vines, with thousands of tiny dark eyes blinking and shifting about the viscous fleshy mass, and little creatures he knew to be named sprites skittering about the spaces between. In the distance, malformed blighters, who once appeared human, chased and attacked their former kin, adding to their mad host.

Such horror.

Such loss.

Such agony.

Powerless to aid them, Aiden dodged and weaved Lenore through a jungle of slick, snotty nether tentacles and angry spritelings until he heard a fresh clamor of shouting voices and shrieking wand magic resounding from some rest nearby.

Magus.

The archivist cut hard at the next corner and found the party hacking, slashing, and burning through a pack of ghouls.

A glimmer of hope.

Four in total.

The spellslinger he recognized from the crowd in Drezhal's throne hall. Likely a twat, though a twat surprisingly adept with a wand.

The second, wielding dragon's flame, looked a dandy smasher and as far as warring went, pranced about like a greenhorn barely off his mum's tit.

And the third was a little girl. A little girl much too young to be dealing in such violence, her skill as sharp as the blade she wielded as she sliced a path beside the...

Fuck's sake.

It couldn't be.

His little birdie gut caught and twisted as the fourth figure spun about to face him.

Be still my tiny, shriveled crow heart.

It may as well have been him she'd just brained.

Lady Misery, take me now.

The gods know, if Lenore had anything at all in her belly, he would have shit it post haste. He nearly kissed the wall at the sight of her, swerving back straight in spite of catastrophe's calling, her voice ringing in his head as though only seconds had passed since the last time he'd heard it. A version of one of her classics.

Of all the bloodbaths on all the moon.

He blinked through his shitty frost-covered bird vision, unwilling to accept it. But the pain in his soul cared little for his acceptance and would not permit such a denial. It was a pain only her presence could purchase. A ghost half a decade buried, looking anything but the fetching young lass that had plagued his memories every night since her abrupt disappearance.

Rhymona.

She slammed a hatchet into the skull of a screaming woman that was carving a knife across her own face. The blade clattered to the floor as a pair of spriteling parasites crawled out of the woman's body like cockroaches from rotting wood, and Rhymona managed to stomp one to death as the other caught flight and flitted away.

Why are you here?

You shouldn't be here.

Anywhere else, but here.

Rhymona! He tried to call to her, catching awkwardly atop a doused torch hold.

She glared up at him as he cawed and croaked madly, her eyes like a pair of dancing candle flames, and flipped him a middle finger with an added, "fuck off, bitch."

Classy. And certainly, no mistaking it now.

Suddenly she halted in her destruction, staring ahead, transfixed as though she'd just seen a hauntling. Her eyes narrowed, a face she'd given him any number of times, and he followed her gaze, unable to locate what unnerved her so. When he shifted back to her, he found her staring at him again.

"The bird?" she appeared to ask a heap of charred corpses in front of her. "Now you want me to follow the fucking bird?" She held out her hand to him. "Oye, spooky arsehole...come..."

Reckon this is happening then. He flew down to her, catching against the top of her index finger.

She gave him a once over. "You are an unsightly wretch, aren't you?"

It's me, Aiden, the archivist croaked at her.

"Rhymona, what are you doing?" the girl called out from up ahead.

"For some daft reason, my sister wants me to follow you," she said to him. "The fuckwit I am, I'm trusting her on this. So, lead on, yeah. And if you try to fuck us, I promise you, there's a cook-fire waiting for you the second I get the chance."

Aiden flapped his wings away from her, cut a hard turn, and glided forward, halting at the intersection of corridors to glance back at the group.

"We need to follow the white bird," Rhymona said as she caught up to the others and each one stared up at him.

"You're sure?" the dracari host asked.

"I'm not sure of anything anymore, Toff. But Fiandrel hasn't steered us wrong yet."

159

This way! Aiden cawed and the group followed him down the corridor toward the library entrance.

The dracari host burned a path through the nether as the others cut through the advancing blight. Rhymona hurled a bottle into the wall that lit up bright, causing the mass of netherflesh to bellow mightily as a part of it began to deteriorate. The girl smashed a second bottle that opened a sink hole in the floor, and it began sucking at everything within the vicinity. Quickly, Rhymona tossed another bottle behind them, causing an explosion that formed a crystallized wall between them and the sink hole. Only it didn't stop at just a wall.

The wall formed rows of icy thorns across its surface. At first, they came in small as baby teeth, but those teeth swiftly grew into fangs, and then tusks, and then spikes large as stalactites, rows upon rows of them, sprouting around and out of each other, stabbing out in a dozen different directions, severing through the netherflesh and anything else daft enough to remain in its twisting path.

"Run!" Rhymona cried.

Aiden recognized it as some form of frost magic before coasting back inside the library.

"Get inside!" the spellslinger called.

"I'll ward the door," the dracari host answered.

Aiden watched from atop a bookshelf as the group scurried in and slammed the door behind them. The dracari host was quick at the spell, sealing the doorway with a flickering ward. One Aiden recognized as an anti-magic hold.

"The killer ice wall was one thing," Rhymona managed through labored breaths, "but what the hells was the hole in the floor?"

"I believe the Chandii named it *dryndl mach*," the spellslinger answered.

"Yeah? And what does that mean?"

"Devil's maw."

"Devil's arsehole, more like." Rhymona gazed at the girl. "You don't have any more of those void juice vials sloshing around your pack there, do you?"

The girl rummaged through her pouch a moment before offering a shrug. "No?"

"Interesting," the dracari host said.

"What now?" Rhymona asked.

"The library has been wrapped in another ward. A very old ward, once considered a trick amongst my kind, not dissimilar to a midaran snare ward, designed to keep in whatever enters the ward's boundary. Though, whoever cast it must be too far away now or too weak to sustain it. It's fading fast."

The archivist rasped out at the group from his perch before soaring further into the archive.

"Watch my back," Rhymona said to the girl as they followed.

Aiden landed beside his body and Rhymona approached cautiously, her hatchet aimed out at the mound of half-burned drylax, before she kneeled next to him. "Stay back," she ordered the girl, as she placed a hand on his shoulder. "He's cold as the crypt," she started and her mouth hung as she rolled him over onto his back. "Oh, fuck."

Oh, fuck, is right, love, Aiden thought. *Welcome to the shitshow.*

"Aiden." Her voice came out raw.

"Aiden?" the girl echoed. "That's...is that him? My brother?"

Your brother? And the truth of the girl's identity washed over him. *Julia Harver,* Uncle Rhonyn's voice returned from the dungeon cellars.

"Toff," Rhymona howled. "Remy, for fuck's sake, get over here. Now!"

Remy?

Aiden twitched his attention to the dracari host, taking him in proper for the first time. The resemblance couldn't be more obvious, now that he had the name.

Remy! He rasped excitedly.

"Do you know who this is?" Rhymona asked.

"Desmond." Remy halted at the edge of the circle, examining the chamber curiously, before turning back to them. "Is he still breathing?"

"Yes," Rhymona answered. "What are you doing? Why have you stopped?"

Remy glanced down at his feet. "This. I cannot enter. This blood ward here...Thira says it's a dracari hedge ring, it's designed to rot a dragon's essence."

Rhymona muttered a series of colorful curses before landing on, "And how do we bloody break it then?"

"It's been scuffed and scratched at places already, which means it has a master source beyond its own. Do you see where the source was drawn?"

As Rhymona and the girl searched around, Aiden took to the air again, landing atop the altar, and began cawing out desperately.

"Forget it for now," said Remy. "Just bring him out here."

The spellslinger took his ankles as Rhymona hefted him up from under his armpits, and they carried his body outside the ward.

"Check the altar stone, Jules," Remy ordered. "See if there is something that looks like a ward up there."

Julia ran up to the altar, made an odd face at him, and traced a finger against Tetherow's drawing. "There's blood here. I think this is it."

"Good," Remy said, as the others lowered his body to the floor outside the ring. "Scratch your blade against the blood there. If you get enough of it up, it should break the seal."

Aiden flew back to the others as Julia began to scrape away, his familiar brand glowing once more as he drew near and landed next to Rhymona.

"Did you see that?" she asked.

"The crow is his familiar," Remy said, shifting azure eyes upon Lenore. "Desmond? Are you in there?"

Fucking yes, finally, Aiden responded. *Gods dammit, I'm going to need a whole ass tavern to put this shit behind me.*

"He must've varged into the bird once his body became too weak to stay conscious," the spellslinger said.

"This wound on his shoulder," Rhymona said. "It looks like he cauterized it himself."

"And doing so likely saved his life," Remy answered. "But I can sense he has lost a considerable amount of blood. We will need to replenish it before reversing the varg."

Rhymona opened her pouch of blood candles. "Will this do?"

Remy nodded, then glanced down at him, black curls spilling down his sweaty forehead. "What say you, big brother? Ready for a proper reunion then?"

CHAPTER SEVENTEEN

AIDEN REELED ONCE the transition settled, the rift going straight to his brain, spinning a half-moon to catch his balance as he flailed through a flock of passing phantoms, each countenance more repugnant than the last.

Shit.

The ghoulish horde danced around them, more than he had ever seen inside The Spellbind before, disappearing and rematerializing in pairs and patches.

"Desmond," a voice echoed through the eerie hush.

"Remy?" the archivist uttered, fixing his brother with a quizzical stare.

Remy's specter allowed a faint smile. "I can't believe it's really you."

"Where the fuck are we?" Aiden studied a strange silver statue of a woman melded inside a robed figure with a skeletal face, her head and arms sprouting from the creature's spine. "I feel as though I know this place, but I don't recall how."

"The last Spellbind was opened inside Lancastle to banish a lichlord."

The archivist poked a finger against the lichlord statue. "You mean to say *you* did this?"

"In a manner of speaking. Though the deed itself actually belongs to Myrenna." His eyes flickered azure.

Aiden rounded the statue, inspecting the woman's face. *Myrenna.* She appeared as ordinary as they come. Someone's sister, someone's daughter, someone's best friend. "And you..."

"Yvemathira. She saved my life when I took a blade to the belly. Accepting her was the only way."

"A blade to the belly, was it?" Aiden scratched at his own version... Tetherow's doorway. "Seems we Lanier boys have a nasty bit of curse there."

"And given by the same rotten bastard at that."

The name echoed afresh. "Vaustian Harver."

"Put to the hatchet's kiss," the youngest said with a particularly roguish smirk.

"Good riddance," Aiden added, as he took in the spectral crowd. Most displayed discernable faces, which meant their tallies against The Spellbind's collection were still quite fresh. Though many of their faces exposed twisted features, and ghastly scars, with a few missing noticeable chunks. "All of these people."

"They were once her citizens. But Lancastle was overrun by the blight. Hundreds perished, thousands, and now..." A quiet agony filled Remy's voice. "Now, a madness curse has been unleashed amongst her remaining populace. Cast by a man named Yurien Tenbrooks. By the looks of the palace library, I take it you and he crossed paths?"

"Tetherow dueled the wretch before abandoning me."

"I suppose the dragonrot ward makes considerably more sense now."

"We...Tetherow injured him. With a dagger laced in nether residue."

"Is he dead?"

"I cannot say. I too found injury and everything became as a blur. I tried to cauterize the wound and the next thing I knew I was inside Lenore..."

"Lenore?"

"The ugly-ass branch goblin. Tetherow has bound her to me." Aiden shook his head. "Fucking hells, what a pair we are. One saved by a dracari, the other by a diseased bird."

"Father would be fulsome proud," said Remy.

"I daresay, brother, you look nothing like what I'd imagined."

"Nor you. Though I suppose I thought you a pile of bones in a fancy box until a few days ago."

"Not nearly off it considering what Tetherow's done with me."

They shared a brotherly snort.

"He did a number to be sure. I'll tell you quite plainly, Desmond, Thira says she won't be able to restore your appearance, at least not fully. But she can make sure you don't succumb to your wounds."

Aiden nodded. "I reckon beggars can't be choosers." He stared up into the ashfall above. "And the others. Rhymona I recognized. And Julia from Uncle Rhonyn's description."

"You spoke with Uncle?"

"He's being kept in the cellars on charges of treason."

"Treason? The gods know, it's always something, isn't it?"

"Aye, and who is the spellslinger?"

"Victor Goss. He's a former Oathsworn."

"An Oathsworn? End of the world arrives and suddenly they're all coming out of the woodwork, aren't they?"

"Such is the way of things."

"I came here with another myself. A dodgy old clip named Ledgermaine."

"We held company for a time only a few hours past if you can believe it, but we became separated in the marches outside the palace." Remy ran a hand through his hair. "Can I assume Tetherow summoned the blood ward?"

"He did."

"And then he just left you?"

"He thought I was a dead man, and rightfully so. I began to pull back some control after he took a knife to the neck. The wound released me from a curse, some bastard variation of a madman's loop. During his contest with Hrathgon's host, I was able to rip the blade free."

"You tried to kill yourself?"

"I meant to bring that fucker down, whatever it took. Prize well, the wretch is more than some clever sorcerer bending black magic. He's bloody cambion."

Remy remained silent.

"I believe he's returned to the nether and now means to go after my sister Autumn."

A queer expression befell Remy's face at the last part. "How do you mean?"

"I saw into his mind before he severed our connection and I saw Tam."

"You know she is not your sister. Not truly."

"She may not be of my blood, Remy, but she is my family, and I'll be damned before I let that fiendish piece of shit take another loved one from me."

Remy held his glare, frowning.

"What is that look for?" Aiden asked.

"It's a lot to take in. You. The way you are. All of this really. You've had this whole other life and you've lost so much from it. As much as we have. Mayhaps more."

"And what have you lost, brother?"

"More than I care to sift through just now. Though you should know, our mother…"

Aiden lowered his chin as a crawling phantom passed through his ankles. *No.* "Do me a favor, yeah, and never finish that sentence." A series of empty breaths passed before Aiden turned a sidelong glance at his brother. "And what of Marsea?"

"In the wind. She went with The Covenant to save me and Rhymona. Apparently. Though she's quite resourceful these days, I'm told."

"No offense, brother, but it sounds like you require more saving than a dull-witted damsel."

"Says the man in need of saving."

Remy was fastly growing on him. "Rhymona," Aiden changed course. "She's different than what I remember."

"Oh, she's different all right, but hand to heart I wouldn't trust another more to cover my back in a melee. All damsels aside, she's saved my ass a dozen times over in the past quintweek alone."

"I reckon she's not entirely without her charms, is she?"

"She told me about you and her. That you were close once."

"Close? Is that how she named it?" Aiden almost smiled. "More like I was a lost little pup, and she was a kind and patient master."

"Did you love her?"

"Naturally." *What's not to love?* "And still do by a certain manner. But you know what they say about love. Be it honey or poison, in the end, we only accept the love we believe we deserve."

"My sons," a voice called from within the phantom mass.

The brothers Lanier turned in unison.

"Father?" Remy uttered. "Do mine eyes deceive?"

A man in his middle cycles separated from the shifting crowd of Spellbind memories, wearing a hard, rugged face, and orbs that pierced like that of a freshly whetted lance. They were much the same as the last pair of haunters Aiden beheld from his father, all those many cycles ago. The archivist recalled the fury in the King's eyes as Vaustian Harver's sword slipped back out of his slight, half-grown body and he stumbled backward until his legs left him.

Had he blood inside this place, it surely would have frozen over.

"There isn't much time," Whit's ghost answered.

"Marsea always believed you were here watching over us," Remy said.

"Always. As well as I could. She nearly had it puzzled out, your sister. She's awfully clever, you know. If only there had been a little more time."

"What did she nearly have puzzled out?"

"My truth. The truth of a grimoire named *Haunt*."

"*Haunt?*" Aiden said. "As in *the Haunt*, from grandfather...rather Aiden Critchlow's collection?"

"It is here in the library, locked away inside a hidden chamber."

"The Cupboard," Aiden couldn't stop the words from coming, imagery of a doorway within a stack of books returning to him as though from a long since discarded dream.

"Yes, the one you shared with Marsea as children."

"You knew about that?"

"I suspected, and Marsea confirmed as much after a time. Prize well, she's kept it warm company ever since. She's got a hunger for knowledge, that one. A hunger mayhaps more ravenous than was my own." His dark orbs lightened, if only by a shade.

"How are you here, father?" Remy asked. "I thought a soul had to exist within the confines of The Spellbind to manifest. And I thought it had to be attached to a living thing to communicate."

"I am attached to a living thing within The Spellbind, though I am but half a soul."

"So, it's true. You've actually gone and split your soul?" Aiden's eyebrow arched.

"What?" Remy shouted.

"Into *Haunt*, yes. Before the coup."

"Whatever for?" Remy pressed.

"A prophecy from my youth that I'd come to believe Tetherow stitched together. As a result, I studied his works, obsessively, putting his past to a hard investigation. I even had some of my closest infiltrate the ranks of his heathen cult. After a time, I became convinced that he may have split his soul into the pages of an ancient grimoire now known as *The N'ther-N'rycka*. Done so in an effort to achieve some fel form of immortality."

"And your response was to make the same foolish decision?" Remy's eyes burned azure afresh.

"A soul is not what he split," Aiden interjected. "Malthus Tetherow was cambion. The demon half tricked a sorceress into severing its essence from his human soul."

"Demon essence." Whit glared at his eldest. "But, of course."

"That is how it became as the nether," Aiden added. "How the fiend controls it. Once released, it wrote its essence into that of the nether's."

"Making them one and the same," Whit finished. "How did I not see this?"

"How could anyone have guessed at such a madness?" Remy said.

"The grimoires. It is more imperative than ever that you find them and quickly. I believe they are the key to closing the rift Tetherow opened inside The Pale."

"The key how?" Aiden asked.

"Each one possesses an ancient script and boon but requires a specific tongue and gift to decipher it. A chosen reader if you will. And there can only exist one reader per passage. For to attempt to harness multiple boons at once could prove catastrophic."

"Well, isn't that just a peach," the archivist murmured.

"Originally, the grimoires were created in response to the elemental incantations scribed by the Chandii. *Earth, Fire, Water,* and *Wind. Dawn, Noon, Dusk,* and *Haunt* followed. Fashioned by the first midaran giftborn magi. Though these were but burn names to conceal their true nature. These eldritch bindings born of body and soul magic. For their true names, once upon a newfangled age, were *Blood, Flesh, Shadow,* and *Spirit.*"

"How do you know this?" Aiden quibbled. "Stella said grandfather made them."

"Tosh! Critchlow was merely their keeper." Whit shifted into the wind suddenly and appeared to listen for something as the ashfall began to swirl about them, coming down thick as lamb's wool. "My hour is almost come," he declared. "Tell me, do you know where any of the other grimoires may be?"

"Marsea may have *Dusk*," Remy said. "She took it with her."

"And knowing Tam, she likely has *Noon* tucked away some place safe, though I fear Tetherow has plans to go after her next."

"Where is *Dawn*?" Whitman set him with an iron glower. "Stella was meant to bind you specifically to the blood book when she brought you back."

"Tetherow passed it on to Pion Harver during my possession," said the archivist.

"Pion." Remy spit the word out like an obscenity.

"Wait, you knew about my resurrection?"

"Of course, I knew, son. Who do you think made the bloody order to bring you back? But that is a discussion for another time. Where are you both now? Are you together?"

"We're in Courowne."

"Grand. There's a nest on the edge of town with a tether to an old tanner shop in Lancastle."

"I'm familiar," Remy said.

"Once you make The Cupboard, there is a tether within the ceiling to Perciya University. The ward requires a watchword. *Sylvoth'yka*. From there you will need to find Autumn and *Noon*. Assuming Marsea has *Dusk*, that will leave just Pion and *Dawn* to contend with."

"Not to be a wet blanket and all, but easier said than done," Remy said. "When I left Lancastle…"

"The curse has been contained to the upper halls and nearly quelled save for a rogue patch holed up in my old solar."

"It has?" Remy's brow wrinkled. "How?"

"The Royalguard. Thanks to your warning and a few capable sorcerers. The boys in blue can be quite resilient when the time calls for it." Whit Lanier's ghost began to fade at the words.

"Father, what's happening?"

"It would seem my time here is up for now. *Haunt* is pulling me back to the page. I can only break my bind from it in short bursts. Another day within and I may be able—"

The King was cutoff midsentence, gone as though snapped from existence, leaving the brothers Lanier once more to the silent gray.

"Well, that just happened," Remy muttered.

Stella's words came round for a stir, a whisper on the wind. Some bit of spurring she used to pass along during his early university days when things became too hard and overwhelming. *Sometimes, son, a thing comes along and the only way out is through.*

"Reckon we should be getting on with it then," Aiden said.

"Sure you're ready?"

"Not even a little bit."

"Same."

"Remy," Aiden turned to the younger brother. "In case this goes sideways and I come back a potato, I'm glad we met."

"Same." A sphere of crackling Eldn flame flickered to life inside Remy's palm.

"Fuck me, that is just top-shelf there." A mad smile fixed upon the archivist's lips. "And on that note, little brother, stack the pyres and light the fires, we've got some dirty old books to find."

CHAPTER EIGHTEEN

RHYMONA CURIE STOOD motionless upon the top step leading down from the hole in the floor, teeth digging for blood inside her bottom lip, inspecting Val's mae'chii, stewing in every dark thought she'd ever conjured over the youngest Alyfain daughter.

She kept reimagining the big-eyed, grotesque version of Val from her meld with the Chandii blood candle. The gore-dripping smile, the unnatural movements, the petrifying stare. Why would her gift show her such a scene? Was that how she truly viewed her most tender companion? As some sort of demon out to bring her harm?

The gods know, you're a bloody fuckwit, Morgan. But you've really outdone yourself this time, haven't you? All of those trust issues and walls. All of your same old bullshit. You know good and well that girl loved you. She would have bought every star in the sky just to have your hand. Not that you ever deserved such a thing. It's not her fault you can't manage your fevered mind for your tiny ailing heart.

The scrape of a blade across stone echoed from some rest below, and she inhaled.

Goss.

The battle-magus had entered the void roughly a quarter-hour past to investigate the strange resonating noises within whilst she and Julia stayed behind to watch over the Lanier brothers. The stone scratching was Goss's signal to let her know he was still in one piece. Though by the length of the echo, he couldn't have covered a whole lot of ground yet.

She turned sidelong to Julia who remained by her brothers on the other side of the altar and exhaled, unable to determine if the smell from below arose from something living or dead. Though, with the count of things lately, it could be coming from something both living and dead.

"How you keeping?" Rhymona asked.

The girl shrugged. "I'm starting to get worried again."

"Thira is with them," Rhymona said as she approached, retrieving Fucker from atop the altar. "She will see them back in standing order, I have no doubts."

"He almost looks like one of them," Julia said. "One of the blighted."

Rhymona glowered at the gaunt husk of her former friend and lover, roaming his body end to end. The girl wasn't wrong. Tetherow had certainly done a number on him, the massive pulls of black magic having bled him entirely of his youth and bonny features.

And a famous line from *The Warlock's Heir* came to call: *Ofttimes, and more oft than not, I've found, the mask is prettier than the thing which lies beneath.*

"Tell me about him," Julia said, "about Desmond. What is he like?"

"Desmond is..." *Broken, damaged, cursed.* "...complicated. He's fiercely loyal to those he loves and stubborn as they come. Just like Marsea and Remy." *When he isn't burning out his brain puffing shufa and drowning his sorrows in the quickest glass of rotgut to hand.* Rhymona forced a lukewarm smile. "Only he's twice as reckless about it. And more than a little mad."

The words felt handsome enough.

"Mad like you?" Julia said with a darling smirk.

"Not quite so bad off, you cheeky little witling. At least not from what I remember."

Though there was no telling what measure of trauma Tetherow had caused him since they'd last shared a laugh.

Julia waved a hand in front of the crow beside him. It hadn't moved since Remy opened the rift to The Spellbind and pulled Aiden through. Hells, it hadn't even blinked since its master's parting, as though some barmy back-alley taxidermist took a frightful turn with it.

"I can't believe he was trapped inside a bird," Julia said. "How perfectly odd."

How perfectly Aiden, Rhymona thought. She crouched next to the girl, laying her weapons down between them as she studied the eldest Lanier sibling a smidgen closer. *What did you do with Val, Aiden? Where is she? And why do you have her mae'chii?*

The abandoned mae'chii was mayhaps the most disturbing sign yet of Val's fate. It was all wrong her being without it.

Once bestowed, an ashaeydir's ka'rym chii was their life. It represented their quality and repute within the High Houses and was considered a great humiliation and dishonor if one were to lose their blade or have it broken outside of proper melee. In Morgan's case, she sold her set to an apothecary outside a township named Temporary for a skin of backwater swill, a sinner's song, and a bag of binders. In fairness, the binders lasted her the road from Temporary to Nightsbridge, so the deal wasn't a total wash, but there was no denying the fact that a fleecing had taken place that evening. She only hoped the drunk old bastard was wise enough to fetch a pretty purse for the swindle. The gods know, his potbellied arse wasn't going to be putting the blades to any worthwhile use anytime soon.

That said, Valestriel wasn't a wasteful rebel like Rhymona. She had a reverence for the old ways and felt an obligation to her House, a problem Rhymona never had much stake in considering her glaring lack of one. And despite all of Val's misgivings and issues with her kinfolk and their ruthless ideologies, she never would have surrendered her blade. Not without good reason. Not unless...

No.

The thought kept creeping back in. The thought she wouldn't finish. Not until she had the words. And not until she saw a body.

She glanced at the brand carved into Aiden's forearm then trailed down the mangled limb to the missing chunk of flesh in the center of his palm. A telltale sign of a hemomancer, there. Unmistakable, really. The wrong sorts of circles named it a warlock's well, its purpose to allow the caster to both release and absorb large amounts of blood at once.

Suddenly his fingers began to twitch and an azure glow erupted between the brothers, expanding and kindling the dimly lit space about them.

"Back away," Rhymona bade Julia.

Aiden's eyes burst open like two exposed eggshells and a pair of intense white rings ignited around impossibly dark pupils. A beastly cry followed as he started to convulse and foam at the mouth.

"The stars save me," Julia uttered.

"Give him space," Rhymona said. "The Eldn fire will cleanse any nether that remains and bring him back round."

At least she hoped.

Aiden jerked away from Remy, turning his shoulder from them as he gasped back to life and curled into a ball, groaning, coughing, hacking, until the sound of bile forcing its way out of him took over.

Rhymona rose to her feet and found a puddle of muddy sick seeping across the floor. She winced at the memory of her own difficulties purging the nether back in the Lancastle courtyards, the ghost of the horrid cramping sensation running through her.

"Desmond?" Remy's voice called.

Aiden spit and moaned as he clutched his stomach. "Not a potato." His voice came out like raw silk. "Though I wonder if I wouldn't be better off as one."

At his rasp, Rhymona felt a spasm of fury contort her features. *Where the fuck is Val?* She wanted to scream at him, the scene playing out in her head. *Where is she? And why the hells do you have her mae'chii?*

He rolled onto his backside and their eyes collided.

"Rhymona," he mumbled, blinking sheepishly like every other shame-faced fuckwit that had ever fucked her over.

And there it was.

The last string holding her heart together snapped at its center and an eye began to twitch.

She knew that face all too well. Hells, she was the queen of that face on her brightest days.

Fuck you, Aiden.

The world became askew and her chest burned as the truth came shredding through her.

Hatred followed, ragged and messy.

Then rage.

You stupid cunt bastard.

Fuck you. Fuck you. Fuck you.

She couldn't tell if the words were actually leaving her mouth so she kept after them, unable to bite them back a second longer despite his paltry state.

"Fuck you, Aiden!"

Oh, but she heard the bitch that time. And so, too, did the others.

"Rhymona?" Remy said as he met her stand, reaching out toward her.

"Piss off, Remy!" She flinched away, turning a cold shoulder on him.

"What the hells is happening?" he argued.

"I won't accept it."

"Rhymona, what's wrong?" Julia uttered.

She turned to Julia as the first tear broke, blistering down her cheek. The girl had slain dozens in the past day, beheld more atrocities and violence than most folks see inside entire lifetimes, and this was the most horrified Rhymona had ever seen her.

Don't care.

She bent down for Val's mae'chii, ripping the hilt from its scabbard. "Where the fuck is she, Aiden?" Murder gleamed in her menacing eyes, running wet and wrathful down her cheeks.

"I'm sorry," Aiden mustered.

"I don't want to hear that shit," Rhymona shouted, extending the mae'chii between them. "That's not an answer."

Aiden held up a bloodied hand in defense. "She's no longer with us."

The hells she's not.

"Where's her body then?" Channeling Thira into Remy was the closest she'd ever come to a proper gravedance, but for Valestriel she'd void herself trying if she had to.

"I know what you're thinking," Aiden said as he eased himself up into a sitting position.

"You have no idea what I'm thinking, you vile little knob-fucker."

"It wouldn't do you any good even if I could take you to her."

Remy said something to Julia and they faded into the background. Or so Rhymona thought they did.

"Fuck you, yeah," Rhymona snarled. "I'll be the judge of what's good for me."

"It cut her into pieces, all right. Every limb off her. And it hollowed out her eyes and mouth for good measure. She can't be brought back, Rhymona. Not as she was. Tetherow made sure of it."

"Fuuuuck!" Rhymona growled into the far archive reaches, the gush of tears weighing down her lashes, blurring her vision—Aiden's words sowing their poison song.

In pieces?

Every limb off her?

Eyes hollowed?

Mouth...

The image from her Chandii candle trip sank its fangs in again.

Val...

She glared up from between Rhymona's legs, dark fluids running down from the edge of her mouth, chased by a grotesque smile.

This can't be real.

She can't be gone.

I won't accept it.

Try as she might, she couldn't shake the ghastly vision loose from her mind.

Not like this.

Not with how it ended.

"Tetherow did it to punish me," Aiden's dumbarse voice again. "And because it hates ashaeydir. And it did it specifically to Val because it feared our bond and what she was capable of."

"What did you just say about ashaeydir?" She shifted back toward him, her eyes unwilling to take him in fully.

"I know the truth, Rhymona. Your truth. Val told me everything." He groaned to his feet, nursing his midsection as though his guts would spill out at any moment. "It would seem I am not the only one masquerading about the hollows under a false name. Shall I name you Morgandrel henceforth?"

"Do so and I'll have that tongue from your throat."

"You must know I cared for her too. She quite reminded me of you, all told. Of us."

"You didn't know fuck all about her, Aiden, I can promise you that much. You only knew what she allowed you to know." *Such was the way of the ashaeydir. Always give the truth, but never give it all.*

"Mayhaps I didn't then, I won't argue it. But I know love and I know a genuine heart when I meet one, and Val harbored both."

"You keep her name out your poxy mouth, yeah." Words of the sharpest steel.

"I also know you, Rhymona. Despite our time apart. And gods, do I know you."

"Oh, come off it with this pass-the-penny bullshit. Comes to me, you don't know your arse from a fucking hole in the ground."

"I would have died to save her."

"Then why the fuck didn't you?"

"Oh, fuck you, Rhymona, Morgandrel, whatever-the-fuck your name is. As though you're innocent in all of this. Val told me about your little trysts. About how you abandoned her and sent her off tatter-hearted and wanting."

Yeah? And die cross about it, fucker.

Rhymona stared him straight in his glowing white orbs as she stepped into his ugly, fucked-up, monstrous face, close enough to kiss, Val's mae'chii raised against his blood-spattered throat, quick as silver. "You don't know the half of it." She hated the words. Dullard's words, they were. And yet, how many times had she spoken them before? How many more had she heard them given?

"Don't I?" Aiden held her glower, iron-hard, breath reeking of blood and vomit and tooth rot, the very epitome of rags and ruin. "You thought you were protecting her, didn't you? Just like you thought with me when you left Kanton."

She fixated on his stupid chapped lips, her eyes flitting back to the massive gap beside his front teeth every time he spoke.

"You tried to kill me." Her voice rose, black stare in tow.

"That was Tetherow and you know it." Aiden veered away from her, the blade grazing pale flesh. "Fucking hells. You know it better than anyone."

"Trust, I'm well aware of fuckhead's involvement."

"Then what the hells are you pissed at me about?"

"I'm pissed because you're still alive and she's not..."

"So am I."

"You don't get to say that."

"Go ahead, Rhymona, hate me if you must, but I promise you, you cannot hate me anymore than I already hate myself."

"Oh, fuck off with the woe is me gobshite."

"I will not fuck off. I was just as much a victim in this, whether you wish to hear it or not. Tetherow killed Val because it's a racist piece of shit and saw her as a threat. It used me and the trust I'd formed with her. Then it made her a sacrifice. How else do you think it completed the gods damned possession ritual? Stella was another victim, likely its first, and I believe there were a few students at university it went after in between."

Rhymona paced down the nearest aisle, shaking all over, cheeks glistening with useless tears. She knew of such a ritual from *The N'therN'rycka's* passages. The Sacrifice of Five Souls, it was named. Designed to allow nether beasts to cross planes and claim a host body.

"If you'd stayed," his voice followed, "mayhaps we could have stopped it before all this shit began."

You're such a fucking foolhard, Aiden. Why the fuck is that what you would say to me right now?

Rhymona's grip tightened on the mae'chii and she imagined rushing back at him with it, stabbing the blade into a ghostly eye and driving it through the back of his thick, idiotic skull. She wondered how Remy and Julia might react to such a scene. Having just met their long-lost brother, having brought him all the way back from the brink, only to watch him get immediately brained right in front of them.

"So, this is all on me now, is it?" she said instead, spinning a half-moon back toward him.

"No, Rhymona. That's not at all what I'm saying. But this is not all on me either." He halted at the aisle's end. "'Tis the folly of fools to count all cards in absolutes."

"Do not piss my words at me, Aiden Ashborough."

"I accept my fair share of accountability, Rhymona, I do. But we're in this together, you and I, one way or another. And in this, we are both innocent and both responsible." The albino abomination landed on his shoulder at the words.

"You sound like a fucking twat right now," she spat. "I don't owe you shit."

"I never said you did."

"You didn't have to. I can feel it rolling off of you like some bastard winter sickness. You Lanier toffs are all the same. The astounding level of delusion. The unearned privilege. The absurd expectations." She was acting the dramatic prat and she knew it, but she couldn't stop it from coming, not now, no more than she could prevent the bloody sun from setting.

"What can I say?" He dared to enter *her* aisle. "What can I do?"

"You can stop where you stand or there will be one less of you." She leveled the mae'chii between them to keep him honest.

"I hate this," he said. "I hate that I've hurt you. And I hate what's happened to Val. I tried to kill the wretch. First chance I got." He pointed to his shoulder. "The fuck do you think this is?"

Her frown deepened.

"But Tetherow's a clever bastard. And a powerful one at that. I'm only the latest pawn in a centuries-long succession. Just another puppet to be used and discarded for the next. That is what it does, Rhymona. It finds a host that will serve for a time, preferably one well-endowed with the gift, uses them up for all they're worth, then moves on. And if our last conversation gave any indication, Tam is next on his list."

"Tam?" An eyebrow arched. "Why the fuck would it go after Tam? She's what? Fifteen? Still a child."

"I don't know exactly. But Tetherow doesn't give a toss about trivial shit like age. The part that found me was all demon essence, and I was younger than Tam when it attached itself to me. To Tetherow, we are all of us, nothing more than instruments to dispense its bidding. As for Tam, it mentioned something about spirits like theirs defying ages. And then I saw her. In its thoughts. And it knew her. And they knew each other. Somehow." Aiden inched closer, stopping so the sharp edge of Val's mae'chii rested against the side of his neck. "You can kill me, Rhymona, once all of this is over. If that's what you must do. If that's how you must define me. And I won't move to stop you. But after everything that whoreson fuckstain has put me through and taken from my family, I've at least earned the right to try to protect what little I have left of it. To try to protect Tam. To make sure she makes it through all this shit-fuckery in one piece."

Rhymona's jaw tightened. *He almost looks like one of them.* Julia's voice rang in her ears, and her vision fell away from his, the blade following.

"My father appeared to us in The Spellbind," Aiden said.

"Your *father* father?"

"The King one, yes. And in good keeping with how absolutely batshit barking mental all of this has become, he's somehow managed to split his soul into *Haunt.* Which is buried away in the Lancastle archives apparently.

"*Haunt?* As in the Critchlow grimoire?"

"Aye."

"Your father is haunting a grimoire named *Haunt?*"

"Reckon so. And he's bid us return to Lancastle to retrieve it. Along with finding the others."

"I thought Lancastle had fallen."

"Think again."

Good news had become such a rare occurrence of late Rhymona wasn't entirely sure what to do with it or how to react.

"He believes the grimoires hold spells and boons that can aid us in banishing the nether and mayhaps Tetherow."

"Baka." Suddenly Rhymona recalled the grimoire she and Remy fought to keep from the Tarborils. "How could you have been so foolish?" She swiped a pair of books from the nearest shelf. "How did you not put it together?"

"Not exactly the reaction I was expecting."

"I think we had another one. It wasn't *Dawn* or *Noon,* so I didn't recognize it. Though it could have been *Dusk.*" *Bloody hells.* It was the only one of the four she'd never actually beheld.

"Where is it now?"

"With Marsea and the Tarborils."

"Who the fuck are the Tarborils?"

"A couple of scheming Covenant cockroaches who think far too well of themselves. The gods only know what they might be using it for, if indeed it is *Dusk.*"

"Do you know where they went?"

"Likely a hollow named Vinth, or so the story went. But this was days ago. They could be anywhere by now."

"Lovely. Though I can't say I've done us much better. *Dawn* was stolen from me by one of Tetherow's lot."

"Of course, it was."

"We'll get it back. Mark my words."

"And what of *Noon?*"

"As far as I know it's still with Tam. Which means we'll need to get to her before Tetherow does."

"Sounds like a plan."

"Hopefully Remy will agree."

"I'm sure he will, though Thira may take some convincing."

"Thank you, Rhymona."

"Keep your fucking gratitude, yeah. You're not by an inch forgiven in all this."

"Believe me, I know."

"Just so we're clear, you will never be forgiven for Val. No matter what cares and kindness you may provide going forward. To me, you are a walking corpse, yeah. A haunter. A throat awaiting the blade."

"I don't want your forgiveness, Rhymona. Nor will I ever ask for it."

A chill stole over her as an ethereal figure, appeared in the space beyond Aiden's shoulder, in plain view for once, short and slender, gray as thunder.

Fia.

Her eyes were practically peeling out of their sockets as she returned the apparition's draining stare.

"Rhymona?" Aiden asked.

"Don't move," she answered.

"What is it?"

"My sister."

"Your what?"

"Fiandrel. She appears to me. Usually from the corner of my eye. But now I can see her plainly."

Fia began mouthing something to her, but she couldn't hear the words.

"I don't understand," the magus said, taking a step forward.

One of the girl's arms rose, a tiny finger pointing straight at her.

"Rhymona?" Aiden whispered.

"Hold on."

"Rhymona, we have to go."

Her attentions flitted back upon him, noticing his bright white eyes wide as the sins between scoundrels.

"Now."

"Rhymona!" Remy cried out.

Aiden shuffled back a step, turning on a heel, and hurried toward the aisle's end as the scent hit her. The scent that claimed all others since they entered the palace. The scent of sweat and sick and unwashed skin, like a swamp ogre shit itself rotten. And Rhymona realized what Fia was trying to tell her. Her haunter wasn't pointing at her but at the unfurling pitch over her shoulder.

The nether had found a way through the protection ward.

Bookshelves behind her began to creak and splinter, giving way seconds later under the weight of the nether's collapsing heap of flesh, creating a hailstorm of falling tomes.

Rhymona ran for all she was worth, chasing after Aiden's shadow into the common area.

Remy remained by the hole in the floor flailing an arm about. "The nether has broken through the ward." he shouted.

"Is that your learned opinion?" she yelled, bitch still at the bridle.

"There is a lever just inside the passage. It should seal us in." He disappeared belowground.

Brilliant, Toff. Lovely. Let's just have a go down the secret stairway in the floor with all the spooky-ass noises. What bad could possibly happen?

As Rhymona bent low to retrieve Fucker, the floor rumbled to life around her and the marble squares by the altar began to separate and rotate.

"Do we want to be sealed in?" Aiden asked as they reached the stairwell.

"I don't see much of a choice," Remy answered from the gloom, "do you?"

Rhymona risked a glance over her shoulder as a giant black mass of tentacles slithered into the common area, moving fast as a boiling basilisk, the nearest appendage sporting a big nasty maw at its end.

Shit.

She descended into the stairwell as the altar rumbled across the floor toward her.

Already halfway in the ground as it is, what's another foot closer?

A pair of tentacles stole in after her, the thinner one with thorns sweeping just inches over her head, the other with a fanged maw snapping at her coattails. The slab settled into place severing the limbs from its greater mass, and they slapped down with a wet thunk into the stairwell behind her.

For a brief moment, the darkness consumed, and the netherflesh howled aboveground, its wail vibrating through the floor and into her bones. It reminded Rhymona of the great Kraken beast from her father's old stories, and the ear-splitting horror it could produce. Fortunately, the dense layer of stone between them spared her the worst of it.

"Rhymona!" Aiden hollered.

A sphere of Eldn fire kindled the pitch and Remy ascended the stairs toward her, illuminating the area as the severed globs of netherflesh shrieked and squirmed about the uppermost steps like beached eels. As the dragonlight neared, the slimy appendages began weaving around each other, spitting and hissing as they melded together around the whining maw, reforming into something that began to resemble a squid-like creature.

Rhymona backed down another step before locking in place, unable to control her own movements, boiling cold blood rushing to the pounding sensation inside her head, her fingers loosening their grip from Fucker's scruff and the mae'chii's bindings.

Enthralled by the twisting monstrosity before her, her body fought futilely against her mind and her desire to race down the stairwell and as far away from the fiend as possible. She could feel the bastard in her thoughts again, just like when she and Remy were in The Spellbind, rooting around, rummaging...

A flood of otherworldly visions rushed before her eyes in quick succession.

The fetters inside the Ayfain's stables.

Halion clutching her into his chest, a quiver's count of arrows protruding from his backside.

Valestriel, crawling up the length of her naked body, a smile bloody as the butcher's block.

Aiden staring into the dead man's rift after her, face warped and wicked.

Remy. She latched onto their spin through the cellars back in Palatia and Westerly's mad reckoning regarding the nether's reaction to his blood sample.

Fear. She reminded. *It's using your fears.*

Now have a breath, sack up, and remember who the fuck you are.

A blaze of azure wailed out from the space beside her, igniting inside the fel abomination's chanting maw, and Remy appeared at her wing a moment later. The nether beast's bulbous red sacs began to bubble up across its impossible shape, rising from the flaking midnight flesh like oven-baked bread and bursting into puffs of ash and obsidian ichor.

Rhymona turned her face into her shoulder as the pungent odor hit her, and she slowly backed down a few more stairs, released from the creature's incantation.

Nose scrunched, she glanced at Remy, his profile in the flames all that could be seen for eternity.

He nodded at her before staring back into the dark underground abyss behind them.

"What is it?" she asked, her wits returning some measure of order within.

Remy's eyes narrowed as a fresh flame pulsed to life in his palm. "It's Thira. She can sense one of her clutch nearby."

"Down here?"

"Yes."

"Are you suggesting Hrathgon may have actually survived Tetherow's attack?" Aiden asked from the Eldn light's edge.

"That would appear to be the situation."

"Fuck's sake," the older brother groaned. "There was a damned maw the size of a Gallean flytrap growing from his backside."

"Then he should be fairly easy to spot, yeah?" Rhymona grumbled, shoving Fucker into his chest. "Here's my husband," she added as Aiden gripped the handle. "Don't break him. And don't you dare lose him." She pressed on into the fathomless depths. "Or I'll make what Tetherow did to you play like a fucking holiday at Old Nan's house."

CHAPTER NINETEEN

MORNING BROUGHT a certain light to the township of Marrovard kept hidden by the night. Most notably that its townsfolk appeared on edge. At least the few Magwyn and Ledge had crossed since strolling passed the gatehouse. Ledge warned to expect trouble at the gate, especially considering he was carrying goldcoat armaments, but nothing of the sort came.

The lone guard standing sentry on the battlements above the gate stared down at them, puffing at his pipe, but otherwise, let them through without so much as a word. The cluster huddled just inside the gatehouse paid them even less bother.

It would only get stranger from there.

Bluecoats congregated silently on every other street corner, multiplying in number as the pair advanced toward the university grounds. Their eyes dark and haunted, almost empty as though their souls had been plucked clean from their bodies. Their tongues stolen from their mouths just the like.

Magwyn had never beheld anything so eerie and unsettling in all her days. All of these people, all of this life, and not a word spoken amongst them.

"Place looks a shell of what I remember," Ledge muttered.

A few blocks further in, Maggie noticed all of the shops and marketplace stands abandoned or completely shut down. Every window either shuttered or dark inside.

It was around this time that an otherworldly murmur replaced the deathly quiet causing the Empress to clench her teeth.

"Do you hear that?" she asked, wincing.

"I hear nothing, milady."

"It's a humming sound."

NOT A SOUND, Emyria corrected. A VIBRATION.

Gods, its dreadful.

WE NEED TO STOP.

"This way," Magwyn ordered as she cut down an empty side street, a pressure ballooning in her head, beating against the center of her brow, primed to burst.

"What is it?" Ledge asked.

Magwyn hunched over about halfway down the narrow passage, clutching the sudden twisting sickness slithering about her stomach, steadying herself against the side of a building. "This place is spooked," she answered.

"You think?" Ledge said dryly.

"I mean literally. I can actually feel it in my bones. A dark energy similar to what I felt from Desmond and the nether back in the palace. Only instead of it being concentrated, it's everywhere. It's everything Emyria can do to keep us hidden from it."

"Are you saying the nether is already here in Marrovard?"

"I'm not sure, but something fel lies behind her stones. And the closer we move toward the university, the stronger its presence." She eased herself back upright as the pain subsided.

"Maggie, your nose."

The Empress dabbed a finger to her upper lip and pulled back blood. "We need to pick up the pace. I fear this will only get worse."

Figures appeared in the corner of her eye at the far end of the alleyway and she glanced sidelong at them. They were a jumble of bluecoats and townsfolk, and though they didn't appear particularly threatening from an individual perspective, the collection of them certainly yielded a certain measure of menace.

"Something's definitely wrong here," she said as the group started toward them, unhurried in their advance. Magwyn gazed back the other way and found a mass of bluecoats gathered at the entrance, blocking escape.

"It's as though they're being controlled," Ledge said, his hand dropping down to the hilt at his hip as he moved closer to Magwyn. "Like some sort of hive mind."

GRAB A CANDLE. WE MAY NEED IT.

Maggie reached into her pouch, her fingers rolling over each blood candle all the way to the seventh, and she gripped it tight.

"Fair warning," the swordsman said. "If they come at us, I'm cutting them down."

Magwyn pulled the blood candle from the pouch and stared down the dead-eyed bluecoat leading the approaching pack from the rear of the alley. As she opened the ring razor an explosion, loud as cannon fire, erupted from some rest back near the gatehouse.

This drew the mob's attention, and instinctually, the Empress spun back toward the alleyway's entrance where beyond the pack of bluecoats a figure appeared on the rooftop across the street, motioning for them to follow.

"Look there," Maggie said. "On the roof."

"The hells?" Ledge uttered.

"Come on," she bade. "Now's our chance."

She rushed toward the entrance, shoving through the distracted group of Royalguard soldiers out into the main drag, chasing after the cloaked figure racing the rooftops. Maggie marveled at the figure's skill and agility, leaping gaps between buildings she would never dream of attempting, not even in her wildest fantasies, not even with access to dracari magic. They passed more dead-eyed bluecoats and townsfolk during their flight, but the citizens of Marrovard couldn't have been less interested in their fresh company, shuffling mindlessly toward the roar of conflagration near the gatehouse. A few blocks down, the figure disappeared between buildings and reappeared at the alleyway's mouth, waving them over.

Magwyn risked a glance over her shoulder and found Ledge giving chase, but not a soul of the bluecoats or townsfolk pursued. Instead, they hobbled and lumbered about like glassy-eyed ghouls in the opposite direction.

As Magwyn turned the corner, she found the figure entering a doorway into one of the buildings and followed.

"This could be a trap," Maggie served Emyria's warning, feeling her dracari companion swiftly revitalized. She turned up her palm and realized that at some point during their mad dash her nails punctured the skin and she'd absorbed the blood candle.

For crying out loud, Maggie.

Down to six.

"We're in it now, one way or the other," Ledge said as he lifted the shield from his back. "Stay behind me." He positioned himself in front of the door, sword poised at the edge of his iron wall.

The Empress gripped the door handle and pulled it open once Ledge gave the nod.

The room was dark save for the patch of light from the doorway.

"Put up your iron, fool," a voice sang from the pitch. "If I wanted you dead, I'd have burned the alley instead of the gatehouse."

"Name yourself," Ledge answered.

"Some bit of gratitude there."

"We are appreciative," Magwyn said. "But surely you can understand our mistrust."

"Solindiel," the figure appeared before them as though from thin air, the shadows bending away from her, dark curls framing chalk-white skin. "You can call me Solindiel."

"Is that ka'rym chii steel you're handling there?" Ledge asked.

"Let's cut the shit already," Solindiel said, easing off her stance. "I'm fucking ashaeydir, yeah. That's why I have them. And for the time being I'm on your side. So, close the fucking door and stay your blade before I have your arm off its elbow."

Magwyn placed a hand on Ledgermaine's shoulder. "Steady on."

"Well, aren't you a peach," the swordsman muttered.

"Fuck your pleasantries, old man."

"Wait a tick. I know you, don't I?" Ledge said. "How do I know you?"

"You don't."

"The Stranger take me, but you're quite similar, aren't you?"

Solindiel's attentions flicked from Ledge to Magwyn. "The fuck is this geezer on about? He senile or something?"

"You said you are ashaeydir, yeah?" he asked. "Any chance you know a Valestriel Alyfain?"

Solindiel's eyes hardened, her grip constricting about her hilt. "What do you know of her?"

"More than you may wish to hear, I'm afraid."

"Then keep the words, old man. They'll only slow me down."

WHAT A PECULIAR CREATURE.

My thoughts exactly.

SHE IS CLEARLY DISTURBED.

That's putting it rather delicately.

"Slow you down from what?" Magwyn inserted herself between the others.

"From killing the bitch that started all this." Solindiel sheathed her mae'chii, quick as a whip. "Dysenia Deadeyes."

"How do you mean started all this?" Magwyn asked. "What has happened to the people here?"

"They've been bewitched. Obviously."

"Right, obviously."

"She controls them, as does a lichlord the blight."

"Are you saying she's a lich then?"

"I didn't think so. Truly, I don't know what she is. But I know she cannot be allowed to carry on a dayfall longer." Solindiel slunk back into the room's shadows, her voice returning as though from just behind Magwyn's ear. "I followed her here from Courowne. Through a ward in the palace cellars."

"And how came you to be in the cellars?" Magwyn questioned. She was certain the woman was not a prisoner herself.

"I was following another ne'er-do-well through the township. One I thought curiously out of place given our history. A devious little snake named Pion Harver."

"Harver?" Ledge grumbled. "Now there's a name."

"You know him?"

"Not closely, but we've crossed paths. I know enough that to name him a snake is a kindness. He and his entire rotten House."

"And who are you two?" Solindiel asked as she inched a curtain back to spy out the window. Her figure bent a strange silhouette inside the screaming pillar of sunlight.

"My name is Xavien Ledgermaine," Ledge started, "and this is—"

"Empress Magwyn Lanier," Maggie finished proudly.

This drew the rogue's attention. "That a fact." They locked eyes. "Helluva time to abandon your kingdom. Though I can't say I'm terribly surprised considering what all I've seen of midaran royals over the cycles."

"And what is that intended to imply?" Maggie asked, growing irritated by the woman's unending impertinence.

"It means for the most of you, your courage keeps well to your shadows."

"We came here after a friend that was being kept in the dungeon. A man named Rhonyn Waldgrave."

"Not sure how wise that was."

"Have you seen him or not?"

"If he was in the cellars, then he was likely taken by the cultists."

"Cultists?"

"Aye, nutcakes loyal to Tetherow from what I've gathered. A fiendish lot to be sure. Had to have been at least a dozen of them down there, Dysenia and Pion included, most brandishing about wands and silver."

Magwyn shared a worried look with Ledge.

"Had a collection of prisoners with them. They forced them through the ward and marched them into the large building with the towers down the cobble. This was a few hours past."

"Was one of them a man with a branded face? Short blonde hair and a beard."

"Could have been. Though I was rather more distracted by the cultists and the not getting caught if you must know. I counted six in total. Mostly old poshers, a couple of them beat up and bloodied. The only one that really stood out was a young girl."

A young girl? Magwyn immediately thought of Marsea, envisioning a youthful Larissa in her place.

"I considered following them inside," Solindiel continued, "but with their numbers and the daylight approaching, I thought it might be best to wait for the darkness to pursue further. In the meantime, I figured I'd get a lay of the township and that's when I came across this lovely little shop of horrors. You'll find in the back there a cupboard full of elixirs and potions and the gods only know what other midaran contrivances. Enough liquid fuckery to save you lot from a horde of braindead wantwits anyway."

It was at that moment Magwyn realized where Solindiel had brought them. Now that her eyes had somewhat adjusted to the dark, she was able to clearly make out the work-tables and all the shelves cluttered with tomes, plants, and queerly shaped jars.

They were inside an apothecary.

Ledge laid his shield down on the shop counter and opened the door just beyond, disappearing inside. "Shitfire, Maggie, she's not lying." He reappeared. "It's a bloody alchemist's treasure trove in here."

"Baka. Keep your voice down," Solindiel bade through a whispered yell. "I can hear someone approaching."

Magwyn joined the rogue by the window, listening closely.

"Every damn time something goes sideways, it's Calem, do this, Calem, do that," the voice quibbled as it neared.

"As I recall, you were the one that wanted in so desperately," a second female voice returned. "These are the dues to follow in Mummy's footsteps."

They both sounded quite young, their accents borne of the Southlands upper crust.

"I looked after that insufferable ingrate for cycles, listened to him whine about how horrible his life was, day in, day out, watched him drink himself black nightfall after nightfall. *Those* were the bloody dues."

Magwyn glanced back at Ledge as he snuck out the door back into the alleyway, steel at the ready.

"At least you didn't have to bed him," the girl said. "You saw what a slob he became. Could you imagine such a wretch crawling atop you every other evening?"

Solindiel took to the swordsman's shadow, and Magwyn quickly followed. The Empress held at the doorway and watched in awe as Solindiel caught a foot on the door handle, her second atop the door, and then climbed onto the roof. Not a sound was made in all that action.

Ledge halted flat against the wall at the alleyway's mouth.

"Wouldn't go that way if I was you," Solindiel's voice rose from the front of the shop.

"What the hells," the one named Calem responded.

Ledge cut around the corner and Magwyn tailed him out into the avenue. Between them and Solindiel were a striking young man and woman in dark robes wielding thin obsidian wands. Such was the weaponry of the dark-dabbling nobility.

The girl stood closest. As she made to raise her wand, Ledge caught her from behind and raised the edge of his blade against her throat. "I wouldn't do that either."

Calem made the mistake of turning around toward Ledge's voice, giving Solindiel the time needed to split the space between them and sink her sy'chii into his lower back. Magwyn had never beheld a creature move so swiftly and ruthlessly. Calem sank to his knees in crying agony and Solindiel struck him over the head with the butt of her dagger to silence his suffering.

A SONG later they had the pair bound with rope from the shop's supply cupboard. Calem was still unconscious, and Emyria was working on mending the blade wound so it wouldn't kill him.

Magwyn listened to the conversation across the room between the others and the girl in the chair. She'd called herself Caitlyn, but was otherwise quite rude and uncooperative, claiming she was the daughter of two of the other members of the cult, which was apparently named Black Lantern, and when she and Calem didn't return, they would send a search party out for them.

Solindiel hovered over the girl with arms crossed. "Listen to me, cunt, you keep up the sass, I'll have you in so many pieces your folks won't even know what they're looking at to comprehend that they've found you."

"We're looking for a friend," Ledge said. "That's all. We just need to know if your people took him or not. He was a prisoner in the dungeon in Courowne. What could your people possibly want with him?"

The girl giggled with marked defiance.

"I warned you, bitch." Solindiel had her sy'chii at the girl's cheek and ran an angry red line across it.

Caitlyn made to scream, but Solindiel put a sharp end to that with a fist to the gut. The girl labored for breath as she hung forward against the ropes bound around the chair, blood dripping from her freshly mutilated face.

"You make that fucking sound again and it'll be your ears, nose, and tongue that follow. You think I give a toss about you or who your fucking parents are?" Solindiel touched the space behind her ear, unveiling her true form as the girl gazed up at her.

Instantly Caitlyn's glower melted to that of sheer terror.

"All right," Ledge grumbled. "I think you've made your point."

The Empress stared at Solindiel, spellbound. Her darkened curls, lilac skin, and those big golden eyes. It was the first ashaeydir she'd ever truly beheld and all the hearthfire haunters from back when danced through her head at the sight, of how frightening they were said to have appeared, and how they had taloned fingers and serrated teeth, and how they wore about their victim's skins like costumes at the masquerade. She remembered how Whit used to frighten her so when they were little. Chasing her about the kingdom halls behind masks and furs, pretending to peel his face off.

Of course, as she grew older, she understood the rumors about the ashaeydir to be greatly embellished, but never in a thousand cycles did she ever think she would actually meet one and, what's more, that she would find it quite fetching.

I HAVE DONE ALL I CAN DO FOR HIM, Emyria crept into her thoughts like a cleared throat. HE SHOULD COME AROUND SHORTLY.

Thanks, Em.

Magwyn grabbed the roll of linen cloth and joined the others. "Caitlyn, do you know who I am?"

"Dish Wench Sally from the local alehouse?" she murmured.

"I say we end this bitch now," Solindiel hissed. "Mayhaps the boy will be more cooperative."

"Give us a moment," Magwyn said.

Solindiel spat out a string of curses under her breath and wandered back over to the window. Ledge went over to keep an eye on Calem.

"Given your allegiances, do you honestly expect me to believe you do not know who I am?"

"I won't betray my family, Empress. Not for all the coin in the commonwealth."

"...That is brave of you to say..." Emyria surfaced and Magwyn could see the azure reflection in the girl's watery eyes. "...But you do not have to tell me anything for me to get what I need out of you. I only hope to spare you as much pain as possible..."

"Your illusions won't work on me," Caitlyn huffed. "Dracari cannot compel people."

"Who said anything about the dracari?" Magwyn returned. "You think one survives the court of Courowne for decades without learning a little cunning? How do you think I managed beside a monster like Drezhal Dalivant for all of these cycles?"

"I'm no turncloak," Caitlyn rasped.

SHE IS A FIERY ONE. I WILL GRANT HER THAT.

"Gods," Calem groaned. "My back."

At his stirring, Magwyn began to wrap the linen cloth around Caitlyn's mouth until it covered the entire lower half of her face. Mayhaps she could use the girl as leverage.

"Calem," Magwyn called as she approached. "Your friend has been most forthcoming about your allegiances with Black Lantern and their plans for the prisoners."

Calem gazed past her to the girl in the chair with the muffled cries of response.

"Shut it, girl," Solindiel said from over Magwyn's shoulder.

"The ritual began hours ago," Calem answered. "So, whatever she's told you, you're already too late."

"Your masters made a mistake bringing Rhonyn Waldgrave here," Magwyn returned, her eyes flickering azure. This caught the boy's full attention.

"You're Eldnumerian?" he uttered.

"I am and I know about Harver and Dysenia and that she's placed a mind control spell on the students and townsfolk of Marrovard."

"Waldgrave is a corpse," Calem said. "One of the five."

A corpse?

THE BOY COULD BE LYING.

"What are you assholes summoning in there?" Ledge questioned. "Hasn't there been enough death?"

"I guess you'll have to stick around to find out, won't you?" Calem sneered.

"The girl?" Magwyn said. "Marsea Lanier, is she one of the five?"

"Marsea Lanier?" Calem replied.

The Empress breathed a sigh of relief at that. If the boy could be believed, whoever the young girl was that Solindiel saw with the prisoners couldn't be her niece.

"Calem!" A woman's voice called from outside.

"Do not answer." Ledge had his blade at Calem's throat.

"Who is that?" Magwyn asked.

"Fuck you, is who it is," Calem spat.

SOMEONE CLOSE. COULD BE FAMILY.

Ledge took the boy up by the collar of his robe and dragged him off the table, forcing him back up to his feet, and shoving him into the counter. "Well, that's what we'll be bringing you for, you mouthy bastard."

"Eat shit, old man. You tried to interfere before, back in Kanton, but you had no idea we were watching."

Solindiel shoved past Magwyn, ripping her sy'chii from the sheath at the small of her back.

"Calem!" the woman called again. "Caitlyn!"

"You truly believe I don't recognize that shrew's cant out there," Ledge grumbled.

"Mother!" Calem shouted. "They're in—"

Magwyn's eyes went wide as Solindiel's sy'chii sank through the boy's windpipe and he dropped limp to the floor, blood spurting and pooling across the hardwood

"Enough," Solindiel hissed as she turned back to the others. "No more games."

"Solindiel!" Magwyn uttered.

"Fuck that brat, yeah. He was more trouble than he's worth and you know it. That bitch out there is the next obstacle, and then I'm going for Dysenia. With or without you lot."

"Calem," the voice spoke from just outside and a blast of magic followed through the window, screaming past Caitlyn, Magwyn, Ledge, and into the supply cupboard.

Magwyn locked eyes with the sorceress through the glowing hole of cinders in the wall as the tip of her wand conjured a fresh sphere of bright white-gold.

Then came the madness.

An explosion behind her sent Maggie stumbling forward as jars containing potions and elixirs began to break and seep into each other causing strange chemical reactions.

Flames ignited the rear of the building and smoke spread into the room. Magwyn buckled to her knees as the chamber shook from another blast of mixing substances and a second scream of magic coiled through the hole in the wall narrowly missing her.

She heard coughing behind her and found Ledge crouching beneath the cloud of smoke. He staggered toward the doorway and into the alley. Next, she glanced back at the girl, who was turned over on the floor, struggling to wiggle free from her restraints.

Em, give me the strength.

Magwyn crawled over to Caitlyn, gripped the back of the chair, and, pulling from her gift, began to drag her across the room toward the alleyway, grunting with every footstep taken.

They barely beat the flames to the alley and Magwyn collapsed next to the crying girl at the doorstep.

A strange popping noise erupted from inside the apothecary, followed by a sound like glass shattering, and Maggie forced herself up, grabbing the back of the chair. Ledge returned to her side and helped pull the girl across the alley as the flames caught at the doorframe and door, dripping a strange liquid substance that fastly crystallized, cracked, and exploded into tiny shards.

"Milady, are you—"

"I'm fine. Where's Solindiel?"

The answer came with the roll of a severed head at the end of the alleyway.

Gods.

"Done with that shit," the ashaeydir said, slinging blood from her mae'chii.

Magwyn glanced at the head of the sorceress before returning to her feet.

More explosions and shattering sounds from inside the apothecary filled the brief silence.

"We need to be moving on," Solindiel said. "This will only draw more of them."

"Maggie, what are we doing with the girl?" Ledge asked.

"She's dead weight," Solindiel answered. A ring of crimson wreathed her golden pupils. "Kill her and let's be done with it. She won't be the last of them."

"She could still be useful," Magwyn argued. "She's our only lead to—"

"Your lead to what? Your man Waldgrave is a corpse. You heard the girl. Besides the target is Dysenia. We drop her, we end this madness."

"*Tun kir mmr!*" Caitlyn screamed into the bloodstained cloth wrapped around her face.

Ledge lifted the chair back upright and lowered the wrap from the girl's mouth.

"Don't kill me," she rasped. "I will take you to the ritual chamber since you're all so keen for the grave."

"Who was this woman?" Magwyn asked her.

"That was Calem's mother."

Magwyn held the girl's glower.

SHE APPEARS TO BE TELLING THE TRUTH.

"And you're wrong about Dysenia," Caitlyn spat at Solindiel. "Killing her won't end this. She is but a piece."

"A piece of what?" the Empress asked.

"Him. It. Of she who dawns the endless night."

"This rotty bollocks again," Solindiel quibbled. "You fucking midarans and your halfwit superstitions."

"It's not bollocks. I'd figure you of all folk, would believe this. After all, your moon was taken from you by the same creatures all those cycles ago. And I don't mean the bloody nether either."

"You're talking about demons."

"Only they aren't just demons, are they? But fallen gods once tainted by the nether. How else do you think they are able to control it?"

"What is the ritual for?" Ledge asked. "Why all the secrecy?"

"They are bringing it back, of course. Tetherow."

"How do you mean?" the Empress pressed. "Tetherow is in my nephew. I saw it myself. Spoke to it not a day past."

"Tetherow was in your nephew." There was a certain measure of disgust to her words at the mention of Desmond. "But Aiden was only a placeholder for the true host. A host that can raze The Pale."

The young girl prisoner, Magwyn thought. "Who is she?"

"It doesn't matter."

"Answer the question," Solindiel leveled her mae'chii at the girl.

"Autumn Ashborough. She's Autumn Ashborough."

Stella's daughter?

"And why is she special?"

"Allegedly, she houses the Chandiian favor as well as the maker's ichor."

"What the fuck does that mean?" Solindiel snapped.

"It means her blood is as pure as..." Magwyn started.

Mine.

"But that's impossible."

Unless.

Magwyn took the girl up under her chin, gripping her jaw tight, and forced her to meet her eyes. "If she has the maker's ichor inside her, then that would make her a Lanier."

"Yes, it would."

"Are you saying my brother and Stella?"

"Were together." The girl jerked away. "You catch on quick."

Affairs amongst the nobility were always quite common, rampant at times, but still, this particular instance took Magwyn by surprise. Not so much that Whit had an affair, but that he did so with a lowborn farm girl. Though Larissa had been lowborn just as well, she reckoned. And to Stella's credit, she was as fair as they come.

"How do you know this?" Ledge questioned, visibly shaken by the divulgence.

"Ravenholme, of course. Stella and my mother were the best of friends once upon a time."

"Your mother?"

"Lydia Ellsbury," Caitlyn answered matter-of-factly. "It would seem your Lord King was not all the man of honor you loyalists paint him as. A married man and father taking bed with a—"

Magwyn slapped the girl like a woman possessed, blood from Solindiel's blade wound smearing across her stinging hand. "I have no interest in recounting my dead brother's forgotten scandals. Do I make myself clear?"

Caitlyn huffed away from the Empress, muttering curses under her breath.

"Yeah, so you want I should kill her now?" Solindiel said. "Or was there more for her to piss you off about?"

"We're not killing her," Magwyn fumed, her fury trailing from the ashaeydir to a bluecoat standing at the end of the passageway. The soldier was quickly joined by another and a group of townsfolk.

"We've got company," Ledge said.

"They won't hurt you unless their master commands them to," Caitlyn said.

In unison, the bluecoat soldiers reached down to their hilts and drew their swords.

"Which appears to be the case presently," Solindiel said, backing up toward the others, assuming a battle stance.

"Who controls them?" Maggie asked.

"Impossible to say. They all took a section of the town."

The mob advanced with a coordinated step.

"They all who?"

"The others in Ravenholme. The guild members."

"You mean to say these bewitched could all have different masters?"

"I mean to say."

"What are we doing, milady?" Ledge asked. "We fighting or running?"

"We cannot fight them," Magwyn said. "These folks are innocent."

"Now's not the time to play hero," Solindiel argued.

"If we kill their masters, mayhaps it will break their curse and return them to their proper wits," Magwyn returned.

As she moved to untie the girl, the mob's vanguard charged at them.

LEAVE THE GIRL.

Em.

THERE IS NO TIME.

We can't—

"...RUN!..." Emyria howled against Magwyn's will and they all turned the other way, rushing down the alley into the next avenue over.

"Don't leave me here!" Caitlyn's voice begged after them.

Emyria cut a hard right in the direction of the university's looming spires as the girl's cries pierced the dead space behind them.

We've killed her.

NOW IS NOT THE TIME FOR SENTIMENTALITIES, MAGGIE.

Give me back control.

Emyria shoved Magwyn's hand into the pouch as they tore down another serpentine side alley, gripping another blood candle. I CANNOT DO THAT.

Emyria, I mean it.

THIS IS FOR YOUR OWN GOOD. The dracari scratched the ring razor across her palm and absorbed the candle.

Do not shut me out, Em!

Her silence was roaring.

You can't keep me buried forever.

Darkness devoured.

Emyria!

And Tetherow's words sank back in for another haunt.

That's right, run and hide, Emyria, just as you've always done.

CHAPTER TWENTY

BLESS *the maidens for small mercies.*

But there were particular things in life one simply had to experience firsthand to truly understand their quality. Little did Marsea know, a dip in a hot spring would prove to be one of these such experiences. And the stars knew, if ever she were to make it back home, she might never appreciate the bathhouses of court in quite the same manner again.

Though all things honest, a number of factors played into her freshly found love for the splendor of a steaming spring. Namely, that she hadn't actually bathed since leaving Lancastle, at least not properly. To wit, it was the longest she could ever recall going without a decent wash. That, coupled with the fact that she hadn't felt the slimmest measure of warmth in over a day and apparently reeked of smelly dog, it was all she could do to leave the welcoming water once she'd settled in.

She could hardly believe the sight of herself in the spring's reflection. *Giving Other a chase for her coin purse,* she mused as she scrubbed vigorously at her dirt-stained cheeks. And Casilvieri's words crept in for another lesson. *There is a certain appreciation beyond value for even the smallest of delights when it's been worked for.*

As for Edgar, to Marsea's surprise, he'd shown himself a gentleman to the letter. Far more so than she had expected from an obvious backwoods bumpkin. He kept his eyes averted while she disrobed to her skivvies and skins, and afterward, when her stomach came calling, he even offered her an apple from his travel sack. It wasn't exactly crisp, and one side wore a questionably dark squishy spot, but she wolfed the rest of it down all the same.

In the carousel of winter winds, her shortened curls dried to an awful frizz by the time they reached the outskirts of Debynshire. Still, she couldn't keep her fingers from combing through the ungodly mess, her mother in her ear all the while asking why she must always act so ill-mannered and rebellious.

Noble thoughts with noble expectations, she reminded. *Expectations that no longer suit your current predicament. What would a town of hicks care about some lowly drifter's odd appearance anyway?*

"We'll be within sight of the guard towers soon," Edgar said after a time. "You may want to stay your imaginary friend."

Marsea glanced at Broenwjar, stalking the forest about thirty paces off the main road where she and Edgar walked. She could barely make him out in the twilit haze.

You probably know these situations better than I do, B, she spoke to the wolf in their special silent language. *Keep close, but stay out of the township unless you feel something terrible coming.*

Old Boy wasn't particularly pleased with the order, especially given her contradictory pitch about campfolk only a few hours earlier, but he accepted it (or so she hoped), padding off a mite deeper into the woodland shadows.

She wondered if Elsymir often let him follow into town and if so, how others reacted to such a scene. Before all this, had such a ghastly creature shown itself amidst the hamlets of Lancastle, she would have locked herself in her chambers post haste until it was gone. Though Vaustian would have had the beast chased off or put down long before it ever reached the upper courtyards.

Marsea smirked at the memory of how craven she used to be. A big ol' fraidy-cat, as Jules would name it. *A housecat amongst strays,* Casilvieri's churlish words followed. Oh, but how that fraidy-cat felt a thousand, thousand cycles away now.

"What's that grin about?" Edgar asked as the tall wooden walls that surrounded Debynshire came into view.

"Nothing," Marsea answered. "Thinking about someone I used to know."

"Once we're in town, best to keep your eyes down and your head uncovered. The bluecoats have become quite ornery as you might expect, what with the goings-on in the north. The last few hollows we've passed through, haven't exactly been inviting."

"Naturally."

"Couple of fetching smiles like ours though, we should be fine." *Subtle.* "The tavern we're to meet at is on the edge of town anyway, so it'll likely just be the lot at the gate we'll have to sing for."

As they neared the entrance, a burly bluecoat shoved another man forward, and the second guard, half his cohort's size, flung a mud-stained travel pack out into the road beside him.

"This is your last warning, scab," Burly called after him. "We catch you sneaking in again, it'll be your throat at the noose."

The dark-eyed man snatched up his pack, slung it over his shoulder, and stomped past them, cursing under his breath.

"Check out these two simps," Edgar muttered. "This ought to be a cinch."

"Hold there," Half Pint ordered. Up close, Marsea realized he was actually shorter than she was. In his royals, he almost appeared a child wearing his father's uniform.

"What's your business in Debynshire?" Burly asked. Marsea found his deep voice strangely attractive.

"We're with a troupe passing through," Edgar answered, all good ol' boy swagger. "Name of Potions Preferred. Anson Wordsworth can vouch for us. He's likely tossing a mug in The Rittermark right over yonder." Edgar made an attempt to look over Burly's shoulder, pointing about aimlessly. "Just over there, if you feel the need for a check."

The guards shared an unmoved look.

"Yeah, the old man mentioned a scout," Burly said, "but not two."

"Who's this then?" Half Pint added.

Marsea kept her expression blank, though she didn't care at all for how the skeevy lech was leering at her.

"This is my damsel, of course," Edgar said with a wink and a winning smile.

Your what? Red crept upon Marsea's face as she turned to him.

"Your damsel?" Half Pint repeated with a snort.

"Come now, kind sir, don't make it any more awkward than it already is. Times are tough on the old tinker trail these days."

"Yeah, and how much is he paying you, sweetheart?" Burly asked, arms crossed, muscles stretching the stitches of his shirtsleeves.

"I...um..." What remained of her pride died in her throat. *Oh, how the favored have fallen.* Marsea pushed up her glasses to hide her flushed cheeks.

Half Pint's eyes dropped to the scabbard at her hip. "What's with the silver, yeah? Not too many whores I've seen toting about a proper length of steel."

Whore?

It wasn't the word itself, but rather how he used it.

The insult sent a sudden tremor of rage tearing through her and Blind Widow latched on to it, game for a fresh hunt, urging Marsea's hand toward the hilt.

Only a man. A slab of meat.

No.

Rhymona Curie flashed in her mind's eye and Marsea channeled the woman's response.

"First off, asshole, I'm no whore. A girl has needs too, yeah." The words just started spewing out of her. "That being what it is, I see something I like, I take it by the bollocks and I make it mine. As for the silver here," her bad hand clutched the pommel, voice steady. "I know you lot are holed up out here in bumfuck, nowhereshire, but mayhaps you've heard tale of a little problem named the blight?"

"Balls of Agault, the mouth on this one," Half Pint snickered to Burly.

"There you are, Eddie," a voice from behind the guards sliced through the mounting tension. "I was growing worried."

The group turned in unison.

"Poppy," Edgar produced one of the worst fish-eating grins Marsea had ever beheld. "Here she is, love. Told you I'd find her."

A bit of madness played upon Poppy's cherubic face. "Mmhmm, yeah, that's her all right."

"What's this about then?" Burly asked, turning an arched eyebrow back on Edgar. "Is this woman your wife, sir?"

"That's uh, yep, that's her." Edgar said, teeth to his eyes. "That's my lady right there. Light of my life. Stars to my moon."

"Love you, Honey Bear," Poppy cooed.

"Love you too, Sugar Muffin," Edgar answered, his smile somehow expanding.

"Your wife fancies men and women?" Half Pint questioned.

"I fancy what I fancy," Poppy said as she strode up to Marsea and dragged a hand sensually through her hair and across her cheek where she pressed a thumb against her lips. "And this one's quite bonny, wouldn't you say?"

Poppy smelled of cloves, reminding the princess of Vaustian, and an unexpected tingle ran down from Marsea's mouth to her fastly beating heart.

"Bloody hells," Half Pint grumbled to Burly, throwing up a hand. "Some bastards have all the damned luck, don't they?"

"Indeed, they do, sir," Edgar replied. "We good here?"

"Go on then," Half Pint sneered, clearly put out. "Off with ya."

"Take cheer, boys," Edgar said, strutting past. "The night is yet young."

Marsea kept her eyes downcast as they crossed onto the township cobble, masking her anger behind pursed lips as Half Pint kept on about all the country slags whoring about the township these days. She could feel Broenwjar close, watching, ready if needed, and had half a mind to call the beast on the ill-mannered fool for a good scare.

"What a legend," Edgar said to Poppy once they were out of earshot of the guards.

"Yeah, yeah, those two have been stirring up trouble since they took the post," Poppy said. "I figured you'd get the same once you came round, and the others are already in fine form, so I thought to play the good troubadour and keep an eye out for you."

"And hand to heart, I love you for it."

Marsea remained behind the pair, listening. It was obvious Poppy fancied him and Edgar was woefully oblivious to the take.

As though the girl could hear her musings, Poppy spun around toward Marsea, walking backward. "And who are you really?" she asked.

"This is Damsel..." Edgar started.

"Selwyn," Marsea appended, the name erupting out of her. "Selwyn Shawley." A pitiful smile followed.

"That a fact?" Edgar offered her a funny look over his shoulder.

"Selwyn," Poppy shifted back forward, staggering a step so she kept pace next to Marsea. "I like your hair."

"Thanks?" It was not at all what she expected the girl to say.

"How do you two know each other?"

"We met at the hot springs," Edgar said. "She's a sellsword looking for work."

"You're a sellsword?" Poppy questioned.

"I am."

"Oh, I love that." Poppy brushed long dark hair behind an ear, wearing a puckishly inquisitive expression. "It's been a dream of mine to interview a sellsword..."

"Interview?"

"Poppy fancies herself a writer," Edgar said.

"I want to be a scribe for one of the universities," Poppy expounded. "A chronicler, if you will. But they require a collection of work before consideration."

"Suffice it to say, I'm fairly new to the profession," Marsea said, as they passed under a sign reading 'The Rittermark,' and into the tavern.

"That's perfect." Poppy's voice rose slightly above the strumming of lute strings from a stage in the far corner. "That means I'll be the first to have your tale."

Marsea followed Poppy and Edgar to a booth in the back of the tavern where she found Wordsworth and Niall sitting across from each other, a collection of empty mugs between them. Edgar slid in next to Wordsworth and Poppy next to Niall.

"Scooch in," Poppy ordered the thin man that reminded Marsea of Remy, long black curls covering half of his sculpted face. Poppy used her curves to spur him into action.

Marsea sat down in the narrow space left her and immediately found Wordsworth staring at her, a big, bushy eyebrow raised to the heavens.

"Made yourself a new friend, Priscilla?" the old man asked as his attentions drifted from Marsea to Poppy.

"This is Eddie's friend actually," Poppy answered.

"I bring you our sword for the road," Edgar said, holding Marsea's eyes.

"And does this strayling have a name?" Wordsworth lifted his mug up for a swallow, plainly unimpressed.

"Selwyn," Marsea answered.

"And tell it true, lass. You ever even glimpsed a wildkin before?"

"I have," Marsea lied. "More times than I care for, all told." She thought back to her sparing session with Vaustian. The sheer madness of his attack. "Not a folk to be taken lightly." She drew her bad hand up to the table.

A grin stole up Wordsworth's grizzled face, all the way to his forest-colored orbs. "I can assume Edgar has provided all the details then. Not that we couldn't use the extra eyes and ears."

"He has."

"There's no promise of coin in it."

"Mayhaps the company is all I seek."

"It's been my experience, if a thing appears too good to be true, it likely is."

Earn it, earn it, earn it, her mind translated. But the maidens knew, mere seconds in and Old Man Wordsworth had proven himself about as crotchety as Uncle Rho a bottle deep into his bitters.

"Take it or leave it then. Keep your coin, if you must. I only ask for a few scraps to keep me standing. I mean to make Courowne, same as you lot, and then we shall part ways."

"And what's in Courowne?"

"An old friend." *And nothing of your bloody concern.* Marsea thought back to conversations she'd overheard about the kingdom by the sea. "Mayhaps a venture to the southern ports."

"Looking to make a name for yourself, are you?"

"Mayhaps. Or maybe I'm looking to bury one."

Wordsworth let out a ripe old laugh at that and turned up another swill. "Oh, you've certainly outdone yourself with this one, Eddie."

"It gets better," Edgar said, meeting her eyes again.

The princess nodded slow. The topic would have to be broached at some point, after all.

"Selwyn has a companion."

"Does she now?" Wordsworth asked.

"His name is Broenwjar," Marsea added.

"Broenwjar? Sounds Bourysh," the old man said.

"That's because it is," she answered matter-of-factly.

"And where is this Broenwjar?"

"He's outside town," Marsea said. "He's not big on large groups of people. And he's also not, well...human."

"The fuck does that mean?" Niall joined the conversation.

"It means he's a big ass wolf," Edgar answered.

"As in an actual wolf?"

"Yes, and the largest bastard I've ever seen. He obeys Selwyn's commands like a well-trained hunt dog. Could be quite useful, going into wildkin woods, especially if we run into a patch of trouble."

"He is my familiar," Marsea said, pulling every eye at the table.

"Familiar?" Poppy uttered. "Does that make you giftborn?"

"I suppose, in a way. I'm no scholared magus, mind you, but it's true my bond with Broenwjar was forged through the gift. To honor a dying friend. Broenwjar's previous master. We are as one, Old Boy and I. Mind, heart, and soul. As such, he will protect me 'til the end, and through our pact he will protect those I bid him to."

"And who is this fair lass?" a voice slurred from the crowd as the other half of the troubadours approached. The question came from Stringer Paul who sported a dashing pair of pink shufa-shot eyes as he dragged a chair up from the empty table beside them to the end of the booth next to Marsea. "Don't you smell lovely," he said as he collapsed into the chair and rested his head against his arms atop its spine.

"Don't mind Stringer," Poppy whispered, "every word that leaves his mouth is a come-on."

"I heard that," Stringer spoke into the back of the chair. "And you're not wrong."

"Our intrepid lute player thought he could smoke his dealer under the table," Xandria said.

"You should see the other guy," mumbled Stringer.

"I trust Simon is watching the van then?" Wordsworth asked.

"Yes, grandad, and feeding the horses like a good little lad," Xandria answered in a sarcastic cutesy tone that Marsea rather thought fit her appearance far better than her actual voice. The songstress settled on Marsea. "Xandria Pelvenyn," she put on airs as though they were noble-women meeting at the gala.

"Selwyn," the princess murmured. The name flowed with such an ease she almost believed it herself.

"My, my, Selwyn, that's a mighty big sword you have there."

"And it's a good thing too," Poppy said. "She's our blade for the road south."

"Is that so?" Xandria murmured.

Marsea couldn't tell if the girl was being sincere or teasing her. Not that she particularly cared one way or the other. By Lancastle's count, girls like Xandria Pelvenyn were ten-a-penny garden variety. What was one more strike for the tally?

"All right, let me out," Wordsworth grumbled. "Gotta drain the snake and check the van to make sure that muttonhead hasn't lost it or set it to the flame already."

"Care to see the caravan?" Edgar asked her as he slid out of the booth. "Wouldn't mind getting an early start on the night. A little mead, a little stew."

Marsea's belly growled at the mere mention of food. "By all means," she answered. "Lead the way."

THE TROUPE PUT down for the night in a camp area just outside Debynshire and it didn't take long before the fire was blazing and the cookpot simmering.

Stringer Paul passed out against one of the caravan wheels, snoring loud as a bear, but the others remained spirited, drinking and dancing and singing to the stars.

A proper troupe, the princess thought, relishing every minute of this most unforeseen happenchance.

Though Marsea wasn't terribly impressed by the girl's personality, Xandria Pelvenyn did indeed possess one of the loveliest singing voices she'd ever encountered. The sort that made even the smartest of men stupid. Between songs, she and Simon danced merrily to the buoyant strings of Niall's fiddle whilst the rest watched and ate and japed, mostly at the poor bard's expense.

Marsea tore through two bowls of stew so fast she couldn't half recall the taste of it. But for the first time in a long time her belly felt full, and near to bursting.

Xandria tried to convince her to get up and join their dance, but Marsea waved her off.

Poppy jumped to the princess's rescue, taking her sister's hand, and capering madly about the camp.

A tale of opposites was the Pelvenyn sisters, at least by personality. One the life of the party. The other a library mouse of a lass. Marsea's kind of girl, being something of an ink drinker herself. Still, there was certainly no denying their relation. They both had the same thick, black hair, honey-colored eyes, and olive complexion, likely of vinteyaman ancestry.

The caravan was quaint and surprisingly spacious, housing two pillowed benches to either side with a table pushed up against the front wall in between. A heap of books lay underneath and a series of jarred candles cluttered the top. Bedclothes, travel packs, and instruments were strewn about in random places. Though, by and large, it seemed comfortable enough.

Eventually the others retired for the evening, drunk as ladies and lords. The girls inside the caravan, and Simon at the steps. Wordsworth found himself a bed atop the caravan's driving bench, his snoring fastly drowning out Stringer's. Niall nodded off against a stump on the other side of the fire, leaving just Marsea and Edgar and the dying flames.

Bundled in a thick wool blanket, laying in the grass, propped up against a sitting log, Marsea gazed up at Y'dema, her emerald hide radiating. Under the mead's kiss with such lively company for distraction, she almost forgot about her loneliness, her frustrations, her growing collection of worries.

Almost.

"Flavor?" Edgar asked, offering the jug of mead.

"Cheers." Marsea took it and turned up a swallow. It wasn't very good, but it helped to numb the cold and heavy the eyes. She felt Old Boy watching her from the edge of camp, letting her know he still wasn't ready to meet the troupe yet. Secretly, she hoped he would never have to, for that meant trouble stayed away.

"I was curious, Edgar," she started, "are you former military?"

"Why do you ask that?" His words had become slightly slurred.

"No reason. I thought I picked up on some of your mannerisms is all."

"Are *you* former military?" he returned.

"I'm not, but I've had family in the service. An uncle and a brother."

"I had to wonder, considering your talent for the sword. What branch were they in?"

"Bluecoats. My brother was part of the Kingswatch for a time." *Always give a little bit of truth.*

"What were their names?"

"I'd rather not say."

"Are they still alive?"

"I believe so, though with the way things are…"

"Is that who you hope to meet in Courowne? Your family?"

"Mayhaps." Marsea offered the jug back to him. "Though I feel like even broaching the topic puts a curse to it."

"I know how that is." He chased the words down with a hearty gulp. "I did get to meet the Prince of Lancastle though. You believe that? Poor bastard had no idea what he was in for at The King's Wall."

"You met Remy…erm…Prince Rembrandt?" *Stars alive, Marsea, you simp. No more mead for you.*

"I did. He was in my company for a few quints before some upstart magus came along and had him reassigned to the Black Stags." Another swallow. "Thought he'd get the preferential treatment, too, given his namesake, but Van Prick put that shit to bed iron-quick. Had the princeling manning the ass-end of the wall his first two nights pulling watchman duty." Edgar snorted. "For a highborn, his favor was about as shite as I've ever seen."

Marsea stared off quietly into the pitch where she felt Broenwjar's presence, silently praying to the maidens above that Remy was still alive. And Jules, and Mother, and Effie, and even Rhymona.

The jug sloshed about again.

"For me, the military was my old life. A life I'd sooner to leave in the past if it's all the same to you."

Marsea nodded, her attentions returning to the firepit's dwindling flame. *He's a deserter*, she thought. *Likely around the time the blight came about.* She wondered if the other troupe members knew and wanted to press him about it further but didn't want to risk showing anymore of her own hand. *What does Selwyn Shawley care about a deserter and a nothing prince anyway?*

"Since we're being honest, and since I've had far too much mead, can I admit something to you?" Edgar asked.

Marsea slowly shifted her gaze from the fire to her drinking companion. "Sure..."

"I know your name is not Selwyn Shawley."

Marsea found her tongue pressed to the backs of her front teeth as her jaw clenched.

A prolonged hush fell between them, spanning the campsite and the night beyond.

"I passed through the cemetery when scouting ahead. I recognized the name Shawley on one of the crypts."

"Edgar—"

"Now hold on, before you go about getting all defensive again, let me finish. I don't know why you need to conceal your identity. And, no, I won't ask you your true name again. I just thought you should know that I know."

"I appreciate you telling me," Marsea said for lack of anything better.

"Now, if you wish to tell me your true name, I'd be more than happy to listen," he added with a dreamy smile.

"Mayhaps another time."

His smile grew into a mighty yawn, and Marsea noticed his eyelids had become heavy. "Another time, then." His eyes closed. "My gut tells me you're one of the good ones, Damsel."

She let the words sink in as she gazed back into the flame, unable to find a proper response.

Silence reigned.

Until she felt something against her shoulder. Edgar's head had listed to the side and now lay next to hers.

What a difference a day makes, she thought, the shivers from the Shawley mausoleum still clinging to her bones.

She waited there, tense and unmoving, her vision eventually rising once more to the moons and stars.

Here I am, she mused, counting her maidens many, a misfit amongst misfits. *The name is dead.*

"What now?" she breathed quietly.

CHAPTER TWENTY-ONE

UNDER THE BLOOD candle's influence, Emyria confined Magwyn inside her gift, suppressed in a timeless expanse, with only her thoughts for company, thoughts that fastly pushed past her dracari companion's sudden betrayal and attached themselves to Caitlyn's revelations.

Maggie trusted the girl about as much as a known slitpurse, but still, she couldn't deny the possibility of her words.

After all, what reason would the girl have to lie about such matters? And what was the probability that she could simply make up such a mad scenario off the top of her head?

The Empress pondered the prophecy at that and did her best to think herself inside Whit's position and mental state. She knew he had become obsessed, and that much more desperate to defy Selwyn Shawley's words. But how far would he have been willing to go?

Apparently far enough to sire a fourth child and one outside wedlock, risking his reputation. Though why Stella Critchlow? What could have been the intention behind such an endeavor? By Julia's birth, Larissa could still bear children, so it wasn't because she'd become infertile. Meaning Whit specifically chose Stella instead of Larissa.

Come on, Maggie, think. Why would he have done this? Why Stella?

She pushed deeper into her well of memories.

Stella. Stella. Stella.

It was no high-held secret the magus possessed quite the talent with the gift in her day. That coupled with the long-standing rumors of the Critchlow's connection to some bygone Chandiian bloodline certainly may have been enough to push Whit to her.

But that can't be all of it. It's never that simple.

What more of the sorceress?

There rose a time of speculation against Stella, she suddenly recalled. Just before Whit's death. Of an inquiry by the Ministry into claims of her dark-dabbling.

Though, eventually the investigation was dismissed, and not long after, she resigned her role as Lancastle's head archivist and moved back to some backwater hollow in the Southlands. That was the last Magwyn heard of Stella Critchlow. But thinking on it proper, with everything Caitlyn had just divulged, Maggie couldn't help but wonder if Whit had something to do with the dropped allegations.

Were you protecting her, Whit? Or were you just protecting yourself?

She knew Autumn was roughly fifteen cycles old, coming along some-time around the coup, which meant Stella could have been with child before leaving Lancastle.

Gracious me. Or was it the child?

And this wasn't even yet broaching the topic of Desmond's fate. Caitlyn said that Tetherow dispossessed her nephew. Assuming the girl was telling it true, what all happened? Was Desmond killed? Was it possible he was exorcised? Could he still be alive?

The thought sat ill with her.

Given his ghastly state upon their last meeting, she couldn't imagine what would be left of him were he somehow still amongst the living.

A sudden spark of azure stole Emyria's shroud, momentarily blinding her, as though she had just come in from the bright of a noontide sun, and she slowed her steps, blinking through the blurry gloom as she wandered away from the wall.

Something gripped her arm and pulled her back to the shadows.

"What are you doing?" Ledge whispered.

"I..."

Magwyn's vision began to adjust, and she found they were inside a long, dark corridor, with tall stained-glass windows on one side and iden-tical oak doors evenly placed along the other. Starlight poured across the stone floor in pale emerald bands, Ledge keeping her from stepping inside the nearest.

"Where are we?" she asked.

"What?" Ledge returned. "We're in the admissions hall."

At the far end of the hall, nearly thirty paces ahead of them, between a pair of burning torches, loomed a towering set of double doors that ranged to the high, rounded ceiling. Two robed figures stood guard, one of them with an ear pressed to the door listening. There was movement inside.

Emyria?

The dracari did not respond, but something did from inside her nose.

Not again.

Once more blood trailed down onto her upper lip and she wiped it away with the end of her shirtsleeve.

"What's going on with you?" Ledge asked.

Magwyn thought about exposing Emyria's deceit to him, but quickly decided against it. She would have Emyria's explanation first. After everything, the dracari had earned at least that from her.

"Nothing," she answered, "just got a bit lightheaded is all."

"Are you fit to keep going? This could be it."

"Yes, of course. We can't stop now. No matter what."

She could feel his eyes narrowing in the darkness. "That chanting up ahead. Do you recognize the language?" he asked.

Magwyn concentrated on the voices, separating them to at least four or five, but the words themselves may as well have been gibberish for all she understood of them.

"No."

"What about Emyria?"

"Emyria is gone," Magwyn grumbled, with perhaps more irritation than she meant.

"Gone? What do you mean gone?"

"She's...resting."

"Could she not do that right now?"

"She's not answering my behests." The Empress did her best to hide her crossness this time. "For that matter, where is Solindiel?"

"Somewhere between us and the end of the hall," Ledge answered.

"She told us to wait here while she did her thing. The gods only know. I've never seen anyone blend to the shadows like that one."

As though she heard them talking about her, the robed figure listening at the door began to stagger awkwardly backward into the hall, while the second guard struck hard into the wall and clutched at his throat before sinking soundlessly to the floor.

Magwyn could barely make out a third figure there in the pitch as it caught the first guard choking on the dagger lodged in his neck and lowered him quietly to the stones.

A most pitiless death for an undoubtedly rotten pair.

"I think we're clear," Ledge said as he hurried forward.

Maggie started after him, the chanting growing in ferocity with every footstep gained. Suddenly her head began to pound again, like it did earlier in town, and she slowed to a plod, using the wall as a crutch. Her jaw clenched and she blinked back tears as she dug inside the pouch at her side and found only two blood candles remained.

Dammit.

"This is the only way in," Solindiel said.

Maggie clutched one of blood candles, holding it tight, before releasing it. *Not yet.* She forced herself toward the others, wiping away the fresh trickle of blood from her nose.

"It's going to be a clusterfuck the second we barge in," Solindiel whispered. "But this is what's left us."

Magwyn knelt by the guard in the center of the hallway and relieved him of the sword at his hip. It was not unlike those issued by the Royal-guard smithies, so at least there would be some familiarity with its use, albeit that familiarity was now decades to the past.

"Ready?" Ledge asked, gripping the massive wrought iron door handle.

Magwyn nicked her offhand with the guard's blade and fished one of the two remaining blood candles from her pouch, squeezing it tight in her palm. *One left.*

"Ready," she said.

Ledge pulled, and Solindiel entered first, drawing a mask up around her face as she tossed a bright green powder into the chamber.

The chanting instantly died by half, replaced by sounds of curses and choking, and chased by bolts of bright yellow magic coursing across the room, to and fro, hither and yon, mad as a summertide tempest.

Had Magwyn been standing a foot to her left, she would have taken a hit directly, but instead it merely singed the edge of her sleeve.

"Shit," Ledge howled, swiveling back into the hallway. "That mad bitch was holding wretchrot."

"What?" Magwyn sprang to the opposite side of the opened doorway.

"It's like acid in dust form. Eats away the insides." he answered. "Fucking hells, I should have known better than to trust a gods damned ashaeydir." He dared a peek back into the room. "Let the green cloud disintegrate first. One breath of that shit could put us down with the rest."

A robed figure stumbled through the doorway, scratching at her neck and chest before faltering to her knees and collapsing in a heap, a bright pink liquid pooling around her downturned face. Magwyn had never seen anything like the substance leaking out of her before.

The song of blades crashing against each other echoed into the corridor.

"Cut their throats!" a voice screamed.

"No!" another followed. "The ritual is not yet complete."

Magwyn glanced back into the chamber and found Rhonyn bound on his knees as a blade settled against his throat. His eyes found hers and she curved into the chamber, holding her breath, reaching out for her gift to sustain her, as she dodged a crackling stream of bright white wand magic.

"Maggie!" Ledge howled.

But it was too late, she'd already committed.

Into the sea of chaos and slaughter. A blur of masks and magic in the dying cloud of green smoke. The stench of shit and vomit, the shouts of the cultists, the static hum of black magic in her ears, chorused by the calculated drone of a most diabolical incantation.

Though Emyria was absent, her gift yet remained, and the fresh blood candle slowed everything by a hair, giving Magwyn some small window to assess the madness.

Half the robed figures were on the ground, coughing and choking, or already laying in a bright pink puddle of their own sickly demise. A few were opened up by Solindiel's ka'rym chii as she carved a grisly path across the chamber toward her target.

The robed figures with masks unaffected by the initial explosion of wretchrot were butchering the other hostages, their daggers running throats red and opening torsos fast as the blade would have them.

From the corner of her eye, Solindiel was crossing steel with a frail corpse of a thing and the corpse was giving every measure she got.

"Rhonyn!" Magwyn cried as she passed through to other side of the dissipating wretchrot.

"Saaa Artem!" Rhonyn shouted through the gag in his mouth just before the cultist's dagger drew a thick cascade of red down his neck.

His eyes darted to the far corner of the room and she followed, finding a motionless girl strapped to a stone altar guarded by a pair of robed figures wielding galvanized wands.

Autumn.

The girl had her mother's fiery hair and then some, but the eyes...the eyes were undeniably Whit's.

Another cultist hunched over her chanting feverishly and a mist the color of stone malachite began to rise from the opened grimoire in his hands. She recognized this one as Raelan Harver's son.

Her attentions returned to Rhonyn as the masked cultist shoved his gurgling corpse aside and charged at her.

Magwyn made to defend as Ledge floated into the space beside her, smooth as a water viper, running the bastard through just before the blade was set to have a taste.

"Fuck," the swordsman growled, finding Rhonyn bleeding red and pink. He covered his offhand over his face.

"The girl on the slab," Magwyn said. "We must get to her. All of this can't be for nothing."

Ledge followed Magwyn's stare. "Here on out, do the opposite of what I say," he bade.

Maggie shifted to Solindiel, who was still in a deadly dance with the corpse woman she could only imagine was Dysenia, their ka'rym chii glancing off each other and into the next strike with blinding speed and precision.

Em, if you can still hear me, now would be the time to come back to us.

A second masked cultist charged at them, and Ledge deflected the strike, spinning around him to a third who found the lethal end of the swordsman's iron.

Magwyn hacked down at the second off-balance cultist catching him across the chest and sending him stumbling behind her. She didn't look back to see if the strike was fatal or not, she just kept after Ledge's path toward the altar and the growing cloud of malachite.

"Left!" Ledge howled.

And Magwyn obeyed his previous order, shifting right in unison with the swordsman, keeping her feet and following his charge.

The first wand blasts hit left and where she previously held.

Something from her right screamed for her gifts attention and she turned to find a length of steel lunging at her. She parried the strike just before it set to flesh, pushing the blade just wide and sending the cultist sprawling across her front.

Ledge was already ranging forward again, and she hurried into his shadow.

Emyria.

"Left!" he barked and she stayed the course, center bound, as he rolled right and a blast of magic shrieked past her.

"Emyria, now!"

She moved ahead of Ledge and flung her sword at the wand-wielder on the right, driving in at the one on the left, as Emyria thundered to the surface, an egg of Eldn flame sparking to life inside her splayed fingers as she caught his mask inside her palm, and melted it into his face.

He dropped to the stones, his screams muffled, and Magwyn turned to Pion Harver as the last of the mist disappeared inside Autumn's nose.

No.

A crack of energy sent Maggie flying backward into Ledge who caught her as they both came crashing to the floor.

She shook the ringing from her ears as best she could, fighting to her feet, as the chamber settled.

A deathly cry rasped out to her left and Magwyn found Solindiel crawling on hands and knees with a blade protruding from her shoulder.

"You little bitch." The hag trailed after her, eyes glowing white as winter's bones, as she ripped Solindiel's sy'chii out of her belly and flung it back down at the owner, nearly every inch of silver disappearing inside Solindiel's backside.

Deadeyes.

Screaming obscenities, Solindiel rolled onto her side, squeezing the hilt of the sy'chii jutting out from the space just above her heart.

"Thas'kon ech vira dhu xarma," the hag called and Solindiel curled into the fetal position, her bones snapping like dry twigs, one by one, her body convulsing and vomiting blackened blood as the clicking sounds set in and a dark oily mass of flesh began twisting out of the blade wound in her shoulder.

Solindiel whimpered out in anguish, her screams strangled, as black ran down her face like an inkwell exploded somewhere inside, and a second appendage burst out of her yawning mouth, splitting her lower jaw from the rest of her skull.

:Fucking hells, that never gets any easier.:

Magwyn shifted back to the altar to find Autumn standing in a shroud of malachite shadows, the remains of her restraints melting away from her wrists.

Her eyes.

They were the same eyes Desmond had worn. Bright, icy, hateful eyes. Dead despite their brilliant color.

"Autumn."

"We have to go," Ledge hollered.

"I failed," she uttered, a sickness flooding over her in crushing waves.

Autumn locked eyes with her and produced the same impish smile that warped her nephew's face back in the throne hall.

Fear and panic hooked its claws in and ripped through her like a violent tremor.

"Maggie, we have to go," Ledge clutched her arm and tugged her toward him. "The girl is lost. We have to go now."

She swung back around to the swordsman as he let her go to deflect a swipe from a cultist before cutting the fool to the ground.

An egg of Eldn fire opened inside her palm, her fury enduring, swallowing her terror, and she spread her fingers out wide to amplify its cast.

:Do it,: Autumn dared from over her shoulder.

Magwyn turned back to the fiend who was clutching a radiating amethyst pendant that hung down from Autumn's neck.

A ghastly grin pulled back the girl's ears, as gray lines streaked down through her vibrant red hair.

Autumn certainly deserved a better fate than all this, but the wretch could not be allowed to endure, no matter what form it took.

Emyria guided the dragon's fire between both hands, magnifying its size further, lifeblood leaking from Magwyn's nose and ears.

Em. She'd felt the drain of magic before, but never as severe as this.

The sphere enhanced in size to that of a watchtower bell before she compelled it at the altar, slumping in the spell's wake.

Autumn raised a palm out in response, cool as you please, freezing the conjured magic midair between them, as though it were merely a leaf on the wind, as though it were little more than a bloody afterthought.

IMPOSSIBLE.

Magwyn gaped in awe, Emyria's fear all-consuming, as the blazing sphere was devoured by a viscous black liquid, snuffing out the Eldn flame, and crumbling its remains to a mound of pale ashes.

"Gods' breath." Her pulse was thumping like mad.

Dysenia Deadeyes cackled.

"Maggie." Ledge jerked at her arm again.

Magwyn backstepped, dodging a cultist's blade, narrowly keeping her insides in their proper place, as she turned away and into a full dash past Rhonyn's corpse and through the pit of lifeless bodies out into the starlit corridor.

Shouts and the hum of magic filled the space behind her as she tore through bandlight, dark to starlight and back to dark again. She was halfway down the hall before she realized she was alone and spun around to find Ledge closing the doors to the ritual chamber and pressing his back against them as they bucked outward at him.

"Xavien, what the hells are you doing?" Magwyn took a step back toward him.

"Go, milady!" he shouted "I'm buying you what time I can."

"Don't be a fool!"

"It's a little late for that, isn't it?" His head jerked to the side. "The old blood must..." tick, "survive."

A dark trail blistered down from one of his eyes.

HE IS INFECTED.

No.

"For House Lanier," Ledge bellowed as the doors bulged out at him again and a blade burst through his chest, caked in nether residue, thick, black fluids coughing up through his airways as he wilted to the flagstones, his twitching fastly escalating to violent spasms, light pouring through from the ritual chamber he guarded. Yet, even with the nether

221

oozing out of him, he shoved himself back against the doors. Defiant to the last.

The Empress ran for all she was worth, chasing the nothingness that filled her with each passing breath, pushing into the dark and out onto the university grounds and whatever the hells lay beyond.

CHAPTER TWENTY-TWO

A FEW HOURS off the tinker's path and Marsea discovered she rather had a fondness for scouting. Though she couldn't help but wonder just what share of that belonged to the bond of her beastly companion. Not that it really much mattered in the end. There was an undeniable freedom in it, like nothing she'd ever experienced before, and it made her question why it was she ever feared such a thing so ferociously.

The forest was such a wondrous place, after all, once taken through the right lens. There was a strange feeling of safety in it. Likely from the lack of people, she surmised. Honestly, she found she might even prefer it given time. Aside from the awkward issue of having to see to her privy business with only a tree for cover. But that was neither here nor there considering.

The troupe broke camp after breakfast, and Edgar showed her some of his wood running techniques, each taking to a side of the kingsroad in the after where she followed the tree growths and patches of broken earth, inspecting here and there for any fresh activity. Though nothing of note stood out in the hours since. It was all quite peaceful.

Almost too peaceful.

Further off in the forest she felt Broenwjar, some place ahead of her, but heading back in her direction. She could still sense his sadness over Elsymir's passing, so she allowed him as much space as she could, suspecting his sorrow would keep to the cut for a good long while. He would let her know when he was ready to resume as something near normal again; in this she had to believe.

She stopped at a pillar of late afternoon sunlight shimmering down through the canopy of treetops, inhaling its warmth, and removed the mask that was attached to the back of her head.

It was a smooth ceramic mask like those typically worn by the carnie folk for theatre, pale lilac base with deep-lavender rings around slitted eyes and smeared across the cut-out mouth, and it was dreadfully uncomfortable, pulling at her frizzy locks with every nod and shake.

Edgar forced the infernal thing on her before they set out, convincing her wearing it could save her life out in wildkin territory. It was something cadets were taught in the Royalguard, he explained, as the wolld were notorious for ambushing their enemies from behind, and wearing a mask backwards was a known practice to throw them off such an attempt.

Who was she to argue?

Marsea fit it back over her head, adjusting the string so it would sit better from around the front of her neck rather than across her forehead, until she was satisfied with the new placement.

Instinctually, her gloved hand returned to the haxanblade sheathed at her hip, as though she could feel a bout of trouble brewing.

Tiny breaths. Tinier heartbeats.

A sigh of the wind.

She gave the hilt a squeeze, tighter and tighter, until she felt the pulse within. It was almost addicting, the haxanblade's vibrations, and she drank it in, simultaneously sending up a prayer that she wouldn't have to use it again, especially not so soon after the madness outside of Vinth with the Tarborils and the ghastly wood witch.

Broenwjar appeared between a pair of mossy trees just ahead and they met eyes.

Welcome back, she offered in their special language.

He padded up to her as she approached him.

What is it? she asked as he gazed back whence he'd come. *Trouble? You're sure?* She glanced back toward the road where the caravan wouldn't be too far away. *We'll need to apprise the others. Best to stay close for now.*

Marsea hurried back for the caravan and a few breaths later heard a chorus of screams and shouting, followed by a horrifyingly familiar sound.

A long, terrible shriek chased with a second that ended messy.

Wand magic.

"No!" she hollered out as she raced the snarl of trees back toward the disturbance, her heart pushing through the gaps of her ribcage.

Every footstep was an age at length.

"Marsea!" A voice called, stopping her dead in her tracks and confirming her fears.

Yongrin.

The sorceress had found her.

One of the troupe members was howling bloody murder ahead, which was likely to draw in unwanted attention, but...

The old blood must survive, Other protested.

I can't just leave them to her.

This is not to be.

Like hells.

Marsea ripped Blind Widow from her scabbard and raced through the Kingswood beside Broenwjar until the caravan came into view, quickly darting behind a tree and peeking out from its side. Simon slumped on the ground unmoving and Poppy held Xandria in her lap, brushing back blood-matted hair. Stringer lay before Yongrin in the road yelling madly from the wand blast that had taken a chunk from his shoulder and now bled profusely. Wordsworth and Niall approached from the side of the caravan at wandpoint and dropped to their knees beside Poppy with their hands cupped behind their heads.

"I know you're out there, you little wretch," Yongrin hissed, looking as frayed and frazzled as Marsea had before finding the troupe.

Did she actually manage to slay the wood witch?

"Are you truly going to leave these innocent folks to suffer in your stead?" Yongrin sent another bolt of magic into Stringer, permanently silencing the cries for his mother. "For every minute you make me wait, another will eat your debt."

Marsea frowned at Old Boy, trembling. *I know, but we don't have a choice.*

Broenwjar let out a frustrated growl.

The maidens watch over us.

Movement from the other side of the kingsroad drew Marsea's attention and her guts rose into her throat.

Edgar, you fool. What are you—

"Run," he barked. "Wildkin! Run!"

A jet of white-hot magic surged after him as he dashed across the road behind the caravan, the strike narrowly missing him, but sending the horses into a panic.

You go around, Marsea ordered Broenwjar as they sprinted toward the caravan. *I'll get her attention.*

"You lot move, you're dead," Yongrin warned the other troubadours.

"I'm here," Marsea called.

Without delay, a twisting spiral of white-gold sorcery screeched at her and she ate leaves and dirt diving for cover, the blast immolating a tree just behind her.

The horses with the caravan raced off down the path.

"This is between me and you, Yongrin," Marsea shouted, as she fixed her glasses and gazed back up to find Yongrin slinging a series of quick, angry spells into the opposite woods at a pack of wildkin savages firing arrows and descending upon the troupe with all manner of crude weaponry.

"Friend of yours?" Edgar arrived at her side, gasping for breath, orbs near out of his skull.

"I'll explain later."

"We have to keep moving," he said, retrieving an arrow from his quiver.

"We can't just leave them." Marsea glanced back at the others and watched as an arrow took a fleeing Niall in the back of a leg and a second through the neck. He clutched at his throat and collapsed, dead before he hit the dirt. Poppy and Wordsworth were nowhere to be found in the wave of onrushing wildkin warriors. The others lay still. Gone as the ghost.

An arrow sailed up at them next, missing by a fair length, but the intent certainly hit the mark.

Edgar drew back his bowstring, settled, and let his arrow loose into the approaching pack, piercing one of the savages in its midsection. It tumbled with a feral whine into a patch of briars.

"There were dozens of the bastards giving chase," Edgar said. "We don't keep running, we'll be joining the others for wildkin supper."

Broenwjar, forget Yongrin. Marsea called as she and Edgar tore through the jumble of trees with reckless abandon. *On me.*

Yowling wildkin battle cries chased after them for what felt like hours as they traversed the woodlands south, leaping roots and ruts, tumbling through thicket and brush, slipping and sliding across puddles of muck and slush. Marsea didn't dare look back. Not once. The maidens know, if she'd learned any one thing in her time since leaving Lancastle, it was that nothing good could ever be found by looking back.

Occasionally the sound of an arrow flitting past or splitting nearby wood spurred her on a mite harder, but despite the treacherous conditions, they managed to stay ahead without contest...

...until they stumbled on a clearing with nothing about to shield them from a volley. They'd have to cross it quickly.

A legion of footsteps closed in behind them.

Her breath quickened.

A third of the way in they noticed figures scattered in bunches at the tree line on the other side of the clearing, bobbing and staggering about aimlessly.

Immediately the pair halted, and Marsea hunched over, hands on her knees, lungs burning, panting heavily.

"More wildkin?" she asked, her chest rising and falling rapidly.

"Not sure," Edgar answered, glancing back to the forest behind them.

Those of the wolld hunting party that trailed them held at the edge of the clearing. Marsea counted eleven of them against the woodland gloom, and that was only those that chose to reveal themselves.

Wobbly, she retreated a few more paces, watching the waiting line of wildkin, and feeling as though she might drop from exhaustion at any moment.

"What are they doing?" she questioned.

"Wolld are extremely territorial, mayhaps we've crossed off their land. Or," Edgar said, shifting back the other way, "whoever it is that lies ahead there isn't worth the trouble of a few trespassers."

One of the wildkin leveled an arrow at them and fired. They were at a middling distance, and able to easily dodge the shot, but the point was made. There would be no return without a fight. Meaning the only option left them was forward into the horde ahead.

Marsea counted at least a score waiting, and she assumed there would be more beyond the trees.

The stars keep us.

One of the patches of figures took notice of their company, growing agitated, and began to shamble out toward them, some moving swiftly, others quite queerly, almost unnaturally. And nothing at all like the wolld savages that sent them here.

"Brace for it." Edgar nocked an arrow to his bow.

Best pluck up that courage, girl, she heard Cas in her ear.

Marsea readied herself, clutching Blind Widow in both hands, expecting a madness as Broenwjar hunkered down beside her, fangs bared, coat bristling.

Whatever it was that approached, it was enough to put off wildkin savages, so it would no doubt become a problem.

A strange clicking noise resounded amongst them, like that of the marsh creatures described in Uncle Rho's old hearthfire haunters.

"Ghouls," Edgar announced a moment later, letting the first arrow loose, downing one of the faster-moving fiends. "They're blighted."

Fuck.

"Aim for the head or don't bother," he added as he sent a second arrow whistling into the nearest ghoul's face.

"All right, asshole," Marsea addressed the haxanblade, "you wanted violence, now's the time for it."

Do your bloody worst.

Broenwjar pounced on a tall, bearded ghoul, taking it to the ground in a wave of dark pulp and fluids, as he leapt for the next. Old Boy had some practice with the undead, Marsea was reminded, and thusly she took to his shadow.

"Follow Broenwjar," Marsea called to Edgar, cutting down the first one to reach her, Blind Widow glowing molten pink as it ate through one side of its balding head to the next. Stars alive, but he was a repulsive bastard, too, missing chunks of skin from his neck and face, not to mention a half-eaten arm that appeared mostly bone below the elbow.

By their dress, most of the blight looked to be townsfolk, which meant they were likely near a village or township. Marsea's mind raced over the potential geography given the time and distance from Debynshire and she landed on Marrovard or, her breath caught…

Wyrmswold Hollow. A shiver raced down her bones from crown to toes.

But of course. Home of Lita Drufellyn. The Wyrmstower Witch. Birthplace of Blind Widow.

Have you led me here on purpose? She asked the haxanblade as she shoved her good hand all the way up to the cross-guard and clasped the pommel with her gloved hand. It was a technique Vaustian showed her to use against multiple enemies in single sword combat, allowing for maximum maneuverability of the blade, for both cutting and defending. Though given the opponents were blighted, she hoped there wouldn't be much need for...

A pitchfork thrust in at her.

Shit.

She parried the clumsy strike and spun around the fiend to bury the width of Blind Widow in the back of its head. The blade stuck firm for a moment, before the Widow began to wail, hissing and spitting, feasting on the creature's lifeblood to stoke its frenzy, chewing through skull like a buzzsaw until enough had been taken to allow proper withdrawal, bloodied skin and hair clinging to the steel upon extraction, dressing the grass in dark red blobs and beads, and it was on to the next ugly wretch, which Marsea made fast work of with a deft lunge that ate through the ghoul's face halfway down the gore-stained length of glowing steel.

Don't stop.

She moved like a dancer, hunting the haxanblade's song, Blind Widow scything through air, splitting body and bone like boiling acid through rotted fruit. One bloodstained ruin to the next. Bodies. Limbs. Crimson. Everywhere.

Always twist at the bone, she heard Vaustian say, *help it come off clean.*

As she removed the haxanblade from the latest victim, a dark pink mist poured off of it and the vibrations intensified.

She studied it for a moment as they made the tree line and passed into the forest, recalling the same effect after she cut into Davrin. It was almost like the blade was becoming more powerful with each kill. She couldn't help but wonder if that meant the witch might return, spinning puddles of blood from its victims' remains. What if Yongrin hadn't killed it? What if she'd run from it too? Marsea shook the thought from her mind, as she chased after Edgar and Broenwjar, clinging to the wolf's monstrous shadow like a leech, slashing at a ghoul here, hacking down another there, weaving between the trees and around the bramble, until the creatures and their clicking noises disappeared behind them.

"I think we're near Wyrmswold Hollow," Marsea called to Edgar as they kept the pace behind Broenwjar.

"Guard your tongue," he answered in a low voice, slowing to her side. "We are, indeed," he added. "And hopefully it's not where these folks came from."

"Hopefully not."

"Your blade. It's enchanted."

"Enchanted might be a touch kind. I'd call it more cursed."

"I've never seen a blade eat through people like that thing, and one of my best mates back home was a smithy."

"As I told you before, the blade is a burden."

"Is that what brought the magus after you?"

"Not exactly," Marsea said, drawing the satchel around to her front. "She's after the book."

"She murdered them in cold blood," Edgar muttered.

"She's a monster, prize well. And she killed my friends back in Vinth just the like. My friends that risked their lives to prevent her from gaining the book."

"What is it, this book of yours? Some sort of fancy-shmance grimoire?"

"Something like that."

"And what's so bloody special about it to send a magus out into wildkin woods slaughtering innocent folk?"

The tale withered on her lips as she mulled over its recounting. It wasn't that she didn't trust Edgar, but that she would be inviting him into a deadly game if she divulged anymore. Though, all affairs considered, he was already well in it now, like it or not. Then again, for all he'd done to aid her thus far, she supposed he was owed some measure of honesty.

Always give a little truth, she reminded, *but never, ever the whole of it.*

"I'm still trying to figure that out myself," she decided to start easy. "Though from what I've read of it thus far, it houses numerous pages with black magic incantations."

"Meaning, she's a dark-dabbler?"

"More than like. She was associated with Ravenholme. As were my companions that gave their lives to keep it from her."

"Edgar," he grumbled to himself, "Edgar, Edgar, Edgar, what have you gotten yourself into this time?"

"I'm sorry about your friends," Marsea said.

"We weren't very close, to have it true," Edgar answered. "Though I was growing fond of them. Most of them at least." He came to a halt, and she held with him. They both stared back into the woods, searching for movement. "I think we may have lost them."

Marsea met his eyes momentarily before shifting away. "It'll be dark soon."

"That woman named you Marsea," Edgar returned.

The princess nodded. "That she did." She was rather hoping he'd missed out on that bit.

"Is that your true name then?"

"It is a dead name," she said, "and a name I no longer acknowledge."

"I knew there was something familiar about you. And here I was believing you were just some toffee-nosed Lordship's runaway daughter."

"Would that I could be," Marsea found herself saying.

"You and your brother are not so different, you know. Like fish out of water, you two."

"There are plenty of noble folk that would say the same. I suppose I'm a bit of a sore thumb to most when it comes down to it."

"I won't pretend to know you or your past, but in the short time we've gotten on, you've proven yourself agreeable enough."

"Thanks, I think."

"Could've said something about the dodgy spellslinger, all told, but I understand why you didn't. That tramp was mad as a bucket of wet cats."

"You can leave me to it, you know. I won't blame you." Marsea felt the heat of useless tears welling up behind her eyes. "I've already caused so much—"

"I'm not leaving you to anything, milady. I want to help you. Whatever it is you're mixed-up in. I'm no knight, hells I'm no squire, but I know the land, and I know how to avoid trouble for the most."

The princess nudged her glasses up. "As plainly indicated by our friendly wildkin display back there."

"Mayhaps we keep this between you and me, but I drew their hunting party on purpose."

"Edgar!" The name came out a whisper drenched in reproach.

"They'd already heard the wandwork and screaming, I merely guided them to the source."

And it likely saved our lives.

Marsea recalled Yongrin's graveyard glower, dirt and mascara smeared across her face like soot from a hearth, her posh robes in tatters, hair all manner of disheveled.

She'd truly meant to take the madwoman on. She and Broenwjar, just like she had the brother. Even if it meant her life.

Even if…

"I didn't see Wordsworth or Poppy," Marsea said, sensing some regret in Edgar's tone. "Mayhaps they were able to escape."

"Mayhaps."

The pair resumed southward, clouds swallowing the last drops of sunlight, creating a fog-like specter over the dense, shadowy forest.

"Milady," Edgar started after a short silence. "What should I call you, if not by your true name?"

"Selwyn will do." Something about the name was growing on her.

"She, of the wandering woods," Edgar said. "Suits you, given our crossing."

"You should know, everyone that's tried to help me since this all began has—"

"Oye, that's enough there, yeah. You can keep the past where it is. I'd rather not know any more."

"Edgar…"

"I've always been an overthinker. Ever keeping to caution's shadow. But this time I'm going with my gut." He looked at her and waited for her gaze to return to his. "This is going to sound barmy, but have you ever felt like you were in the right place at the right time, even when everything seemed horribly wrong? Or like you've been somewhere with someone before? Someone you couldn't possibly have ever met? As though you were close in a different place in another lifetime? As though you were somehow—"

"Connected," Marsea finished, sifting through the same strange familiarity she found in his presence since their meeting.

"That is how I feel with you. From the moment I first saw you across the woods. There was this energy. Like something was calling me to you. I didn't really understand it…"

"I know," she said. "I've felt it too. Like a distant voice on the wind."

"Aye. And typically, I'd be the first to bite the thumb at such romantic tosh, but—"

"It's real. This bond." Marsea swallowed. "You're not the only one I've felt this with before. There was another."

"Another?"

"Her name is Rhymona. She was a dear friend of mine." The ashaeydir version flickered through her mind, lilac skin, orbs of poison gold.

"Was? Is she…dead?"

"I cannot say. When I left her last, she wasn't in the best of ways, but she was still alive. She's one of the hardest women I know, so I have to believe she pulled through. Just like with you now, I can hear the voice when she's close. Almost like an echo from a dream."

It's what started all this mess in the first place.

Listen.

Broenwjar came to an abrupt standstill.

"Down," she bade, scanning the woods ahead, where a creeping mist stretched out toward them.

"I see someone," Edgar whispered. "No, there's a few of them. Fuck all, I think they're blighted." He reached into his quiver for a fresh arrow. "Nearly out."

"There's no telling how many there may be in this fog," Marsea said. "We'll have to keep close."

"This isn't fog," Edgar answered, drawing in a long whiff of air. "Something is burning."

SIXTEEN.

That was her tally on downed ghouls before they reached the squalid township. And she notched another twelve by the time they found the source of the burning, Blind Widow becoming more ravenous with each felling, her deathly mist darkening to a strawberry scare in the trail of carnage.

The smoke belonged to the blighted themselves, their scorched bodies ringed around a spectacular field of heather and producing a urine-colored stench worse than anything she'd ever crossed amidst the Lancastle cellars.

Quite fastly Marsea found an actual use for the mask Edgar forced on her back at camp, removing her glasses as they approached the line of corpses, and stuffing them in a pocket sewn inside Remy's old hunting jacket.

Nothing moved within the patches of gray and yellow smoke, the insufferable clicking sound mercifully silenced.

Deep inside the field of heather, some thirty yards in, stretching high as the sea of stars was a tower like no other this side of the Morrigar Mountains, at least no other Marsea had ever heard of.

Wyrmswold Tower, it was named, and the maidens know, the stories and accounts from Lancastle's collection did her magnificence remarkably little justice. She was swathed in rust-colored lichen and caped by a tangle of bright scarlet vines that collected at its base like a fishtail train, ranging out long into the heather beyond.

"You reckon it's a hex?" Edgar asked.

"It has to be some sort of protective spell. It's the only thing that makes sense." *And if the tales of the Wyrmstower Witch held any merit at all, it most certainly did.* At the thought, Marsea felt a change in the haxanblade's vibrations and her arm swung up like a needle point directly at the tower.

"What the?" she uttered as the blade yanked her forward. "No, wait." She tried to let go of the blade as she stumbled after it, but it wouldn't allow her, its vibrations forcing her grip to tighten upon its hilt.

"Stop!"

She tried to pry her fingers loose with her bad hand, but it was little use. The enchantment was in her blood and using it against her, pulling her toward the great spire.

It jerked her again, and Marsea squeezed her eyes closed as she approached the line of burnt ghoul carcasses, expecting a shitshow.

Not like this.

Feeling the procession of corpses coming, she opened her eyes and leapt awkwardly into the field of heather, expecting to burst into flames promptly, Elsymir's prophetic words ringing afresh.

Possessed swords are assholes.

"Selwyn!" Edgar howled.

But she remained whole on the other side.

I'm alive.

"Good gravy! You bitch!"

The haxanblade's *fuck you* scowl was practically palpable.

Broenwjar followed as the blade kept tugging her toward the tower steps.

"Selwyn, what's happening?" Edgar shouted.

Marsea threw a desperate glance back at him. "I can't let go of it. I can't control it."

"Fucking hells," Edgar reached a hand slowly over a smoldering blighter onto the other side and waved it around. "Please gods."

Marsea watched as he let himself go, stepping through into the gentle sway of purple. *You fool*, she thought, smiling somewhere inside the horror scrawled upon her countenance. But the maidens know, his idiotic bravery was quickly beginning to grow on her.

Within in a blink he was at her side, studying the quivering blade as it rained wine-colored tears at her footsteps, its point never leaving that of the aged tower steps.

"Blind Widow, enough," she scolded. "We're going to the tower. You don't need to force me."

"That's one hell of a curse on that thing," Edgar said.

"Who are you telling? I can't even feel my hand anymore."

"I'll check it out, and see if we have company," Edgar said, nocking an arrow to his bow and ranging ahead.

Follow him, B, Marsea commanded.

Broenwjar's brow furrowed.

I'll be fine. Go on.

Red door, Other returned, because shit wasn't already batty enough.

"Other? Is this your doing?"

Look.

Marsea stared ahead at the tower door. It appeared more like a jewel than a traditional man-made door, three times her height and twice her width. Like some bit of madness out of bloody *Mervold Chronicles*. "I see it. And as I recall, you said a red door with no walls."

Here is where we meet.

"You're not going to believe this," Edgar called out. "There's a keyhole here. And I'm going to bet your blade fits it." He knocked against it. "The hells kind of door is this?"

Marsea hurried up the stairs, feeling the doorway's beating heart like a loadstone drawing her in, drawing Blind Widow in, like distant lovers that had spent far too many cycles apart.

There was no handle or knob, only an ornate silver slit in its bright ruby epicenter.

Gallows glass, she thought as the blade pierced the aperture, twisting her hand right then left, a movement which produced a snapping noise like ice cracking.

Blind Widow released its hold on her as the gallows glass groaned.

Broenwjar let out an anxious whine.

"I know, B," Marsea clutched her throbbing hand, the lines of the hilt's leather wrapping scarred into her palm like a turncoat's brand. "I feel it too."

Iridescent magic shimmered from within as the giant jewel-like door yawned out toward them, releasing a sweet, cloying odor from inside. The odor of old magic, stored magic, like the kind Nan used to natter on about in her endless collection of bedtime fables. Magic from those who came before.

Marsea lifted the mask over her head and returned her glasses to bring the chamber into focus.

"I..." she started, a faint dizziness taking hold, her mouth suddenly dry as a dustland alehouse. She caught herself at the edge of the entryway. "I've been here before."

She stepped inside the tower, fighting the spins, the symbols of the ancient arcana sparking to life upon her presence, tall as the hallowed heavens.

"Marsea!" a voice shouted from behind them.

Shit.

"We are not finished, you and I."

"It's her," Edgar said, nocking an arrow as Marsea glanced sidelong over her shoulder into the meadow. "And she's got Poppy."

Yongrin approached, another woman behind her with a blade raised to Poppy's throat. Marsea recognized the woman's face from those she'd passed in her brief stay at the Ravenholme enclave. Another one of Elsymir's betrayers.

"Come out here and find your death, Marsea Lanier," Yongrin called. "Or the girl will find hers for you."

CHAPTER TWENTY-THREE

"Keep your bow on the bitch in red," Marsea bade Edgar, tearing Blind Widow from the gallows glass keyhole, feeding off the sword's fury as she descended the steps, Broenwjar prowling at her side.

Her good hand still smarted something dreadful, but Poppy needed her, and despite Elsymir's warning, she'd already abandoned enough folk in the past quintweek. Had it been just her out here, she would have caught the wind again and never looked back, but this one here she couldn't abide, this one here she couldn't turn the cold shoulder to, for despite the fact that she barely knew the girl, Poppy didn't deserve a knife at her neck, not by Yongrin Tarboril and her ilk, and certainly not on her behalf.

No, this was a contest that would not be denied, could not be avoided, her wishes to the nine, the luck stones be damned, for good or ill, all favor to the fates' preferred. A promised ruin between them. A dance to the death. Enough was enough. Yongrin Tarboril would have to be put down. Or she'd find her own grave in the effort.

Only a woman. A slab of meat.

Watch the spare, B. That knife so much as moves a whisker you make her regret it.

"I didn't want this, Yongrin," Marsea called.

"And I didn't want to lose my brother."

"Mayhaps you lot should've thought better on stealing me away from my kingdom and family then."

"Orders are orders, girl, and the masters I serve you do not disappoint."

"And will they meet your wrath as I have? Are they not just as responsible for Davrin's expiry?"

"A problem for another day, that," Yongrin said. "All this. My brother's murder. You will not walk away from it. I will see Davrin avenged." She glanced at Poppy, her face stained with tears. "The girl may go free in exchange for the grimoire, but only one of us will leave this field alive."

Marsea didn't believe Yongrin would let Poppy free for a second.

"Selwyn?" Edgar called from the tower steps.

"Steady on the target," she returned, halting midway between the tower and Yongrin, lifting the satchel off her shoulder and letting it fall to the ground at her heels. "There it is. But you want it, you're going to have to go through me to get it."

The princess brought the haxanblade up into her defensive stance, absorbing its intensifying vibrations, recalling the remains of her courage from the depths of their coffers.

We shall see who the maidens prefer. She'd never beheld Yongrin with a blade before, mayhaps it would grant her a sporting chance to come out of this fool's charade the victor.

Blind Widow's battle cry came out a shrill wail.

After gorging through the undead, old girl was starved for the blood of the living, for a taste of the gift.

"And suddenly the wretch has grown a spine, has she?" Yongrin stepped forward, wand humming and spitting hot golden tears across the endless heather.

"If you raise to fire, my archer will put the rest of his quiver in you."

Yongrin glowered through columns of streaking kohl, sweat, and dirt stains. "Have it your way," the magus quashed her crackling gift and dropped the wand to the ground, reaching over her shoulder for the hilt that rose up behind her, unsheathing the blade slowly. "It seems only fitting Davrin's sword would see out his revenge."

"Tell your crony to lower the knife from Poppy's throat or Broenwjar will have a fresh feast for the spectacle."

Yongrin nodded at her companion to comply. The woman brought the knife down over Poppy's chest.

Marsea retreated a step, maintaining her stance as Yongrin advanced with deliberate theatrics.

Still your mind, Casilvieri commanded from the Hall of Glass.

The sister moons had all but swallowed the sunset whole, great Y'dema seizing the lion's share, casting a yellowish emerald tint across the field of lavender. Ghouls were arriving and burning up upon their fallen as they became attracted by the commotion, their stench filling the air and surrounding the scrap like mindless spectators at the arena.

Marsea drew a breath, her skin prickling as she soaked in the haxan-blade's budding temper and returned her own.

As one.

Yongrin lunged, spanning the distance between them in a blink, poised to take Marsea through the heart. Marsea stepped back and parried, but the attempt surpassed her expectations of the woman.

So, you can wield the blade then?

Yongrin was back after her, quick as the cutthroat's call, lunging and swiping as Marsea faded from the rapid flurry. She recognized the style as classic helanderan, popular amongst the northern territories. It was an approach Marsea was quite familiar with, as it was the first Vaustian ever taught her.

Wait for the breath. She told herself as it came, Yongrin slowing for the smallest window, and Marsea sent a riposte whistling just wide of Yongrin's neck, Blind Widow pulling at the tiniest hairs thereabouts.

They broke from the contest for a moment, rounding an invisible sparring circle from about ten feet apart. Nothing outside their scowls registered.

"You know your way around a sword, but you are overly cautious," Yongrin said, touching a hand to her neck with a sneer. "Vaustian's student to the letter."

"And you are unbalanced."

"That a fact?"

"A blade always mirrors its master."

"Save your bookworm rhetoric, wretch. You left nothing of my brother." Yongrin's eyes hardened. "And then you sent that thing after me to do

239

the same. I don't know how you managed to summon a blood wraith, but it'll take a good measure more to push me under."

A blood wraith? So, her speculation from *Dusk*'s bestiary section was correct.

"What? Nothing to say, princess?" Yongrin sneered. "Truth is you're just as much a monster as the rest of us."

"What happened to Davrin, was not intended. I had no idea about the blood wraith until it was upon us."

"Keep your excuses. It won't change any of this. I mean to have the grimoire and your grave."

Yongrin dashed at her again, forcing Marsea on the defensive, each strike like a hammer to the anvil, clumsy, but a damned sight stronger than anything the princess would have anticipated from the woman before their crossing.

Dodge, parry, feint, parry, dodge. This became their song for minutes on end, Marsea gasping for air as Yongrin gained in confidence and became that much more ruthless in her pursuit. It was a barrage amongst the worst Vaustian had ever put her through, and harder still than what Ganedys had given her, the magus's gift on full display. But Blind Widow would not be undone so easily. Not by some upstart hayseed with a vendetta, and certainly not by its soft and half-tutored bearer.

And then the strikes began to slow. The haxanblade screaming as much as the bloodlust intensified, the ache from Blind Widow's pull to the tower all but a distant memory. She couldn't feel any of it now. Only the haxanblade. Only the length of metal nightmare rising from her fists.

"You're heavy," Marsea spat the haxanblade's ire as the dance shifted, and she caught the offensive, pushing Yongrin back, forcing her to better her footwork or risk the ugly end of Blind Widow's wrath.

Fever poured down her skin, cherry blossom steam chasing strawberry steel, desperate to sate an unsatiable hunger.

Yongrin managed a few commendable strikes between parries, but nothing of true concern, as Marsea pressed her into a retreat.

"You do not know what you wield, girl," Yongrin managed through tired breaths.

"I know plenty well what I wield."

Marsea stole a quick glance around at the others, before returning to Yongrin. Edgar held at the base of the tower steps, arrow trained on

Yongrin's every move. Poppy remained perfectly still, and bedsheet pale, with prowling Broenwjar ready to pounce at a moment's notice. Only kept at bay by Marsea's order.

"A haxanblade cannot be controlled. That's what summoned the blood wraith."

Kill her and be done with it, Other demanded. **She is the one this time.**

The one for what?

We've been here before. Us.

Blind Widow let out an ungodly screech and Yongrin charged at her.

Marsea brought the haxanblade up for the defense, its steel a ruby-colored horror...and Yongrin was on her...and there was a ringing sound, followed by a second, and a glint of shattered steel hurdling end over end into the field behind her, as a tremor ran the length of her arms. Instinctually, she bent around her foe, like a water serpent, dropping low, toes sliding in the dirt, just as Vaustian taught her, she and the haxanblade moving as one, carving a gash deep into the sorceress's exposed flank.

A stream of blood trailed the princess, hanging midair, as she followed her momentum through and whirled around to face her opponent.

Yongrin staggered forward, away from Marsea, dark red blood soaking through her clothes as she pressed a trembling hand against the gushing wound. A shriek thence followed, rupturing the spring of dusk, and all was red, bright and blinding, spiraling from the sorceress like the inside of a rose.

Color drained from Marsea's countenance as the blood wraith appeared from inside the tower entrance; tall as a wngar, sickly gray skin, face concealed behind a veil of long snow-white hair, moving its hands in a similar esoteric motion as before with Davrin, scratching and ripping Yongrin apart from the inside out.

The sorceress crumbled into the flowers, flesh chunks and dark red paste rising from the stain that was her shriveling body.

A command snapped from Marsea's mind to Broenwjar and Old Boy leapt at Poppy and her captor, driving Yongrin's accomplice down into the heather. Poppy scrambled away from the bloodbath on hands and knees, crying and cursing hysterically as Edgar raced out toward them.

Steaming entrails spouted from Yongrin's opened side as the blood wraith wrung her once humanoid shape free of its contents, ounce by bloody ounce, organ by severed organ.

Oh, and how the sorceress wailed, until enough of her had been torn away as to end the possibility. Her agony concluding with abrupt finality, replaced by wet, fleshy sounds, and the groans of the surrounding ghouls.

Whispers danced like phantoms all around her as the floating mass of Yongrin Tarboril called her back to the tower, back toward her destiny. Just as Other had promised. Marsea had been here before, indeed. In this very moment. She knew it for truth as she watched the river of gore pool into a sloshing, spinning vortex. It was slightly different than the last time, but the sensation, the familiarity, could not be denied.

Before the blood wraith, a sigil sparked to life, and Yongrin's insides amassed around it forming a watery puddle not unlike a translocation ward. Though she had the thought to, Marsea realized she could not turn away from it. The portal was drawing her in. Drawing in the haxanblade, which she found once again she could not release. Step by step, she neared, fighting the sickness in her belly, her eyes widening as the pool of blood swelled.

"Selwyn, what are you doing?" she heard Edgar holler.

"Get away from there," Poppy shouted.

They were safe. For now.

Watch over them, she implored her maidens many, halting at the last step and staring into the pool of blood at her crimson reflection.

Broenwjar appeared at her side, the satchel containing *Dusk* in his mouth, and Rhymona on her other, her face unreadable in the gurgling murk.

Rhymona? Marsea glanced to the space where her friend stood, as an invisible force compelled her through the portal.

CHAPTER TWENTY-FOUR

TIME DOES NOT HEAL OLD WOUNDS, Thira said as they pressed further into the labyrinth's stench. *IT INSTRUCTS YOU HOW TO LIVE WITH THE PAIN. ELSE, WHAT IS THE POINT OF PAIN IF YOU DO NOT LEARN FROM IT AND CHANGE WITH THE KNOWLEDGE EARNED?*

Easier said than done, Remy returned, as he squeezed through another slender cut within the palace underbelly, like a blade between ribs, passing into a much larger chamber. The others joined him one after the other. Fortunately, they were all able to fit through, though he and Desmond only just. It went without saying, really, but the path was growing more treacherous the further they progressed.

"Let's hold here for a moment," he said, inhaling the seawater scent of the unshapely cavern.

An eerie timelessness had begun to creep in, and the group had grown quiet and inward. A result Thira suspected belonged to her trickster brother, borne of a similar sort of warding madness as what he unleashed in the upper halls of Lancastle.

NOTHING ABOUT LIFE IS EVER EASY, REMY. TO LIVE IS TO SUFFER. THIS IS UNDENIABLE. NO MATTER THE COUNT OF YOUR COFFERS OR THE WARMTH OF YOUR HEARTHFIRES.

No matter the record of mine bloodline?

THE GIFT IS CHAOS, PRIZE WELL, EVEN FOR THOSE OF THE GODSBLOOD.

Remy glanced over at Desmond, who had remained suspiciously quiet since they started on into the dark.

IT IS NOT FOR US TO UNDERSTAND. SAVE THAT IT WILL TAKE EVERYTHING IF PRESENTED THE CHANCE.

Then what does that make the nether?

I BELIEVE THE NETHER A PERVERSION OF ORDER.

You think this madness order?

WE CAN AGREE THE ORIGIN OF THE GIFT CAME FROM THE GODS, YES?

Yes.

AND WE KNOW IT WAS STOLEN BY THEIR MORTAL SUBJECTS HOWEVER LONG AGO AND THEREAFTER STREWN ACROSS THE UNIVERSE. AN ACT FOR WHICH THERE WOULD EXIST NO REVERSAL.

That is speculation.

BUT LIKELY TRUE. WITH THAT IN MIND, IS IT NOT WITHIN THE REALM OF POSSIBILITY THAT THE NETHER MAY BE THE GODS' WAY OF PUNISHING SUCH A THEFT?

A chill ran through him.

Speak it plain, Thira. What are you trying to say here?

I AM SAYING THE NETHER IS A CURSE BORN OF THE GIFT. FASHIONED BY THE GODS TO PUNISH THOSE WHO WOULD ABUSE THAT WHICH WAS STOLEN. THAT IS HOW THE GODS WOULD CONTROL THEIR OVERSIGHT. BUT I THINK TETHEROW AND ITS KIN HAVE SOMEHOW CONTRIVED A METHOD OF CORRUPTING THE NETHER SO THAT IT TARGETS THE GIFT REGARDLESS OF ITS MISUSE.

Its kin?

YOUR BROTHER HAD QUITE THE INSIGHT DESPITE HIS SUFFER- ING. HE SPOKE OF A DREAM EATER EARLIER. AN INCUBUS SPAWN. A DEMON ESSENCE.

Demons cannot cross over to this plane. The Pale...

THE PALE IS RIVEN. AS PROVEN BY THE NETHER'S ADVENT. DEMONS CAN CROSS OVER JUST AS THE NETHER HAS. IT MAY REQUIRE SOME SPELLWORK AND A RITUAL PARTY, BUT IT IS NO LONGER WARDED AGAINST AS CENTURIES PAST.

Then we find a way to close it again. Once we have the grimoires. There must be a way.

I HAVE NO DOUBTS THERE IS, BUT I FEAR WHAT IT MAY REQUIRE OF US. HOW IT MAY ALTER US.

Remy scanned the chamber, spotting strange markings carved into the stone walls.

"These markings are ashaeydiri," Rhymona said, tracing fingers against a line of runes.

"Ashaeydiri?" Remy echoed as he approached. *Ashaeydir script beneath one of Midara's most heavily guarded citadels?*

"It speaks of a temple and wreckage from the sky." Rhymona trailed down the wall to another set of runes. "This bit here is y'deman. Devil wards looks like." She stopped a little further down. "But these," she shook her head, "I don't quite follow. They look Chandiian."

Remy inspected the symbols.

"*...And so, they are...,*" Remy repeated Thira's words. "*...Old Chandiian, too, well before the more modernized alphabet that was used once they came to Midara. From what I can tell, it appears to be a list of names, noted as celestial beings. None that I recognize though...*" Thira moved on to the next plot of runes. "*...I believe it a memorial. The names of fallen warriors...*"

"What the hells is this place?" Rhymona asked the obvious question. "Why would a chandii warrior or an ashaeydir ever venture here?"

"*...Fine questions, both...,*" Thira spoke through Remy.

"Celestial beings?" Rhymona kept on. "How long has it been here, you reckon? Did the vinteyamans build a kingdom on top of an underground city?"

"*...It would not be the first time. You might recall Svegaldt was once a dwarven settlement...*"

"Hate to butcher the history lesson, but anyone have a clue how long we've been down here?" Desmond asked.

"*...Impossible to say...*" the watchman prince answered. "*...I believe Hrathgon has placed wards within that toy with the mind, not to mention time and space...*"

"And you're just telling us this now?" Rhymona grumbled.

"*...I could not be sure because it may not affect me as it does you...*" Remy glanced at the group, one to the next, at what remained of his family. "*...Also, I did not want to alarm you all any more than was necessary. As I have* *cautioned before, Hrathgon is a tactful trickster, and he loves to use fear to manipulate his enemies..."*

"What should we expect?" Rhymona asked.

"I would say hallucinations," Remy resumed control, "but you already suffer those apparently."

"Bit of a dick thing to say, but fair."

"Thira says we'll need to hold each other accountable going forward. If one of us starts to muck off the carriage, we'll need to—"

A howling noise resounded from some rest up ahead, collecting in the chamber, before squeezing back through the narrow fissure and into the darkness whence they'd come.

They all looked at each other with varying expressions of distress.

"What did that sound like to you lot?" Rhymona asked.

"Damned if I know," Desmond answered. "But nothing at all like the growling sounds from before."

"Could it have been Goss?"

"Possibly."

Goss's scratch marks on the walls halted some time ago, and the further inward they traversed without finding him, the more Thira began to fear the good magus had become lost to one of Hrathgon's madness spells. Had there been more time, had she known about Hrathgon's attendance, she would have warned the others to stick together in her absence, and certainly not go exploring alone.

This coupled with the fact that they hadn't come across a single living creature since entering the catacombs, no insects, no flora, not even a stray rat, she suspected devilry would soon find them, and warned Remy thus to remain vigilant.

"Shall we on then?" Rhymona said, starting toward an arched opening in the rocks that led to another narrow passageway.

"Take the lead," Remy said, as he stopped next to Julia. "You seeing anything out of the ordinary, Jules?"

"No, I don't believe so. I keep thinking of mum though. Of what happened."

Remy nodded. "Me too. And that's normal. It's all right to think of her."

"Yeah."

"You'll tell me if it starts to get in too far, yeah?"

"I will."

"Good."

They followed after Rhymona and Desmond.

"We'll find a way out of this place," he said. "And we'll find Marsea and the grimoires, and we'll bring an end to this all this horror. I promise."

She nodded and they walked in silence again for a while, side by side.

"I'm glad we're together, Remy," Julia said after a fork and a few more awkward twists and dogleg turns.

"Me too," he forced a smile for her, not too much of one, but just enough to let her know he appreciated her saying so.

"What the fuck is that?" Rhymona asked from up ahead and a bright green flash of light followed.

"Rhymona!" Remy cried out, rushing toward the others, conjuring a fresh egg of Eldn fire.

"Stay back!" Desmond warned through a coughing spell, dropping to his knees.

Lenore flew back toward them, perching atop a mantle in the stone wall, cawing feverishly.

Remy and Julia halted at the edge of the vapor that surrounded their companions.

Thira, what is this?

BY THE SCENT AND COLOR, MY BEST GUESS IS GHOST BLOSSOM.

Cute name.

NOT SO CUTE SIDE EFFECTS.

Will it kill them?

NOT PHYSICALLY UNLESS THEY HAVE AN ALLERGY TO ONE OF THE COMPONENTS. PSYCHOLOGICALLY WILL PROVE A DIFFERENT STORY.

Care to elaborate?

Manic laughter answered.

Desmond stared up from beneath his lowered brow with a resin-fiend grin stretched across his malformed face, bloodshot eyes pissing tears down his boney cheeks, cackling hysterically at them.

"Des?" Julia asked.

"Stay behind me, Jules." Remy reached an arm out in front of her, pulling her back.

"What's wrong with him?"

"What's wrong?" Desmond echoed, running fingers down from his watery eyes, red and white. "What's wrong?" He gripped Fucker and leapt to his feet. "We're all fucked, that's what's wrong."

"No," Rhymona started from further down the passageway. "This isn't where it happened before. This isn't the same place."

"Rhymona," Remy called. "Are you all right?"

"Rhymona's not here right now," Desmond answered.

Remy raised his watchman's blade at his brother. "Where is she?"

"Head Fuck City, population fucked."

Classy.

"Hand me the hatchet, brother," Remy ordered.

"I think not, *brother.*" Desmond cracked a deranged gap-toothed smile. "A promise is a promise, yeah. Head Fuck City back there won't like I betrayed her husband. Even to you. Besides me and cutter here, we're old mates now."

More batshit mental then. Lovely.

"You can trust me," Julia said.

"Trust *you?*" Desmond echoed. "I saw what you did in the halls upstairs, you murderous little slip. You may not rightly look it, but you're a killer just like the rest of us."

"Back the fuck off," Rhymona shouted, swinging back around toward them, cutting her mae'chii at open air. "I said away, or I'll have you open cunt to crown. This isn't the place."

Desmond turned back toward her, and Remy quelled the Eldn flame, jerking his brother back from the cloud of ghost blossom, wrestling him to the ground, and pinning him down beneath the flat of his watchman's blade.

"Well, that wasn't very sporting, was it?" Desmond chuckled. "What's the plan now, little brother? You going to have me a red smile?"

"I'm trying to save you, you fucking bellend."

"I said, fuck off!" Rhymona shrieked into the nothing between them before turning away and rushing into the black beyond.

"Rhymona!" Julia cried out, chasing after the magus.

"Jules, no!" Remy hollered.

LET HER GO, Thira bade.

Are you mad?

THE SPELL HAS NEARLY DISSIPATED.

"Shitting the bed with a flourish, little brother. Delighted to know I'm not the only fuck-up in the family."

"Dammit," Remy hissed. "Would you piss off with the little brother wag already?"

"Touchy-touchy." Desmond's eyes hardened and his smile evaporated. "You...you bastard!" he screamed into Remy's face. "You killed her!"

"What?" Remy returned.

HE IS HALLUCINATING. THE GHOST BLOSSOM IS A FEAR INDUCER, NAMED AS SUCH FOR THE THINGS THAT HAUNT US MOST. HE LIKELY SEES YOU AS AN ENEMY OR SOMEONE HE IS AFEARED OF.

Bloody hells. Remy strained against his brother's flailing. *How long do the effects last?*

Desmond caught Remy with a punch to the side of his head, struggling against the youngest's weight. Remy removed the sword from his brother's throat before the mad fool accidentally opened it himself with his wild squirming, all the while, blocking the eldest's thrashing blows.

"Desmond, snap out of it. I am not your enemy."

"You can't fool me." Desmond gripped Remy's neck and began to squeeze. "I'll do you like you did her, you fucking whoreson." Remy grasped his brother's wrists as fingernails split into skin, and ripped them off him, opening Desmond's defenses, and chased the effort with a downward strike that stung like a son-of-a-bitch and a second to the nose that set him straight.

Desmond spit blood with the contact, his eyes rolling about inside their sockets, mumbling something incoherent.

"Bloody lunatic," Remy grumbled through tired breaths as he retrieved Fucker and the watchman's blade and stood over his dazed brother, staring into the darkness after the others.

CHAPTER TWENTY-FIVE

No.

Rhymona walked the walls, teetering from one side of the passageway to the other, footsteps crossing awkward one before the next, her vision spinning fast as a carousal, digging at the sick in her stomach. Not that she had much in her to offer up for it.

No, no. No, no.

Sweat hemorrhaged from her pores, leaking down her body and through her clothing like the wringing of a wet wash rag.

Not like this.

Suddenly she became acutely aware of her own stink. Ripe in spite of the dank cave cellar air. Her gift complaining, letting her know something was coming, and would quite soon find her.

This is wrong.

A dull pressure ran the shape of her skull, conjured from nothing and everything at once.

This is all wrong.

The shards were everywhere and anywhere her eyes fell, like hail in a blizzard. Twinkling slivers of radiant crimson. Amassing as though for war. Merging into shimmering glass battalions. Their presence accompanied by a rumbling like a stampede of oni. Putting her to the huntsman's chase.

But this is it, isn't it? This is how it happens.

One would figure she might have become used to such a shitshow by now given the terrible nature of her dreamscape, but these mirrorspawn were different from those of her night terrors. For these lot showed others amongst her own warped reflections.

Versions of Stella.

Of Fia.

Of Marsea.

And the white-haired crone.

She could feel them raging inside the whirling fragments of gallows glass. Sense their violent shivers. Each more hateful than the last. More hateful than she on her worst days.

"What would you have of me?" Rhymona implored the pulsating darkness. "Where would you have me go?"

"Rhymona, wait!" A voice answered.

The magus spun around, mae'chii at the ready, tears flooding down her face.

"Rhymona, it's me."

Torchlight neared from around the bend.

"Julia?"

The girl rounded the corner and slowed her advance, their eyes meeting. "Munchkin?" she asked.

As Rhymona let the silver fall to her side, a bright golden spark crackled in the passageway between them, twisting and arching like in her dreams, causing the floating pieces of gallows glass to sparkle like a burst of fireworks.

Portal magic.

The rune began as a spiral, looping round and round, creating three circles, stopping at the largest circle's base and shooting straight up through the others like an arrow where it arched out to form a small triangle for a crown. Rhymona recognized the language as Chandiian, and the spell as a translocation ward, but nothing came to her regarding a proper name for it.

At the rune's completion, the shards of gallows glass all snapped together simultaneously, a rippling egg of red fluids gushing forth from their union, pulsing waves spraying into the passageway and spewing

251

viscera across the stones below, a dark river forming and snaking out toward her.

"Munchkin," Rhymona uttered, staring at her antlered crimson reflection in the blood mirror as it stretched unnaturally, ceiling to floor, more scar on her face than actual face, her hair growing impossibly fast down her expanding torso, near to her feet, her fingernails lengthening to the size of scullery knives.

"I'm here," Julia said as she appeared through the ghastly reflection, unaffected by its fount of gore.

"So is she," the magus whispered.

"Who?" the girl inquired.

"The witch god." Rhymona could smell her now. Close by. The scent of old fish at market sending her insides lurching again, drowning out the rotten egg stench of the gurgling blood ward. "And she won't be denied this time."

Julia followed Rhymona's gaze and turned back to her in confusion. "It's the smoke. It's causing you to see things."

You will hear it like a thunder through the stone. Feel it deep inside your core, pulling at every fiber of your being. Taste it like an abscess in your mouth. And when it comes...

"You must let it move through you," Rhymona said.

"What?"

"For only then will you move through it. With it. As it."

"What are you talking about?"

Wisps of bright white hair materialized around her, fine as spider's silk. Had they always been there? In the ether? Or were her eyes finally exposing the truth? Peeling back the shroud of The Pale.

"I've been here before." Rhymona approached the floating pool of blood and guts, passing Julia, slogging through slick entrails, clawing through layers of cobwebs. "All of this. Since we arrived in Courowne. I've seen all of this before. Lived it before. Or something very near to it."

"Rhymona, you're not making any sense."

"You cannot see it because you are not controlled by this curse."

"I don't understand. What curse?"

"I've been running from it for far too long now. Hoping it would never catch me up. Praying Stella was just taking the piss."

"Whatever you're on about, wherever you think you're off to, I won't let you go alone."

"The portal is not meant for you, Jules."

"What portal?"

"It won't have you try as you might to stand my side. And if I'm right about this, where I'm going, I won't be alone. Your sister calls to me."

"Seasea?"

"We are spellbound to this curse, she and I."

"Julia!" Remy howled.

"You must stay with your brothers, yeah. Strong women like us keep halfwits like those two out of the dirt."

"Rhymona."

"Tell them I'm with Marsea," Rhymona said, before pushing into the boiling puddle of gift rot.

CHAPTER TWENTY-SIX

THE RIFT RAIDED her insides like a plowman's plague, wave after crimson wave, drowning her within its blood vessel burrow, cruel as a whore mother dunking her delicates, worse than raw-dogging a beggar's drop into The Spellbind off a bottle of black, flaying away at her body, layer by layer, until it had the bone of her and split her apart at the sternum, where it proceeded to dig in at her exposed organs, prying them from their proper placement one after the other, squeezing each one, slick and soupy, before fastly reversing course and stuffing them back inside her all helter-skelter.

All the world became red, smothered in every gruesome shade of it imaginable, as the blood portal released Rhymona upon the steps of a great ranging tower, the word *Wyrmswold* rattling ruthlessly about her mindscape.

Twisting movement overhead drew her attention to the pale pink heavens as ruby-colored bloodflakes drifted down from the fleshy tentacle-like appendages dangling about the endless mass of cloudworks like severed arteries.

Reckon it'd be too much for one of these damned portals to find a fucking tavern for once, she thought as she sheathed Val's mae'chii and proceeded to push along the seams of her reconstructed body. Despite all the agony, she found herself in one piece, apparently no worse for wear.

Crimson bubbles of various sizes floated up from the ground and the magus poked at one about the size of an apple. It popped covering her hand in a dark, syrupy goo.

What the fuck?

A sudden stir of watery vapor beside her drew her attentions and a familiar figure surfaced.

"Marsea," she rasped through the dustland pitch the blood portal left in her mouth.

"Rhymona?" Marsea grated in return.

Love the hair. "With respect, you look about as fit as a boiled turd."

"Pot meet kettle."

"Still alive though, so there's a thing."

"And little brother?"

"Still a pain in the arse."

"The stars save us." A smirk twitched upon the princess's lips as she reached down to retrieve a satchel from the largest wolf Rhymona had ever beheld.

"Desmond too," Rhymona offered with considerably less enthusiasm, though she reckoned the girl deserved to know.

"Desmond?"

"What can I say? We've been a busy bunch."

"Desmond's alive?" Marsea's face twitched about in search of a proper expression. "As in *alive* alive?

"As in." *For now.*

"But how? I don't understand…"

"Do come in," a woman spoke from inside the tower.

They froze for a moment, eyes widening, before turning in unison to the flicker of firelight through the doorway.

"Quickly then. Our window will be limited."

"After you," Rhymona curtsied, waving a hand out for the princess to proceed.

"Oh, but you're too kind," Marsea answered with a wrinkle of her button nose.

Same old Marsea, she thought, grateful the girl's time away from Lancastle hadn't yet made of her a complete ruin.

Inside, they found Stella sitting in a high-backed armchair at the far wall. Though this version appeared a far cry from the beauty Rhymona met all those many cycles past, most notably altered by a thick, uneven traitor's brand swallowing the entire left side of her face from cheekbone to jawline. She shifted in the seat as they approached, turning the ugly half into the gloom.

"A fresh loop it is then," Stella said. "I'd begun to suspect." She focused on Marsea. "Though I reckon by your being here, sending you into the past was a failure."

"Me?" Marsea asked.

"Please, have a seat, if you like," Stella gestured to the quartet of armchairs facing her. "I'll explain in due course." Her eyes trailed to the wolf at the princess's side. "That's new."

"His name is Broenwjar," Marsea said, finding a rest in the leftmost chair. "He is my familiar."

"Your familiar, is it? Oh, but he's a frightful beastie, isn't he?" She smiled at their furry companion. "Welcome aboard, Broenwjar. We'll take whatever hands we can get." Her attentions returned to the girls. "I must say, you both appear in considerably better shape and spirits than the last time."

Then what the fuck happened last time? Cause shit's pretty shit right now.

Rhymona plopped down in the furthest chair to the right, taking in the glowing sigils circling the tower walls around them, not a one familiar to her at first inspection. "I know *where* we are, but what the fuck is this place?"

"We call it The Bloodbind, or rather our prior incarnations did. Though, to my knowledge, there isn't a proper name for it." Stella let her bad side slip into the fireglow, the scarring from the traitor's brand having warped her face to such an extent that only one side of her mouth moved naturally when she spoke.

Prior incarnations?

"It's almost as though we've been transported inside the belly of a living creature or some such," Marsea said, wiping her glasses clean with the hem of her shirt.

"In a way, you have, milady. It is similar to Spellbind Theory, if you are familiar. Created in a similar fashion anyway, as a pocket dimension, a place outside of time and space with restorative properties and what have you. However, it is not astral like The Spellbind, it is corporeal."

"Meaning we're actually physically here?"

"Meaning just. There are portals called by the elements and ancient runes, after all. And the gods know, we've used the body to pervert every other aspect of the gift to this point. Is it truly that much more far-fetched they can also be called from the flesh and blood? I'm assuming that's how you both came here. A carnomancer's cast during dusk with that there haxanblade."

"Yes," the princess answered, returning her odd-shaped spectacles to their perch. "At least that is how I arrived."

"The portal opened up before me in a labyrinth beneath Courowne," Rhymona said.

"Courowne?" Marsea gazed at her, an eyebrow arched inquisitively.

"It's a long story."

"And one we may not have time for just now," Stella said.

"Prior incarnations, last times, previous loops. What in vaelnation are we talking about here?" Rhymona folded her arms and squeezed them in close. "What's happening to us?"

"That blade in your hand," Stella held Marsea's eyes, "how long has it been in your possession?"

"A few days. It was given to me by—"

"Beldroth, I presume," Stella finished.

"Yes."

"And is he still alive?"

"Not in the proper sense." The princess bowed her head as though in tribute.

The fuck does that mean? Rhymona thought, curious to know what all went on between the princess and Ravenholme after their parting.

"He was poisoned by the nether," Marsea continued, "and it turned him into a creature called a gnaudrylax."

"As was his fate in prior loops, the poor soul." Stella shifted in her chair, placing her elbows at her knees, holding her audience with an intense stare. "I take it you both have been experiencing sensory recall over the past few days then? Since you took up the blade. The feeling like you've lived through the passing events before?"

"Yes," Marsea answered.

Rhymona shrugged, lips thinning, not loving the conversation's present course.

"It is because you have, in a manner of speaking. In this loop, did I find you, Morgandrel? Did I give you the ward key to Lancastle Library?"

"Sylvoth'yka," Rhymona said, as though Stella plucked the word forth from its last utterance half a decade past.

"Grand," Stella breathed, "we're already leagues ahead of the last one then."

Rhymona blinked at Stella realizing the woman had spoken her true name. Oh, but how the questions were mounting now. *Keep it to the plot, girl.* "I'm sorry, but there you go again with the last one bit? Are you saying we're actually reincarnated souls living inside of a time loop? As in we are living the same life over and over and over again?"

"To name it the *same* life is a bit of an oversimplification, but, yes, that's nearly the sum of it. We've been taking what we can from previous loops and using it to alter the next."

"Fucking hells," Rhymona stood, fearing such an affirmation, her chair scraping back across the flagstones, and she began to pace, the urge to run fingernails over the long scar on the inside of her arm rearing its nasty fangs again.

"We remember fragments from before. And something about the haxanblade there unlocks those memories in us once one of us melds with it."

"Just to clarify," Rhymona spun back around to face the group, "we're talking about chronomancy here."

"We are, indeed."

"Right. And chronomancy is a fucking myth."

"Says the girl who taught me its language," Stella said. "I take it by my absence I'm already dead in this loop?"

Rhymona lowered her vision from the sorceress and offered a grim nod.

Stella frowned. "Can't win them all, I suppose."

"I'm still trying to wrap my head around this prior incarnation business," Marsea said. "How many loops have there been?"

"Seven, eight, nine-ish...that I'm aware of," Stella answered. "Though, honestly, it could be any number. There was at least one or two before mine, and likely more as I have an assortment of memories from them. And there have been six since my caging including this one."

"Your caging?"

"Aye. Something we did, or I did, in my loop created a time slip that trapped me here, which I'm finding both a gift and a curse."

"How do you mean trapped you here?"

"At dusk's end in your respective plane, you'll both be pulled back to Vaelsyntheria, to your proper lives. For some reason I don't go back with the rest of you when this happens."

"Odd."

"Well odd and properly fucked, if you'll have my grievances. It's actually pulled back every other version of me since, but for whatever reason won't have this old ghoul."

"How long have you been here?" Marsea asked.

"Would that I could name it. Quints, mayhaps months, though time works differently here."

"How have you even survived that long? What do you eat in this place?"

"Hunger no longer betides me. Neither does sleep. I suspect this is due to the restorative properties of The Bloodbind, though to have it true, I haven't the foggiest. And prize well, these are but a few of the dozen some-odd anomalies I've encountered from previous loops."

The fucking rabbit hole to end all rabbit holes, this.

"Well, let's just do the bloody thing already," Rhymona said. "What else do we need to know?"

"Where to begin?" Stella returned. "Ah, the blood wraith for one. The one that conjures The Bloodbind at duskfall to bring us here." Stella favored Rhymona with a look of pity. "That one's you. Or a past version of you."

"Me?" Rhymona asked.

"Her?" Marsea said at the same time, a look of sheer terror scrawled across her countenance.

"From one of the loops before, mayhaps the prime loop. I can only assume she attempted to split her soul into the blade for whatever purpose and it came back sour."

"Split her what into the what?"

"Merely speculation, mind you, but that creature is indeed some bastard version of you. She may not have known at the time, obviously, but my theory is there was a curse on the sword in her loop that twisted her enchantment against her and bound part of her to it in a similar manner that I am now bound to the tower. No doubt you've both experienced strange irregularities of the like. Memories from lives unlived. Division of self."

"Division of self, yes," Marsea said, trailing her half-hand through the scraggily mass of wolf fur at her side.

"Milady, pardon the dance of topics, but did I overhear your brothers are still alive?"

"Apparently." Marsea gazed from Stella to Rhymona.

"I was with them in Courowne when the portal opened." Rhymona expounded. "Aid...Desmond was possessed by a creature named Tetherow, but somehow managed to expel the fiend."

"Malthus Tetherow," Stella hissed. "He is cambion, if you weren't already privy. And the demon half has been at the root of every loop I'm aware of."

"Desmond explained as much."

"In nearly every instance the demon took a different form. King Whit twice, Prince Desmond, a Chandii magus named Effie Cavendish, and a Baron named Vaustian Harver."

"Vaustian?" Marsea said.

"Fuck's sake, this is a bloody madness," Rhymona harped, driving a fist down into the nearest tabletop. "This rewrites everything. Literally rewrites everything. I mean, fuck it. The way she's mugging about, who's not to say we're not all just different versions of the same bitch?"

"Oh, don't be absurd," Marsea said.

"What's absurd about it? We're talking alternate timelines and resurrected souls here. At this point what's a little more spice?"

"I'm merely relaying what I know."

"Everything we've done, everything we've been through, and now we're just reduced to pawns in a fucking loop?"

"You say that like it's a bad thing," Stella said.

"Right," Rhymona made a quick shake of her head as though nothing in the history of existence could have been more obvious. "Unless you have some positive news to share with the class."

"Paltry as it is, it's still your life, isn't it? And silver lining, two of us made it this time, neither one of you bleeding out or missing any eyes or limbs..."

"Well," Marsea held up her bad hand.

"Not to diminish your suffering, milady, but losing a few lengths is about the best I've seen from your prior count. You were a corpse already in three of the five since mine. Couple that with your familiar there and the fact that your brothers are both still breathing, and it sounds to me like you've swindled the gods of their coin and supper both. To wit, this is the best shape I've seen us in this far into a loop. I'm not exactly thrilled that I'm one of the casualties in this one, but if what you lot say is true, this is as good as I've seen us coming off a haxan egg, so I'll take the loss and send up a prayer."

"Well, hu-fucking-zzah then," Rhymona spat. "Shall we on to the wine? Have a caper about The Bloodbind elite."

"Piss on it all you like, Morgan. But, given our state from loops before, this is the first one I believe we might actually stand half a chance to end it."

"Yeah? And how many loops before have you spat out that wishful ass gobshite for the lessers to shit it?"

"I only know so much, Morgan."

"It's Rhymona, in this one, yeah. Rhymona Fucking Curie."

"Rhymona Fucking Curie, fine." Oh, but this Stella had a chip on her shoulder tall as the tower that trapped her, and a devil's tongue to fit the ire. "Ridiculous as it is, I believe the three of us have been caught in this time loop mess for a reason. I believe someone or something has put us here to end all this with the entity, however many loops it takes."

"The what?"

"The entity, the nether, giftsbane, the all-things tomb."

"Colorful, truly."

"I believe this something pushes parts from previous loops into our minds for us to deconstruct and use against Tetherow and the nether. I believe it uses our gifts, our dreams, our sorrows, whatever it can, and I believe it's just as desperate as we are to break the cycle."

"How long does the loop progress after this?" Marsea asked.

"It varies."

"Meaning you don't know," Rhymona quibbled.

"Meaning it's up to you lot, isn't it? I've had those from the same loop return before, which means multiple days, dusks, rot, rot, bloody rot and onward. As far as I know, it ends and begins again once the four of us die."

"The four of us?"

"Us three and Lita Drufellyn."

"The Wyrmstower Witch?" Marsea uttered. "She's a part of this too?"
Of course, she is.

"Aye. Though I've only ever met her in one other loop. My loop, coincidentally. But I know she also existed in the loop prior." Stella glared at Rhymona. "In that loop, you and she were, shall we say...together."

"The Wyrmstower Witch is fairytale folly," Rhymona spat. "A hearthfire haunter old fuckwits bugger on about to pass the darkly hours."

"I know what I know, dear."

"Oh, now don't do that. Don't fucking dear me, yeah. You're bent is what all this amounts to. Far as I can see."

"Given my tale, you think I give a mummer's wet toss about lying to you? What purpose would that possibly serve me? Chances are I'll be looking at another one of you lot before too long anyway. Especially if you keep on with that attitude."

"Why are we coming at each other?" Marsea asked. "We're all on the same side here. Aren't we?"

"You had a burn name for her," Stella said, orbs hard as pitted iron. "You named yourselves as sisters beyond blood."

"A burn name?" A certain scar upon Rhymona's thigh began to itch.

"Yes, you named yourselves as each other's balance. Two sides of the same coin. Opposites. Equals. Twins. And she took up your House name through a silly anagram of her own. A special name that was only meant for your tongue. Fiandrel, as it were. Fiandrel Tully."

What remained of Rhymona's heart caught.

"She preferred the name to her own, in truth."

Rhymona circled back round her chair and collapsed upon it, heat filling the dark spaces behind her eyes. "All right." She searched the corners of her vision for her sister's ghost, but neither hide nor hair nor a shudder of movement would permit such an indulgence. But how could she deny the woman's words now, mad as they were? How else could she possibly know of these things if not for some barmy chronomancy bollocks?

"Rhymona," Marsea whispered.

Her head shook around a scowl for the ages, and a middle finger split the space between them.

"Let her sort it a second," Stella said.

"You said others had returned once dusk becomes nightfall," the princess started. "What happens after this? After we leave The Bloodbind?"

"Nothing good, I assure you. I think it best we concentrate on what we do know from this one. You said Desmond *was* possessed by Tetherow. Do you know who the current host is?"

"No," Rhymona muttered. "Wait." She shook her head to clear her thoughts. "Aid...Desmond mentioned something about Autumn. His sister."

"His what?" Marsea was quick to the cut.

"Step-sister, I should say," Rhymona held Stella's eyes. "Your daughter."

"My...daughter?" Stella's jaw slackened. "But that's not...I can't have children..."

"You can in our loop," Rhymona said. "You did. I've met her, in fact. And you were the one that brought Desmond back from the dead."

"I did what?"

"You gravedanced that bastard back from his coffin, a quint after Vaustian Harver shoved a blade in him. Brought him back and raised him as your own and then you had a baby girl."

"Gravedanced? Maidens' mercy, I would never. You. You were always the gravedancer. You and Lita."

"Our loop it was you."

"Gods' bones this loop has gone completely off the trolley then, hasn't it?"

"The what?"

"I...bloody hells, how different are our timelines? What cycle is it for you?"

"1829."

"In mine it was 1828, so not far off. Anyway, your me has a daughter named Autumn and Tetherow may be coming after her?"

"That would appear to be the gist of it, though I've only just become privy to the news myself."

"Right, then let's break this down," Stella wandered past their circle into the chamber. "If she's my bloodline, mayhaps, is Tetherow..." She stopped before a bookshelf and leaned back against it, scratching the side of her neck. "No..."

"What?"

"Could it be targeting Chandii blood? Would it know?"

"Haven't formally met the bastard just yet, but seems a fair assumption it would. Our Tetherow is rather known to be a cunty piece of shit, all told."

"Who is the father?"

Rhymona shrugged. "Some Southland arsehole named Vincent Ashborough. Seemed pretty nondescript to me. Had little to no interest in me the one time we shared a chamber. Aiden, fucking hells, Desmond, seemed rather unimpressed all the same. Gods know, you get that Aiden and Desmond are the same fucking knobend in our loop, yeah?"

"I gathered as much, but appreciate the clarification. This is the first loop I've heard of a Vincent Ashborough."

"He's a winemaker in Gallea's Grace, and that's pretty much the story as far as I know it. As just-some-tosser as one gets."

"Tetherow is adapting then, just like we are. It must know of the loops. If what you say is true, if my daughter is the target, then that could spell grave trouble for this loop if Tetherow takes possession. Chandii blood is dreadfully dangerous, especially if it hasn't been tapped before."

"Right, right, now pretend I'm a fucking dullard when it comes to all things Chandii," Rhymona said. "How bad are we talking here?"

"*Bad* bad. Cataclysmic bad. The girl could harness abilities surpassing even the Eldnumerian. Especially if she's gone through her burning."

"Her burning?"

"Do you know her age?"

"Fifteen, I think. And what the fuck do you mean by *her burning*?"

"It is what the Chandii call the gift maturation period, which occurs during adolescence, where we burn through our original skin and become one with our gift."

"Meaning what exactly?"

"Meaning we get more powerful. A lot more powerful."

"Fantastic, that. Just brilliant. More bullshit to deal with." Rhymona thought of Aiden and his declaration to protect his baby sister and couldn't help but wonder just how much of this Chandii business he was actually aware of.

Marsea reached into the satchel and retrieved the grimoire. "Do you know if this would be of any help?"

Dusk. Rhymona could shit herself rotten. Through it all, the girl still had the bloody wretch. *Never again*, she told herself. *Never again will I underestimate you, Marsea Lanier.*

"May I?" Stella reached out for the grimoire.

"Maidens' breath, this is one of the eldritch bindings." Something like a smile pulled at the good side of her face. "It's been an age since I've beheld this one." Her eyes flickered back to Marsea. "Is this the only one?"

"As far as I know."

"There were three others in prior loops. What luck that we've managed one this time."

"What are they exactly?"

"Potentially, a way to combat the nether. It is said they can be used to open portals beyond founts and tethers, hells, beyond the known universe. That they amplify the gifts of their chosen who together can summon a greater ward called a godsgate."

"You mean a plane ward?"

"Spot on."

Now we're on to realm jumping, are we? You're officially off your fucking tits, woman.

"Do you know where the others might be?" Stella inquired.

"Desmond believes Autumn has one named *Noon* and a second named *Haunt* is still tucked away within Lancastle Library," Rhymona indulged. "Though *Dawn* presently lies with the enemy."

"These names are unfamiliar. In my loop they were named as *Blood*, *Flesh*, *Shadow*, and *Spirit*, after the base spells they concealed."

"Frayed are the threads that cast shadows," Marsea began.

"Lush is the drear in their unforgiving wake," Stella said. "As within, so without, where soul doth shed its skin, else mind dither non with doubt."

"That is from the *Kingstome*, my father's writings, how to you know this?"

"Because it is written upon the last page of *Spirit*. It is part of the binding's riddle. The only way to unlock the grimoire's true text is to solve it."

"Have you done this before?" Marsea asked.

"No. But in my loop you did."

"I did?" the princess asked. "How?"

Tethers.

Threads.

Phantoms.

265

Shadows.

"The Spellbind," Rhymona answered. *Why is all of this actually beginning to make some measure of sense?* "It's true text can be read inside The Spellbind."

"How do you know this?"

"Fuck if I know, Marsea, I just do. Mayhaps something from one of the other loops I retained? Given everything we've had thrown at us here, what's not possible anymore? And your father's grimoire, this *Kingstome,* he's apparently split his soul into it."

"He's done what?" Stella blurted as a chime sound rang to life from the edge of the table's clutter beside her.

"That can't be good," Rhymona said, a shiver racing through her at the dreadfully familiar din.

"Shit." Stella retrieved the timepiece, holding the face out towards them. Gray with a series of gilded numbers etched around its edge in a circle. Nearly identical to the one Aiden lost back when. "It means dusk is almost at its end." She clutched it in a fist. "I set it every day at the start of dusk just in case something like today happens. Dusk generally begins at some point between the five and eight, so I set it for five and hope it's enough time. For today, I would have to say not nearly enough. Another few minutes and The Bloodbind will pull you both back."

"Where will it send us?"

"This is as far as I've gone." Stella handed the grimoire back to Marsea.

"How can we return?" Rhymona asked.

Stella offered a severe expression. "The blood wraith, at dusk, in the same manner that brought you here this time."

"You mean to say we have to murder someone to come back here?" Marsea fussed. "The portals are literally made of the haxanblade's victims."

"I am aware, dear, but it's the only way I'm privy to, I'm afraid. Only once has there been a second return from a party during the previous loops."

"What is the strategy here?" Marsea asked. "What do we need to do?"

"We need to find the other grimoires, obviously," Rhymona said. "Mad as it sounds, we were already on course for this back in Courowne, your brothers and I. We know who *Dawn* and *Noon* are with and we know where *Haunt* is, so my vote is we storm Lancastle Library and retrieve what's left of the old man. Aiden said he and Remy spoke with the King in The Spellbind, mayhaps we can beg another chat and he can provide us some insight into this realm jumping business. Grimoires, godsgate, and we send the nether off to pasture. Either that, or we send ourselves."

"Ourselves?" Marsea questioned. "Rhymona, be serious."

"Oh, I am deadly serious, yeah. The way this world is shitting itself, you better believe we open a fucking godsgate I'd be just as apt to send myself through it and hope for the best."

Suddenly, Rhymona felt a cramping in her belly and Marsea let out a cry to match, lowering to her hands and knees.

"You must go to the archives in Marrovard," Stella said. "Name the ward in the south wing supply cupboard and it should take you to Lancastle Library."

Rhymona dropped to the floor, a hand reaching out for Marsea's, drawing the princess's attention as the world became a watery blur. "See you on the other side," she said, as dark fluids pooled beneath them, burbling up through the cracks between flagstones.

"Famous last words," Marsea returned.

"What?" She made to ask as the ground gave and they became swallowed up by a deep sea of scarlet.

CHAPTER TWENTY-SEVEN

THE RETURN PROVED TWICE AS cruel as the leaving, lancing through her like a fishmonger's blade, dragging her back through The Bloodbind abyss, jerking her every which way imaginable, until finally birthing her screaming across the Wyrmstower flagstones, Broenwjar a sodden heap at her side; Rhymona joining them an instant later spewing rift residue down the side of a stack of books.

"Selwyn!" Edgar's voice enveloped her like a maiden's kiss.

"Edgar…" Marsea uttered, blinking through the syrupy tissue of the blood portal froth, swallowing down the sickness that pushed at her throat.

"Note to self," Rhymona rasped from her rest a few feet away. "Never open your mouth before entering a portal."

"Are you injured, milady?" Edgar asked Marsea, arriving at her side.

"I'm fine. It's only portal leavings." She made to stand but found the rest of her was not quite as obliging.

"One step at a time, yeah." Edgar held her close as she eased back down. "Where the hells did the portal take you?"

"If only I could properly explain it," Marsea said.

"To a pocket dimension called The Bloodbind," Rhymona did her best with it as she leaned back against the leg of a work-table. "Tall, dark, and fetching, beggar a smoke?"

Edgar patted his chest. "Would that I had one."

"Not to be a royal cunt or anything, but it'd be a damn sight sweeter if you did."

"So, Edgar, Rhymona. Rhymona, Edgar," Marsea went ahead with the requisite introductions.

"Pleasure," Edgar said.

"Is it, Edgar? Is it really?" Rhymona worked herself up to her feet, slicking portal goo out of her hair.

"How long were we gone for?" Marsea asked.

"Half an hour or so," Edgar answered. "The blight just keep on pouring in, but fortunately whatever ward has come to find this place, hasn't yet faltered."

Marsea glared out past the field of heather at the expanding wall of ghoul parts.

"The bastards are growing clever," Edgar said. "Not all of them are pushing in after us."

"We'll need to make our way through," Marsea said. "There's a lot to catch you up on, but we're on to Marrovard next."

Poppy appeared at the top of the tower steps and they locked eyes, a grin curling her lips. "Selwyn," she uttered. "Thank the gods."

"How near are we to the university?" Rhymona asked.

"Reckon an hour on a good pace," Edgar answered.

"Right," the magus fixed on Marsea. "And what's all this Selwyn shit about?"

"Had a go at a burn name," the princess replied. "Asked myself what would Rhymona do?"

"Did you now?"

"Not my finest moment, as you might imagine." Marsea pushed up to her feet.

"No, I wouldn't imagine so." A wry grin twitched her lips.

"And it went about as well as an arranged marriage, all told."

"Only to be expected."

"Yongrin rather spilled the beans in spectacular fashion."

"That fucking bitch," Rhymona hissed. "I've got a grave with her name on it next time we cross."

"Do you remember all that talk about victims at dusk?" Marsea asked.

"Yeah." Rhymona looked at her squinty-eyed, catching her meaning.

"No." An expression Marsea could only assume might be respect danced across her friend's face. "You?"

"Me." Marsea removed her gran glasses and cleaned the film of rift residue from their surface. "Not that I'm greatly pleased about it, but she gave me no other choice."

"She got what was coming to her, you ask me," Poppy said.

"Hunh," Rhymona's head tilted slightly. "Not for nothing, but you're something else, Marsea Lanier."

"It's Selwyn out here," Marsea said. "Selwyn Fucking Shawley."

"So it is," Rhymona shook her head. "I daresay, a quint at the Kingswood and she's gone fucking legend on us."

"I wouldn't go that far."

"I would," Poppy said. "We survive all of this you better believe I'll have your stories running the kingsroad from Stone's Throw to Synner's March."

"Speaking of which," Marsea produced *Dusk*. "Stella said they could amplify the gifts of their chosen, which I'm assuming would be myself, Remy, and Desmond." Maidens' breath, given everything that had come at her in the past hour, she'd nearly forgotten Des was still alive. "But who would be the fourth?"

"Autumn, of course," Rhymona answered.

Stella's daughter. "You're sure?"

"Cycles ago, our Stella tried to tell me about all this, but I didn't understand. Hells, she didn't either. Honestly, how could we have? She told me about the grimoires. About their bindings. That *Dawn* was bound to Aiden, *Noon* to Autumn, and *Haunt* to you."

"Which means *Dusk* is bonded with Remy."

"And likely how it made its way to him in the first place."

"The stars keep us."

"You following any of this, Sugar Muffin?" Edgar asked Poppy.

"Not even a little," Poppy answered.

"To the point, there are four grimoires," Marsea began, "one of which we have. If we gather all four and find my brothers, we may be able to open a portal that we can banish the nether through. First, we need to go to Marrovard, evidently there is a secret portal in the university archive that will take us to Lancastle where a second grimoire is hidden."

"That is assuming Bloodbind Stella can be trusted," Rhymona said. "And there's no difference in this particular piece of our timelines..."

"And for our worries' sake, let's just say that there aren't," Marsea appended, ever the air of optimism.

"Aye, and once in Lancastle we'll grab *Haunt*, and," Rhymona held her gaze, "reckon you're not privy to this bit yet...there is a ward nest in Illery that will take us to Courowne."

"A girl after my own heart," Marsea said.

"And if I've been following for half a shit, Courowne is where your brothers currently are, yeah?" Edgar asked, scratching at the tuft of hair on his chin.

"There's a lad," Rhymona answered.

"Brilliant," Poppy said, "so nothing terribly difficult then. Had me worried for a second."

"Oh, I like this one," the magus said.

"Aww," Poppy twisted a finger into her cheek.

"Shall we crack on then?" Edgar asked.

"You don't have to join us," Marsea said. "As before, there's no promise of safety in this."

"The way I see it, milady," Edgar collected his bow from a nearby work table, "there's no promise of safety anywhere anymore. Not until this evil is dealt with."

"And I doubt I'll ever find a better story than that of the princess that saved the moon," Poppy said.

"Very well," Marsea said. "Gather what you can from this place. We leave for Marrovard without delay."

———

THEY CLEARED a path through the blight of Wyrmswold Hollow with relative ease and behind Edgar's scouting savvy made fast work of the woods between the tower and Marrovard Township.

During the trek, Rhymona filled Marsea in on all the happenings since she left Lancastle for the Ravenholme enclave. Namely that Remy was now Eldnumerian, housing the dracari soul of Yvemathira the Undying and wielding Eldn fire like the dragonriders of yore. That Julia was with them, and quite a smart little stitch with the sword. And that Desmond, though still alive, looked more lich than living after his apparent self-exorcism.

Woefully, she saved the worst of the news for last.

Somehow, astonishingly, Marsea kept her feet at the telling, though a gray tide of numbness washed through her and heavied her feet in the after.

Rhymona kept talking, and Poppy comforted from her opposite side, but all she heard over and over is *your mother is dead*. In the depths of her sorrow, her vision vacillated between her own and Broenwjar's, and she wobbled in the spaces between consciousness, sick at the thought of the last word she left her mother with. A word she'd thought about numerous times over the past quintweek. A word she'd resolved to apologize for at first chance. A word born of impertinence and misplaced anger. A word she'd never truly meant. A word she'd never use again. Not in this lifetime.

Lovely chat, Mother, as always.

Bitch.

"WHAT'S WRONG WITH THEM?" Poppy asked, as the group passed into town under cover of nightfall.

"They're bewitched," Rhymona answered. "At least some of them are."

Marsea watched as a man waved a torch before a woman's face calling her name. Though no response came. She only stared ahead with dead eyes; the flames be damned.

"Which likely means trouble," Edgar added.

"Likely," Rhymona answered. "Keep close."

"It's like he's fucking one of them," a voice said from a street corner where a pair of bluecoats stood before one of their own, snapping fingers in his face. "Georgie, wake up, mate."

"On toward the spires," Poppy said, having some familiarity with the university grounds from her tenure as a dormitory chambermaid. "The library is just off from the one on the left."

Stay out of town for now, Marsea bade Broenwjar in their special language. *Something foul is afoot here, but nothing to fret on just yet.* She could feel him padding the outskirts of Marrovard just inside the forest's edge.

"Stars!" Marsea cried, stalling beside a crowd, and pulling the hood of her cloak up.

"The fuck is wrong with you?" Rhymona asked.

"Do you see the group just up the avenue by the bend?"

Rhymona casually gave a glance. "Aye."

"They're Ravenholme, I recognize the tall one with the beard from the enclave."

"He certainly has the scowl of a spellslinger," Edgar said.

"We'll want to be avoiding that lot to be sure." Rhymona's hand lowered to the hilt of her mae'chii.

"It appears as though they are investigating something in that burned down shop."

"Aye," Edgar agreed, "and the festivities appear quite fresh."

"This way," Poppy said, waving them over and drifting down the next alleyway over. "This should be a less conspicuous route."

They hurried down the starlit alley to the next street over and found Poppy's prediction mercifully accurate. There were a handful of towns-folk idling about, though none of which that wasted more than half a thought on a band of riffraff outsiders. Pacing the dark between street-lamps, they made the university grounds without complication and soon arrived at the library courtyards.

"Place looks abandoned," Edgar said as they approached a building of dark stones and pointed arches with queerly carved statues of saints and grotesques guarding the spaces between.

It appeared nothing at all how Marsea had envisioned of a university library, especially one as storied as Marrovard. But there was no time for disappointment just now.

B, we're at the archives. Be ready to come soon. It wasn't the best plan, but Broenwjar barreling through town once they had the library's location was the least conspicuous strategy she could come up with.

Quickly, the group hurried across the cloister and through the main doorway.

Utter silence spanned the library's insides, which in contrast to its tragically drab exterior, displayed some of the most stunning architecture the princess had ever beheld. Her vision darted about in every direction, absorbing as much of it as possible, as she trailed the others toward the supply cupboard, passing aisle after lavish aisle. The colors painted across the ceiling immaculately placed, the scenes divinely illustrated, accentuating the cherry red bookshelves, which themselves produced an exquisite glow as though fashioned from some ancient strain of magic dust. And that wasn't even to mention the tomes. Oh, the tomes. Maidens' breath, the tomes.

"This must be it," Rhymona said, halting at the last door at the far wall.

"How do you know?" Edgar asked.

"Sylvoth'yka," she said, staring the bowman straight as something came to life on the other side.

"I'll shut up now," he said.

We're at the portal, B.

The magus tried the doorknob, but it wouldn't turn. "Damned thing. Must everything be a massive pain in the arse?" She kicked at the doorknob, driving it to the side.

"Rhymona, what the fuck?" Poppy whispered.

"Without the key, we're going to have to break in."

"Won't that leave it exposed to others?"

"Obviously, yes, but they'll also need the name to call the ward back to life. A risk I'm willing to take given our rather short time frame here." She kicked again and the doorknob broke away from its body, the door squeaking slightly ajar.

Eyes closed, Marsea held out her bad hand, searching for Broenwjar's location, guiding him through their gift bond. She could feel his agitation as he charged through the gate and into the township, in the company of so many others, so many eyes, so much fear and panic. He followed the same avenues and alleys they took, chasing after her scent.

"The space this opens in is quite small, so give it a moment after I enter," Rhymona ordered.

"We'll have company soon," Marsea said as she turned toward the others, Old Boy's tear through the township drawing all manner of notice. "Go now."

And with the word, Rhymona was through.

"Give it a ten count," she told the others.

Poppy went through next.

"Milady," Edgar gestured for her to go through.

"Not without B," she said. "You go."

274

A burst of pain shot through the small of her back, burning hot as iron fresh from the flame's kiss. She grimaced.

"Selwyn?" the bowman made to assist her again.

"I said go, Edgar," she gritted.

Without another word of contest, he backstepped through the portal.

"Maidens' bones," she rubbed at the phantom pain in her back, realizing it had risen from her link with Broenwjar. Which meant Old Boy was coming in off a knock.

And he was there with her before the thought passed, favoring his right side.

Following her command, he went through next.

The princess gave the archive one last glance, breathing in the wondrous assemblage of tomes. In another lifetime, she could have spent days, nay quints in this place, scouring the shelves from end to end.

May we meet again.

She froze mid-turn as she shifted back to the rippling portal, catching a figure down the far wall from the corner of an eye.

Quick as a cutpurse, Marsea drew the haxanblade from its scabbard and leveled it at the shadow figure.

"I mean you no harm," a female's voice echoed from the shadows, "but would it be too much trouble to beggar a jaunt?" The woman staggered into the torchlight, her eyes catching fire as Marsea's jaw dropped.

The azure stare was new and the lines of dried blood twice as unsettling, but the princess recognized the face at once from portraits hung about the Lancastle halls. 'Twas a face she could not have mistaken were she a bottle deep. A face she never would have expected to find in this of all haunts. A face, were she being honest, she never thought she'd ever see again. But a face, given the recent tidings regarding her mother, she needed more than ever.

She took a step forward. "Aunt Maggie," her voice came as a pitiful whimper, heat forming behind her eyes.

"Marsea?"

CHAPTER TWENTY-EIGHT

MAGWYN DASHED across the university grounds toward the township, burning through her energy in a blink as the blood candle's boon faded, her pace slowing with each footfall until she was reduced to an awkward hobble and the pains of battle and gift-exhaustion washed over her, in particular from a nasty cut across her left leg that stiffened her movements the moment she noticed it.

Ledge, the loyal fool, had bought her a few precious seconds, but it wouldn't be long before the cultists caught her if she tried to make the gatehouse. Hiding was the only option left.

Fast as her aching body would allow, she limped to the closest building, hugging the walls for support, out into the cloister, shadows in the starlight, through the doorway, and found it housed within a library lush with tomes and bindings. Blood dripping down her thigh, she navigated the maze of bookshelves until her body finally gave out, unwilling to push on another step further, and she lowered herself to the mottled flagstones.

I'm sorry, she thought, the faces of Xavien, Rhonyn, and Ilfaeyda flickering through her weary mind. *I'm so sorry I couldn't do more.*

WHY THE GIRL? Magwyn asked Emyria after a time, bundled up against a bookshelf near the back wall of Marrovard Library, shivering from the lack of food and loss of gift. *What's so special about her?*

SHE IS OF THE CHANDII BLOOD AND SHE HAS RECENTLY COME OF AGE.

Come of age? What does that have to do with anything?

CHANDII GO THROUGH A METAMORPHASIS AROUND THEIR FIFTEENTH CYCLE WHERE THEY BURN THROUGH THEIR YOUNGLING SKIN AND BECOME ONE WITH THEIR GIFT. AS YOU MIGHT IMAGINE, SUCH AN OCCURRENCE HAS BEEN A HIGHLY GUARDED SECRET BY THOSE THAT YET REMAIN.

DURING OUR ALLIANCE, IN THE YORETIMES, THIS MATURA-TION PERIOD WAS WHEN WE WOULD ACCEPT ONE OF THEM AS A POTENTIAL RIDER AND CHAMPION AS THEIR NEW SKIN COULD BETTER WITHSTAND OUR FIRE AND THE WARMTH OUR BODIES PRODUCED.

You had a rider?

I HAD TWO BEFORE THE DRAGONSFALL.

What were their names?

THEY WERE OF THE SAME HOUSE. AUNT AND NIECE. OF HOUSE LEDRANGE, THE HIGH HOUSE OF CHANDII SOCIETY BACK WHEN. THEIR NAMES FYR AND FARADOR.

Magwyn found them both within flashes of Emyria's memories. One short and stout, the other even shorter and thin as a reed, each with long, braided, fiery red hair that trailed down to their ankles like a phoenix tail. And then a feeling of shame bubbled to the surface. A guilt so deep the dracari could not keep it quiet.

What happened?

The younger one, Farador, stumbled desperately through a forest, grunting and puffing, her veins radiating bright blazing azure, melting through her bones, muscles, and alabaster skin, boiling her body away from the inside out, glowing giftblood pouring from numerous puncture wounds and gashes.

THEY HUNTED US. EVEN AFTER OUR SOULBOND. AND EVENTUALLY THEY CAUGHT US UP.

Eldn fire engulfed Farador's body, igniting her blood gush as the flaming girl flung it out at her attackers like a taskmaster's whip, screaming high holy nightmare.

AND IN MY DESPERATION TO FEND OFF THE MILITANTS, I PUSHED HER GIFT TOO FAR. I TOOK TOO MUCH.

Dozens dead around her, Farador collapsed before an old stag hall, her skin stained dark as a mid-winter hearth.

Emyria...is that...?

THAT IS THE FATE OF THOSE WHO HARBOR DRACARI SOULS. EVEN THOSE OF THE CHANDII BLOOD. OBVIOUSLY, FARADOR'S DEATH WAS NOT MY INTENT. TRUTHFULLY, I THOUGHT THIS WAS THE END FOR US BOTH.

A pair of boots rose up before her as the last of her breaths writhed across scorched earth.

A survivor. A young boy. No more than a dozen cycles to his count.

BUT I WAS SELFISH.

You took him, didn't you? You took him against his will?

I WAS NOT READY FOR THE ETERNAL SLEEP.

He was only a boy.

Emyria said nothing. Thought nothing. Felt nothing.

How many have you taken against their will, Emyria? How many have you fooled into harboring you? How many have you burned through?

"This must be it," a nearby voice echoed out and Magwyn's breath caught.

Another voice spoke afterward followed by a third, all distinctly different in tone and accent.

Grimacing, Magwyn forced herself up from the floor and hobbled to the end of the aisle, tense as a fugitive turncloak, peering down the back row at a group gathered about the other end.

The mouthy one kicked at the door and a bright glowing light poured out into the archives from inside the room.

A PORTAL. WE MUST HURRY.

They could be killers.

THEY MOST ASSUREDLY ARE, BUT WE WILL NEVER SEE A BETTER OPPORTUNITY FOR ESCAPE. THE CULTISTS ARE LIKELY MANNING EVERY STREET CORNER BY NOW. AND THE NETHER WILL NOT BE KEPT LONG IN THAT RITUAL CHAMBER.

Magwyn fell back against the bookshelf and stared up at the ceiling with a heavy sigh. *They could be cultists.*

THEY ARE NOT. YOU MUST TRUST ME, MAGGIE.

"I don't know if I can, Em," she whispered. "Not after everything you've done. Not after you pushed me under…"

But something else was pulling her toward their unexpected company. Something deeply buried yet eternal. Something beyond Emyria. Something beyond mere survival. Beyond necessity and desperation.

With all her strength, the Empress pushed away from the bookshelf and groaned out into the aisle, stumbling forward a series of steps, only to collide against the back wall, utterly exhausted. She hobbled on, using the wall as her crutch, as she neared the glowing chamber, halting when a great furry mass appeared before the figure at the end and entered the portal.

The last of the mysterious figures spun around to face the light and stopped, her head twisting toward her, as a sword leapt from its scabbard.

"I mean you no harm," Magwyn said, braving forward a step, her words wavering, "but would it be too much trouble to beggar a jaunt?"

The girl advanced a step, deep purple rings surrounding a pair of haunted silver orbs. "Aunt Maggie?"

Magwyn eased away from the wall, swaying, doing her best to keep her feet under her. "Marsea?"

YOU KNOW THIS GIRL?

By the gods, I do. Maggie's heartbeats thundered. *She is…my niece.*

Beneath all the grime and gore, the girl still favored Larissa's features, but there was no denying the scowl. A deathly scowl that only a Lanier could spawn.

"Is…is that really you, Marsea?" the Empress asked, on the verge of tears. "Or am I hallucinating?"

"I could ask the same," the ghostly girl answered. "But we haven't the time just now." The Lanier princess hurried to her aunt's side and offered a shoulder for support.

She certainly felt real. And fit for warring.

"Where will the portal take us?" Magwyn asked as they staggered toward it as one.

"Lancastle Library."

"Lancastle?" she breathed.

A quarter century since Whit shipped her off to the Dalivants, and this was how she would return home? Lame of leg and bleeding out on the arm of a girl both family and foreign? The gods had a most peculiar sense of humor indeed.

Maggie shielded her eyes from the ward's blinding name as the pair pierced through the standing pond of rippling waves and touched down inside a small alcove lined with all manner of tome.

"About bloody time," a snow-haired woman quibbled, her darkly eyes immediately befalling Magwyn. "And who the fuck is this?"

"Curse me for a clod," the bowman beside her uttered, lowering his vision from Magwyn's regard. "You don't recognize her?"

"Obviously not."

"Obviously not? She's the ruddy Empress of Courowne."

"Rhymona, spare a candle," Marsea bade.

The snow-haired mouth rummaged through the pouch at her waist and fetched a bright red finger-sized stick.

"You have my thanks," Magwyn said, taking the candle and easing back onto an old wooden chair Marsea pulled forth from inside the alcove.

Marsea slid a tome from a stack by the doorway and a smile sprouted. "Halfway there."

Magwyn gazed at the girl's prize. The gods only knew, the thing appeared ugly as a rotten prune.

"That's it?" Rhymona grunted as the ward died out upon the secret room's ceiling, leaving them to the flicker of torchlight.

"Yep, it's just this old thing," Marsea said. "What were you expecting?"

"Hells, I don't know. Given all the bollocks we've faced to this point I figured we'd have to fight or fuck something. Or solve some dodgy old geezer's dumbshit riddle."

THE TONGUE ON THIS ONE.

"All's quiet," a woman's voice whispered from down the aisle, joining the group alongside a massive beastie. "Who's this then?" she asked, meeting Magwyn's stare.

"Empress Magwyn," the bowman answered as Maggie gently pressed the blood candle into the gash on her leg.

She could feel her eyes light up instantly with dragon's aura as the blood candle set to the cut and raced her bloodstream. "Gods," she uttered. Cycles had passed since the last time she'd felt the euphoria of the chandiian gift. Everything became heightened: her hearing, her sight, her movements, her sense of smell.

What is that scent? She'd caught it before, many moons ago, during her deviant days at court Dalivant, high on shufa, cooked on chandii candles, and dreaming of Elysia's pastures, but never so potent as this.

IT BELONGS TO YOUR NIECE. Emyria answered. SHE IS WITH CHILD.

With child? Maggie could hardly believe the words. *Whit's granddaughter. In this world?* The thought terrified her.

"Those eyes," the approaching woman gasped, her words big and loud.

"We've got us another Eld," Rhymona said, an uneven grin forming.

Magwyn exhaled, focusing her gift on the wound's restoration, as she settled on Marsea and the misshapen hand clutching The Vael's most hideous patchwork of parchment. She couldn't help but wonder if the girl knew yet. "Emyria offers her warmest regards," she said instead.

"The luck stones are having a proper tug with this one," Rhymona scratched at the back of her head. "I mean what are the fucking chances?"

"Better question," Marsea said. "What in vaelnation were you doing in Marrovard of all places?"

"Chasing ghosts," Magwyn answered, the Chandiian gift leveling out as the wound began to close and scab over.

"And did you find any?"

"I found more than I care to name to have it true and lost a few in the meantime." She gazed at Marsea. "Rhonyn amongst them."

"Uncle Rho is dead?" The girl's shoulders sank, her excitement from the tome's retrieval dissipating thusly.

"He was part of a ritual to summon a demon back across The Pale. We tried to stop it, but..."

"And there it is," Rhymona spat, turning up to the heavens, "you fucks couldn't even give us half a damned minute to pretend?"

"The demon is named Tetherow, and it's taken possession of a chandii girl named Autumn."

"And there's the fucking knife," Rhymona stomped down the aisle a few paces and then back, scratching at the inside of an arm. "The old nutter was right."

"The hells is she on about?" the bowman asked.

281

"Goss...and some barmy prophecy scrawled within the pages of *The N'therN'rykca* about the nether's champion. The bastard born of summer's blood and winter's kiss. We thought it was Aid...Desmond, but mayhaps it's the sister."

"None of this changes what must be done," Marsea said. "It only proves Stella's theory true."

"...And what must be done?..." Magwyn dished Emyria's words.

"We must gather the four grimoires and summon a godsgate to banish the nether. Then we'll see to Tetherow."

"...A godsgate?..." Emyria breathed.

"We have two of them already," Marsea added, opening the satchel and retrieving another tome bound in twine and chains that somehow shown twice as ghastly as the first. "And father's bound himself to this one." Marsea held forth the prune.

Father? It took a moment for the girl's meaning to find its teeth. *Whit.* "He's what?"

"He's split his soul into *Haunt*," Marsea answered. "And I mean to commune with him post haste."

Commune with him? Magwyn stood. "Not without me, you won't."

"Very well," the daughter said.

"The nether is a problem, Marsea, make no mistake, but prize well, the demon Tetherow is the true menace and it's not alone. There is another."

"Another?"

"There were two of them in the ritual chamber. The one that took possession of Autumn and a second that wore the face of a woman named Dysenia Deadeyes."

"Dysenia," Rhymona growled.

"You know this wretch?" Magwyn inquired.

"She's my...well, she's my you. My auntie. Or, rather, she was." Rhymona turned to Marsea. "And she's the one responsible for your mother."

"What about Larissa?" Magwyn asked, returning Rhymona's glower.

"Dysenia murdered her."

Magwyn's mind began to swim at the divulgence. *So much at once. So much loss. Both Rhonyn and Rissa?* And a realization befell her. "If you're her niece, then that would make you?"

"Ashaeydir. Yes, yes, old hat, all that."

"What the fuck?" Edgar stepped back from Rhymona, producing a dagger from his waist. "You're fucking ashaeydir?"

"Edgar, no," Marsea said, filling the space between them. "She's with me, with us, on my word. The ashaeydir are not all what you think. And Rhymona is certainly not what you think."

"I'm much, much worse," Rhymona appended.

"Not helping," Marsea quibbled.

"The girl speaks it honest, Edgar. You've nothing to fear from me. As for Dysenia, I'll have that bitch a grave before the end of all this. Or find my own trying." At the telling's end, she started away from the group.

"Where are you going?" the woman asked after her.

"The ramparts," Rhymona said. "We should be able to see it from there."

"See what?"

"The Spellbind's heart."

EVEN WITH ALL THE horrors she'd crossed in Courowne, Magwyn was still in shock over the state of Lancastle Proper.

The faces struck the hardest. Those that remained of Lancastle's court and cobble. A few yet old enough to actually remember and recognize her, bowing in respect, recalling her name in whispered breaths, as she and Marsea strode side by side through the halls toward the ramparts.

As they neared the outer walks of the castle, they found all the telltale signs of a Spellbind summoning; dancing flecks of ash, soot-covered stones, thinning air, the static cling of the gift used to excess.

Into the pit of gloom they pressed.

The woman, who Magwyn came to know as Poppy became so light-headed and ill from the lack of oxygen that she had to stop several times. Eventually, she and Edgar had to split from the group and return to the library, both showing severe reactions from The Spellbind's effects.

Out atop the battlements, all was caked in cinder dust. Even the sky fell prey to it, all the stars swallowed up by a thick layer of moving gray. It was so dense had she not already known the time of day it would have been impossible to tell.

They found The Spellbind's heart below in the center of Kristof's

Courtyard. A strange four-armed statue stood alone inside the largest bloodstain Magwyn had ever beheld. A soulmeld chrysalis; the consequences of tearing a hole in The Pale and resealing it.

"Stars' alive, what was the thing?" Marsea asked.

"*They* were a cloth maiden and a lichlord," Rhymona answered.

"A cloth maiden?"

"You knew her as Effie."

"That's Effie?" Marsea asked, at once cross and crestfallen.

"Effie and Myrenna. Turns out the girl was keeping a secret of her own."

"...Myrenna sacrificed herself to stop the lich..." Emyria's deduction spilled out.

"Aye. To have it from Remy, she refused to allow Thira to sacrifice herself again."

JUST LIKE MYRENNA. EVER LOYAL TO HER QUEEN.

"Is she...are they dead?" Marsea asked.

"...Yes and no..." Magwyn spoke Emyria's words. "...Their souls yet live, trapped inside the chrysalis..." She gazed at Rhymona. "...As you found with Yvemathira, a soul can be removed from its chrysalis and placed inside another with the proper quality of gift. However, if I am following correctly, this particular situation is quite complicated and that much more volatile, namely because there are three separate souls contained within that chrysalis..."

"Speak plainly," Marsea bade.

"...From my knowledge of soul retrieval and second melding, attempting an extraction from such a scenario could prove unpredictable and disastrous. I do not know how a giftborn could tell the souls apart to withdraw the correct one. Or how they might only withdraw the one and not all three for that matter..."

"Last candle left," Rhymona fished a blood candle from her pouch and held it out. "Better make it count."

"You're not coming?" Marsea asked.

"Three on a candle is a shitshow, trust me," Rhymona answered. "Besides someone's got to play the watchman, yeah." She glanced over to Broenwjar. "Me and old mutt over there are going to have a frowning contest."

"Have a care," Marsea cautioned. "B's on one today, and he's come after folks for far less."

"And I'm sure in his mind, he's named me far worse."

Marsea couldn't resist a smirk. "Prize well, in his mind he's named just about everyone far worse."

"Ready?" Magwyn asked, offering Marsea one of her ring razors.

"Does it hurt?" the ghostly girl asked.

"Oh, yes," Magwyn answered. "Just like any other thing worth its weight in this sour whelp of a world."

CHAPTER TWENTY-NINE

S<small>OUND SHATTERED</small> and Marsea felt the wrist of her good hand twist as the blood candle kissed the cut, cold as the evening crypt, slithering inside and expanding up the length of her arm, skin shriveling and constricting around the bone, near to snapping.

Half a beat later the rest of her followed, and the next thing she knew she was covered in the candle's wax plummeting backwards; unable to move, unable to breathe, some unseen force squeezing tighter and tighter around her belly, her eyeballs rising into the back of her head, her thoughts disappearing inside the spiraling vacuum of suffocated screams.

Only a woman. A slab of meat. Other echoed in her ear.

But the pain was unbearable, nigh on numbing, every measure as cruel as her trip into The Bloodbind, and yet entirely different. For where the bloodrift felt physical in its torment, this felt spiritual and categorically wrong, hunting the span of her essence down to its very core.

She wanted to howl, sensing Broenwjar's anguish from some distant rest, to push out every ounce of agony trapped within her, but air no longer filled her lungs in this place, the last of it frozen at the base of her throat.

"Just a moment more," her father's voice sang to her from the ether as the blood candle's coating began to crack and flake away, her eyes

opening to a sea of shrieking symbols, disjointed visions, and memories that didn't fit in context with her own.

There was a jerking motion and the cramping around her stomach ceased as her body spun violently forward, end over end, the ground coming at her fast, feeling returning to her limbs as the rift opened up, releasing her topsy-turvy, and she reached out to her gift for guidance as the battlements rose up to greet her, landing into a prowling squat on all fours, *Dusk* and *Haunt* spilling out of the satchel at her side.

Haunt fell open and a gust of wind passed over it, sending the pages fluttering this way and that, the writing within glowing bright as shimmering starlight.

Heartbeat thumping, Marsea fastly retrieved the fallen grimoires and rose to her feet, where she found a face she thought she'd never see again only a few feet away.

"Father," she whispered, meeting his inquisitive gaze.

He appeared as she remembered him from before the coup, dark curls and full beard, no bloodstained bandages, nothing yet cut away from him. She wanted like fire to wrap her arms around him in that moment. Though she knew he was but a phantom in this place. Merely a whisper on the wind.

"Daughter," he returned.

Oh, but what a calming whisper it was, she thought as Magwyn materialized into the space next to them.

"And sister," Whit added. "Isn't this an unexpected surprise?"

"Fuck you too, Whit," Magwyn met his words.

"Yes, well I suppose I had that one coming."

"And you'd have far worse if you weren't already a corpse, you selfish git."

"For what it's worth, I am sorry, Maggie, and I'm sorry I cannot give you your proper due just now, but time is of the essence. I can only break from the grimoire for a short turn and there are things that require attention." He glanced at the grimoires guarded closely in Marsea's arms. "You've managed a pair, I see. A damned sight better than I can say for your brothers."

"Stella told us about their abilities," Marsea started quick, as though they hadn't gone fifteen cycles since last speaking, as though they were old mates down at the pubhouse chatting the daily over a pair of pints, "that together they can be used to call forth a godsgate."

"Indeed, they can. And just as well, they can be used to stitch a rift inside The Pale."

"I think we've also figured the order," Marsea said as she stuffed them back inside her satchel. "Des with *Dawn*, Autumn with *Noon*, Remy with *Dusk*, and me with the *Kingstome*."

"And so you have."

"I understand the connection for myself, Remy, and Desmond, but why Autumn?"

"Is it not obvious?"

"Obvious? Why would it be obvious? I've only just heard of this girl within the last day."

"As you know the grimoires are attached to the old blood. Lanier blood. *Our* blood."

"Are you saying she's a Lanier?" Marsea loathed the words as they left her lips, knowing good and well she wouldn't approve of their answer.

"I am saying Autumn is mine and Stella's."

"Oh, Whit," Magwyn said, covering a hand to her mouth.

"So, you admit to it then?" Marsea knuckled her glasses up. "You had an affair on mother?"

She'd heard the rumors of her father's philandering over the cycles, from mother, from the socialites of court, from a number of council members, and especially from the Harvers, but she refused to believe them. Most were had from folk that had it out for her father, after all. Folk that would prefer his name buried with the worst of the empire's scum.

"Your mother and I, we tried after Remy. For cycles we tried. But, suffice it to say, nothing ever came of it. And there was a prophecy given to me in my youth, a prophecy ugly as a crone's curse, a prophecy that I could not let go of, and in turn it would not let go of me, a prophecy that I came to believe genuine with every strand of my soul. It was about my heirs, my three children and their inevitable ruin. Your ruin, Marsea. I thought if I could sire a fourth, if I could prove the words fallible..."

"Whit, you bloody foolhard," Magwyn murmured. "You used that poor woman to sate your madness."

"On the contrary, the prophecy proved quite true, though only half imparted. Because its bearer only held but the half of it to give." He glanced at Marsea. "Isn't that right, Selwyn?"

"Wha…?" Marsea uttered.

"Selwyn?" Magwyn echoed, giving the girl a once over.

"Examine the sword, Maggie, and you'll find it's the same blade as the hag's from the churchyard all those cycles back."

Magwyn's eyes fell to the scabbard. "How is this possible?"

"I don't know the whole of the how, but I do know the who," Whit said. "It's been made haxan by a chronomancer named Lita Drufellyn from an alternate timeline or some dodgy nonsense of the like."

"What?"

"I know it sounds barmy, Mags, but somehow she used it to fray the threads between realities."

"She was so much older then," Magwyn said, staring utterly confounded at her niece.

"Not older," Whit corrected, "She was likely near the same age as our Marsea is now, only Selwyn was withering as an adverse effect from the slip between space and time. Jumping realities would be rather frowned upon by the fates, I would imagine.

"I believe the lads at uni name it a dead man's rift. But they misunderstand the school of magic. It's not actually necromancy at all, but chronomancy. For you're not actually raising the dead to commune with them, you're traveling back to a pocket in time when they were still alive. Selwyn Shawley did that *and* jumped realities. As you might imagine, things were bound to go awry."

"I should say so."

"Lita Drufellyn was that which told me in our timeline. During my studies regarding soul-splitting Stella summoned the Wyrmstower Witch to court."

"And father would be turning in his tomb to hear it," Magwyn remarked.

"I presume she did so to deter me from further inquiry into the like, but instead Lita helped me perform the ritual, and then she explained to me about the alternate timelines. She told me that the haxanblade was not of this moon. Rather it was forged of some ancient artifact ages ago, an artifact named trezsu that doesn't obey the laws of nature, time, or space. At least not how we understand it. For time is not linear as the scholars claim. It exists above, around, below, concurrently, within, without, rot, rot, bloody rot, kick about the chamber pot."

"You know about the time loops then?" Marsea asked.

"I am aware of them, though I understand very little about their science." Whit returned.

"And do you know about the blood curse?"

"Blood curse?"

"That's what Stella, rather Bloodbind Stella named it. She said there were four of us caught up in some sort of bizarre blood curse. Lita, Rhymona, Stella, and myself."

"How do you mean caught up? What is the curse's intent?" Whit asked.

"I don't know exactly, other than it seems when all four of us die in each iteration, the loop resets itself."

"Fascinating," Whit said, turning away from them. "If that's true," he said, shifting back, "then Selwyn must have been the last of the four from the previous loop. Which means she likely knew she wouldn't last long and tried to give us as much information as possible to end it this go-round. Bugger me blind."

Marsea's gasped at her father's foul language.

"Wait…Bloodbind Stella? Why did you name her that?"

"Because she's not our Stella," Marsea answered. "She's Stella from a previous loop that has become trapped in a pocket dimension she named The Bloodbind."

"No further explanation required," Whit said.

"No further explanation required?" Magwyn quibbled, her eyes glowing azure.

"And what have we here?" Whit returned. "Sister, you've gone Eldnumerian on us, have you? The surprises just keep on coming."

"And it's a damned good thing too or I'd be a corpse right along with the others. We've already lost so many, Whit. You, Rhonyn, Drezhal, Xavien, Stella…"

"Mother," Marsea added.

"Rissa?" Whit uttered.

"Rhymona told me she perished during the blight attack, murdered by a demon named Dysenia Deadeyes."

"Of which, apparently there are now two," Magwyn added. "Dysenia and Autumn have both become possessed."

"You know this for sure?" Whit asked.

"I've witnessed both with mine own eyes. Emyria made to attack the one in Autumn, but the girl quelled our Eldn fire conjuring as though it were merely that upon a candle's wick."

"This certainly complicates matters," Whit said.

"You think?" Magwyn groaned.

"But only in terms of banishing the nether," he continued. "I daresay, if there is a silver lining to it, it makes our next actions plainly clear."

"We must exorcise the demon from Autumn, so she can help us complete the godsgate ritual," Marsea said.

"Correct you are, Daughter. And to do so you will need to find Tetherow's *N'therN'rycka* and destroy it. By doing so it should sever its connection to this world."

"Assuming it can be destroyed. And that it hasn't fashioned another."

"That is where our dear friend Lita comes into play."

"How do you mean? Is she not dead?"

"Oh, she is quite dead. Took a bad fall off her mare some decades back if you can believe it. But part of her yet remains. And you wear it handsomely there at your hip."

Marsea's hand lowered to Blind Widow's hilt.

"As much as Elsymir took from our family, he did manage one decent thing in the end, and that was keeping the blade from his rotten master. That haxanblade there is designed to cut through just about anything if fed enough of the gift, but it especially prefers flesh and blood."

"There's an understatement." Marsea snarked.

"And that is all the original *N'therN'rycka* is. Flesh and blood. Created over the cycles from the remains of Tetherow and his hosts."

That was what you were trying to tell me? Marsea thought back to her conversation with Other in the mausoleum.

"As for how many grimoires he may have bound himself to, that's anyone's guess. I pray just the one. But with each one destroyed he will weaken." Suddenly his vision cut to the satchel at Marsea's side.

"What?" Marsea asked.

"It would seem I am nearly out of time," he answered.

"When can you return?"

"A day or so might buy us a few minutes. Keep *Haunt* safe, yeah?"

"Of course."

"I wish I could hug you, Marsea," her father said. "I am proud of you. You and your brothers, you've all come a long way..."

And just like that he vanished leaving Marsea and Magwyn to the gray silence.

"Same old Whit," Magwyn said.

"Yeah?" Marsea asked, having fit fifteen cycles of expectation and wishes into the span of a few short minutes.

He said he was proud of me.

There was a time she would have had a spin and dance at such words, especially from one of her parents, having never had them before that she could recall, but that time was long passed. Proud meant fuck all in this steaming pile of a world. Proud got a girl nowhere.

AN HOUR hence and they were out amongst the somber faces of the king's cobble, traveling the lantern lit walks torch to crackling torch, striding past bleary-eyed townsfolk and clusters of bluecoats that appeared as though they hadn't slept in quints, each one that dared to meet her eyes in lieu of Broenwjar's hunting within for answers. Hunting within for hope. For something to believe in. A strange occurrence, indeed, considering their cycles of dismissive treatment under the reign of the Midnight Men. And she was just as lost as they were to have it true, barely managing to keep her own life in order, what with alien swords and blood portals and haunted grimoires turning up every five seconds, but, through it all, it fell as Elsymir said it would be.

Folk know the name Lanier, and desperate times are coming. And in desperate times, folk are always looking for a savior—a leader to step up and take the reins—a voice to follow.

The word savior sat ill with her, especially when used to describe anyone of the mortal populace. Mostly because it put mankind on the same level as the star maidens, which was horribly misguided, not to mention dangerous. Titles of the like put monstrous thoughts in the minds of men, or such had been her experience.

But, savior or no, she'd give it her all going forward. As though there was any other choice in the matter.

Sensing Broenwjar's tension within the presence of so many, Marsea coursed fingers through his fur. *I'm here*, she said, attempting to return the same soothing presence he so effortlessly provided her.

"We're nearly there," Rhymona called back over her shoulder, Aunt Maggie maintaining a brisk pace at her side.

Rhymona did her best to warn Marsea of what might lay ahead at the shop, sparing few details at Marsea's behest. Still, the princess couldn't quite accept it for reality. Her mother. Larissa Lanier. Dead. Meeting her maidens in some dingy old shop off the shoddy side of town. A wand curse eating through her face, leaving but the half of it. Such a cruel fate, even for the worst of the Vaelsyn Empire. She shook the imagery from her thoughts. There was certainly enough horror to mind without her imagination taking part.

As for Edgar and Poppy, it was decided they would stay in Lancastle for the time being, both of them still feeling the ill effects of The Spellbind. The chronicler put in her most compelling protests, but Marsea wasn't having it. For her part, Magwyn ordered a quad of bluecoats to keep watch over their friends in the library until they returned.

Afterward, Marsea and Magwyn met with Captain Arkham, the acting High Commander who explained there were still those infected by the madness curse running amok the upper halls, including Raelan Harver, who at last report had barred himself inside the King's Solar. Marsea commanded the Captain to oblige his confinement as long as possible, and if he made to escape, to keep him alive by any means necessary. She had no doubts the good Captain would see the order through to the letter.

The princess had always favored Arkham amongst the coats, one of the highest-ranking female officers in the entire Royalguard. She was hard-nosed, elite in the tourney yard, and firm in her beliefs. A born leader, as they say. And with the way things were shaping up, it was possible by week's end, should she survive it, the good Captain might very well find herself at the crown of the Royalguard pecking order.

Marsea kept her eyes to the fore as they pressed into Illery, the stench of voided bowels and death rot killing all sense of proper smell after a few seconds in.

Oh, but how the dark was a boon in such a haunt.

It appeared nothing outside the upper commons had been touched, at least not with any conviction or purpose. She imagined patrols had swept through any number of times, cutting down what ghouls they found wandering about, but no clean-up had been performed, and truthfully, given the paltry state of the upper cobble, it would likely be days if not quints before such an operation were even possible.

Three blocks in and Rhymona halted at the corner of Market and Aft, a cloud of smoke rising from her lips as she flicked the roach of a shufa stick into the breeze.

The princess blinked out of her trance to find bodies all around them, far as the eye could see, some blighted, others half-eaten, more yet in severed pieces, double what they'd crossed in Wyrmswold, nay triple, and that was just the one avenue and what lay plainly before them.

"If you want, I can move the body," Rhymona said. "You don't have to see her if it's too much."

Marsea swallowed. "But I think I need to."

Lovely chat, Mother, as always.

Bitch.

"I'm here, yeah," Rhymona added.

"Cheers," Marsea managed, her stomach beginning to turn as she approached the shop, and not because of the corpse stink.

Aunt Maggie entered first and a bright azure glow lit the inside.

The Lanier princess glanced down at Broenwjar meeting his good eye. "I'll be fine," she answered his gaze. "I won't run this time. Not from this. No matter what."

Despite the many bodies, Marsea found her mother's almost immediately, drawn in by the dress, a gown far too glamorous for such a hovel. Someone moved her body, laid her out neatly on her backside. From the neck down she appeared almost normal, save the lines of dried blood.

Marsea's steps slowed.

But what remained of her head was a horror, gore-matted hair clung to her sagging cheek, her lone eye sank unnaturally inside its socket, as though it were slowly being devoured by the skull from within, and her tongue dangled down from the blackened hole half-cauterized by the passing of magic through flesh and bone…

Marsea shifted away. *Mother.* No sequence of words could have ever prepared her for this.

Her hands curled into fists as she watched Rhymona pulling bodies from a heap until she found the poor bastard at the bottom. He was barely recognizable, given the chunks torn from his face and neck, but Rhymona made mention of his sacrifice during the retelling of her mother's murder.

Cas.

Rhymona knelt before him. "It's me again you old fuck. No better off than our last meet."

Marsea turned back to her mother. *You must face this.* She glanced to Magwyn, who nodded, then she lowered herself to her knees, staring her mother straight, refusing to look away.

"Mother, I'm sorry."

Broenwjar came to heel at her side.

"We never much saw eye to eye. And I was unforgivably awful to you." She concentrated on the remaining half of her mother's face. "More so than you ever deserved. And now..." Tears streaked down to her jawline. "And now I can't tell you...I can't tell you how much I love you. How much I appreciate you. I can't hug you. I can't even..." She hid within the watery pitch behind her eyes, searching for proper words, doing her damnedest to settle her thoughts against her spiraling emotions.

"I'm sorry," she started easy. "I'm sorry I was always so selfish when it came to you. And I'm sorry I took it all out on you. It wasn't okay. But neither was I." Her eyes opened. "*I* wasn't okay, mum. I wasn't. No matter how hard I tried to be. I'm still not, but I shouldn't have hidden that from you."

A sigh pushed out of her.

"Though I have a keen sense you always knew this about me. I was never as strong as you were. Never as clever. And nowhere near as cunning. I couldn't repair what was broken inside me. And I certainly couldn't pretend as well as you. The best I could do was hide from it. Why else do you think I spent so much time holed up in the library? Because as awful as some of the character's lives were, at least they weren't mine. At least they had a purpose. I despised you, Mother. Truly despised you. And I blamed you for all of it. For the coup. For father. For all of my inadequacies. For my lack of purpose and passion."

A warm ache radiated from her chest and into her arms as she spoke.

"And yet, despite my constant temper and disrespect, you always asked after me. About how I was doing. About what ailed me. Which, ironically, only made me despise you more. For reminding me of how weak I was.

295

How cruel and arrogant I'd become. Though I now know that was never your intent."

She sniffled back her running nose.

"I think I just needed time away from it all. Time away from you, from Remy, from House Harver, from Lancastle. Time to actually miss something."

Marsea cupped her good hand atop her mother's. It felt colder than the stone floor she lay upon.

"I just...I hated you so much for your dismissal of father, and your marriage to Raelan so soon after, as though our House meant nothing. It burned me up to grant it thought. That you would take bed with that monster. And that I had to see you with him every single day. But I know now it's never that simple. Nothing ever is. I know now you were doing what was necessary to protect us. To keep our family safe and together. You sacrificed everything for us." She swallowed back mucous. "And I gave you all the hells for it. I treated you the worst, and you were the one that most had my best interests at heart. Even more so than father."

Old Boy nudged her gently with his snout and she felt his condolences, as well as his pain at the loss of his pack all those many cycles back. She wanted to wrap her arms around him but knew if she did it would unseat what composure she still had remaining.

Her attentions swayed back to Rhymona as she performed some queer manner of salute before relieving Casilvieri of a small leather pouch and a handful of blood candles hidden within the inner folds of his coat. Without another word, the magus paced to the far wall and began tracing her fingers against it.

The truth about worth, Cas once told her, *is it's only after you've lost a thing that you truly understand its value.*

The maidens knew, but her old mentor held far more wisdoms than any bastard of his repute ought.

Marsea's vision returned to her mother. "I'm going to do everything in my power to uphold your legacy, mum. And Father's. And Rhonyn's. For both House Lanier and House Waldgrave. I will never forget what you did for us. For me and Remy, despite the impossibly dreadful circumstances."

She retrieved a luck stone from the drawstring pouch at her waist, said to have once belonged to the maiden Vesper. It was stardust white with a gilded interior that shown through the engraving on its face. Nan had given it to her the night after the coup and told her it belonged to her mother and her mother's mother before her, and that the rune inscribed upon it meant divinely protected, and that as long as Marsea kept it close and called to her maidens many they would always keep her safe.

"Nan gave this to me. She named it divinely protected. And it's done a consummate job, in spite of my reckless behavior. Especially these last few quints. The maidens know, I've been a lord amongst fools. And I'm like to be even more foolish in the days to come. But there was something I once heard you say to Uncle Rho, though you knew not of my attendance. And for some mad reason it's stuck with me all these cycles. You said, *ofttimes there is but a hair's breadth between foolishness and bravery. And both sides bear their own weight in suffering. But sometimes, more times than not, in fact, it's simply at the luck stones' decree which side of that favor we fall on.*

"I pray I'm on the right side, mother." Marsea pushed up to her feet, closing the luck stone inside her fist. "I pray most of us are. And I pray we have enough foolishness yet in us to do what needs doing and enough luck to make what's left worth it."

She felt a hand on her shoulder and she crossed over her chest to it with her bad hand.

"You honor your mother as a good daughter should," Magwyn said.

Marsea wished she could give her mother a proper burial. That she could take her away from this infernal shop. But there was no time for it. No time at all for ceremony. For decorum. For reverence. For decency.

"It doesn't feel like enough."

"One daughter to another, it never will. But your words just now, your actions and intent, know she would be proud of the woman you've become. Just as your father said. Just as I am."

There goes that word again. Proud. Though Marsea felt the sentiment behind it this time. Sure, it was a touch romantic, but the world, in its present state, could use as much kindness as possible. As much family possible.

"Goodbye, mother," she said, stuffing the luck stone back inside its pouch. "I love you." A quivering frown accompanied the words, and the princess glanced over at Rhymona as Magwyn left her and approached the far wall, expanding the egg of Eldn fire in her palm.

Maidens, make me thine instrument

Marsea wiped the tear marks from her cheeks.

Where doubt may dwell, may I find faith

Magwyn placed her hand flat against the wall, calling forth the ward's name, and a sigil crackled to life melting the wall around it into a watery mirror-like surface.

Where despair may haunt, may I find your hope and grace

Rhymona entered first, Broenwjar right behind her as Marsea strolled up to the portal from the dark of his bulky shadow.

Where hate may tread, may I find your gentle love

The princess gazed back one last time at her queen mother, her hand falling to the haxanblade's hilt.

Where the nether grows, in blackest dark, may I find your light

And with the prayer's end, Lancastle was gone once again, fast as she found it, and replaced by a song of warring steel and violent screams.

CHAPTER THIRTY

"BAG OF BONES is heavier than he looks," Remy grumbled as the labyrinth opened upon a vast chamber. He lowered Desmond from shoulder to stone then mopped his brow with the back of a sleeve, the dank air turning deathly as he gazed long into the lightless abyss.

They'd been navigating the maze of tunnels for an indeterminate amount of time since Rhymona's disappearance, only stopping for short spells here and there. It could have been an hour. It could have been five. In the damp, whispering dark, it was impossible to tell. Though some time had passed since they'd last heard the groaning noise echo through the sprawling passageways. Remy hadn't yet decided if that was a good thing or not.

"What is that?" Julia asked, waving her torch back and forth as she stepped inside the chamber. "Are those people?"

"They were people," Remy answered, studying the pair of corpses lying motionless within a few feet of each other.

"Stay with Desmond," he bade his sister, conjuring a fresh egg of Eldn fire in his offhand, sword at the ready. "If anything comes at me, you run and hide, yeah."

"I don't like this, Remy," Julia offered as she took up a defensive stance next to the eldest. "Be careful."

HE IS HERE, Thira warned as they crept deeper into the pitch, Hrathgon's aura growing stronger the further inward they progressed, the connection between dracari siblings radiating through him like a midsummer sickness.

Remy studied the first corpse, which found the azure kiss and bore the scent freshly. It was unrecognizable, though by the shape the watchman suspected it belonged to Goss.

The second, a little further in, was that of Yurien Tenbrooks. The mage's lower jaw had broken away from the remainder of his skull on one side as though something from within forced its way out of his mouth.

Do you suppose they fought?

NO. GOSS WAS MET WITH TRUE DRACARI FLAME. NOT ELDN FIRE.

What are you saying?

YOU ARE A FOOL TO HAVE CHASED THIS DEEP INTO MY LAIR.

"...Hrathgon..." Yvemathira spoke through her host. "...*Has it been so many cycles you no longer recognize the scent of your own kin?...*"

MY KIN ARE ALL DEAD.

"...*Brother, how have you come to be in this place?...*"

Not only could Remy sense Hrathgon's aura, but now he could feel the beast itself. Some haunt above and around him. He cast the flame up high and released, its light expanding, illuminating the chamber's depths. In the shadows before him he caught the movement of a large, glistening serpentine mass.

Thira's memory flashed to her brother, dark green scales, golden underbelly, claws like an eagle, the long, crooked antlers of a dire stag.

Remy prepared his watchman's blade as a massive head broke into the light, jagged fangs bared, silvery orbs sharp as the executioner's axe, a thick, black ooze dripping down the sides of its camel-like face.

BY CURSE OF A CHRONOMANCER WITH A KNACK FOR DEFYING THE NATURAL ORDER OF THINGS.

"...*You are infected? How is this possible?...*"

BLIGHTED BY TENBROOKS. A MISCREATION OF MY OWN DESIGN. AND SO, THE FATES MOCK ME IN THEIR CONTEMPT ONE LAST TIME.

I CAN ALREADY FEEL MY BODY BEGINNING TO BETRAY ME, SUCCUMBING TO THE NETHER'S WILL, MERGING WITH IT.

IT HAS NEARLY DEVOURED ALL OF MY MAGIC. AND SOON IT WILL HAVE WHAT REMAINS OF MY SOUL.

"...Is there a way out of this place?..."

FOR YOU AND YOUR HOST THERE ARE MANY, BUT ALL OF THEM REQUIRE A SACRIFICE.

"...What manner of sacrifice?..."

Hrathgon slunk in tighter around them, his broad snake-like torso surrounding them on all sides.

I CAN LEAD YOU FROM THIS PLACE, BUT ONE OF YOUR COMPANIONS WILL HAVE TO BEAR THIS SOUL FROM ITS NETHER-FED DOOM.

No, Thira! Remy argued. I won't allow it.

"...I thought you would rather have death than take a midaran host. Were those not your words to me before you abandoned us?..."

I WARNED YOU AND RHYVARIATH TIME AND TIME AGAIN THAT CONFERRING WITH THE MIDARANS WOULD ONLY END IN WAR. HELLS, YOUR RIDER LEDRANGE BACKED ME IN MY CAUSE. AND YET I AM NAMED AS THE VILLAIN BECAUSE I REFUSED TO PARTICIPATE IN A WAR I VEHEMENTLY SOUGHT TO AVOID?

"...I made a mistake, Hrathgon. Is that what you wish to hear? As though any of this could ever be undone..."

YOU ARE FORTUNATE I DO NOT DEVOUR YOUR HOST WHERE HE STANDS. HE AND THE OTHER GODSBLOOD BASTARD IN THE HALL.

"Why would you want to kill us?" Remy inquired. "We mean you no injury."

TO RETURN THE SCALES TO THEIR PROPER PLACEMENT. TO PURGE MAGIC FROM THE MIDARAN BLOODLINES. THAT WAS HOW IT BEGAN. BUT I UNDERESTIMATED THE DEMON SEED AND ITS CONNECTION TO THE NETHER. AND I UNDERESTI-MATED THE DEPTHS OF GREED IN THE HEARTS OF MEN. TRAPPED IN THIS OLD HAUNT, BUT HALF A SOUL TO COUNT, I HAD NO IDEA HOW MUCH YOU LESSERS STOLE FROM OUR GODS' GIFTS.

AND NOW, AFTER EVERYTHING, I AM REDUCED TO A
BEGGAR ON THE VERGE OF EXPIRY. DECADES LEFT TO THE
ROT. AND WHO SHALL ARRIVE AS MY DEATHBED SAVIOR, BUT
THE SISTER WHO ORCHESTRATED MY EXILE, AND ONE OF THE
VERMIN I RESOLVED TO END.

"We could just leave you to it," Remy grumbled.

YOU COULD, LITTLE MOUSE, BUT NOT WITH YOUR LIFE.
BESIDES, YOU WILL NEED MY AID IN WHAT IS TO COME.

"Will we?"

THOUGH I MISJUDGED ITS MENACE, I KNOW YOUR FOE
BETTER THAN ANY OTHER. YOUR DEMON TETHEROW. AND I
KNOW WHERE ITS PRECIOUS PHYLACTERY RESIDES.

"...The N'therN'rycka? Where is it?..."

FREE ME FROM THIS PLACE AND I WILL SHOW YOU.

"...Why should I believe any of this? You are a liar, Hrathgon. A deserter, a
trickster, and a fiend..."

AND YOU ARE A FOOLISH IDEALIST THAT MURDERED HER
PEOPLE WITH WISHFUL PROPAGANDA.

"...How dare you..."

BELIEVE WHAT YOU LIKE ABOUT ME, YVEMATHIRA. BUT I
KNOW YOU. AND MY DEATH WOULD NOT WELL SUIT YOUR
CONSCIENCE.

WHAT WOULD EMYRIA THINK? OR RHYVARIATH? OR YOUR
DARLING   MYRENNA?   ASSUMING   THEY   YET   REMAIN
AMONGST US.

Thira, we cannot do this. My brother has been through enough against his
will and Julia is just a girl. I will not allow that monster to twist her any more
than what's already found her out here. We don't even know if she harbors
enough of the gift to withstand such a spell.

I UNDERSTAND YOUR RESERVATIONS, REMY, BUT TRY TO VIEW
THIS FROM MY PERSPECTIVE. HE MAY BE AN ASS, BUT HRATHGON
IS MY FAMILY, AS DESMOND AND JULIA ARE YOURS. WOULD YOU
NOT DO ANYTHING TO SAVE YOUR FAMILY IF YOU HAD THE
ABILITY?

IT LIES WITHIN THE SCAR. BURIED DEEP IN ITS RUIN.

"...The Scar?..."

As in the one place humans cannot survive? Remy quibbled. Convenient.

MOST HUMANS CANNOT SURVIVE THERE. BUT THE CHANDII CAN AND MAYHAPS THOSE OF THE GODSBLOOD AS WELL.

Hrathgon is a liar and trickster. You've named him this yourself. Can't you see he is playing you?

HE DOES NOT DESERVE DEATH, REMY, AND YOU WILL NOT CONVINCE ME OTHERWISE…

TICK TOCK, SISTER. I CANNOT KEEP THE NETHER AT BAY MUCH LONGER. Hrathgon slithered back into the dark, allowing them a path back to Desmond and Julia.

THE NETHER WILL MAKE OF HRATHGON A DRYLAX. IF THIS HAPPENS WHILE WE ARE STILL DOWN HERE…

There won't be any family left to speak of at all. I get it.

I KNOW THIS IS UNFAIR, REMY. AND I ALREADY KNOW WHICH OF YOUR SIBLINGS YOU WOULD CHOOSE. BUT I MUST HAVE YOUR CONSENT TO PROCEED.

The watchman settled on his brother's slumped form as they approached. *The gods know, I thought my luck was shit.*

Julia stared at him owl-eyed. "Is it letting us live?"

"It's dying," Remy said as he knelt next to his brother. "Desmond," he called, gripping the eldest's shoulder and giving him a shake. "Des, wake up."

He refused to stir.

Remy slapped him once, held a beat, then a second time, slightly harder.

Nothing.

Though Lenore certainly let him know of her displeasure, cawing down madly from a nook in the wall above them.

THE GHOST BLOSSOM IS A SEDATIVE. IT HAS LIKELY DUG ITS FANGS IN DEEP.

"He'll never forgive me for this. I would never forgive him were our roles reversed."

SACRIFICES MUST BE MADE BY ALL OF US.

"Remy, what are you doing?" Julia asked from the space just over his shoulder.

"The beast out there is Thira's brother," he answered. "I mean to soul-meld him with Desmond."

"Soulmeld? But you can't…"

"I don't see any other choice. The nether will soon consume Hrath-gon's body, and we'll be stuck down here with it."

"The stars save us," the girl uttered.

"He knows a way out, Jules."

"How can you know for sure?"

"I don't, but the nether is eating him alive right now and I have to believe he wants out of here every bit as badly as we do." His eyes fell to the pouch at her side. "Do you have any more candles?"

"I think so," Julia lifted the flap and rummaged through, retrieving a couple.

"Good girl," Remy nodded.

"Is there anything I can do?"

Remy hefted Fucker from the inside of his belt. "You can keep guard in the passage." He loathed the words as he said them, the idea of placing his baby sister in any kind of danger, but what other options were there? The best he could do was keep her as far away from Hrathgon as possible in case shit went sideways. "I will be in a fugue of sorts, just as you saw in the library."

"For how long?" Her voice trembled, but only just.

"I hope not very. A few minutes. I don't think we can afford much more than that. Just be ready to move whatever happens." He offered the hatchet to her.

Julia sheathed her short sword and gripped Fucker at its scruff.

"Rhymona would shit herself rotten to see you with that thing," Remy said.

The girl returned a determined scowl of the like only the ill-tempered magus could produce.

"You have her look down, that's for certain," he added as he sheathed his blade, then lifted Desmond up from under the armpits and began dragging him out into Hrathgon's lair.

The monstrous dracari slithered up to the brothers Lanier, a leathery hand opening up wide. It was big enough to crush them both if the beast so desired, not to mention the creature's talons, where a single errant flick of a finger could have them squirming about the stones in halves.

Remy sucked in a heavy breath then lay Desmond inside Hrathgon's palm.

A tick twisted the dracari's head to the side.

NOT LONG NOW.

WE MUST MAKE HASTE.

The watchman drew his blade and ran them each a cut, letting his sword clatter to the ground before pressing a blood candle each into Desmond and the dragon.

The Nine Fires took them and in seconds they were back in the Lancastle courtyards amongst the phantom legion, Hrathgon towering over the battlements.

Desmond shifted up from the stones, a series of grunts rolling off him, as he clutched at his temples. "Fucking hangover from hell."

"Des," Remy was at his side, azure flame igniting the shroud of gray mists.

"Are we back in The Spellbind?" Desmond asked, languidly.

"We don't have long, I'm afraid."

"If I had a schill for every time I've heard that one in the past week..."

"Right. And do you recall when you thought conjuring Eldn flame was top-shelf?"

"Mmhm..."

"Then you're going to love what comes next."

"Why do I mislike everything you're doing right now?"

Hrathgon let out a growl of anguish behind them drawing the brothers' attentions.

"Shit's sake," Desmond gasped, backstepping and falling on his ass. "That's a bloody dragon."

"You're very much correct, brother, that is a bloody dragon. And much like Thira, this one is dying and in need your help."

"My help?" He shook his head. "Hold on a tick. Where are we now? In the real world, I mean?"

"Still beneath Courowne. With Hrathgon here and he is plagued with nether rot."

"You were what I heard down below, weren't you?" Desmond asked Hrathgon, returning to his feet.

A bright cerulean glow began to screech from the cuts between them and Hrathgon lowered his claw atop the battlements. **IT IS NOW OR NEVER, PRINCELING.**

Desmond clutched his wrist, gritting his teeth at the agony of the meld's pull, Hrathgon's soul shrieking as it hungered after Desmond's vessel.

LET ME IN OR WE ALL PERISH.

Desmond shifted to Remy. "What's he on about?"

"He knows how to get us out of the labyrinth. Once you two meld, you must let him take control. The nether will consume his dracari form and make of it a—"

"Drylax," Desmond finished. "It's going to become a fucking dracari drylax."

"Now you're getting it," Remy said. "Head Fuck City, population fucked."

"What?"

"I don't know, brother. I'm all out of rousing words at this point. You do this, we might live. You don't and we're buggered six ways to Sunfell. The choice is yours."

Hrathgon's spirit began to fade, his massive form slumping.

"Ready?" Remy asked.

"Fuck no," Desmond rasped. "But when has that ever made a shit?" And he pressed his radiating hand into Hrathgon's.

"Don't look back, Jules!" Remy shouted between ragged breaths as they chased Desmond through the crooked corridors, slipping fissures, skirting bends, ducking stalactites, and dodging stalagmites twice as wide. The labyrinth seemed to stretch on forever, a jagged, unforgiving blur. Relentless in her darkness, countless in her halls.

"Just up ahead," Desmond called over his shoulder, his echo ranging far into the passages behind them.

Fastly, Remy spun about, tossing back an egg of Eldn flame that formed another magical barrier behind them, it was about all of the gift left to him without a proper rest, but the clicking and shrieking of the nether beast only grew closer.

"Here," Desmond said, skidding to a halt before a pitch-black pit.

"Here what?" the watchman asked. "What is this?"

"Do you not smell it?"

Remy inhaled and caught a thick salty aroma. A scent like the ocean.

"Freedom," Desmond said, azure in his eyes. "And now we jump."

"Are you off your fucking tits? Where does this lead to?"

"Compose yourself, yeah. It will drop us into an underground lake."

"It damned well better."

The nether bellowed from some nearby rest in the gloom behind them.

"Trust me," Desmond said with a daft grin as he casually whirled about and backstepped off the cliff into the darkness, Lenore diving down after him.

"Remy, I'm scared," Julia said, clutching Rhymona's hatchet tight with both hands to her chest.

"As am I, but this is our only path left. I will be right behind you."

She stared down into the void and turned back. "I don't know…"

They heard a splash below.

"Take my hand." Remy offered. "We'll go together, come what may."

A screech tore into the corridor just behind them and Remy jerked the girl with him, losing his grip on her in the screaming descent…

Though it had to have been close to a hundred feet, the fall lasted no more than a few seconds before they both plunged down through the lake's surface like a pair of arrows, thousands of bubbles surrounding them as they sank to the depths and swam back up in unison.

"Remy," Julia puffed as she burst from the water's face, "if you ever do that again…"

"Under," Desmond howled, and they all sucked in a gulp of air and submerged.

Above the lake's surface, a dense, scaly, black mass soared through, skimming across the water's edge, silky smooth and swift as the serpent it governed, chilling the water's crest before disappearing out the other side of the cavern.

Remy kicked back up to the surface, arms propelling through chunks of icy slush, Julia and Desmond emerging just after him.

"Was that?" Julia started.

"Hrathgon," Desmond answered, wiping the wet out of his eyes.

"It let us go?" the youngest asked.

"More like we weren't worth the effort," Remy said.

The trio stroked and paddled forth in the beast's wake until starlight broke through gaps in the stone and the cave opened up into the Graylem Ocean, where the water warmed considerably.

Exhausted, barely able to keep their bodies afloat, they watched in quiet horror as Courowne burned in the distance, a serpentine shape with wings breathing azure flame up and down the shoreline before crossing deep into the kingdom cobble toward a second gargantuan mass of thrashing appendages.

GLOSSARY

GENERAL TERMS

Blight, The – Sentient beings reborn as ghoulish creatures by black magic incantations. They are typically controlled by a lichlord or a necromancer and operate in a hive mind.

Chandii, The – An ancient race highly attuned to the gift. They are also known as flamekin, summerblood, and summerkin of the Summer Isles due to their distinctive bright, fiery orange and red hair. They were once believed to be beast whisperers, familiars of the dracari, and, thusly, dragonriders.

Charonisk – A man-made concoction with similar effects to eldn fire.

Dracari, The – The race of dragons. Dracthonir is the name of the dracari language.

Dragonsfall, The – The event comprising both the fall of dragons by man and the spreading of the gift into the elements that would result in The Giftborn Age.

Drylax – A physical curse of the nether. There are two forms: A gnaudrylax, which is a being fully consumed by the nether. This form is fluid and ever-shifting. And a phaedrylax, which is a partially consumed being. This form still experiences some confines of the host's body.

Eldnumerian, The – A chandiian term. "eldnu" meaning ancient, "meria" meaning master. They are also known as the old ones.

Nether, The – An ancient cosmic entity that feeds off of the soul and the gift. It can be physically manifested on the mortal planes using reverse wards and necromantic incantations. It incapacitates its victims using their fear until madness consumes them. The result of the madness, once the soul and gift have been purged from the body, is known as the blight.

Oathsworn, The – The knights of the round. They are a clandestine order formed to serve the realm of men. There is no head or foot. All are equal. The Oathsworn was founded decades ago by King Cameron Lanier. They protect the realm against darkly creatures and the supernatural.

Quintweek (quint) – A fluid term indicating a general passage of time. There are five days in a week. Six weeks in a month. Nine months in a cycle. Ten cycles in a decade. Ten decades in a century.

Ravenholme – Now synonymous with The Covenant, Ravenholme is a rogue guild created by Malthus Tetherow that split from The Covenant (original). Originally The Covenant was created in opposition to The Oathsworn. Members of Ravenholme believe that the darkly and supernatural should be revealed to the public, not kept hidden.

Shufa – A powerful drug that can be smoked or consumed with food.

Star maidens, The – The angelic beings followed within the Omedran faith. They are also known as the Amendeiya. Within the order of the cloth maidens are Lirae (a house mother), Rin (a handmaid to a Ve'Lir), and Ve'Lir (a cloth maiden in study).

Wretchrot – A deadly poison that eats away at the insides of any poor bastard unfortunate enough to ingest it, resulting in the discharge of a strange bright pink substance.

THE KNOWN UNIVERSE (the sister moons)

Ashira – The crimson moon. It is now wasting away and nearly uninhabitable.

Dalynisa – The big blue planet thought to be completely ocean.

Lumos – The smallest of the sister moons. She is known for her pale white appearance.

Vaelsyntheria – The golden moon.

Y'dema – The giant green moon. It was said to be razed by the ashaeydir after the fall of Ashira.

MAGIC TERMS

Bloodbind, The – It is a pocket dimension, a place out of time and space, much like The Spellbind. Unlike The Spellbind, however, it cannot be breached by any giftborn, rather it appears to be a curse tied to a haxanblade and specific group of giftborn (Lita Drufellyn, Marsea Lanier, Morgandrel Tully, and Stella Critchlow).

Blood candles – They are the stored mold of a giftborn's blood. It allows the user to enhance their inherited abilities, sometimes by considerable margins. They are known to be heavily addictive and can be deadly. The use of varying types of blood can alter and sometimes poison the blood system. Though not entirely banned by the Ministry, the use of blood candles is generally frowned upon through The Midaran Commonwealth especially at the universities of magic.

Blood merchants (warlocks) – Those who hunt fellow giftborn to drain them of their blood for wholesale.

Codices and Grimoires – Tomes and grimoires contain spoken word magic, including spells, recipes, sigils, wards, and bestiaries. This type of magic existed in previous ages, but has become more archaic in the Age of The Giftborn. It is largely considered an inferior form of magic by comparison to gift conjuring.

Eldn fire – A form of magic conjured and controlled by the dracari. It is the most powerful form of known magic and is one of the few defenses left against the nether. It manifests when called forth as azure and white flame.

Giftborn – A person with magical abilities. They can inherently perform great magical feats. The quality varies and is typically bloodline-based. To conjure magic the person must sacrifice something in return. They are less commonly referred to as warders and spellslingers.

Godsblood, Of the – Also referred to as the maker's ichor. It is the term the dracari use to describe giftborn descended of the older bloodlines with a deep connection to magic.

Gravedancer – A giftborn with the ability to resurrect the dead.

Haxanblade – A possessed weapon. This unfortunate soulmeld occurs through a curse or a mishandled enchantment.

Kindleblade – An iron-forged weapon, typically a ritual dagger or a sword, that is enchanted and soulmelded to a master.

Night writing – Raised code substituting for words. It is often times used with codices.

Soul magic (black magic) – Magic that feeds off of the soul rather than the physical body. This form of magic is very powerful, but also that much more risky and dangerous. Too much use can twist and deform the conjurer's appearance. It can whiten the hair, pale the skin, and rapidly age the conjurer.

Spellbind, The – A sliver of The Pale that was long ago cut away. It is a pocket dimension. A place out of time and space. One must be greatly gifted or use a blood candle, sacrificing something of their own health to enter. A studied giftborn can transfer their consciousness to The Spellbind. It can be a place of great healing or great destruction.

Totems – Enchanted trinkets, typically made of whittled wood or carved stone.

Varg – The ability of a giftborn to enter the mind of a soulbound familiar and take command of their actions. This ability leaves the conjurer in a vulnerable, almost corpse-like state during its casting.

Wands – Enchanted weapons created by giftborn to channel magic. They form a bond with a master through a soulmeld and will only react to that user's gift.

Wards – There are two primary forms of magic. Elemental-based magic and Soul and body-based magic. Elemental magic consists of Fire (Pyromancy), Water (Hydromancy), Earth (Terramancy), and Wind (Aeromancy). These forms of magic were common during the Age of Dragons. Soul and body-based magic consists of Shadows (Necromancy), Spirit (Psychomancy), Blood (Hemomancy), and Flesh and bone (Carnomancy). These forms of magic are common in the Age of The Giftborn. Powerful giftborn can merge two and three mantia at once.

MILITARY TERMS

Crownswatch, The – Liveried in crimson, they are also known as bloodcoats and redcoats. These soldiers man the northern highlands from The Straights to The Scar.

Emperorswatch, The – Liveried in gold, they are also known as goldcoats (and derogatorily as pisscoats). These soldiers man the Vinteyama swamplands and the flatlands between the highlands and southlands. They are noted for not allowing women to enlist in their guard.

Kingswatch, The – Liveried in blue, they are also known as bluecoats. These soldiers man Lancastle and her surrounding hamlets. They also man The King's Wall, a massive construct that separates the highlands from the lands now occupied by the ashaeydir.

Lordswatch, The – Liveried in gray, they are also known as graycoats. These soldiers man the lands east of the Morrigar Mountains, from the north to the southland provinces just outside Six Ports.

Royalguard, The – The overarching term referencing any coat of arms inside the midaran military.

WEAPONRY

Helanderan sword – A one-handed sword of varying lengths, edged on both sides, and generally paired with the use of a shield.

Ka'rym chii – A set of ashaeydir weapons primarily indicating a mae'chii and sy'chii.

Mae'chii – A long, slender, single-edged blade.

Sy'chii – A shorter single-edged blade.

Trezsu implant – An implant surgically embedded in ashaeydir soldiers that allows them to alter aspects of their appearance.

ACKNOWLEDGMENTS

First and foremost, I want to thank the team at Falstaff Books, Melissa McArthur, John G. Hartness, Erin Penn, Tuppence Van de Vaarst, Kristen Gould, and Joe Crowe, for helping usher my dream of becoming a published author into reality. My craft as a writer has grown by leaps and bounds in just a few short years and it's all thanks to the advice and efforts of the amazing group mentioned above. I may be a misfit, but when it comes to writing, I am no longer lost.

Additionally, I want to thank my family for continuing to support me and asking about my story, process, and progress. It may seem a small thing, but there were days, (many, many days, in fact), when it meant everything. I wrote this particular book during an especially dark and difficult time in my life when I didn't know if certain people who meant the world to me would make it through their ailments and troubles. As fortune fared, their luck stones would eventually prosper, and so too would mine. For this, I am eternally grateful.

To the readers of the first two (maybe three) volumes, a massive thanks from the bottom of my heart to the crown of my soul. I used to only write for me and told myself that was enough, that writing for me was all I needed, but I've since seen how my stories can affect people. I've received so many positive responses from readers of The Giftborn Chronicles series that are looking forward to the next entry and I can't tell you how much that means, how much that spurs me on. Only that we're in this thing together now. So, a thousand and one thank-yous for taking a chance on this old talebearer and his crazy little hearthfire haunter.

As before, as always, may you count some measure of hope and inspiration from some place within.

ABOUT THE AUTHOR

Drew Bailey is an emerging author of horror and fantasy. Though he attended college to expand his knowledge of Literature and History, it still took him the better part of a decade to actually mold it into something worth chasing after. Better late than never, as they say. The Royal Nothings is his first novel. In his spare time, Drew is a chronic coffee drinker, avid movie watcher, and follows Liverpool F.C. and the Green Bay Packers. He currently resides in Charleston, South Carolina.

STAY IN TOUCH!

If you enjoyed this book, please leave a review on Amazon, Goodreads, or wherever you like.

If you'd like to hear more about or from the author, please join our mailing list at https://www.subscribepage.com/g8d0a9.

You can get some free short stories just for signing up, and whenever a book gets 50 reviews, the author gets a unicorn. I need another unicorn. The ones I have are getting lonely. So please leave a review and get me another unicorn!

FRIENDS OF FALSTAFF

Thank You to All our Falstaff Books Patrons, who get extra digital content each month! To be featured here and see what other great rewards we offer, go to www.patreon.com/falstaffbooks.

PATRONS

Dino Hicks
John Hooks
John Kilgallon
Larissa Lichty
Travis & Casey Schilling
Staci-Leigh Santore
Sheryl R. Hayes
Scott Norris
Samuel Montgomery-Blinn
Junkle

Printed in the USA
CPSIA information can be obtained
at www.ICGtesting.com
LVHW051318101123
763332LV00007B/134/J